THE RETURN OF BUCK DUANE!

THE RIDER OF DISTANT TRAILS brings back one of Zane Grey's most memorable characters, Buck Duane, in four new stories by Romer Zane Grey, son of the famous writer. In the novel LONE STAR RANGER, we learned how young Buckley Duane was driven to ride the outlaw trail, and of his thrilling and dangerous life. Pardoned through the efforts of Captain Jim MacNelly of the Texas Rangers, Buck Duane served as Ranger agent in breaking up the infamous Chelsedine gang. In these new adventures, Duane continues to answer the call of the man who gave him his chance to go straight!

This is the second in a series of new adventures featuring characters created by Zane Grey. Other volumes spotlight LARAMIE NELSON, ARIZONA AMES, YAQUI, and NEVADA JIM LACY.

Also in the ROMER ZANE GREY Series:

ZANE GREY'S LARAMIE NELSON: THE OTHER SIDE OF THE CANYON

ZANE GREY'S BUCK DUANE:
THE RIDER OF DISTANT TRAILS

Romer Zane Grey

Based on characters created by Zane Grey

LEISURE BOOKS NEW YORK CITY

A LEISURE BOOK

Published by

Dorchester Publishing Co., Inc.
6 E. 39th Street
New York City

THE RIDER OF DISTANT TRAILS: THE LURE OF BURIED GOLD Copyright© MCMLXIX by Zane Grey Western Magazines, Inc.

HIGH VALLEY RIVER: LONG TRAIL TO NOWHERE Copyright© MCMLXX by Zane Grey Western Magazines, Inc.

All rights reserved. No part of this book may be reproduced or transmitted in any form or by an electronic or mechanical means, includung photocopying, recording or by any information storage and retrieval system, without the written permission of the Publisher, except where permitted by law.

Printed in the United States of America

CONTENTS

THE RIDER OF DISTANT TRAILS........5
THE LURE OF BURIED GOLD..........90
HIGH VALLEY RIVER.................190
THE LONG TRAIL TO NOWHERE......267

THE RIDER
OF DISTANT TRAILS

I

Buck Duane stood silently in the entrance of the Osage Saloon, his hands parting the batwings. Behind him, the late morning sun climbed slowly out of the jagged foothills and threw his shadow into the saloon.

The shadow did not reveal the man. His apparel was the ordinary outfit of the cowboy, without vanity, and it was torn and travel-stained. His boots showed evidence of an intimate acquaintance with cactus. He was a giant in stature, well over six feet of hard bone and muscle. Another striking thing about him was his somber face with its piercing eyes, and hair white over the temples.

He packed two guns, both low down—but that was too common a thing to attrack notice. The flaring butt of an ivory-handled Colt .45 which had belonged to his father was in a polished holster that was tied to his right leg. Another .45, a twin of his father's gun, was holstered on his left side.

Duane took in the interior of the saloon, noted the men at the bar, and the four men at a table at the end of the bar. A den of thieves, he thought. He had been persuaded by Captain MacNelly to return to the Texas Rangers, on secret Ranger service, to run down, capture or kill the bandit gang warring against banks, mail cars, and stagecoaches throughout Texas.

Captain MacNelly, who had obtained a pardon for Buckley Duane from the Governor of Texas after Duane's three years as an outlaw, was a slightly built man with a black mustache and hair, sharp black eyes, regular features, a peace officer who was dedicated to the law and determined to rid Texas of rustlers, bandits, and killers.

"Buck," MacNelly said, "I did you a good turn when you needed one. You served me well, that I allow. I can't forget that you rid Texas of Cheseldine and his gang. You were the only man who could have done that. I need you again. This gang is even tougher than Cheseldine's was. I need the fastest gun in Texas and you're it."

"You're making it awfully hard for me to refuse, Captain. I owe you a lot, I know, but I was thinking of setting up a little spread, finding me a wife and settling down. But—"

"Buck, you do this for me and I'll see that you get your little spread. The Governor is a friend of mine. He'll deed you some land, a good piece of property on which you can really build your spread. Well, Buck?"

"What's the deal on this mission?"

"Well, my information is that a so-called solid citizen, a man with a big spread just north of Rio Grande, is the brains of this gang. He's behind all the bank robberies, the mail car and stage-coach robberies. The leader of these bandits is a man named Tulsa Harrow, a gun-slinger with a rep of having killed twenty men. He's fast. That we know.

"But I *know* you're faster. I've seen the likes of Billy the Kid, Wyatt Earp, and Johnny Ringo. They were fast too. But you've got something they never had. Speed and calculation. You play to the other man's weakness, that delicate, split-second timing the other man uses up and you use to advantage.

"You can break up this kind of gang by taking their leader. You take him and we'll take the gang. But most important, I want the man behind the gang. That's the rancher. His name's Jonathan Finley. That much we know. I'm asking you as a friend for this favor. Come back to Company A. The Rangers need you."

Duane thought a long time before he answered. There was his mother, sister, and Uncle Jim. They needed him too. They were dependent upon him. He said as much to Captain MacNelly.

"I know," MacNelly answered. "I'll see to it they are well cared for. What's your answer now?"

Duane stuck out his hand and MacNelly shook it, a broad smile breaking the corners of his mouth and lighting up his face.

"Write me, or wire me if you can, care of the adjutant at Austin, just as you did before. But be careful. Don't risk your safety or your life."

So Buckley Duane set out on his mission of death. His horse, Bullet, seemed delighted to be out in open country again. The animal was a magnificent specimen, coal black, big, strong, and fast, and his endurance over grueling hours of riding was astonishing. Bullet carried a huge black, silver-ornamented saddle of Mexican make, a lariat and canteen, and a small pack rolled into a tarpauline.

There was a strange rapport between man and beast that held within the character of its existence a wonderful mystique most men would find puzzling. The animal seemed to know, by its own sixth sense, just where and how his master wanted him to go.

Buck Duane treated the horse with the greatest of kindness and understanding. A low whistle would bring the black to him at a gallop, its beautiful head shaking up and down, its eyes alert, standing with restrained but eager impatience to be mounted and to run with the wind.

Duane had ridden slowly as often as he had with the great speed of the black, resting himself and the horse. He slept in the quiet of the night that was lighted softly by a silver moon and soothed by the murmuring sounds of a caressing wind and a flowing stream.

Buck Duane came at last to the crest of a hill that overlooked the town of Tafton and was absorbed in a view of the country. The country wasn't as rugged as some bits he had seen. Its hills were lower, its valleys were shallower, its gorges not so wild, its mountains not so gigantic.

He visioned something here that he had not been able to

see in other parts of the country—the evidence of a man's efforts to turn a waste of world into a garden spot. He wondered why and for whom.

The Ranger dismounted and let Bullet graze while he searched far up the gorge behind the town, saw the frowning wall of a great dam blocking the gorge, the glint of the sun on the spraying water of the spillways. He looked over Tafton into the vast level country beyond it where man had left his mark on the soil. Herculean, persistent effort, stubborn patient, heroic sacrifice, had been contributed to the accomplishment.

Beyond, at a distance of perhaps three or four miles, the rimming hills, silent, immutable, seemed to watch indifferently. It was a wild section, wooded, with stretches of dense undergrowth. Tall sacaton grass grew here; there were great stretches of it. Farther south were low, rounded hills and timber. He marked the section in his mind. It would be a good place in which to take refuge if it ever became necessary.

As he stood there looking down at the valley and the big white house which he had already decided belonged to Jonathan Finley, he heard the sharp crack of a breaking twig below him. He stood rigid, listening, and saw a man come into view around the shoulder of the ridge, on the ledge.

The man was tall, slender, old. He wore a faded woollen shirt, trousers that were stuck into the creased and wrinkled tops of well-worn high-heeled boots that were adorned with spurs. A cartridge belt encircled his waist, supporting a holster in which was a heavy six-shooter. A battered wide-brimmed hat was in his left hand, while balanced in his right hand was a rifle.

He was directly below Buck Duane. Looking down, Duane could see the crown of his head, a bald spot where the sparse gray hair had fallen out.

There was a sinister stealthiness in the man's manner. He moved along the ledge until he was behind some dense brush. Then he dropped his hat on the ledge, and sank to his knees behind the screen of the brush at the edge. He stuck the muzzle of the rifle through the brush and waited.

Several times during the next few minutes Duane heard the man muttering to himself. He could not catch the words, but from the voice he gathered that the man was beset with a terrible impatience. Twice he raised the rifle and glanced along the sights, only to lower the weapon and curse audibly.

Although Duane could still catch glimpses of the tall man walking about the yard that surrounded the white ranch-house, he was reluctant to believe that the man kneeling below him meant to kill him. But if the tall man was Jonathan Finley, then perhaps he had good reason.

Duane waited, watching, his muscles tensed, for the kneeling man's intentions to become plain. When he saw the rifle come up again, and observed that the muzzle seemed to be following the movements of the tall figure in the yard, he leaped outward and downward. He did not want Jonathan Finley dead yet.

He landed on the ledge beside the man, lunged against him, and grasped the rifle as it exploded. As he bowled the man over upon his back and sat astride him, he had a mental picture of the white smokestreak from the rifle belching downward into the gully. Therefore, he knew that the bullet had not found its mark.

He said nothing, but his movements were swift, sure, and vigorous. He wrenched the rifle from the astonished would-be murderer and hurled it into the gully. Then he jerked the heavy six-shooter from the holster at the man's waist and threw it after the rifle. Then he settled his weight heavily upon the man's stomach and pinned his arms to the floor of the rock ledge in spread-eagle fashion. A cold wrath blazed in the man's eyes.

"Why did you want to kill him?" Duane said. "Who is he?"

"Jonathan Finley, that's who he is. A gol-danged murderer. He ain't no good. He's choked all us homesteaders, taken the good bits of land and left us dirt nothin' will grow in. Now leave me be. You've done what you were sent for, but how you knew I'll never be able to reckon."

He struggled under Duane, although he knew that his strength was not equal to that of the man who had thwarted him, and he lay back breathing hard, his eyes glaring with hatred.

"You're one of 'em ain't you?" he gasped. "One of Finley's guns. I ain't seen you before, so who be you?"

"I'm not one of Finley's men. That ought to be enough. I just don't want you killing him. You would have been in bad trouble for sure." Duane got up, yanked the old man to his feet. "You had better get out of here before Finley wakes up to the fact that you were trying to kill him."

"That I didn't is thanks to you, and you'll be regrettin' it, mister, whether you be one of Finley's men or not."

"That's strange talk at a time like this. I could be one of Finley's men and just throw you over this hill into the gully and no one would be the wiser. Get back to your home and forget about this. You'll be better off."

The old man uttered a low curse and half-stumbled as he ran from the scene. Duane brushed the dirt and dust from his clothes and stared down toward the west where there were grouped the rough houses of homesteaders set in level country through which ran the dark gashes of irrigation ditches. The level was dotted with the shacks, tent-houses and outbuildings of the homesteaders, and scratched with new roads and trails. Here and there went thin lines of fence, between which were small emerald stretches of growing crops.

II

Buck Duane heard a sudden rasping and crackling behind him, then a light step on the rock floor of the ledge; heard the rustle of garments. Then, when he still did not turn, a voice, calm, even slightly challenging, came close behind him.

"Stranger, I expect you saved Uncle Jonathan's life."

Her voice was distinctly and mellowly Southern. But in it seemed to be a note of mockery, elusive, gentle. She was tall, although her head did not quite reach his shoulder.

She was slender, graceful. She stood with her hands hanging with unconscious ease at her sides as if she took no thought of them whatever. Nor were they brown and rough as he had expected they would be after hearing her. Instead, they were slender, shapely, and white.

She held her slim young body erect with a dignity that rather astonished Duane although he could not understand why he had gained the impression that he would find her undignified. That she had concealed herself behind the bushes may have furnished the foundation for the impression.

"I didn't know who he was, and I didn't know he was your uncle. I just didn't care to see him killed."

"Why?" There was a curiosity in her tone and in the way she accented the word.

The Ranger thought her eyes held a vague twinkle in them. They were deep blue eyes, clear as pools of sparkling water, steady, and confident. He saw a rifle balanced against a sapling at her right hand, then looked back to her and noted that her hair gleamed like burnished gold in the sun that was streaming down upon her. It was coiled about her head in heavy, bulging waves.

"I just said why. I didn't care to see him killed."

"You go about caring about not seeing anyone killed? Is that your business?"

"Nope. But if I see someone trying to kill a man I wouldn't feel right unless I tried to stop it. Your uncle was defenseless. It was like shooting a pig in a pen."

"My uncle wouldn't like that."

"I didn't mean to imply he was a pig. I was just trying to draw a comparison."

"Between my uncle and a pig?" Her mouth turned upwards into a thin smile. She was obviously enjoying Duane's discomfort, the manner in which he kept getting deeper and deeper into a flustered condition.

He said on a note of mild defiance, "Your uncle isn't a pig!"

"Mister," she said, "lest you think of yourself as a hero, I want to tell you that I had a bead on him. I saw you too. I saw you watching him, and then when you leaped on him I waited to see what would happen. So, you see, you just beat me to him. Matter of fact, you didn't save my uncle's life, you save that old coot's life. Understand?"

He smiled at her. "Just as you say, Miss—"

"Miss? Yes. Miss Catherine Finley. My father was Jonathan Finley's brother. He was killed in the War Between the States when I was still a child. Were you in the war?"

"Nope."

"If you had been, would you have been a Blue or a Gray?" Her eyes looked directly into his and she obviously wanted an answer.

He smiled showing even white teeth. "A Gray. I was born in Texas. Both my parents were Southerners. Does that please you?"

"I'm not sure. What's your name?"

"Duane. Buckley Duane. My friends call me Buck."

"Buck. All right, Buck. My friends call me Cathy. You can call me Cathy too. But that's as far as you can go. My uncle doesn't cotton to strangers. What are you doing in this neck of the woods?"

"Looking for a job."

"There aren't any. There's nothing but trouble in Tafton. I'd advise you to move on."

Duane's senses had grasped her first as a complete picture. In his astonishment of the beauty of it he did not attempt to fix details in his mind. Now he observed the white, rounded firmness of her chin and throat, and his gaze rested momentarily on her lips, which were what a woman's lips ought to be. Without warning he took her in his arms, held her tightly, and kissed her.

She didn't struggle and she didn't respond. When he let her go, she asked, "Why did you do that?" There was no anger in her voice, merely curiosity.

"You looked too beautiful to resist, that's all." He smiled broadly. "If you intend to kill me, go ahead. It was worth it."

"I just may do that." She paused. "Did you just want this one kiss or are you interested in me?"

"I'm interested."

"Why?"

Her manner of asking one-word questions was a little upsetting to Duane. He thought that perhaps it was her youth, her candidness, ingenuousness, for she could not be more than eighteen or nineteen.

"Well, that's hard to say," he said. "I think that perhaps it's—well, because you're natural."

"What do you mean?" She was looking straight at him, her clear eyes unshadowed by any sign of duplicity or guile. But for all that he felt she was probing him, seeking indications of insincerity, of equivocation, of levity. "Why shouldn't I be natural? Do you mean there are people who aren't?"

"I'm pretty certain I mean that," he told her. "There are folks who aren't."

"I don't think I'd care to know them," she declared, her eyes appearing to snap scornfully, and her wonderfully firm chin tilting upward a little. "Why should anyone pretend to be what they aren't? Can't people see they are pretending? You're not pretending, are you?" Her eyes gazed at him with an unwavering steadiness.

"Of course not."

"Do you like people who do pretend?"

"I keep as far away from them as possible."

"And yet you know people who are natural?"

"Quite a few."

"Then why do you say you are interested in me? Why are you not interested in other people who are natural?"

"I am, of course."

He thought he saw a shade of disappointment in her eyes, and he observed that the toe of one of her shoes was digging into a small hummock of earth with a movement that was almost vindictive.

"I suppose those natural folks are girls," she said, not looking at him.

He wanted to disclaim that. He did, and he could not repress a smile over the astonishing thought that she resented his admitting interest in other girls.

She had been watching him covertly; she saw the smile and her cheeks flamed, paled. She stood erect and looked at him disdainfully.

"Mr. Buck Duane," she said coldly, "I think you are pretending. You are pretending, aren't you?"

"No, I'm not."

"I see. Would you like to kiss me again?" she asked.

"Yes, I would. Very much."

"Then why don't you?"

He started to take her in his arms; but before he could, her hand lashed out and she slapped him across the face. She turned then and walked westward on the ledge. She held her head very high, and her little body was defiantly straight.

Duane stood watching her until she disappeared behind a jutting shoulder of the ridge. Then he smiled again, this time thinly, although with a strange feeling of satisfaction that she had so unmistakably betrayed jealousy. Amazed, and unaware of his own feelings, he did nonetheless experience an exhilaration he had never before known. He stood staring at the ledge where she had disappeared.

Suddenly, a rifle crashed. He felt his hat rise and settle down again. He knew that a bullet had gone through the crown, for he had had that experience before. Disdaining to run or even to turn his head, he stood rigid, defiantly facing a clump of brush from which the shot had appeared to come.

The bushes parted and Cathy Finley's face appeared. She stepped into view, rifle in hand. For an instant she stood, looking at Duane. Her eyes were flashing; her cheeks were strained a bright crimson. But despite her evident scorn and anger there was the merest shadow of a reluctant smile on her lips.

"Mr. Buck Duane," she said, "you've got nerve. Why didn't you run?"

"Cathy," he said, and bowed low, "I never run from anyone who interests me." He straightened up and saw that she was smiling.

"I'll remember that," she threw back, and then, obviously on impulse, blew him a kiss and was gone.

He whistled low and Bullet came trotting over, his head bobbing up and down in eagerness to be off again. Duane mounted and rode slowly towards town. He saw that Jonathan Finley's land made a cosmic sweep upward toward a distant mountain range. Through the slumberous haze of the morning he saw the green of gigantic stretches of grazing land; the knobs of hills with their films of pine, their bases linked with purple shadows.

The sun, now swimming high, was streaming down into a clearing that surrounded the ranch-house. He could see the white gravel walks curving around the grounds and the tall man whom he now knew to be Jonathan Finley walking about aimlessly, a cigar in his mouth.

He saw the big white house, a two-story affair with a peaked roof and three chimneys which rose majestically toward the blue sky. The house, grounds, and the man who walked about seemed to hold a strange fascination for him. It also troubled him because of Cathy.

III

Duane came into town at a leisurely gait, was struck by the atmosphere of quiet calm which pervaded it. There was a vacuum-like silence. The Osage Saloon was a combination saloon and hotel. It was a rambling frame building with a wide porch running across its front with a sign hanging under the eaves bearing the legend: OSAGE SALOON AND HOTEL.

Across the dirt road was a row of other frame buildings, low and squat which housed a general store, a barber shop, restaurant, blacksmith shop, express office, and several other buildings that were occupied by merchants. He dismounted and tied Bullet to the hitch-rail, walked up the two low steps to the batwings, opened them and stood there for a long moment.

As Duane stood there he saw four pairs of hostile eyes turned on him from a table at the farthest corner of the saloon to the left of the long bar which ran from the entrance to the end of the room. Half a dozen men stood at the bar drinking and talking but these paid no attention to him. He walked in slowly, with a measured step, and the four pairs of eyes followed him each step of the way as he moved to the center of the bar.

"Whiskey," he told the bartender. As a bottle of whiskey and a glass were set on the bar before him, Duane sensed that the bartender, a man of medium height, slim but wiry, agile in his movements, and carrying a six-gun strapped to his left leg in a short holster, was somehow connected with the gang.

The Ranger wondered if the mark of the lawman showed so much in his face and appearance that the bartender recognized it, or if, possibly, the fact that he was a stranger in town was responsible for the interest in him. As he poured himself a drink, one of the men at the table stood up and walked to the bar, stopped a few feet from where Buck Duane stood.

The man was Slap Wilson, a gunfighter. Duane took him in with a quick glance, saw how Wilson's holster was tied to his right leg, at the right distance to permit a swift and easy draw. He saw, too, that the leather of the holster was greased slick and bright to allow the .44 Colt an unhampered draw.

"You riding through, stranger?" Wilson asked.

"Don't know. Been riding a long time. Thought I'd look about a bit."

"Ain't nothin' to look about in this town," Wilson answered. "It's a nice, quiet little town. Ain't much doin' hereabouts."

"So I noticed. Must be nigh onto eight o'clock. Don't nobody work around here?"

"Yep. But not before eight thirty. Half an hour from now all the stores will be open and people will be comin' into town."

So late?

"Kind of queer, ain't it?"

"Not so queer. There's goin' to be a trial today. Fella by the name of Tulsa Harrow's goin' to be on trial."

The name struck a bell in Duane's mind. Tulsa Harrow. The man Captain MacNelly had said was the leader of the gang. "What's he done?" he asked.

"Ain't done nothin'. Some crazy homesteader says he burned his shack and killed two of his cows. Ever hear of Tulsa Harrow?"

"Nope. Can't say I have."

"Where you from, stranger?"

"Galveston."

"That's a long way from here. How come?"

"You really want to know?"

"That's why I'm askin'."

"Well, kind of had to leave quick like, if you know what I mean."

Wilson eyed him narrowly. "What kind of job you lookin' for?"

"Don't matter. I'm good at a lot of things."

Wilson pointed to the guns strapped to Duane's legs, "I see. Includin' those."

Duane hesitated a moment then said, "Including those."

Wilson flipped a silver dollar from a pocket in his shirt, held it between a thumb and forefinger and suddenly threw it into the air and yelled, "*Draw!*"

Duane's movement was so fast that Wilson's word had barely died down when the shot exploded, and the silver dollar tumbled crazily in the air and then fell to the floor, creased dead center. Every pair of eyes stared at him with fascinated wonder.

Slap Wilson said, "I think you'll do. I think Tulsa Harrow will be inclined to hire you." He hesitated a moment then said, "He's that fast too. Maybe faster."

"Tulsa Harrow? But you said he was going on trial today."

Wilson laughed. "That I did, but I didn't say he would be convicted. He won't be." He turned to the bartender. "Sal, give this gent a drink. That kind of shootin' calls for a drink. Come on, boys, belly up to the bar. Drinks on me."

"No," Duane answered. "On me. I did the shooting."

"You didn't give me your handle, stranger. If you're buyin' the drinks we ought to know who you are."

The Ranger looked around the room as the men came to the bar from the table at the far end. "Buck Duane, boys."

"This here's Buck Duane, Sal. Hear? Looks like he might be with us. Set it up!"

Wilson introduced him to each man at the bar. "Stu. Harry. Bob. Frank." The first three were the ones who had sat at the table with him. Frank, obviously, was the leader of the group that had been standing at the bar when he came in. All the men were dressed in blue jeans, boots, wool shirts, kerchiefs around their legs, and guns tied low on their legs.

Gun-fighters all—one faster than the other, Duane thought. None of them mattered, he told himself. None, that is, except Slap Wilson. He recognized him instantly from the description of Captain MacNelly had given him of the gang. So there would be two Duane had to watch, and perhaps fight in a gun duel. Slap Wilson and Tulsa Harrow.

About a half hour later Slap Wilson said, "Well, boys, I think it's 'bout time we went to the courthouse to watch that there trial. Let's go." He turned to Duane. "Come along, Buck. I think you'll find this kind of interestin'."

The courthouse was in a frame building a block away from the Osage Saloon and Hotel. As the men emerged from the saloon, Buck Duane saw that the street was no longer vacant or quiet. Benches were occupied by visitors who evidently had reached Tafton while he had been in the saloon. Women in calico gowns dotted the place with color; children were racing over the grass and the walks; men walked about or stood in groups talking.

Around the edge of the square where the courthouse was situated were wagons, buckboards, buggies. Ponies bearing saddles were hitched to various racks. The space in front of the courthouse was thick with vehicles of various descriptions.

Duane stopped to buy a hat in a store near the courthouse. He crumpled the other and threw it into an empty barrel that stood near the entrance. Duane turned and addressed the storekeepr.

"Expecting any trouble today?"

The storekeeper looked Duane over quickly. "I hope not. This Tulsa Harrow—well, I don't know. Better not say anything. If you go to the courthouse you'll understand. Judge Grant lives right here in Tafton. Didn't want to handle the case but couldn't get anyone else to sit in."

"I see. Well, I think I'll just go over to the courthouse and have a look at the proceedings."

Duane crossed the square and entered the courthouse. The large square room was already filled to capacity but Duane found a space in a corner and stood there, his eyes taking in the men who stood around him and Judge Grant, who sat behind a desk at the back of the room. Inside the railing which separated the spectators from the court officials and the defendant he saw Cathy. Seated next to her was a tall, distinguished looking man who could be Jonathan Finley.

At a table a few feet from where Cathy and Finley sat was another tall man, obviously the defendant, Tulsa Harrow. On the opposite side of the table was a small, slim man in a loose fitting dark suit who, very likely was the prosecutor. Duane's eyes were fixed on Tulsa Harrow.

He saw that Tulsa Harrow was young, no more than thirty, broad of shoulder, slim of waist, with long arms and strong hands with long tapering fingers. Duane felt he could beat this man in a fight. He had been told Harrow was fast, maybe even faster than he was. If that were so, then the thing that was in his favor would be in the split-second error in movement, the timelessness when the draw for the gun would be made. He dismissed the probability of his own error as Cathy turned, saw him, gave him a quick smile and turned her head.

A voice beside him broke up his thoughts of Cathy. "Watch the show, Duane. This'll be good." It was Slap Wilson.

Duane nodded.

The prosecutor was looking over some papers. His face was in profile to Duane, so he couldn't tell much about him. Judge Grant rapped his gavel on the desk and nodded to the bailiff, who held up his hands for silence and then announced that Court was open and in session.

"Mr. Meadows," Judge Grant said, "you may proceed."

The prosecutor arose from his seat, looked about nervously, then said, "Your Honor, we are concerned in this trial with the defendent, Mr. Tulsa Harrow, who is charged with burning down the home of the plaintiff, Mr. Clem Abbott. I call Mr. Abbott to the stand."

The plaintiff called out in a loud voice, "Mr. Abbott is here. I am ready to testify." He turned and pointed a finger at Tulsa Harrow. "He burned down my house and killed two of my three milk cows."

There was a loud murmuring of voice among the spectators and Judge Grant rapped his gavel for silence. "Mr. Abbott, you will have to take the stand and testify from there. Take the stand and be sworn in."

The plaintiff, a slight man in his fifties, bent, his hands showing years of work with hoe and rake, was dressed in a pair of bib-overalls, a brown wool shirt, and dirty, worn boots. He strode to the stand, was sworn in, and sat down. He seemed to be staring at Tulsa Harrow for several seconds and then turned his eyes.

Buck Duane saw that Tulsa Harrow was looking straight into the face of the witness, his gaze fixed intently on Clem Abbott, who began shifting around nervously in his seat. There were many more homesteaders in the audience than Harrow men, or Duane thought, Jonathan Finley men. The homesteaders obviously were looking toward Abbott to make a break in the hold Finley and Harrow had on the town. If a conviction could be gotten, and it all depended on Abbott's testimony, on his courage to face down the gang, then there was some hope for them.

Duane looked around at the various members of the gang—Slap Wilson, Stu, Bob, Harry, Frank and the others. Some were smiling, others had sneers on their faces as they looked toward the witness stand. He felt sorry for the homesteaders.

These people who were striving for fairness in the law, for an opportunity to build lives for themselves in this outlaw-infested community, to progress in a civilization that was still raw and untamed, were defeated and thwarted by that faith in the law and the court which administered its justice. That was obvious to him. Judge Grant was a weakling. The prosecutor was no better.

The homesteaders would not fight with guns, and if they did they would die doing it because they were no match for this gang of thugs, all of whom were gunfighters, one better than the other. Still, they were there to voice their protests, to demand that a guilty man be punished for his crimes, that the sovereignty of the law be upheld.

How many times they had been defeated in this courtroom Buck Duane didn't know, but he was certain it was more than once. The law that operated in Tafton was not a constitutional law but a Jonathan Finley law. That, too, was obvious to Duane.

The prosecutor asked Clem Abbott to describe the events of May second. "What happened on that day and what did you see?"

"Well, it was nigh onto dusk and me and my wife Bessie was in the field working when I looked up and saw my house burning, and then this man rode up to where my milch cows were grazing and he shot one of them, and I hollered at him, and then he shot the other cow, and I started to run to where he was but afore I got there he rode off."

The prosecutor said, "You stated in your testimony that you saw 'this man.' Who did you mean? Is that man in this court now? Do you see him here?"

Clem Abbott rose from his chair and pointed a finger at Tulsa Harrow. "That's him right there! He did it!"

IV

There was a loud murmur of voices again, most of the sounds coming from the homesteaders who, no doubt, were certain this positive identification would result in a conviction. Judge Grant would have no alternative but to hand down a guilty verdict.

The prosecutor turned in several directions, uneasy, nervous, not knowing how next to proceed. He very likely had hoped for a vauge identification that would take him off the hook, because he didn't want to convict Tulsa Harrow. That was as plain to Buck Duane as the brightness of the day. The proesecutor looked toward Judge Grant, shrugged his shoulders.

At this point, Jonathan Finley stood up. Duane fixed his eyes on him, saw him full face and in profile. Finley was tall, straight as a ramrod, with hair as white as seeding clematis and gleaming like snow on a mountain peak with the sun shining upon it. It was rich and abundant, with a virility that made it stand out upon his head with a hint of waviness, suggesting the ghosts of curls that had been there in his younger days.

Finley was as erect as a well-trained military officer standing at attention. But he was infinitely more at ease because he was apparently unconscious of himself, was giving no thought to himself. He stood there for a long minute and stared at Clem Abbott, his keen blue eyes flecked with tiny points of fire, of challenging inquiry. It was as if this white-haired man mutely demanded to know why this miserable wretch, this poor tenant farmer, a homesteader without a piece of land of his own, could voice an accusation that was so groundless.

Duane studied him intently, saw that the man's features were large, bold, his skin a raw bronze. Perhaps the face had once been handsome, for there were still signs of an intensely masculine comeliness in the lines of nose and mouth and chin; but character, developing, had set its stamp upon his countenance. That character was similar to the shark or the barracuda. The man was arrogant, inflexible, a persuader of robbery and murder, a man surely with no conscience, no compassion.

Duane marked him as a dangerous man, more so even than Tulsa. He could understand, however, from whose side of the family Cathy had inherited her looks. The blue eyes, chin, nose, and mouth were Finley, more finely formed, true, more delicate, but the lines were all there. He wondered if she had also inherited some of his nature, and as he wondered about it he told himself that he hoped she hadn't.

Jonathan Finley looked toward Judge Grant, pointed a finger at the ceiling as he spoke. "Judge, any evidence that's been given here ain't worth a damn!"

The homesteaders began to murmur again, some in loud voices, as they saw their hopes for a conviction in the case dwindle and fade with each word Jonathan Finley uttered.

"I've known Tulsa Harrow for ten years. I've never known him to do a mean or low thing in all that time."

The Ranger saw the broad smiles on the faces of the gang. They were smiles of amusement. The faces of the homesteaders were grim.

"This here homesteader, this man, Clem Abbott, comes into this court and says he saw Tulsa Harrow. He said it was dusk. He said he was in the field. I know his place. The field is a good hundred yards, that's three hundred feet, from his shack, and from where his cows were grazing. How the hell is he going to recognize anybody from that distance?"

Judge Grant nodded his head.

Jonathan Finley turned his attention to Clem Abbott. "You wear glasses, don't you?" he asked in a towering voice.

Abbott stood up from his chair and stared mutely at Finley.

"I asked you if you wear glasses!" Finley repeated.

"Yes I do. But I can see without them too," he answered defiantly.

"Sure you can," Finley declared. "You can see your two feet and hands, and that's about all. For all you know, some wild kid could've rode up and burned your shack as a prank, and then shot your cows. Isn't that right?"

Abbott didn't answer, just stood there and looked back at his tormentor with tired and defeated eyes. There was dead silence in the room. Duane saw the homesteaders bow their heads, their backs bend, their shoulders droop. The whole scene stabbed at him with a mixture of sadness and anger.

27

Judge Grant was visibly disturbed. He reddened, fumbled with the papers that lay before him on the desk. He finally spoke. "I'm inclined to believe the defendant is innocent, since there has been no positive proof presented here that he was the man who committed the offense charged."

Abbott's eyes filled with tears. His wife, who stood near the rail which separated the spectators from the court officials wiped at her eyes with a handkerchief. So did several other women.

Jonathan Finley spoke coldly. "This seems to end this case, Judge. Abbott has proved nothing. His eyesight ain't what it used to be. He was very clearly mistaken. I'll allow that maybe his intentions were honest, but it's just as dishonest to make an accusation unfounded on fact as it is to tell a downright lie, a lie that could send a man to prison or hang him. I hope Tulsa Harrow will forgive this man who tried to do him evil."

Duane felt his stomach turn over. He had seen some raw things in his life so far but this one took the cake and all the crumbs.

Jonathan Finley walked over to Tulsa Harrow and touched him on the shoulder. "Come on, Tulsa. Get out of that chair, and let's get out of here."

Tulsa rose, brushed an imaginary fleck of dust from his coat, looked around the courtroom. He was a fox, a cheetah, a grim hunter of his fellowman, a ravager, despoiler, and a murderer. This was his native habitat and in it he was indisputably master.

Cathy stood up and joined her uncle and Tulsa, and the three started out from the courtroom. As they came to Buck Duane, Cathy said, "I'll wait for you outside."

Duane nodded his head.

When they had passed, Slap Wilson came over to Buck Duane. He was smiling broadly. "Well, how did you like the show? That Mr. Finley is really something, ain't he? Took right over. Better than any lawyer man. Come on, Buck, I'll stand for the drinks."

"Have to talk to someone first. You go ahead and I'll join you in a little while."

"Sure. I want you to meet Tulsa Harrow."

"I want to do that," Duane answered in a strange tone but Slap Wilson missed the significance of its meaning.

Duane moved out with the rest of the homsesteaders who were talking intently among themselves. Their faces showed plainly the great disappointment they felt. He went down the short three steps to the wooden walk and saw Cathy standing with her uncle. He went over, removed his hat.

"Uncle Jonathan," she said, "I want you to meet Mr. Buckley Duane. His friends call him Buck. He's the man who saved your life this morning."

"Thanks very much, Mr. Duane," Finley said, and held out his hand. "What made you do it?"

"I don't like to see a man shot in the back," Duane answered pointedly. "That's what he was fixin' to do to you."

"I see," Finley said thoughtfully. Then, "My niece tells me you're looking for a job. That right?"

"Yes, sir."

"Cowhand?"

"I can do that too."

"Meaning you prefer something else?"

"If it's available."

"Well, let me think about it. Come see me tomorrow afternoon and I may have an answer for you."

While they were talking, buggies, spring-wagons, buckboards, and other vehicles were wheeling away amid dust that swirled in clouds. Horses bearing riders were cavorting around the square, then heading for open country. The square had been magically cleared, with the exception of about a dozen people who were walking toward the various stores on the street. A man approached Finley from the south, stopped before him.

"Mr. Finley," the man said, "my name's Kelly. Jeff Kelly. I own a piece of land 'bout three miles south of town."

"What can I do for you, Mr. Kelly?"

Kelly was a short, stocky man with a full mustache. He wore the blue jeans and boots of the rancher, the typical horseman. He appeared to be in his mid-thirties, strong as a blacksmith.

"I was in the courtroom this morning. I heard everything. I have something to say to you."

"Say it," Finley replied. His tone was challenging.

"Mr. Finley, there ain't so much law in this country but what a man's got some right in the place where he lives. You bluffed that judge and you bluffed the prosecutor. I don't know what kind of hold you got on 'em but what you did in there this morning was to destroy every law on the books and every right a man has to live under it peacefully.

"If your man Harrow didn't burn down that farmer's shack and shoot his cows then there ain't a steer in Texas. That's what I think."

Finley's face paled with anger for a fleeting second and his eyes glittered with rage, but he took hold of himself quickly. "Mr. Kelly, I hold to the idea that every man has a right to his opinion. That's yours."

Cathy's blue eyes narrowed and remained so as she spoke. "Mr. Kelly, I think you're a damned fool! You're accusing my uncle of running the court. What he did was to defend an innocent man. That right was his!"

"I've got no quarrel with you, Miss. I wouldn't think of it. But like your uncle said, everybody has a right to his opinion."

As they stood there talking, Tulsa Harrow strolled over from across the street. He was wearing his gun, a Colt .44 with a silver handle. "Howdy, folks. Something I should listen to?"

"Yes, you should," Cathy said. "This is Mr. Kelly. He's accusing Uncle Jonathan of having bluffed the judge and prosecutor into freeing you this morning."

Tulsa looked down at Kelly. He was at least six inches taller than the man he faced. "Mr. Kelly, eh? I know who you are. You got a spread south of town. Nice place. You also got a wife and two kids, a boy and a girl. Right?"

Tulsa's tone was even, smooth, as if he were discussing the weather. His voice didn't change as he said, "Mr. Kelly, Mr. Finley is a friend of mine. I don't like anybody talking dirt to my friends. The next time you do it you'll die so fast you'll think somebody is shovin' you. Understand?"

"Yes, I understand," Kelly replied, but there was no fear in his tone. "I don't wear a gun. I'm not a gunfighter. I was brought up to respect the law and to live under it whether it be a good law or a bad law. Every homesteader in this territory has been pushed farther and farther back from the land Mr. Finley wanted. I reckon he wants the land Abbott is working. I reckon you'll get it for him."

"Your mouth is goin' to dig you a quick grave, Mr. Kelly," Tulsa said softly. "Take my advice and put a button on it. That's all. Understand? *That's all.*" The last two words were said in an unmistakably menacing tone.

Duane noticed a peculiar thing at that moment. When Tulsa spoke those two words his left foot moved just a fraction to the left and his right shoulder drooped. He marked it down in his mind.

Jeff Kelly nodded to Cathy, turned and walked toward the buckboard across the road, got in, and drove away.

"Don't worry about him none, Mr. Finley," Tulsa said. "He'll never bother you again. I'll see to that."

"I wasn't worried none, Tulsa. Oh, by the way, this young man is looking for a job. He saved my life this morning. Some damned fool tried to shoot me from atop a hill whie I was walking in the yard. This man jumped him, disarmed him, and booted him away."

Tulsa turned to Buck Duane, extended his hand. "Glad to know you. My name's Tulsa Harrow."

"I know. Slap Wilson told me about you this morning. I met him in the Osage. My name's Duane. Buck Duane."

"Were you in court this morning?" Tulsa asked.

"Yep. I was interested."

"What'd you think of it?"

"I didn't think about it," Duane lied. "The evidence didn't prove a thing. That's all I went on." That part was true. Yet if the evidence hadn't upheld the letter of the law, it had, in fact, upheld the spirit.

Tulsa Harrow looked Duane over a little closer, a quick glance from head to foot. "Handy with those pieces of iron?" he asked, and pointed to the guns strapped to Duane's legs.

"Pretty handy."

"Mr. Finley said you wanted a job."

"I'll talk to him tomorrow, Tulsa. After you and I talk abouit it. Well, let's go, Cathy. See me after lunch, Tulsa."

"Sure thing, Mr. Finley."

Cathy Finley gave Duane a quick, secret smile, winked at him, and then she put her hand in one of her uncle's and the two walked toward home, heads high, a king and a princess of a small domain.

V

It was apparent to Buck Duane that Jonathan's one weakness was his niece. It wasn't hard to explain. She was all he had in the world other than his money, land, the stock, possibly the largest in the state of Texas, and power. Dangerous? Duane let out a low whistle.

Tulsa Harrow said, "Did you say something, Buck?"

"Nope. Just whistled. I promised Slap Wilson I'd meet him in the Osage. Care to join us?"

"Now now. I have a few things to take care of. I'll see you tomorrow."

Harrow cocked his head a little and gave Duane another once-over in that quick way he had, turned without a word and walked to his horse, mounted, and rode away.

Duane watched Tulsa until he was out of sight and thought, "So that's Tulsa Harrow. I guess I'll do a little practicing on quick draws. Yes, sir. It sure calls for it."

The Ranger walked slowly toward the Osage, his mind tumbling. Finley. Cathy. Tulsa. Wilson. It all fitted, and yet it didn't fit. There was a piece missing the puzzle, a very small piece, an important and integral piece. That could be the key to the whole thing.

In the Osage, Slap Wilson met Buck Duane with a loud

yell. "Been waitin' for you, Buck. Drink up! Sal, another bottle!"

Most of the men, and there were about fifteen in the group, were about half-drunk, celebrating Tulsa's freedom. They were noisy, laughing, telling ribald stories, slapping each other on the back and yelling for more whiskey. Duane drank moderately. Then Slap suggested a shooting contest.

"Five dollars a man. Stu, me, and you, Buck. What do you say? One time only. Winner pick up the money, and buys the drinks. You on?"

Duane shrugged. "What've I got to lose? How we going to settle it?"

"Give us three empty bottles, Sal. We'll take these outside and set 'em up on a fence, alongside the barber shop. There's about twenty feet of field there. Just right. First one to break the bottle wins. One shot only."

"Who'll call?" Duane asked.

"Harry. He's good at callin'. Once called me in a poker game when I had an ace full." He laughed and everyone laughed with him except Harry.

"I thought he was bluffin'."

"That's the big trick, Harry," Wilson said. "To know when a man's bluffin' an' when he's tryin' to run a whizzer. Let's go, boys!"

The group filed out, ran to the side of the barber shop where Harry set up the bottles about ten feet apart. The three men took positions in the field some twenty feet from where the bottles stood on the fence.

Slap and Stu adjusted their holsters, moved their guns up and down to test their slide. Duanne watched each man as he did this but could note nothing that would reveal a possible flaw in their draws.

"Ready?" Harry asked.

"Not yet!" Bob yelled. "I want to make a side bet. Ten dollars on Slap. Any takers?"

There were none, either because the men didn't want to reveal a disbelief in Wilson's prowess or because they feared to bet against him. Duane decided to lose. Not by much. A split second would be enough considering the fact that both Slap and Stu had been drinking heavily.

"All right," Harry yelled, "when I yell *draw*, then you pull and shoot. Ready?"

"Ready, ready!" Slap yelled back.

Harry waited several moments then yelled, "*Draw!*"

The three guns exploded simultaneously and all three bottles shattered.

"A tie!" Harry yelled.

It wasn't exactly true. Duane's bottle exploded a fraction of a second before the other two, and this despite the fact that he held back on his draw. It didn't mean anything, he told himself. Both men were drunk. But both were unmistakably fast. How much faster they were when they were sober was something he'd have to contemplate, to watch, and to note.

And again, there would have to be the split-second of time that would be his advantage. This, he told himself, was not going to be any pie-eating contest. This was going to be life and death, requiring the steadiest of nerves, eyes, mind, and body.

The group filed back into the Osage, more noisy than before. They continued drinking for another hour, when Buck Duane said, "Boys, I hate to leave. Must find a place to stay and get some rest."

"Say, Sal," Slap yelled, "ain't you got a room for Buck?"

"Nope. All filled up, Slap. Let him try the Widow Crowe. I think she has a room to rent. It's up the street, Buck. A brown house with green shutters. Can't miss it."

"Thanks. I'll ride over there."

Buck Duane didn't. Instead he rode south. He wanted to find Jeff Kelly's spread. Three miles, he had heard Tulsa Harrow say. Should be easy to locate. The Ranger made certain no one was following him as he rode out, located the spread, rode in, found a bucket, filled it from the well and gave Bullet a long drink. As he was doing so, Jeff Kelly came out from the house.

"Can I help you stranger?"

"Yes, you can. My name's Buck Duane."

Kelly looked him over, recognized him. "Yes. You were

with Mr. Finley and his niece this morning. What do you want?"

"I want to talk to you confidentially. I don't want my horse to be recognized. Can I take him around the back?"

"What do you want to talk about, Mr. Duane?"

"Something that will interest you. Something you spoke about to Mr. Finley."

Duane's manner of speaking and appearance told Kelly he could be trusted. "Yes. Bring him around to the back of the house and tie him there. Come in through the back door."

Duane led Bullet to the rear of the house, tied him to a pole, went into the house. Kelly met him at the door. Mrs. Kelly, a small, attractive woman in her late twenties, was in the kitchen.

"Sara, this is Mr. Buck Duane. I think he's a friend come to help us. Let's go into the parlor, Mr. Duane."

"Would you care for a cup of coffee, Mr. Duane?" Sara Kelly asked.

"Yes, that would be fine, thank you."

Duane noted that the house, which held several rooms, was furnished tastefully and was scrupulously clean. It reminded him of his own home, the way his mother kept the house. This was the home of a man who cared about his family, an honest man, the kind necessary to a growing community, the kind that would be interested in improving things, building schools, churches, civic projects. Mrs. Kelly brought in the coffee and left.

"You came to talk things over with me, Mr. Duane. I'm ready to listen."

"Mr. Kelly, I have to trust someone around here and you appear to be the one. I took in everything you said this morning to Mr. Finley. I liked what you said and how you handled yourself with Tulsa Harrow."

"He's a mean man. Rotten to the core. A killer. He's driven out about twenty homesteaders and gobbled up their land for Finley. He wants Abbott's land, and then he's going to move south, step by step, until he comes to me."

"I figured as much." Duane leaned forward as if to

emphasize a point. "Mr. Kelly, I'm a Texas Ranger, assigned to Company A under Captain MacNelly. You can check me out any way you want."

Kelly's eyebrows raised. "No need to. I believe you. I'm at your service, Mr. Duane. How can I help?"

"My job is to break up this gang, any way I can. The way I figure it, I'll have to have a showdown with Slap Wilson and Tulsa Harrow, when the time comes. Mr. Finley, when I get the goods on him, will go to prison. The gang robs banks, mail cars, stagecoaches. I'm here as an undercover man, so I'm joining the gang. Only way I can get the goods on them.

"However, I'll be tipping off Captain MacNelly any time the gang is ready to stage a robbery. That's where you come in. I very likely won't have time to post a letter or send a telegram. I'm asking you to help in that way."

"Just tell me how and I'll do it."

"I think the best way would be for you to drive into town, say every other day, at exactly ten o'clock to the general store. If I have a message to send I'll find a way to slip it to you."

"That won't be necessary. Hiram Callahan is a friend of mine. Our folks came from the same town in Ireland. You give him the message and he'll get it to me, as fast as he can. However, I will go into town every other day, just to be sure. A telegram will have to be sent from the next town. That's Anderson. Ten miles south of here. I'll ride in. I've got a fast horse."

"You'll speak to Mr. Callahan?"

"Tomorrow. I'll have him come here so there won't be any danger of anyone overhearing anything. It'll be all set. Is there anything else I can do to help?"

"No, that will be enough. For the time, don't antagonize Tulsa Harrow or any of the gang. Play it meek, submissive. Like you were scared off by Tulsa. If you should run into Mr. Finley I would suggest that you apologize to him for what you said."

"God! It would turn my stomach!"

"A turned stomach, Mr. Kelly, is better than one shot full of holes. Try to do it my way."

"All right, Mr. Duane, just as you say."

Duane rose. "I think it best that you don't tell anyone other than Mr. Callahan about our conversation. Not even your wife, for her protection and everybody else's."

"Of course, Mr. Duane." Kelly held out his hand. "You don't know how much better I feel since talking with you. I've prayed for someone like you to come along and straighten things out in this town. So has every other honest person here. It's been a nightmare, I can tell you."

"I believe it. Don't worry about it. I'll take care of it."

The way Duane said it, his manner, his complete air of confidence, authority even, made Kelly smile with relief and satisfaction. He looked now at Duane as if he were a delivering angle.

As they walked back to the kitchen, Jeff Kelly said, "Sara, Mr. Duane is a real friend. Shake hands with him."

Sara Kelly wiped her hand on her apron, held out out. "We've needed one, Mr. Duane. Any time you're hungry, please stop by. I'm a good cook." She smiled apologetically.

"I'm sure you are, and I may take you up on it, sooner than you expect."

"It'll be a pleasure."

VI

The next day Buck Duane rose early. The widow Crowe, who was much younger than he had imagined her to be, and twice as attractive, offered him breakfast.

"It goes with the room, Mr. Duane."

"Thank you, Mrs. Crowe. I guess I could stand it."

"You may call me Abby, if you wish," she said and smiled. "It's short for Abigail, which I loathe."

"All right, Abby."

The Ranger sat down at the table in the neat kitchen, watched her as she puttered around the stove in efficient movements. He judged her to be about twenty-four, perhaps a year or two less. It was always hard to judge a woman's age, especially a small woman. She was small. About five feet two.

The bright yellow calico dress, while it did not reveal the trim figure, did not hide it either. She was round and firm in all the right places. Her skin had the moist, luminous glow of perfect health, and her dark hair was combed in soft waves and into a knobbed chignon.

What Duane liked about her most was her candid brown eyes and her brilliant smile. She had the whitest, most even teeth he had ever seen.

She made him a platter of bacon and eggs, and fried potatoes, took hot biscuits from the stove, and set out a jar of homemade jam.

"I preserved those myself," she said, and unscrewed the jar. "You will try some, won't you?"

"Sure. Aren't you eating?"

"Oh, Lord, I ate hours ago. I rise quite early. You see, I can't afford to loll around in no bed. I pick berries in season, put them up in jars and sell them. Also, apples, cherries, pears, plums, and vegetables. You know, I'm rather famous for that around here. Besides, I have to earn my living."

"Won't you sit down, have some coffee with me?"

"Yes, I think I will." She poured herself a cup and sat down at the opposite end of the table.

They were silent for long moments, strangers trying to bridge the gap that intervened and separated them from knowledge of each other, friendship, and intimacy. She kept her head lowered, but her eyes were raised to him in shy glances.

"Abby," Duane said at last, "what happened to your husband? You're mighty young to be a widow."

"He was killed about three years ago. He was a fine young man. I sorrowed for him for a long time."

"How was he killed?"

"In a gun fight with Tulsa Harrow."

Duane was silent for several moments, the fork of food he was holding half-raised to his mouth. "Why?" he asked.

"I don't know." She brushed a quick tear from her eyes. "It happened in the Osage Saloon. An argument. That's what I was told. That man Harrow came around after the funeral and tried to explain, said he was sorry it happened and would like to help me. He offered me some money but I wouldn't take it. Then he tried to kiss me, said some awful things to me."

The Ranger was thoughtful for a while then said, "You're a very attractive woman, Abby. This may be harsh, but do you think Tulsa deliberately picked an argument with your husband in order to kill him and leave the way open for him?"

"With me? Yes, I've thought of it. He came around several times after his first visit but I wouldn't allow him in the house. He's a terrible man. Everyone in the territory knows about him but they can't prove a thing, or are afraid to do it."

"I see." He changed the subject. "Abby," he said with a smile, "aren't you afraid what the townspeople will say about you having a man in your home, you being so young and pretty?"

"No, Mr. Duane, I'm not concerned. You see—"

"You're unfair, Abby. You said I could call you by your first name but you won't call me by mine. Try it. It's Buck."

She gave him a bright smile. "All right, Buck. I started to say that if I bothered to care about what people say I'd have moved from here long ago. No, I live my life. That's my privilege."

"Good girl. Abby, I want to tell you something. I'm going to work for Jonathan Finley."

Her face grew darkly serious.

"No, wait. I know all about Finley, and Harrow and the gang. I'm asking you not to judge me yet because of it. I'm asking you to trust me and believe in me. I can't tell you any more now. I hope you will, that's all."

She looked into his eyes for a long time, saw something there that satisfied her. "All right, Buck. I won't ask any questions, and I'll trust you."

He reached out and took her hand in his. "Thanks. I

appreciate that."

When he let go of her hand she put her own over her breast and held it there for several moments, her breathing increasing in tempo. "It's been a long time since a man held my hand, Buck. I—I—oh, I don't know." She gave a nervous little laugh, and rose. "I guess I better wash up the dishes. More coffee?"

"No, thanks." He rose from the table, stood very close to her, put an arm around her shoulder in a friendly gesture. "Don't worry about a thing, Abby. Not a thing."

He turned from her and started out the door, looked back and saw that she was weeping softly. But he didn't know why.

Buck Duane saddled Bullet and rode up into the hills. He thought about Finley, Harrow, and Kelly. Jeff Kelly concerned him most. The West was full of his kind—pioneers steeped in the glamor of the past, of men who blazed the trails across the nation and opened up the virgin territories, built towns, railroads, developed trade, gave to the nation its blood and energy.

Kelly was needed and had to survive; and in order to guarantee that survival, men like Finley, Harrow, Wilson, and the rest of the gang had to be destroyed. It wouldn't be easy. But as he rode over the hills and verdant valleys under the brassy sky he was aware that he was giving more thought to Cathy than he was to her uncle or Harrow. She was loyal to her uncle. He had seen that. She wouldn't admire anyone who became his enemy.

Duane loped Bullet to the top of a hill, paused there, saw the winding river which tumbled down the gorge near Tafton to splash at last over the rocky edge of a red scoria butte with a funnel-like chasm cut in its end, and go swirling and broadening to the lower country. He could see the falls from where he stood, saw that the river vanished somewhere behind the cottonwoods that surrounded the big white house. In that house were Jonathan Finley and Cathy. They bothered him, in different ways.

Duane dismounted and stood there looking out at the view before him, lost in his thoughts. His sixth sense gave him a sudden warning, and he turned to see a lone rider gentling a big roan gelding toward him. The rider came to within twenty feet of where he stood, and dismounted.

Buck Duane recognized him as one of the gang, a man in his mid-twenties, clean of face, with narrow eyes and an aquiline nose. He was wearing a brace of Colts.

"I been followin' you, Duane," the man said. "You know why?"

The Ranger eyed him thoughtfully. He had a vague idea that the man knew him for what he was. If so, there would be trouble, something he didn't want at this stage of the game. However, it seemed unavoidable.

"No, I don't know why you've been following me. Why have you?"

"You ain't that much of a fool, Mister," the young man shot back. "You know damned well why I've been following you. What I should've done was tell Tulsa Harrow who you are and let him and the boys take care o' you. But I wanted that chance myself. All alone, see? Right out here in the middle of nowhere, just you and me under the big sky."

He grinned maliciously, cocksure of himself, eyeing Buck Duane intently for any untoward move.

"You're wrong whatever you think," Duane replied. "I'm a loner, rode in looking for a chance to make some money."

"Sure you did," the young man sneered, "reward money. I got a good memory, especially for faces of lawmen. I recall you good. Cheseldine. You fit, don't you?"

Buck Duane shifted his feet a little but made no move with his hands.

The young man said, "My name's Johnny Black. Mebbe that name don't ring a bell with you but I'm better known as The Gumdrop Kid." He grinned crookedly. "That recall something to you, Mister?" he asked, a boastful pride in his voice. "The Gumdrop Kid!"

Buck Duane knew his reputation. He had killed ten men, was a braggart, dangerous as a coiled rattlesnake. The Ranger decided to try to make a deal.

"Suppose I am a lawman, Johnny? Wouldn't you be better off to turn yourself in to me, help me break up the gang?"

The Gumdrop Kid gave a short laugh. "Turn myself in to *you*?" he mocked. "I don't make no deals with no stinkin' lawmen. That's what you are, a stinkin' lawman!" As he finished speaking, Black's hand flashed to his gun.

He was a split second slow. Buck Duane's gun leaped into his hand and exploded twice, the slugs striking Johnny Black in the chest. His gun flew from his hand and he toppled over on his back.

Buck Duane walked to where the Gumdrop Kid lay, looked down at him. The glassy eyes moved slightly, centered, and were still. The Ranger knew he was dead. The killing presented a problem to him. Johnny Black would be missed, and if his roan gelding came into town without its rider the gang would go looking for him. Well, he'd just have to bluff it out, play it by ear.

Duane led Bullet away from the scene, walked back and covered his tracks, reloaded his gun. He gave Johnny Black a last look, shook his head in a regretful gesture, mounted and rode away.

VII

The sun was high in the heavens when Buck Duane finally rode back into town and toward Finley's big white house. He opened a gate and walked in after tying Bullet to a hitching post, knocked on the door. His knock was answered by Cathy.

"Hello," she greeted him brightly. She was dressed in a blue skirt and blouse and a blue ribbon was tied in her blonde hair. She was beautiful. "Come in," she said, and held the door wide.

"I came to see your uncle," he said.

"I know. He is in the parlor with Tulsa Harrow. They've been expecting you. I was thinking of riding out this afternoon, into the hills. I know a pretty place alongside a stream surrounded by cottonwoods. It's a wonderful place for a small picnic—and things."

She looked up at him for his answer.

"Maybe your uncle wouldn't like that, having a picnic with one of his hired hands. If he hires me, that is."

"Oh, bother that! He lets me do what I want. Well?"

Duane smiled. "All right, if you say so."

"Good. I'll meet you on the hill, where we met yesterday. I'll pack a lunch in a saddlebag."

She led him into the parlor where Finley and Tulsa Harrow sat. The house was in perfect order, the plush furniture expensive and in good taste. It was a home that had known the touch of a woman's hand, a woman of culture. Duane wondered who she might have been, and how a woman like that could have known a man like Jonathan Finley, known him, married him, slept with him.

"Come in, Mr. Duane," Finley said. "Buck, isn't it?"

"Yes, sir."

Finley rose, shook hands with him. Tulsa remained seated. He nodded briefly to Buck. Duane saw that Finley was strangely neat in his dress: boots, trousers, shirt were of the best. The string tie added to his appearance. The silver-handled guns didn't escape his notice either. Finley motioned him to a chair and he sat down.

"Buck," Finley said, "we'd like to know something about you. I've heard you're very fast with those guns. That tells me a lot. Where do you hail from?"

"Galveston. The guns?" He looked from one to the other, saw that Tulsa was gazing at him intently. "I've used them."

"How?" Tulsa asked. There was a twofold meaning in his tone.

"Well, let me put it this way. "I was an outlaw. I—"

"*Was?*" Finley asked.

"Had to leave Galveston. Things got kind of hot for me around there. Haven't done a thing in months. Frankly, I don't know what I want to do. But I'm telling you this so there won't be any kind of misunderstanding."

"I see," Finley said. "You mean in case someone comes

looking for you?"

"They might."

"You met some of the boys yesterday in Osage," Finley said. "You know they're no cowhands, don't you?"

"I figured as much."

"What else did you figure?" Tulsa asked.

Duane gave them a small smile and spread his hands. "I got it they made their living dishonestly."

Finley let out a loud laugh. Tulsa Harrow just stared. It was hard for Duane to tell exactly what Tulsa was thinking.

Finley said, "Tulsa, take him in. I think he's all right."

"I'm not sure, but I hope you are, Duane. If you aren't, you and I will have a little meeting in the street. I'd just like to find out how fast you are with those Colts."

Duane grinned back at him. "It might be interesting at that."

"All right, boys," Finley said. "Let's have none of that. Buck, you're hired. You do just as Tulsa says and you'll get along fine. Now, how are you fixed for money?"

"I have a little."

Finley rose, dug a hand into a pocket of his trousers and counted out some gold. "Here's a hundred dollars. That's on account. I'll deduct it from your pay. What you earn will depend on what you do. I hope we understand one another."

Duane took the coins, put them in a shirt pocket. "I'm sure we do, Mr. Finley."

"Good. I understand you're living at the Widow Crowe's. Is that right?"

"Yes, sir."

"Fine woman. Too bad about her husband. Well," he said then, "I'm sure I don't have to tell you not to discuss anything with her. We like to keep our business private."

"I understand perfectly, Mr. Finley."

"Good, good." He turned to Tulsa. "You have something to tell Buck?"

"Yeah. Stay close to town. Slap will tell you anything I want you to know. There'll be something in the next few days."

"I'll be around."

Tulsa eyed him narrowly. "I don't mind telling you I don't particularly like you. There's something about you don't hit me just right. If you make any wrong moves—"

"That's enough, Tulsa!" Finley said harshly. "He's one of us now and I don't want any ill-feelings between you. All right, Buck, go on. I want to talk to Tulsa."

Buck Duane gave Tulsa a quick sidelong look and went out. He whistled for Bullet who came trotting over, mounted, and rode out to the hill to keep his rendezvous with Cathy. He found her already there when he rode up.

"Let's ride over to the spillways," she said. "I know a quiet place there where no one ever goes."

"Shortly. I want to ask you something. I'm not hankerin' to get in bad with your uncle. He just hired me."

"So? Are you saying you're afraid of my uncle?"

"No."

"Of me?" she asked coquettishly. "Come on," she urged, "I promise not to lead you astray." She paused and eyed him with a mischevious glance, a smile playing around the corners of her mobile mouth. "Unless," she added, "you're willing."

He gave her a short, mirthful laugh. "You might be biting off more than you can chew."

"I've got enough teeth. Let's go."

They rode out, over the hills, through a valley, out where the western slopes and valley stretched for miles, where once buffalo roamed and war parties of Indians had crossed, out where there were no trees and endless grass, where the antelope ran and coyotes slept waiting for the night. They came at last to a running stream.

"This is it," she said, and dismounted. "It's lovely, isn't it?" she cried, and stretched her slim white arms to the sky.

He nodded his head. "Yes, it's really nice. Like a slice of another world. You come here often?"

"Occasionally. When I want to get off by myself." She took hold of his hand. "Come on, let's sit by the stream."

They sat down together, side by side, she leaned her head against his shoulder and they sat there like that for a long time. Suddenly, he put his hand around her waist and pulled her gently down. She gave him no resistance, and when he bent his head over hers, she parted her lips, closed her eyes, and waited for his kiss.

The world beyond was shut out, walled off, a planet millions of miles from their own little planet with its own sun, its slice of blue sky, a murmuring stream, and between them no space, and over them no time. They had reached a compromise with a union as old as the ages. He wanted her, as much, no doubt, as she wanted him.

But Buck Duane had held back, contenting himself with the sweetness of her lips and the thrilling closeness of her young body, the warmth of it, the softness, the way she turned in his arms, snuggled against his chest. Cathy was so young, so terribly young and virginal, so gifted with the precious jewels a woman's love could bestow.

They lay on their backs now, eyes closed. There was a dreamy expression on Cathy's face, and her lips were pursed in a faint pout. She reached out a hand, found one of his and held it.

"Why not, Buck?" she asked in a plaintive tone. "Don't you find me attractive?"

"Sure, Cathy. But it wouldn't be right. Not for you, and well, not for me either. I can't explain why."

She didn't understand entirely. She didn't understand that what he couldn't tell her was that he was in Tafton to break up her uncle's gang, to break it up, arrest him, and perhaps even have to kill him. That would hurt her. It was enough. He couldn't hurt her more by deceiving her entirely.

What bothered him was the question of how much she knew of her uncle's life? If she did know, the truth, that is, did she accept it and condone it? Approve it? Or turn her mind away from it and ignore it because she was tied to Jonathan Finley by blood, duty, debt, and and affection a daughter might have for a doting father, for he was more like her father than he was her uncle. It was more difficult, he thought, to understand a woman than to love her.

Cathy opened her eyes suddenly, turned her head and gazed at Buck, studied him for a long time, his every feature, the fine forehead, straight nose, strong mouth and jaw, and the long lashes covering his closed eyes. He was very handsome, she thought. She nudged him with her elbow and he opened his eyes.

"Thinking?" she asked.

He stretched his arms to the sky and then forward toward the sinking sun. "A little."

With feminine logic, she said, "About me? You were, weren't you?"

"Yes, I was."

Her blue eyes reflected a great gentleness and tenderness. She thought, perhaps, that here at last was the man her young-girl dreams had conjured, the lover, the husband to help her by love, passion, the bright and desperate taking and giving that was like liquid velvet coursing through her veins. She thrust herself into his arms.

"Hold me, Buck," Cathy whispered. "Hold me tight. I love you, Buck. Don't ever let me go. Don't ever let anything happen to you."

Duane realized that she had been washed over with a great emotion too much for her to bear alone and that she needed him to damn it up yet contain it and at the same time release her from the panic it wrought in her.

He held her to him tightly for a long time, and when, at last, the sun threatened to sink into the horizon, he took his arms from around her.

"I think we should be getting back, Cathy. Your uncle will be wondering what happened to you." He stood up, held out a hand to her and lifted her to her feet.

They rode back in lighthearted silence and when they reached the edge of the hill where they had met, he said, "I think you should ride on ahead. I'll take the north path around your house and ride home so I won't have to pass the Osage."

Cathy moved her horse close to his, leaned over for a kiss. And then another. "Tomorrow," she threw at him as she spurred her horse. "Same place. Same time."

He watched her ride, marveled at her horsemanship, and then turned Bullet's head and headed for home.

VIII

Buck Duane rode into the large back yard behind Abby Crowe's house, and made it without anyone seeing him. He unsaddled Bullet and put him in the barn then walked into the house. There was a tantalizing aroma of food cooking—roast meat, vegetables, and fresh-baked bread. It transmitted itself to him in such a way that he became immediately hungry.

Duane inhaled the aromas several times before stepping into the kitchen, and wondered where he would eat. The afternoon's riding and the hours with Cathy Finley had sharpened his hunger. Abby was in the kitchen, standing over the stove and stirring something in the pot.

"Hello," she greeted him brightly. "You look like you've been out in the sun."

"Yes," he answered lightly. "I rode out into the hills a ways. I like doing that, getting off by myself at times." He was very close to her. She smelled clean, as if she had bathed only a short time ago. There was a subtle scent of jasmine about her.

Duane said, in a small-boyish way, "You smell pretty. Like flowers touched with early morning dew."

Abby turned her head sharply and stared at him in wonder and then her face broke into a bright smile. "Well!" she replied. "I do declare, Buck, that's the nicest thing that's been said to me in years. I'll repay that by asking you to share my supper. I hope you're hungry."

"I shouldn't ought to. That wood costs a lot; and after all, you have to work for it."

"I won't hear another word about that, Buck. Now you go wash up and get ready." Abby looked up into his eyes, and her intuition told her he had been out with a woman during the afternoon. She felt a sharp pang of jealousy.

She shook it off and said, "You know, Buck, one of the great pleasures a woman has is cooking for some man. And I haven't had that pleasure for a long time. Would you deprive me of that?"

"I wouldn't deprive you of anything you wanted, Abby," he said. "I think you're one of the nicest persons I've ever known."

They stood there in silence for a while, gazing at each other awkwardly, each with his own personal thoughts although they were miles apart in what they were thinking.

"All right, then," Abby said, and her tone was that of a wife talking to her husband, "you go and wash up. Bring in fresh water from the well. Here's the pail."

Duane went out to the well, pumped the pail full of water and brought it in. While he was out, the picture of his having been with another woman assailed Abby and tortured her. She knew she had no right to those thoughts, that he had said nothing or done anything to encourage her feeling about him. That she had feelings about him she couldn't deny.

She brushed an errant wisp of hair from her forehead, noted that her face was suddenly damp, and wiped it quickly with a dab of the towel she held in her hand.

When Buck Duane came in she turned to look at him in a swift gaze she felt her pulse hammering, along the lines of her throat, her forehead, and at her wrists.

"Take the pan out on the back porch," Abby said without turning around. There's soap and a fresh towel in the cupboard." She pointed to the cupboard over her head.

He reached up to get the soap and towel and inadvertently leaned against her. She turned swiftly, and as swiftly was in his arms, her head on his chest, her arms around his waist.

"I can't help it," Abby moaned, "I can't help it. Just hold me for a little while," she pleaded. "Please, please, hold me."

Duane held her, understanding the problem that was buried deep within her, the frustration, the lost and wasted years of her life alone since her husband was killed. But he couldn't get involved, and he couldn't let her get involved with him. It wouldn't be fair to her.

Abby remained in Duane's arms for a long time and then she looked up at him with misty eyes, a toilsome hungering within them, shadowed, burning, fading, glowing brightly as she fought her feeling or gave way to them.

"I'm all right," she said at last. "That was foolish of me, I know," she said in an embarrassed tone. "Forgive me." She turned abruptly away from him but he put his hands on her shoulders and spun her around gently.

"It wasn't foolish, Abby. There was nothing foolish about it. I understand. I've been lonely many times, wanting someone to talk to, someone to look at, a friendly face, a man, a woman, especially a woman. But out there in the hills or the plains there was nothing but the night and the howling of coyotes. I know what it is to be lonely. Don't be sorry for what you did. I'm glad you did."

She looked up at him with great tenderness in her eyes. "Are you really, Buck? Really glad?"

"Yes, I am," he answered truthfully.

"Thank you," she said softly. "It helps a great deal. Now," she said briskly in a sudden change of tone, "go on and sit down and I'll serve our supper."

Duane met Cathy the next afternoon at the top of the hill and they rode out to the same place where they had spent the hours the day before. He saw things this afternoon he hadn't observed yesterday. There were mesquite flats along the trails, some of them broken by tenacious cedars, red sandstone canyons, and in the brassy haze of the boundless plains, scattered cattle outfits which held only small herds.

The Ranger believed that Jonathan Finly was responsible for what he saw. He envisioned the broken hopes, the despair, the shattered emotions, the desperate struggles against a hardened villainy and the guns of hired killers who were backed by the power and the law contained in a single man. His absorption in his thoughts irked Cathy.

"Buck, say something! You haven't said a word in five miles! I'm *here*, Buck," she said peevishly and in a mocking tone. "See?"

He turned to her and smiled, "Sure, Cathy. I've just been thinking a little is all."

"About me, I hope. You aren't shilly-shallying around

with the Widow Crowe, are you?" It was said in a teasing tone, but there was a mild challenge in her voice.

"No, Cathy. One woman at a time. You're all I can handle."

"Come on then!" she shouted, and spurred her horse.

They reached over the hills and the valleys, running at breakneck speed. Her superb horsemanship forced him to exercise all his skill to keep up with her. They came at last to the stream, dismounted, shooed their horses away, and flopped down on the grass, exhausted and laughing. Cathy stretched her arms toward the bright sky.

"It's wonderful, Buck. Everything's wonderful. The whole world is wonderful." She turned to him. "And you," she whispered, "are the most wonderful." She sighed and went into his arms.

Cathy Finley was so young, he thought for the second time. So young and enthusiastic. So full of dreams, romance, the springtime of love. It ennobled her in a way, created life out of life, spirit out of spirit, contained her, sailed her into a new world, a new adventure each day, each hour, each minute.

"You're very beautiful, Cathy," he said softly, and caressed her hair with tender fingers.

She murmured words he couldn't hear, soft words trailing off into a misty atmosphere beyond where they lay. It was as if she were talking to herself, which she most likely was, personalizing this idyllic splendor, cherishing, nurturing it, possessing him in this moment of quietude more than he ever could possess her.

She traced a finger up and down his chest, moved closer to him, sighed, closed her eyes and let the world around her vanish into a void, and suddenly she was alone with him in the small planet no one else could reach.

Riding back to town he was silent again, thinking in terms of the incongruity at the magnificence of her youth, her obvious affection, the explosive manner in which she reacted in their intimate moments though they remained innocent in character. She was still in her teens, in the last year of them, of course, but she was a woman in every sense, mature and sophisticated.

IX

Jonathan Finley's day of using a gun were over, but he had transferred them to the gang he used for his depredations and raids around the countryside.

Duane had been unable to learn anything about Cathy's father. He asked Abby about him in a discreet way, but she knew nothing of him.

"There have been rumors from time to time from the folks in the territory that he had been involved with some outlaws, with men like Wesley Hardin, Doc Holliday, and Johnny Ringo. But these, too, were just rumors. No one really knows for a certainty."

"I see," he said reflectively.

"It is important that you know, Buck?"

"No, not too important."

He asked Jeff Kelly about it but he, too, knew nothing other than information he had heard at church picnics or when the men got together at roundup time. Hiram Callahan, the owner of the general store, although he had been in Tafton for years, knew no more. Someone in the Osage hinted that Morris Finley had been hanged as a rustler. It wasn't hard to believe. If that were true then he could understand why Cathy wouldn't talk about him.

One thing that troubled the Ranger most now, ten days after he had arrived in town, was why he hadn't been included in the raid the gang had made on a small bank twenty miles away. Another sore question was what Cathy would do when Captain MacNelly and his men came to arrest her uncle.

Duane did not understand her for a moment. He was certain she would consider him a traitor of the worst sort, of having used her shamelessly, leading her on, accepting her affection only to destroy her only living relative and her along with him. The Ranger visualized the anger that would possess her. Well, it was too late to break off with Cathy now. Perhaps he had been foolish in taking up with her in the first place.

Duane didn't think, however, that it would go on as it had. When they continued seeing each other, there was no stopping it. Duane cursed himself for a fool and wondered what Captain MacNelly would have to say about it. Probably nothing. All MacNelly was interested in was the breakup of the gang. How Duane did it was his business. He could almost hear MacNelly said, "All's fair in love and war, Buck. Hope you enjoyed it."

Buck Duane tried to shrug off the involvement and its potential consequences, but a sense of guilt assailed him. The long corridor of his honesty since the day when he had given up being an outlaw suddenly became murky in his mind. He had been untrue to himself, false to the code by which he had chosen to live. Duane wondered what Jeff and Sara Kelly would think about it when they found out. And Abby.

The Ranger came to a quick awareness of the fact that he cared what the Kellys would think, but most of all what Abby would think. She knew him so slightly and yet trusted him so much. She had been torn on the jagged edges of life by the violent death of her husband. It was unfair to betray her confidence in him.

Two weeks later Duane was in the Osage and Slap Wilson said, "I got a message for you, Buck. Mr. Finley and Tulsa, they want to see us at Mr. Finley's house at two o'clock this afternoon. I was agoin' to ride over to the Widow Crowe's house to tell you but you saved me the trouble. It's 'bout that time now. Let's go."

They rode to the big white house, paused at the wide gate. Wilson reached down from his horse and unhooked the gate and they rode in, dismounted behind the house, tied their horses. A Mexican maid, young, pretty, opened the door for them.

"Buenas tardes. El Senor Finley los esta esperando en la biblioteca. Pasen." She held the door wide and they entered.

"What'd she say?" Slap asked.

"Mr. Finley is in the library. He's expecting us."

"You speak Mex?"

"A little. She spoke Spanish. Excellent Spanish."

"Yeah? What you know! I thought all them Mex were dumb."

"Their culture is older than ours." The Ranger grinned without humor.

In the library they found Finley and Tulsa Harrow sitting in large armchairs smoking cigars. Neither man rose.

"Come in, boys," Finley said. "Take chairs."

They sat down opposite Finley and Tulsa. Duane noted something about Jonathan Finley that had escaped him in their previous meeting. The thin, grudging line that was his mouth. There was cruelty there, as there was in the suspicious clear blue eyes.

Finley said, "Buck, I'm sure you know all about our operations by now. We figured we would give you enough time to think about it, even to ask around a little. I'm sure you have. If you haven't, then I've underestimated you."

Duane nodded his head.

Tulsa leaned back in his chair, took a long puff from his cigar, then leaned forward, the cigar in his hand, pointing it at Duane as he spoke.

"Duane, I've tried to figure you from the beginning. Maybe I have and maybe I haven't. I thought at first you might be a saddle tramp, but changed my mind when I thought of your guns. Bounty hunter? No. I couldn't figure you for that either, although you may be just sneaky enough to be one."

There was a sudden silence in the room, heavy, awkward, and threatening to burst into violence. Duane didn't move a muscle, just sat and stared at Tulsa.

"I said to myself," Tulsa went on, "what the hell is he? I did a little checking. I know about your old man. Got the word from Abilene. Ever been in Abilene, Duane?"

"Nope."

"Ever know a man named Bill Longley?"

"Nope."

"Cheseldine?"

"I've heard of him."

"That's all?"

"That's all."

"How about Captain MacNelly?"

"He tracked me for a long time."

Tulsa eyed him narrowly. "He's head of the Texas Rangers. A tough lawman, they say."

"So I've heard." Duaned paused a moment. "He never lets up."

Tulsa sneered. "MacNelly couldn't find a prayer in a Bible. All right, Duane. I've said my piece. You know exactly what I was fishing for. Don't make any wrong moves."

"You said that once before."

"I'm saying it again. Keep it in mind."

Finley and Tulsa exchanged glances of complete understanding. It was a swift, gliding gesture but they had told each other something which, if spoken, would have taken a thousand words. These two, Duane thought, were models for the old saying, *Thick as thieves*.

The Ranger gave a slight, noncommital shrug and told himself that whatever passed between them didn't matter a damn to him. Unless, if he made a wrong move, they decided to shoot him in the back. He doubted this. Egoist that Tulsa was, with an overbearing pride and confidence in his ability to beat any man alive to the draw, he would want to meet Duane in the middle of Main Street, at high noon, and with the whole town gathered there to witness his performance. That suited Buck Duance just fine.

Jonathan Finley rose from his chair. "All right, Duane. I think you understand Tulsa, and that means you understand me, too. We have to be careful. We have to choose our men with caution. You did me a good turn by saving my life. I'm paying it back by giving you a chance to make more money than you ever made in your life. This is your first opportunity."

Finley nodded to Tulsa Harrow and Slap Wilson. They rose and went to a long narrow table where Finley spread a map. He pointed to a small circle on the map.

"This, gentlemen, is the town of Hope. It's near the Del Rio-El Paso supply road. Used to be Comanche country but the redskins ceased to threaten the territory years ago. It's a very thriving town with big spreads all around. The ranchers use the bank to deposit their money after they sell their cattle. I have the word that something like thirty to fourty thousand dollars will be in the bank next week. I figure it to be Tuesday.

"There's only three people in the bank. Man by the name of Colby owns it. He'll be there. Always is. He's a big man. Over six feet, with thick black hair and bushy eyebrows. Can't mistake him. Most of the money will be in the safe. He's the only one has the combination, so don't bother with the other two. Don't give Colby a chance to go for a gun. He has several under the counter and is known to use them.

"The town has all the usual shops, and four saloons. The bank is between the general store and a saloon known as the M & M. It's run by two men known as Tony McCrann and Mario Lubichek, a couple of wild men out of Deadwood, big and fast. They kinda look after things in town because there isn't a sheriff there. Watch these two. They're dangerous.

"When you ride in, have half your men go into the saloon, Tulsa. Post one man at the door to give the signal for them to leave after you take the bank. But don't let Tony or Mario get the drop on your men. This here—" he pointed to a black pencil line—"is how you come back. It's hilly country and offers a lot of protection just in case they form a posse."

The three men followed the pencil line, took in the towns and the marked-off trails. Duane knew the territory well. So did the other two, and said so.

"You decide who goes into the bank with you, Tulsa."

"I already have. Slap and Duane."

Harrow looked hard at Duane. "Any objections?"

"None at all. That's what I'm here for."

"Good," Finley said. "I suggest you leave tomorrow morning. That will get you into Hope Tuesday in plenty of time. That's all, gentlemen. Good luck."

As they started to leave, Finley said, "Tulsa, you stay a minute. Want to talk to you."

Duane and Slap Wilson walked through the kitchen and were let out by the Mexican maid, who smiled shyly at

Duane. He said something to her in Spanish and she laughed, thanked him and closed the door behind him.

When they rode out the gate, Slap Wilson turned his horse's head toward the Osage. "You comin' with me, Buck?"

"Don't think so, Slap. I want to get some stuff together for the trip."

"What's there to take? All you need is your bedroll."

"Sure, but I want to rest my horse, clean my guns, things like that."

"'Course. Well, I'll just mosey over to the Osage and tell the rest of the boys to be ready. We'll leave at sunup. Meet at the Osage. Get a good rest and clean those guns good."

"I will."

X

Abby had bathed an hour before Duane left Jonathan Finley's house. She thought deeply all the time she was in the big tub, and told herself with quiet resignation that she had no chance with Duane at all, or at best a very small chance. Yet she was helpless before him. His very presence unnerved her so that she could barely breathe at times. When he passed close to her she trembled as with a sudden attack of ague and her legs turned to water.

Buck Duane had brought her great distress, made her feel inadequate, less a woman, yet if he weren't there she couldn't bear it. With hope in her heart, she told herself that perhaps time would play in her favor. This was her secret. She held it within her because she was proper, prim, even—to all outside appearances, that is. The morality to which she held, which restrained her from throwing herself at him, was what she couldn't deny. It was like a form of religion.

Yet she argued with herself, a moral significance which held within itself a tragic consequence, which harbored loneliness and physical hunger, couldn't be entirely right. The meaning of her life was spinning away from her.

"Buck!" she cried aloud. "Help me. help me!"

She did odd chores around the house for a while, then went into his room, picked over his clothes to see if they needed mending, or a button sewed on somewhere. She found a shirt that had a tear in one sleeve. She got her sewing basket, sat on his bed and began to repair it. Duane came in just as she finished.

She held up the shirt. "There was a small tear at the elbow. I fixed it. You don't mind, do you?"

"No, Abby, I don't mind. Thank you." He took her by the hand and led her into the kitchen. "Sit down, Abby. I have to talk to you."

He was so grave that it frightened her. Her first thought was that he was leaving and she grew faint at the thought. As always, she repressed her emotions with difficulty. She uttered a silent prayer. "He's not leaving. God, he's not leaving." She sat in a chair and he took one opposite her at the table.

"Abby, when I first came here I asked you to trust me no matter what happened or what you heard."

"But I've heard nothing, Buck. I wouldn't believe it anyway."

"Yes, of course. But I now have to ask for your trust in a different way. I have to trust *you*."

"Oh, Buck, you can trust me with anything. I'll do whatever you say."

"I knew you would. Abby, I'm a special agent, assigned to the Texas Rangers under Captain MacNelly."

She could not hide her astonishment. Her mouth opened and her lips moved wordlessly as she stared at him.

"My job here, Abby, is to wipe out the Finley gang. Tulsa Harrow. Slap Wilson. All the rest."

She found her voice. "My God! You? Alone?"

"Just about."

"But that man Harrow is a devil! A killer. He killed my husband. A score of other men! Oh, Buck, I'm afraid something dreadful will happen to you!"

"No," he replied, and shook his head. "Don't be

afraid. I have to ask you to do something for me."

"Yes, yes, Buck. Anything."

"I'm going to write a note that I want you to take to Mr. Callahan at the general store. Be very sure that no one sees you giving him the note. When you give it to him just say one word. 'Kelly.' He'll understand. While you're there, buy something. Groceries. Anything. Here." He handed her half a dozen silver dollars.

"I have some money, Buck," she protested.

"Take that. It's not one hundredth enough for what you are going to do."

"Oh, Buck, Buck, I don't want to be paid for this. I—"

"I didn't mean it in that way," he broke in. "Go on, honey, get dressed while I write the note. Give me a pencil and paper."

She hurried to get the writing material and shivered as she hastened to a small desk in the living room. Had he meant what he called her, or was it a slip of the tongue? Honey! Abby could scarcely breathe as she came back with the pencil and paper. He took it from her hand and saw that it trembled.

"Are you scared?" Duane asked.

"Oh, no. No. I'd do this a hundred times if it meant that we would at last be rid of those men. I'm not afraid, Buck." She hurried away lest he see the flush that suddenly rose to her cheeks.

Buck Duane wrote:

Hope. Tuesday morning. Bank. No time. Will have to go through with it if you don't make it. May be trouble with posse.

He folded the sheet of paper into a small square. Abby came into the kitchen with a shawl over her shoulders and a market basket under one arm.

"This is the note," Duane said. "Be careful. Don't pass it if you think you'll be seen. It might mean the death of Callahan."

"I'll be careful. Trust me."

"I do trust you," he told her firmly. "Completely." He took told of her arms, held them tightly. She hurt but she didn't make a protest because she felt, for the first time since his coming that he was touched by a realization of her presence as a woman.

"I hate asking you to do this, Abby," Duane finally said. "But I'm sure either Tulsa or one of his men is on the lookout for me, for anything I may do that would betray me. They suspect me. Tulsa does, anyway. That's why I asked you to do this."

He gripped her arms tighter. "But, for God's sake, be careful. Don't let anyone see you hand Callahan the note."

"I won't, Buck. I'll be very careful."

He let go her arms and she stood there looking into his eyes, searchingly. What Abby saw gave her a great lift. She turned and went out the door and into the street, her heart singing.

There were two ladies in the store whom Abby Crowe knew. They greeted each other and spoke of everyday things women talk about. Another woman came in when Callahan had finished waiting on the first two women, and he turned to Abby.

"What would you like today, Mrs. Crowe?"

"Over here, Mr. Callahan. Will you please lift this bolt down for me? I think it's something I want."

He came from behind the counter toward her where she stood behind a counter laden with more goods. Abby looked to see if the woman was watching. She wasn't. She handed Callahan the note in a quick gesture.

"Kelly," she said softly, and watched his expression.

He put the note into a pocket of his trousers without looking at her and said, "Yes, Mrs. Crowe, that's a very fine piece of goods. Cotton. A beautiful pattern."

"So it is, but I think I'll wait until next week. I'd like two steaks. Cut them thick, please."

He bent close to her. "I'll have this to Kelly in an hour, as soon as my old woman comes in," he whispered.

Abby smiled at him and sighed in relief. She bought some fruit, a box of salt, some spices, and a pound of butter, paid her bill, and left with the satisfied feeling that she had accomplished a great deed, something that would help to rid the town of its robbers and killers.

She almost ran home, hurried into the house, put the basket down and cried, "I did it, Buck! No one saw me. Mr. Callahan said Kelly would have the note in an hour!"

She was flushed with excitement of the thing and her dark candid eyes were shining. He reached out his arms and took her in them, and gave her a tight hug.

"Good girl. I'm very relieved."

She was suddenly enveloped with a mixture of feelings, excitement and exhilaration over what she had done, involvement in a conspiracy that had broken up the routine of her life, and concern over what might happen to Buck.

When he released her she said, "I can't help worrying about what may happen to you, Buck. That whole gang. If they should find out—"

He gave her a reassuring smile. "Don't worry about it, Abby. Nothing will happen to me." He lifted her chin. "Just trust me. Everything will turn out all right."

"I hope so. I'll pray for you, for things to go right."

"That'll help," he answered soberly.

"Are you hungry? Would you like me to fix supper now?"

"Not right away. I have a few things to do. How about six o'clock?"

"All right, Buck. Whatever you say."

Duane was up early the next morning, as was Abby. She was in the kitchen busy making his breakfast. They ate in comparative silence, each unwilling to talk about the impending events of the day. When he finished he stood up and looked down at her, wanting to say the right thing but unable to call the right words to his mind.

Abby had been thrown into a sudden and startling void now that he was ready to leave. She, too, groped for something to say but couldn't find the words.

"Well," the Ranger said at last, "I'll be seeing you in about four or five days." He started for the door.

She jumped up from her chair, ran to him as he reached the door. "Buck, be careful," she said in a tormented voice. "Don't let anything happen to you."

"I won't," he said firmly, and gave her an affectionate

pat on her back. "Don't worry about me. I'll be back."

Duane turned then and went out the door. He didn't see her when she bent her head to her hands and burst into tears, her whole body shaking with the sudden breaking of the dam that had held back the surging emotions of her fears.

The Ranger rode out to the Osage, found the gang already gathered in the saloon, all but Tulsa. The gang was boisterous, drinking and yelling, pounding each other on the back, spilling liquor on the bar and calling for more.

Duane had moved to the farthest end of the long bar and nursed a glass of beer. And then Tulsa Harrow came in. He was dressed in tan Oregon pants, a tan shirt and jacket, and tan cowman's boots that had been highly polished. His silver-handled Colts, loose in the two holsters, shook a little as he walked in and stopped just inside the door.

He said nothing for a long time, just stared at the group who quieted down much as a classroom of kids might have done with the sudden appearance of an absent teacher.

"That's all," Tulsa said in a low voice. "I said to meet here, not to meet and drink. If anyone has a hankering to take along a bottle of whiskey, I advise you not to. Let's go."

The words dripped from his mouth like so much acid, and his eyes followed every man as he left the bar and went out the door. When Buck Duane reached him, he said, "I'm hoping you make a wrong move, Duane. I'll be at your back every second. When we reach the bank, you go in first and throw your gun on the guy that owns it."

"Sure, Tulsa. Anything else?"

"Yeah. If he reaches for one of those guns he's got under the counter you better shoot him. If you don't, I'll get you first and then him. We understand each other?"

"Like a couple of lovebirds, Tulsa," Duane snapped and went out the door.

XI

The lush colors of early autumn, gold, green, purple, red, and orange, shone under the rising sun as they rode out of town toward the trail leading to the hills, valleys, and the flatlands that would take them into Hope.

Slap Wilson rode in front, the other ten members of the gang behind him, and behind them, Buck Duane. Bringing up the rear, some twenty feet behind Duane, was Tulsa Harrow. They rode leisurely, paused at a stream to rest and water their horses when the sun was straight over their heads.

To the west of the stream, a row of new poles went straggling away toward a slope; copper wires, gleaming in the sun, sagged from narrow cross-arms. The smell of burning hair and side told them someone was branding cattle or had finished branding them a short while ago. Duane caught Tulsa looking at him intently while he watered Bullet and he stared back without wavering his glance. Both men tired of staring at each other and turned their gaze.

Tulsa waved an arm, yelled, "Let's go!"

The paused again in late afternoon beside another stream, took food from their saddle bags, ate, dipped hands into the stream and washed their dust-covered faces, then scooped up water into their hands and quenched their thirst.

By dusk they had reached a flat stretch of ground beyond which was a row of ragged hills, and in the middle of the ground a narrow stream ran between a thicket of scrub-oak. Beyond the trees, on the far side of the stream, brush grew thick and tall.

Tulsa yelled to the gang to halt. He rode up to their midst, said, "We'll camp here for the night. Stu, pick up some branches or stray logs for a fire. We'll make some coffee."

The gang dismounted, unsaddled their horses. Most of them led the animals to the stream for a drink and then turned them loose to feed on the grass. Duane led Bullet to the stream, watered him, then led him back to a tall patch of grass where he could feed to his heart's content.

Night fell swiftly, the darkness hemming them in but for the glow of the camp-fire and the faint light of the silver moon that hung low in the sky. Duane found a place against a tree a short distance from the camp-fire around which the rest of the gang had formed a circle and leaned against it. He sat there for a long time with his thoughts and wondered if Captain MacNelly would get his message in time, and getting it, if he would be able to notify sheriffs in towns surrounding Hope in time to stop the holdup and the murder of the owner of the bank.

The Ranger was sure that Tulsa intended to kill him the moment they entered the bank. Duane knew he wouldn't have a chance to kill both Tulsa and Slap. If he shot Tulsa then Slap would surely kill him. The thought of having to shoot the owner of the bank troubled him. This wasn't in the plan at all. But how to avoid it? That was the problem.

Duane got up, stretched, and headed for the stream, bent down and threw water on his face and over his hair, took a long drink, rose, wiped his face and hair with a bandana, and started across the stream toward a hill. He had expected Tulsa to stop him, yell at him, ask him where he was going, but he didn't. He waded across the stream, the water coming to just over his ankles, the boots keeping his feet dry, and made his way up the hill.

He walked to the outer edge on the farther side, saw a declivity that formed one side of a gully. There was a tangle of wild, virginal growth in the bottom of the gully, and then a long, gradual slope that led to some timber. Behind the timber was a small ranch house. A light shone in one of the windows facing him.

Duance raced down the slope of the hill and ran toward the house. He knocked on the door and a tall, slim man in his late twenties, bronzed, with wide shoulders and slim hips which told of years in the saddle, stood framed in the doorway.

"What is it, stranger?"

"I have to talk to you," Duane said. "It's important."

The urgency in Duane's voice struck through to the

man. He held the door back for Duane to enter. A tall, graceful young woman, with the copper-hued skin of an Indian or a half-breed, came out from the kitchen, stood there and gazed first at Duane and then at her husband.

"What is it, Josh?" she asked in a nervous tone.

"A stranger, Yolanda, who needs help."

"I'm sorry if I frightened you, Ma'am," Duane said, "but I need help." He looked from one to the other, decided he could trust them. "I'm a Texas Ranger. I joined a gang to break them up. They're going to rob the bank in Hope."

The woman turned pale, put both hands to her face. "Ohhh—"

"Why did you come here?" the man asked.

"How far is Hope from here?"

"About twenty miles."

"I must ask you to ride in tonight. Get to the owner of the bank and warn him. Tell him who I am. Tell him I'll be wearing a red bandana around my neck, that I'll be the first one in the bank, not to shoot me but to protect himself against the other two men when we come into the bank."

The man looked bewildered.

"How will I tell him to do that? Besides, it's dark. The trails are treacherous. It would man forty miles of riding, there and back. It would mean leaving my wife alone. I can't do it. There's no way."

"A man may be killed. Maybe two, three or four. Don't you understand? You have to do it! I can't stay any longer. What's your name?"

"Lerner. Josh Lerner."

"All right, Mr. Lerner. You can make it up and back in four hours, be back shortly after midnight. I have to go. I'm depending on you."

As Duane reached the door, the man yelled at him, "I can't do it!"

Duane didn't wait to argue but ran back as fast as he could, to the top of the hill, across the stream, slowed down, took several deep breaths and walked slowly to the tree where he had left his bedroll. As he was unrolling it,

Tulsa walked up.

"You walk around at night, Duane?"

Buck Duane looked up. "Sometimes," he answered slowly. "I was a little stiff from the day's riding and thought I'd take a walk to loosen my legs. Why?"

"I'll ask the questions, Duane," Tulsa retorted coldly. "From now on you stay put with the rest of the boys. I'll tell you when to go, and where. Understand?"

"Perfectly."

"That's good for you," Tulsa said meaningly, and walked away.

Duane finished unrolling his bedroll, wrapped himself in the blanket and tried to sleep but couldn't. He believed that he had made clear to Josh Lerner the urgency of the situation. If he was any kind of man at all, he would ride out to Hope and warn the owner of the bank.

On the other hand, Duane thought, it might have been a very foolish move. If Tulsa suspected anything—and he was just the kind who would, especially where Duane was concerned—then he might take a walk up the hill and have a look. That look would reveal the ranch house. Lerner struck him as a man who would first want to protect his wife, and himself, and if Tulsa threatened the woman first then surely Lerner would reveal their conversation.

All the work Duane had done so far would be lost. Moreover, Tulsa and Slap would decide to kill him and throw his body into the thick brush where he would never be found. It was an irritating thought, and the Ranger cursed himself for having given in to the impulse to reveal himself to Lerner and his wife. He tossed around for a long time and finally fell into a troubled sleep.

Just before daybreak, Duane felt a boot against his back, turned and looked up into Tulsa's grim face. "Get up, Duane."

Duane moved around under the blanket he had wrapped around himself, every sense alert to Tulsa's manner. All he could determine was that Tulsa's tone held no more animosity toward him than it usually did. But that was his way. He had never raised his voice in all the times that

Duane had talked with him. He hadn't raised his voice when he had talked to Jeff Kelly, but the threat in it had been unmistakable.

The Ranger peered through the haziness of the early morning darkness up at Tulsa's face, at the cold gray eyes that were barely visible to him, so that it was difficult for him to tell exactly what lay behind them. He reached a hand to his gun and unrolled slowly from the blanket, stood up with his right side away from Tulsa. He reached down, picked up the blanket, and held it in such a way that Tulsa could not see the right hand that held the gun half-drawn from its holster.

"You have a funny way of waking up a man," he said with mild irritation. "I don't like a man using a boot on me. You wanted to wake me, all you had to do was call my name. I sleep with my mind half open. I'd have heard you."

Tulsa Harrow stared at him for a long, hard minute. "You'll get used to me after a time, Duane," Tulsa said in that even tone. "Most men do. If they live long enough."

"I'll live long enough," Duane retorted, "but I won't ever get used to you, Tulsa. There's a lot about you that gripes me as much as I gripe you."

Tulsa grunted on a low note. "We'll settle that some day," Tulsa retorted, and snapped off the words. "Right now, get yourself together. We're moving out. Hard riding. We have to be in Hope by nine o'clock."

He turned away from him without another word and strode toward the group, all of whom were up and saddling their horses.

Duane walked to the stream, washed his face, took a long drink, and whistled for Bullet. So Tulsa hadn't gone to see the Lerners. Now, if Josh Lerner had ridden into Hope to warn the banker of the impending robbery, all would come off well. If he hadn't, then everything depended on Jeff Kelly having been able to send off the message to Captain MacNelly in time for MacNelly to warn someone in Hope. Duane saddled and mounted Bullet.

They rode out onto the trail single file, Slap Wilson

leading the way and Tulsa Harrow bringing up the rear. The fore-running glow of the sunrise in the east touched the emerald green of the trail's lush growth, and the fragrant moisture of the morning air poured into Duane's lungs as he rode along breathing in deeply. Light came suddenly and Tulsa yelled to ride hard.

Duane would have been dismayed if he had known how completely Tulsa Harrow's suspicion of him had jelled into certainty. He would have been more dismayed if he had known that Tulsa meant to kill him immediately after they walked out of the bank with the money. The crystallization of Tulsa's suspicions into firm belief that he was other than what he represented himself to be, and possibly a lawman, had persuaded him to kill Duane.

Harrow couldn't do it before the eyes of the gang without provocation because even they, under the code of the West, would have held him low and jeopardized his position as leader. But, coming out of the bank, and under the pretext of shooting at defenders of the town, Tulsa could get away with it.

XII

The gang reached Hope shortly after eight o'clock. It was a town weaned on gunsmoke and death. The M & M Saloon had seen a hundred gunfights and as many killings, and the owners, Tony and Mario, had been involved in a dozen of them. This was something Finley had neglected to say, and only because he hadn't been informed of it by the man who had given him his information on Hope.

Tulsa Harrow yelled a signal and the gang halted on the outskirts of town. He waved a hand and they dismounted as he rode up.

"It's too early to ride in," Tulsa said. "Rest your horses and yourselves. We may have a hard ride out of town and you'll need a fresh horse under you."

Harrow looked the gang over, gave each one instructions. "Slap, Duane, and I will go into the bank. Stu, you stay just outside the door of the saloon, Tony and Mario's, and give the rest of the boys the signal to leave when you see us come out. Bob and Harry, you two kind of mosey around in front of the saloon and have your rifles with you, just in case.

"The rest of you go into the saloon and take care of those two bad men, Tony and Mario if they start trouble. All right, that's it. Lie down and rest."

At ten minutes of nine, Tulsa gave a signal and the men who were to go into the saloon got up from the ground, mounted, and rode slowly into town. They dismounted in front of the saloon, tied their horses to the hitching post with slip knots and went in. The saloon was filled with about twenty cowpokes, all armed. They were drinking beer. There wasn't a bottle of whiskey on the bar. The gang did not notice this highly unusual circumstance.

Five minutes later, Stu rode in, tied his horse, and sat down on a wooden bench to the right of the entrance to the saloon. His rifle was across his lap. Bob and Harry rode up then, tied their horses, and split up, taking positions about fifteen feet from the saloon, looking up and down the street, across the street, and along the side of the street where the saloon was situated.

It struck Bob as odd that not a single soul was on the street. The stores were closed. Shades were drawn behind each window. The only noise audible came from the interior of the saloon. At that moment, Slap, Duane, and Tulsa rode up before the bank and tied their horses to the hitching post.

Tulsa looked around, up and down the street, and motioned to Bob and Harry to be ready in case of trouble. The two men moved to their positions about ten feet from the entrance to the saloon, one on either side.

"All right, Duane," Tulsa said, "this is it. This is where I find out if you're with us or a dog. If you're a dog, you're goin' to die like one. Let's go."

Duane looked up and down the street hoping for a sign that would tell him Captain MacNelly had received Jeff Kelly's telegram. He was certain that Josh Lerner had not ridden into town to warn the banker. That poor young man was scared to death. Well, he couldn't blame him. Why get mixed up in an affair like this? It was none of his business. Besides, he had his wife to think of.

"What's the matter, Duane?" Tulsa sneered. "Got cold feet?"

"I'm just wondering whether you have," Duane retorted. "You wanted me to go in first. Again, I don't like you at my back."

As he spoke the Ranger was bleakly sure that his plans for breaking up the gang had been shot full of holes.

Tulsa drew one of his silver-handled Colts. "Move in, Duane, or I'll drop you right here. In the back. I've never shot a man in the back in my life but I'm willing to make an exception in your case. Let's go."

Duane moved toward the door of the bank. He took a last quick look up and down the street. It was hopeless. No one was about. He drew his gun, pushed open the door, and stepped in. Tulsa Harrow and Slap Wilson followed him.

"Raise your hands!" Duane ordered. "This is a holdup. Raise 'em and you won't get hurt. All we want is the money!"

Tulsa swore. Duane didn't know why in the instant that Tulsa uttered his curse, and then he saw why. The owner was not in the bank. The only ones behind the narrow counter were the two clerks, both of whom now held their hands high in the air.

"There isn't any money here," the smaller of the two clerks said in a quavering voice. "Mr. Colby was in early this morning and took all the money to Walden."

Tulsa's eyes narrowed and his face was blue with anger. It was the first time Duane had seen him lose control.

"Come out here, you!" Tulsa said to the clerk. "Come out!"

The clerk came out from behind the counter, his hands still in the air only now he was shaking with fright as he approached Tulsa.

"Who warned Colby about a holdup?" he demanded. "Talk!"

"I don't know anything, Mister. Honestly. I—"

Tulsa slapped the man across the face—hard. The blow sent the slight man sprawling. Tulsa pointed the gun at him.

"Talk or I'll kill you!"

The man began to blubber. "I don't know anything," he cried in stammering tones. "Please don't kill me. Mr. Colby told us nothing."

Slap Wilson yelled, "Kill him! He's lyin'. I'll kill this other coyote!"

The Ranger had no chance to stop Wilson. The gun in Slap's hand exploded. The clerk behind the counter toppled over. Duane saw the rush of blood that swam over the hapless man's face before he fell. He saw the pale blue smoke drift slowly up from the muzzle of Slap's gun.

There was a haunting stillness for a quick moment as Duane fought indecisively with himself. His first reaction was to shoot Slap but he saw Tulsa's eyes on him and he changed his mind. All this flashed through his thoughts with the speed of light.

"Let's get out of here," he said.

It was the weakest thing he could have said, but it was all he could think of at the moment through the deep, keen disappointment over the turn of events. Slap's features, hard, tough, his ugly mouth twisted into a snarl, his beady eyes fixed on Duane were a shade less in harshness than the look on Tulsa's face.

Duane was certain Tulsa wanted to gun him down there and then but the gun in Duane's hand must have changed his mind. A gunfight here would gain Tulsa nothing.

Suddenly there was the sound of gunfire in the street, a staccato of pistols and rifles. Tulsa and Slap hurried out, and Duane followed them. Stu and Harry lay dead on the wooden walk outside the saloon. Bob had backed off the walk and was firing into the saloon with his rifle, the Winchester smoking as he triggered shot after shot in rigid fire.

Tulsa and Slap screamed oaths, and both ran toward the spot where Bob stood and began firing into the saloon. Shouts from inside the saloon mixed with the sound of the gunfire. Moses Pratt, one of the gang, stumbled out into the street. He was bleeding badly.

"Ambush!" he managed to say in a half-croaking sound and spat up blood. "Too many guns. Run for it!" He coughed up more blood and then collapsed to the ground. He was dead.

Duane raised his Colt, somewhat sickened. Tulsa and Slap were perfect targets—two shots, and the men who were on the point of killing him seconds ago would be dead. But it would not be a lawman's victory, or even a gunfighter's, and it went against the grain. Yet even now they were sending lead into the saloon, perhaps killing the town's defenders while he hesitated.

He leved the .45 at Tulsa—then a searing pain in his arm blended with a thunderclap of sound; the Colt spun from his fingers and he staggered forward.

"Hold it right there!" a voice rasped behind him. "This buffalo gun's got two barrels, and th' second one's trained right on yer kidney."

Duane turned to face a wizened figure clad in rank buckskins, grizzled of hair and beard. Old though he was, the hands that held the massive, ancient weapon were steady, and the Ranger had no reason to doubt the asserted destination of its remaining round.

"Listen, old-timer," he said, "I'm not—"

"Old-timer, is it? I'm about forty years older 'n you're ever goin' to get to be, without you raise yer hands jest as high's they'll go," his captor retorted indignantly. "Rights, I should drop ye where y'are, but I'd kind of like to keep y'alive long enough to tell folks how I got me a bandit. Not much longer'n that, though," he added, wanting to be fair.

Duane raged as he heard the sounds of battle die away behind him. The short, fierce fight was over. He risked a backward glance and saw Slap and Tulsa pounding off down the dusty street, unhit by the following fire from the townspeople.

"I'm a Texas Ranger," he said desperately.

"An' I'm the mighty Yeller Hand, feared sachem of the Pawnee," said the ancient cordially. "Which I eats Texas

Rangers for breakfast, 'specially when I catch 'em robbin' banks. Hey," he called to the townspeople now hurrying up from the saloon, "here's an owlhoot with gumption. Caught him blazin' away at the saloon, then he says he's a Texas Ranger. Knocked the gun outen his hand with the neatest shot I ever—"

"I am a Ranger," Duane grated. "And I'd have got those two killers if it hadn't been for that 'neat shot'!"

"I don't know that he's a Ranger," a voice spoke up. "But I do know he's the man who warned me about the raid and did it strong enough so I rode twenty miles here and gave you people time to set up that ambush!"

Duane's heart leaped up as he saw Josh Lerner. So his gamble on the young rancher's nerve had paid off!

Within minutes, the superficial graze on his arm had been bandaged and he was once again astride Bullet and headed out of Hope, followed by the old hunter's mingled apologies and insistences that it had, after all, been a damn' neat shot.

Tulsa and Wilson were on horses as fresh as his, and they knew the route back to Tafton better; Duane had no illusions about overtaking them. Duane and Bullet covered the miles steadily, but without urgency. The drama was approaching its end, and the last act had to be played at Tafton. Slap and Tulsa would be waiting for him there, and so would Jonathan Finley—and Cathy.

Finley: a tricky proposition. Buck Duane had been sent on his undercover mission to bring the ringleader of the robberies to justice, not to gun him down. Either way, the threat Finley represented would be over; but a live Jonathan Finley, standing trial and getting a fair verdict from a jury meant a lot more to law and to the Rangers than a gray-haired corpse leaking blood into the dust of Main Street.

Finley would be tough to take, but somehow or other, Duane would have to find a way to arrest him and bring him safely to jail. It could be done—maybe.

Cathy: sorrow was what Buck Duane felt mostly. He had disturbed her life, and his own. He had come out of nowhere, given her a dream, and, within a day at the most, would explode that dream and shatter the very fabric of her life. He shouldn't have let himself get involved with the girl—but not often did any man, let alone one whose life was set in the harsh but haunting open spaces, encounter such a woman.

"She has grit," he told himself. "She'll hate me, but maybe that will make it easier for her to take the rest."

Slap Wilson and Tulsa Harrow: death, plain and simple. Duane smiled wryly as he pictured himself telling either, "You're under arrest." As well try to serve a warrant on a cougar! He knew full well that he could have a battery of cannons trained on them at point-blank range, and if he called on them to surrender, they would draw and fire on the gunners.

Yet he also knew that if either were at his back, he would walk safely until the moment they called the challenge. His known prowess with the revolver—and his successful imposture as an outlaw, which had gained him their grudging acceptance—made it necessary for men such as these to face him on their own terms. Unless they shot it out with him, there would be no savor in seeing him dead, no inflation of the one value they cherished, their reputation as gunfighters.

So. . .he would find Slap and Tulsa, or they would find him. And Death would complete the foursome. The only question left was, whose?

And, to something in Buck Duane's deepest self—perhaps a remnant of his outlaw years, perhaps a legacy from his father—the challenge was not entirely unwelcome.

When night fell Buck Duane made camp, and fell into a troubled sleep. When he awoke, the first gray patch of dawn shone in the east. He rose, stretched wearily, walked to where Bullet was tied to a tree, and patted him fondly.

"Hard ride ahead, Boy," Duane said in a low tone. "Got to move." He saddled him, mounted, and rode off, slowly at first because it was still too dark for fast riding.

XIII

Then the sun came up and the sky showed blue. Buck Duane found a spring with a group of cottonwoods beside it. He dismounted and let Bullet drink his fill while he washed his face and quenched his own thirst. He let Bullet graze in the thick grass for about fifteen minutes then mounted him and rode hard. He reached Tafton about ten o'clock and skirted the town, riding directly to Jeff Kelly's spread. He rode in toward the back of the house, dismounted and tied Bullet to a post. As he did so, Jeff Kelly came out of the house.

"I got the message out to Captain MacNelly," he said.

"Good," said Duane.

"Come in, come in, Mr. Duane," Kelly urged.

Duane followed him into the house. Mrs. Kelly was in the kitchen. She appeared excited, trembled a little.

"Would you like some coffee, Mr. Duane? Yes, I think you would. And some breakfast? I'll fix you some breakfast."

"No, thanks. Just some coffee." The Ranger sat down at the table opposite Kelly.

"It's all over town, Mr. Duane. Slap Wilson has been in the Osage the last hour screaming for your blood. He said you got the whole gang killed. All except him and Tulsa Harrow."

Sara Kelly set two cups of coffee before the men. "What will you do, Mr. Duane?" she asked, deep concern in her tone. "Those men will surely kill you."

He shook his head. "Not both at the same time. They'll have to make a fair fight of it. Even Judge Grant, weak as he is, could not chew a killing like that. Two men against one. No. That would be outright murder and I'm sure he knows that if that happened it would blow things sky high. Besides, I think that Tulsa Harrow wants a chance at me first."

He took a swallow from the cup in his hand. "Good coffee, Mrs. Kelly."

"What's the next step, Mr. Duane?" Kelly asked.

"Well, assuming that Tulsa beats me to the draw, I want you to tell Captain MacNelly when he gets here that—"

"Are you sure Captain MacNelly will come? How will he know? All I did was send the message to him about the holdup."

"He'll get the word from Hope about what happened and will know the next step is to come to Tafton and clean things up. As I said, if Tulsa should beat me to the draw before Captain MacNelly gets here I want you to tell him that Jonathan Finley planned this holdup of the bank in my presence, that Slap Wilson killed the bank clerk in Hope. The other clerk will bear witness to that."

"My God!" Mrs. Kelly cried. "I didn't know. Those murderers!"

"I'll tell him all that you've said. Anything else?"

"Yes. I want you to ride out to everyone you know around here and tell him to go into town, move around in the stores and in the street. Tell one and tell him to tell another and those to tell another. That will get most of the people there in about an hour. I'll take it from there."

"I'll do it now."

Both men rose. Duane said, "I have something to take care of first, and then I'll ride into town. I'll give you and your friends an hour."

"I think that's all it will take."

"Good. Thanks for everything. Maybe you'll get a clean town when this is over with." He extended his hand to Kelly who shook it firmly. He turned to Sara Kelly. "Thank you, too." He held out his hand and she took it, tears coursing down her cheeks.

"You're a very brave man, Mr. Duane," she murmured, "the most courageous man I've ever known. God bless you, and good luck."

"Thank you. I'll need both."

The Ranger went out with Jeff Kelly, mounted Bullet as Kelly hurried to saddle his horse. He waved to Kelly and turned Bullet toward Abby's home. He rode over a back trail and reached the house without being seen by anyone. When Duane came in through the back door, Abby ran to him and thrust herself into his arms.

"Oh, thank God!" she cried. "I heard about it. I thought you had been killed. I was frantic."

She clutched him tighter, with a fierceness beyond her strength as if she wanted to mold herself to him, murmured against his chest. He suddenly felt a great affection for her wash through him. She was fine, decent, honest, and more than anything else she needed him, desperately. He realized that now with an overpowering sense of dismay. What, he wondered, could he say to her that wouldn't completely demoralize her at this moment when despair had turned to a great flooding of joy at his return.

There was the possibility, too, that he might die before the guns of Slap or Tulsa. He took hold of her arms and pushed her gently away from him, looked down into her face. He saw a great yearning for something intangible in her candid brown eyes. Her eyes always spoke her thoughts. They never hid anything.

She had been soft and yielding against him, eager, still a little frightened but the pleasure of being in his arms was the strongest emotion. She had quivered several times when he held her. He had a new vision of her. Now she was a little taut as she looked up at him.

"Abby," he said softly, "you have to face facts. I'm going to meet one, or two, very likely two, experienced gunfighters in the next hour. I think I understand how you feel about me. I wish you wouldn't. You may be hurt more an hour from now if you don't tell yourself there is nothing for us, for each other."

Abby dropped her hands and looked up at him through tears. She was dumbfounded, the intensity in her slim body conveying itself to him. The shock left her face but the paleness remained.

"Suppose," she said in a halting tone—"suppose it won't be that way? Suppose you—you win?" She half-turned from him, clasped her hands together and put them to her lips, biting the knuckles.

"Oh, God!" She turned back to him. "Help me, Buck," she pleaded. "Help me with the words." She was suddenly in his arms again. "I love you, Buck," she murmured emotionally. "I've loved you from the first day."

Buck Duane put his arms around her and held her close, bent his head and kissed her on the mouth, felt the salt of her tears against his lips. She was trembling again, and then she became a wild thing in his arms, her own arms clasped around his neck, her lips burning him with her frantic kisses. He tried to pull away from her but she held on. She held on desperately, the fear of losing him racing through her with a dizzying speed.

"Let me have my memory of love of you," she said then, and her shy woman's soul bent her head deeply into his chest. The words came muffled but unmistakable. "There's time. Let's have this hour."

It was no good. It would be no good for her and no good for him. The Ranger needed every emotion that possessed him now and in the next hour or two. His life depended on it. He tried to find the right words to say to her, the words that wouldn't leave her scorned, bring shame to her for having been refused, for what she was offering was the spirit and the life of her body and soul.

"If I could say what I would like to say, Abby," Duane said in the tenderest of tones, "I would tell you how much what you've said means at a time like this. Let's wait it out. Let's see what happens."

She stood there completely demolished in spirit for a long moment and then she turned away from him, but he reached out and took hold of her arm, pulled her to him.

"Not like that," he said softly. "Abby, things may work out. Let's hope for them. And say a prayer for me." He kissed her softly on the mouth. "Will you make some coffee? I have a few things to do. I'll be finished in about five minutes."

Abby seemed to recover herself and gave him a wan smile. "I'll hope," she said. "And I'll say a prayer."

The Texas Ranger went into his room, took off the belt that held his guns, got a piece of wax and a small bottle of oil and started to work the insides of both holsters, rubbing the wax and oil into the leather with the palm of his hand. He dropped a gun into the holster, pulled it out, then dropped it back. The action was smooth. He then examined both guns, cleaned them thoroughly, tested the trigger action. That, too, was perfect.

He put the belt back on, tied the holsters to his legs, moved them around in just the right positions for his draw. There was a grim look on Duane's face as he visualized what lay ahead. He heaved a heavy sigh and went into the kitchen. The coffee was on the table. He sat down and took a drink from the cup.

"Aren't you having any?" he asked.

"No. Not now. I have something to do." Abby turned swiftly, went into her room, closed the door, threw herself on the bed and gave way to the great sobbing that had threatened to burst forth all morning. Her body shook with her sobs as she lay there, her small hands clenched into fists, her face buried in the pillow to muffle the sound of her weeping.

She came out after a while, the ravages of her weeping erased from her face. Buck Duane was still at the table. She sat down opposite him.

"What will I do while you—you're gone?" she asked. "I just can't sit here and wait, and hope, and pray, and wait." Her tone was becoming desperate again.

"Would you rather come into town? Would you feel better if you were there, no matter how it came out?"

"Yes," she answered resolutely. "At least I'd know. There wouldn't be that terrible uncertainty, the torture of waiting to learn what happened."

Abby was in full control of herself, and he saw a new side of her. She had courage. She was willing to watch everything that mattered to her dissolve into nothingness with a single shot from a Colt.

"Are you sure you'll be all right?" Duane asked anxiously.

"I'll be all right," she answered firmly.

He rose. "You go into town now. Find Jeff and Sara Kelly. Stay with them. I think that will be better for you."

"Yes, I think it will." She stood up. "I'll go now."

Abby went into her room, picked up a shawl, threw it over her shoulders, came back into the kitchen, bent over him where he sat, and gave him a light kiss on the cheek. He stood up and smiled down at her.

"Don't miss," Abby said lightly. And then they both laughed and the tension dissolved. A deep surging of confidence went through him. It was all right. Everything was going to be all right. She went out the door without turning around.

Duane waited about ten minutes then walked into the rear yard, untied Bullet and mounted.

The center of town was crowded with people. Buggies, wagons, horses hitched to posts on both sides of the street met Buck Duane's gaze as he rode slowly in. His gaze probed the wooden walk outside the Osage. A group of men stood on either side of the batwings. The sun was high, the day bright. The Ranger looked up into the sky to note the slant of the rays. He wanted nothing to hinder him, not even a speck of dust an errant wind might throw up.

People stopped to stare after Duane as he rode past, whispered among themselves. Children pointed to him and shouted. Several small dogs barked at Bullet, who ignored them. He seemed to know that he was on an important mission and had no time to give to barking dogs. Duane rode up to the saloon, dismounted and ground-hitched Bullet. A man dashed into the saloon, and then another.

Duane waited patiently. He knew it was just a matter of a minute. He was right. Slap Wilson stalked out of the Osage and faced Duane. His facial muscles were corded, his face flaming with rage, his eyes gleaming with fury. His hands clenched and unclenched, and his voice was choked with passion as he spoke.

"You dirty night-crawling snake!" Slap Wilson yelled. His tone was hot and murderous, the hate burning through his words.

Duane gazed at him but did not answer. There was a glint of contempt in his eyes and his lips were in a straight, hard line. He said then, "I'm a Texas Ranger, Slap. You know that now. This is where you can settle your quarrel with me."

The crowd around the Osage scattered, the men taking placed against the buildings and the women huddling together in tight little groups. The street behind both men had miraculously cleared as Duane backed away, a step at a time, never taking his eyes off Slap Wilson.

Buck Duane knew one thing more than he knew anything else, that when you stepped out into the street to face the challenge of a gun you were more alone than if you suddenly had been violently thrown by some great force onto a strange and uninhabited planet. Survival now depended on your nerve, wits, speed of hand, keenness of sight, but above all, chain-lightning speed.

The wild anger in Slap Wilson diminished to some degree his judgment of time and distance, time measured in those cold and bitter instants that were like separate little eternities. Duane knew he had that much advantage.

As he backed away, Slap kept yelling at him, cursing him, spitting on the ground. "I'll kill you!" he cried. "I'll kill you! Kill you!"

Abby stood with Sara Kelly, their hands clasped together so tightly the blood had faded from the skin. Jeff Kelly stared at the scene before him, his eyes on Duane, who now was almost directly in front of him.

Abby Crowe turned her head for a brief moment and uttered a prayer. Sara Kelly whispered something to her and she turned her eyes back to the street. The whole tableau had a nightmare quality about it.

Duane stopped at a point in the street where the sun was just to his right and out of his eyes. There was not a rustle of wind, nor a sound from the crowd. All that was audible was a quick barking from a dog, and then it happened.

Slap Wilson cried out an oath. The depth of his hate could not go deeper, and it exploded into action. It was the moment Duane had waited for. He was sure that Slap would make that last oath and when he did he would reach for his gun. The sound of the oath had not yet died down when both men drew and fired. But Duane's gun had flashed a split second faster, so fast that few men saw the pull.

Slap's shot threw up dust a few feet in front of Duane, and then he stood there, stiff and erect, his head rolling a little from side to side, blood poured from his mouth, and he toppled forward. Abby let out a wild cry, started to run toward Duane, but Sara held her back.

"Don't!" she cried. "Not yet. Look!"

"Here comes Tulsa!" a man in the crowd yelled.

XIV

Abby Crowe turned into Sara Kelly's arms, unable to take more of the hot liquid tension that had piled up inside of her. Sara held her close, whispered words of encouragement.

"He'll kill Buck," Abby moaned. "He's killed twenty men. Oh, my God, my God!"

Jeff Kelly went between the two women, put his arms around them and spoke in a low tone. His words seemed to buoy up Abby's spirits as she turned her eyes to the road again.

The crowd remained stilled and the mischievous little dog that had barked was now held in the arms of a little boy who stood on the wooded walk staring fascinated at Buck Duane. He had seen something he had heard his elders talking about but never had believed it would come to pass before his eyes. Now there was going to be another time, in the next few minutes.

Duane had holstered his gun and stood there in the street watching Tulsa Harrow approach. There was a slight sneer on Tulsa's face as he walked up the street. He ignored the crowd completely. His eyes were fastened on Duane. He lifted a silver-handled Colt from its highly polished holster, inspected it briefly, spun the cylinder, dropped the gun back into the holster, then pulled it half way out and back several times to test the smoothness of the draw.

Satisfied, Harrow smiled a quick smile and looked directly at Buck Duane. He had moved just a few feet from where Slap Wilson lay dead, directly in front of the body.

"A Ranger, eh, Duane?" Tulsa sneered. "A damned

Texas Ranger. I might have known. Well, Ranger, this is where I wanted to meet you. Right here in front of all your goody-goodies. You've done a pretty good job. Got all my men killed and killed Slap. You're goin' to try me now, Duane. You know what? I'm goin' to see your guts spilled right where you stand."

Duane said nothing, just kept his eyes focused on Tulsa's right hand and his right foot, keeping them both in full view. He knew from things his father had taught him, that a gunfighter will make an untoward move with some part of his body just before he reached for his gun. The nervous movement might be made with the opposite foot, shoulder, or hand, but when he was ready to pull it would be made with the gun side.

Duane remembered that when he had talked to Kelly that day outside the courtroom he had made a movement with his left foot. If what his father had taught him held true then Tulsa would make the movement with his right foot.

Tulsa stood erect, his hands at his sides, his eyes holding Duane, watching him intently, those steely eyes never wavering for a moment. The hush that had fallen over the crowd was like the silence of death itself. It seemed that nature, too, had been stunned into silence for not a leaf rustled, a speck of dusk moved, nor even the mildest gust of wind drifted over the stretch of ground where both men stood.

Absolute silence had taken over as the crowd watched first one man and then the other. Abby stood there next to Jeff Kelly with her lips moving in prayer.

A man coughed just outside the door of the Osage. It seemed to be the signal for Duane and Tulsa to draw. Duane's eyes had kept Tulsa's right foot and right arm in constant view, his eyes glued to both members. When the man coughed, Tulsa's right foot moved imperceptibly, and Duane drew. If his draw against Slap Wilson had been fast then this one belied belief.

Both guns exploded at once, Duane's shot threw Tulsa violently backward and his gun fell from his hand and clattered into the dusty street. Tulsa's body and the shot from his gun seemed to coordinate in action for he fell at the split second that his gun went off. That was the speed of Duane's draw and the firing of his Colt.

Abby burst from between Jeff and Sara Kelly and ran sobbing toward Duane. The crowd began to mill around the two bodies and to stare at the fallen men. A doctor emerged from the crowd and bent over Tulsa.

"Through the heart," he declared. "Never knew what hit him." He looked toward Duane. "Never saw such shooting in my life for sure. That man is the fastest gun alive."

The crowd began to mill around Duane who held the sobbing Abby in his arms. She was weeping hysterically now, the deep relief at the outcome overwhelming her. Duane patted her shoulder and whispered to her soothingly. Sara Kelly came up and Duane motioned to her to take Abby and comfort her, help her to regain her composure.

Sara Kelly took Abby's arm and pulled her gently away. "Come on, dear. It's all over. There's nothing more to worry about."

Abby allowed herself to be led away, but not too far. She wanted to stay as close to Duane as she could. Jeff Kelly talked to Duane.

"It isn't over yet, Buck," he said. "There's Jonathan Finley. What about him?"

As Kelly spoke, Jonathan Finley came into view, a Winchester in his hands, his gray hair gleaming in the sun, his tall figure striding determinedly toward the street where Buck Duane stood.

The Ranger stood where he was, his eyes fixed on Finley, on the Winchester, waiting for the first movement that would warn him of Finley's intent to shot.

"God!" Abby cried. "Jonathan Finley!" She turned into Sara Kelly's arms. "This is awful, awful! I can't take any more," she sobbed.

"All you people get out of the way!" Finley yelled. "I want that white-livered skunk Duane!"

"Finley," the Ranger yelled, "drop your gun! You're under arrest!"

"Arrest?" Finley shouted back. "You dirty, two-timing snake! Come and arrest me!" He stood there shaking with rage, his head moving up and down and from side to side, his mouth working as if he were chewing something he couldn't swallow.

The crowd had scattered out of direct range of the guns, moved to the wooden walks fronting the streets. And at that moment Cathy came running up the street.

"Uncle Jonathan! Don't!" she screamed. She was weeping wildly. "Uncle Jonathan! Uncle Jonathan! Don't shoot! Don't shoot!"

She reached his side and pulled at his arm. He jerked away from her.

"Get out of the way, Cathy!" he yelled at her. "I'm going to kill this snake!"

"Finley," Buck Duane yelled, "don't make me kill you! Let's talk this over. You've still got a chance."

"Talk?" Finley shouted. He laughed on a high, eerie note. "You did things up fine with your damned talk. Killed off all my men, you did! Now you want to arrest me! Put me in jail, eh? Or hang me! I'll give you talk!" he raised his rifle and snapped off a shot.

As he raised his rifle, Buck Duane dropped to the ground, rolled, was up on his feet, ran in a zigzag line to the safety of a doorway. He couldn't shoot back, not while Cathy stood next to her uncle. The crowd that had taken refuge on the side of the street where the Ranger had run now scattered to the opposite side.

Abby and Sara huddled together holding each other, both women whispered anguished prayers. The drama of the situation had caught the crowd up in its depths and a greater stillness than that which had pervaded them before hung over them.

"You sleazy lawman!" Finley yelled. "Come out into the street!" He leveled the Winchester and fired, the slug tearing splinters of wood from the building where Buck Duane had sheltered himself.

"Cathy," the Ranger yelled, "get out of the way!"

But Cathy refused to leave her uncle's side. She was still making an effort to tear the rifle from his hands. Finley turned toward her and pushed her violently aside. As he did so, Duane threw his hat out toward the street and the anxious and half-crazed Finley fired.

The Ranger took two quick steps from the doorway, leveled his gun and fired. The slug caught Finley in the left shoulder and the rifle fell from his hands.

Duane moved toward him, gun in hand. "Stand right there, Finley. Don't make a move. If you reach for that rifle I'll drop you!"

Cathy leaped to her feet and ran to her uncle's side, took him in her arms. He was bleeding profusely. There was no more fight in him. He was a beaten old man, shaken, wounded, in obvious shock, and tottering on his feet.

The Ranger reached down and picked up the rifle, motioned to the crowd. "Send out the doctor!"

The doctor emerged from the group a short distance away and hurried to the wounded man.

"Patch him up," Duane ordered. "He's under arrest."

Cathy looked up at Duane, a great sadness in her eyes, her lovely mouth trembling, great beads of tears rolling down her cheeks.

"Why did you do this to me?" she asked in a tremulous tone. "Why?"

"I'm sorry, Cathy," Duane replied softly. "Truly sorry. There was no other way, no other way."

"It was cruel. You—you made me believe—" She turned her head away unable to continue, and followed the doctor, holding on to her uncle's arm.

Buck Duane motioned to Jeff Kelly. "Go with them. You won't need a gun but take the rifle anyway. It will probably be some time before he'll be able to travel. By that time Captain MacNelly should be here with the Rangers.

Abby ran toward him. "Oh, Buck, it was terrible! I've never been so frightened in my life. I'm glad you didn't kill him. And that poor girl. I'm sorry for her."

"So am I. I'm convinced she didn't know of her uncle's doings. She tried to stop him from shooting at me. It's a shame, all around."

The crowd stared at the Ranger in fascination. They had seen a man with great courage stand up before two vaunted gunfighters and best them. They had seen him react valorously in the face of powerful rifle fire and succeeded again, a feeling of vague satisfaction in them that he hadn't killed the old man, even though many of them felt that Finley had deserved killing.

Abby said, "Can you come home now, Buck? You must be awfully tired." There was a pleading in her tone.

He looked into her eyes and saw a great tenderness there, and a promise of things she wanted so much for him to take.

"Not yet, Abby. I have a prisoner in the doctor's office. I have to wait to see how he comes out. Why don't you go on home. You must be tired too."

She sighed heavily. "No, I'll wait. I'd like us to go home together."

Some of the crowd began to leave. The undertaker of the town called for volunteers to help him remove the two bodies from the street. Several men picked up Slap Wilson and Tulsa Harrow and carried them into the undertaker's parlor.

A group of young boys gathered on the walk opposite where Buck Duane stood with Abby and stared at him in awe, whispering among themselves.

About twenty minutes later, Jeff Kelly and the doctor came out. Abby gripped Buck Duane's arm, certain of what the doctor would say.

"Mr. Duane," the doctor said, and shook his head, "too old. Shock. Jonathan Finley died a couple of minutes ago. Anything you want me to do?"

The Ranger shook his head. "No, there's nothing left to do. Where's Cathy?"

"With him," the doctor replied. "She won't leave him."

Duane nodded his head in understanding. "All right,

doctor. I guess that's all there is to it. See that she's all right, won't you? Do everything you can for her."

"I understand," the doctor replied. "I'll do my best." He paused a moment. "I'd like to ask a favor, Mr. Duane."

"Certainly."

"I'd like to shake your hand."

The Ranger held out his hand and the doctor shook it, and the understanding between the two men was all in the handshake.

Buck Duane turned then to Abby, and took her arm. "Let's go home," he said. He looked into her eyes, and all the tension flowed out of him as they walked slowly up the small town's dusty main street.

THE LURE
OF BURIED GOLD

I

Captain MacNelly, Commandant, Special Force, Texas Rangers, and his companion, Sergeant Buck Duane, lounged in two of the shabby rockers that lined the lobby of the Buckhorn Hotel, on the Plaza de Armas, San Antonio, overshadowed by the great twin-spired cathedral.

"Figure you could locate a ton of looted gold, Buck?" MacNelly fired the question as casually as though he was asking for a cigarette.

He was a slightly-built, frail-looking man in his early thirties, possessed of a driving energy and stark courage that already had made him an outstanding figure in a frontier force whose exploits were the talk of the nation.

Duane's unsmiling pale blue eyes, set in flat-planed features, gave his face a somber cast. His blond hair, cropped short, showed white around the ears, and there was a taut wariness about him ingrained by years spent along the Border among desperadoes who usually had at least four dead men to their accounts. The notches on the ivory-butted .45 protruding from Duane's holster told their own sinister story, but Duane had never notched a gun in his life. That Colt was the legacy of his father, a veteran on the gunsmoke trail. Lead had finally cut him down, but he'd loosed his last two rounds with a bullet in his heart. Men called it muscular reaction, motivated by an ingrained urge to kill. The same dark passion lingered deep in Duane, although he fought to subdue it. In his hand that same gun had downed six, seven, eight men—he'd lost count, but every killing had been forced upon him, and had left its scar.

The Rangers wore no rigidly prescribed uniform. But the one Duane wore conformed enough to how a Ranger was supposed to look to make it unlikely that anyone would mistake him for a cowpuncher.

Texas Rangers packed a Winchester .44, Colt .45 and a sheathed knife. They fought like Indians, unencumbered by surplus equipment. A Mexican blanket, a small wallet in which were salt and ammunition, a little parched corn, and tobacco, and they were equipped for the field. Wild game provided food, when that failed a horse had sometimes to be sacrificed.

If Duane felt any surprise at his Captain's unexpected question, he showed none.

"You really believe there's that much gold in Texas?" he drawled, half humorously.

"I'm damned sure of it," returned MacNelly, with a touch of grimness. "That gold, one hundred and fourteen ingots, worth over three-quarters of a million dollars, was en route from the Consolidated Mining Company, Hillsboro, New Mexico, by wagon—Texas gold, consigned to the State Treasury in Austin. It was highjacked north of Hertzburg, Camino County, Texas. The four guards were killed, and only a teamster survived to tell the story. He died later, from wounds. That was a year ago."

"A year!" exclaimed Duane.

"The hold-up was played down," said MacNelly. "With an election coming up, the governor figured it would cost votes. He set the State Police, Pinkerton's, a slug of deputies, onto the trail. To date they've turned up nothing, beyond the abandoned wagon."

"So when the trail peters out they call in the Rangers," said Duane dryly.

The Captain shrugged. "You know how many men we can muster—two companies, not half enough to handle the Border gangs, which is our job. I guess the Governor figured it was out of our bailiwick. But now he's dumped it right in our lap!"

Duane rolled a smoke. "Any ideas?" he asked.

"Just one," said MacNelly. "My gamble is that the gold's cached. They found the wagon abandoned in the Aridos Hills. The county sheriff moved fast to block trails and waterholes. That gold weighed close to two-thirds of a ton, too much to slip through the cordon. I'd say those ingots are buried somewhere within a day's ride from the holdup spot. They'll stay buried until a chance offers to smuggle 'em across the Border."

"And our job is to locate 'em first?"

"Not our job," corrected MacNelly gently. "*Your* job. I kind of hate to load this on you, Buck, so soon after that business in Tafton."

Duane nodded grimly, remembering his desperate masquerade as a member of Jonathan Finley's gang of robbers in the Border area. Finley, a respected rancher, had been suspected by the Rangers as the ringleader of the outlaw gang, but no proof could be obtained. Duane had gotten himself taken on as a gunhand, witnessed an abortive bank robbery, and finally had killed Finley's ace gunslinger. He had managed to wing the maddened Finley when the rancher opened fire on him; but the outlaw leader had died of his wounds soon after.

"It didn't leave a good taste in my mouth," Duane said slowly. "Maybe this will be better. Gold-hunting's a more friendly thing than man-killing, any way you look at it."

Buck Duane sat chewing his cigarette and gazing out through the open doorway of The Buckhorn Hotel. The Plaza de Armas was a maelstrom of men and vehicles—trains of unwieldy carratas, solid wooden wheels shrieking on ungreased axles; huge Pittsburgh freighters grinding over the ruts behind long strings of plodding mules; dust-grayed prairie schooners hauled by weary oxen; jouncing yellow stages swaying on leather springs. Men swarmed there thicker than maggots on a carcass, dozens of men—straw-hatted mestizos, bronzed punchers, frock-coated gamblers, sober-clad traders—crowding the plankwalks, blackening the Plaza, bunched around cockfights, swirling in and out of saloons.

A lusty, riproaring city, Duane thought, crossroads of the Southwest, queen of the southern plains. Colorful, crazy, capricious. Then he became aware that MacNelly was waiting for his answer.

"Sure," he said. "I'll take a stab at it—my own way."

"Which is?"

Duane raised his shoulders. "If the gold's cached, someone's keeping cases on it. Maybe I'll just mosey up into Camino County and poke around."

MacNelly's eyebrows lifted. "Wearing those stripes! Dammit Buck, you'll stand out like a piebald in a dun herd."

"Labeled Ranger!" Duane's sober features creased into a grin. It took half a dozen years off his apparent age. "No—as a saddlebum. I'll buy myself some denims, rub them in the dust to make them look trail-stained, chuck these stripes and I reckon I'll pass."

"Don't forget to wind a loose-knotted bandana around your neck," MacNelly said, grinning back at him.

II

Buck Duane was loading his gear on his horse when the distant reports punched into his ears—three shots, two so closely welded that they seemed almost to blend as one, then a third. Following which, brooding quiet again enveloped the dreary spread of hills, their rounded summits yellowed by the early morning sunlight.

Somebody out at dawn to bag a little fresh meat, was his first thought, as he remembered a deer sign. But that, he decided, tightening a loop around the roll, just didn't make sense. The first two shots had the whipcrack quality of a Winchester; the third a deeper note, like the boom of a shotgun. Even in throwing lead at a herd of deer, who would manipulate a Winchester and a shotgun at almost the same instant? Clearly two hunters had been responsible for those shots. But why would one tote a rifle and the other a shotgun? A shotgun for deer! That didn't make sense either.

Vaguely bothered, Duane adjusted the roped roll behind the cantle of his leggy horse, as trailworn as himself. Bullet was a proud-looking horse ordinarily, but Duane had taken pains to give him the aspect of a dust-caked mount such as a saddlebum would have to settle for.

Still pondering on the three shots that had disturbed the serenity of a new day, he set a boot in the stirrup, swung into leather and raised the reins. At his customary jogtrot, Bullet proceeded down canyon.

This was wild, arid country and Buck Duane had no more than a vague idea as to his location. All he knew was that he'd ridden through a vast spread of sunblasted terrain and had made dry camp the previous sundown in what he had believed to be the Aristos Hills. From the appearance of the country, he'd figured there wasn't another human being within miles—until he'd heard those shots.

The sun had risen higher above the distant blue-shadowed mountains and the air began to hold a promise of furnace heat ahead as horse and rider wound between boulders that littered the canyon floor, between which squatty greasewood and thorny mesquite clung tenaciously to life.

Gradually the canyon walls dropped away and the pony jogged across a high bench, clothed with stunted growth, and grayed with alkali dust. Through a break in the hills, a wide valley, now washed by sunlight, came into view, spread like a map before the rider, a vast dun stretch of the country, spiderwebbed with the green of chaparral. Duane drew rein and sat inhaling the fragrance of a lazy breeze, laden with sage scent, and eying the vista.

So distinct through the crystal-clear air as to seem almost within rifle shot—though he judged it to be at least five miles distant—a ranch spread out below him, its rock-and-adobe buildings surrounded by a screen of tall cottonwood. Duane's eyes took in the long, one-story ranch-house, bunkhouse, barns and corrals. The blades of a tall windmill spun steadily, flashing as the sun struck them. Ponies moved antlike around a wire-fenced pasture.

Dotted here and there over the great shallow bowl were other ranches. But the Ranger's gaze followed the course of a creek that meandered down the valley like a thread of silver and focused on the batch of buildings, rendered toy-like by distance, which clustered on its bank and were still partly veiled by the clinging mists of dawn. That must be Hertzburg, located on Dead Horse Creek, he reflected.

Bullet's ears pricked up. Harsh on the breeze came the bawling of a mule. Very likely it was owned by whoever had been out shooting at sun-up. Duane kneed his mount into motion, angling across the bench in the direction of the bawling, bent on satisfying his curiosity as to the nature of the game that needed to be hunted with both rifle and shotgun.

The ground began to slant downward. Rock-etched slopes rose in either side and Duane found himself traversing a gulch, thick-grown with chaparral, the branches of which whipped his head and shoulders as Bullet breasted through.

The pony broke out of the brush and the Ranger eyed a cabin, set upon a patch of partly cleared ground. It was low-built, sturdily constructed of peeled logs, clinked with mud, with a flat roof from which sprouted a verdant growth of grass and weeds.

The windows were glazed with sheets of transparent *veso*, or gypsum, Mexican style. The plank door, on raw-hide hinges, gaped open. From a small shanty barn adjoining a pole corral, a shaggy mule, head outstretched, extended raucous greeting. There was no other sign of life about the place.

Duane walked Bullet across the clearing, drew rein when he was within hailing distance of the cabin and yelled, "Hello, anyone there? Hello—"

The mule continued its braying. Beyond that, Duane's

shout was ignored. He lifted his reins, and rode closer. There seemed to be something ominous about the open door, the silent cabin, and the braying mule.

Suddenly, he stiffened. Midway between himself and the cabin, the windlass of a bricked well protruded above low brush. By the well, a lean-framed man was sprawled, face downward, his hooked fingers dug into the earth as though in agony.

Appalled, Duane darted another quick glance in the direction of the apparently deserted cabin, kneed Bullet and rode toward the prone form. Dismounting quickly, he paused for another swift look around, then turned the body over onto its back. Dark eyes, wide open, stared sightlessly up at him.

The dead man was clad in gray shirt and shabby overalls. Thinning iron-gray hair straggled over his ears, and his features were dour and deeply lined. A stubble of beard sprouted from his lantern jaw, and even the in death his rat-trap mouth was clamped shut. Close by, lying where it had slipped out of slackened fingers, lay a stubby double-barrelled ten-gauge shotgun. But what took Duane's eye were two puckered holes, crusted with dry blood, where the death-dealing slugs had punched into the hairy chest.

III

The mule had stopped braying. Silence enveloped the gulch like a shroud as Buck Duane stood staring down at the slain man. Almost automatically he reached for the shotgun, and ejected two shell cases. One was spent. That, he mused, would account for the shotgun blast he'd heard at dawn. And the two holes in the victim's chest tallied with the two rifle shots. Clearly someone had been hunting a man, not deer.

Lips pursed, he considered the killing. There were no powder burns on the dead man's shirt, no scorching, which had to mean the killing had not been close up. From the position of the body, the victim had apparently stepped out of the cabin and had been moving toward the well when he had been cut down. Apparently, also, he had been braced for trouble, or why would he have packed the shotgun. The odds were that some sound or challenge had pulled him outside.

Duane turned, eying the terrain beyond the well. It had been partly cleared of brush, but several thick clumps of mesquite still botched the ground, the nearest twenty paces distant. He moved toward it, and circled the clump, searching the sandy earth for some telltale sign. Quickly, he struck pay dirt—scuffed imprints of riding boots impressed on the loose soil, the sharp heels plainly defined.

The sunlight glinted on a brass shell case, nestling in a tuft of grass. He bent and picked it up, holding it on his palm for a moment while he studied it.

A picture took shape in his mind now—the killer crouched behind the thick-branching mesquite, a yell that had made the slain man pick up a rifle and dash from the cabin. The bushwhacker had loosed two shots. Hard hit, the victim had blindly gotten off one shot in return, dropped—and died.

The motive for the killing? Unconsciously, Duane shrugged. An old feud maybe, or robbery. He dropped the two .44 shell cases into a pants pocket, and headed for the open door-way of the cabin. When he stepped across the threshold and peered around in the muted light his eyes widened with surprise. He had expected to find the customary crude, homemade furnishings of a squatter's shack, knocked together from discarded boxes and scrap lumber. But there was nothing homemade here. The furnishings were handsome and for the most part of solid oak.

A leather-upholstered rocker stood by the fireplace, a half-filled bottle of Bourbon and a glass on the hearth beside it. Two chairs with woven rawhide seats were drawn up to a center table.

But it was plain an intruder had been foraging around;

for books had been swept from the shelves of an oaken case, and lay scattered over the packed-earth floor.

Moving past the table, Duane opened a door in the rear and eyed a lean-to kitchen, with iron cook stove, a deal table and bench and pots and pans dangling from nails on the wall. Nothing appeared to have been touched here.

But in the boxlike bedroom adjoining the living room, everything was in wild disorder.

The drawers of the bureau had been yanked out and its contents—shirts, towels, underclothes—strewn across the room. The top of a trunk that had apparently been locked had been pried off, and more clothing, sheets, books, papers, littered the floor, scooped out by fiercely impatient hands.

Surveying the wreckage, Duane noted a tintype lying face down on the bureau top. He straightened the photograph mechanically, and his eyes quickened with interest when he saw that it portrayed the head and shoulders of a young girl. An extremely attractive girl, he realized, eyeing it with appreciation.

Her features were well-formed and crowned by smooth-plaited hair wound in thick coils around a proudly-poised head. The level gaze of her large, dark eyes, combined with a touch of austerity about her mouth, conveyed an impression of cool self-assurance. Across the back, in an angular feminine hand, was written in ink, *"To Uncle James with love—Mildred."*

Well, she certainly was an extremely pretty girl, Duane thought and carefully set the tintype back on the bureau.

Moving outside, he stood considering his next move. It seemed plain that the motive for the killing was robbery. The ransacked bureau and trunk furnished evidence of that. Maybe the dead man was a prospector and had struck it rich. The Border was infested with desperadoes who would murder a man for his horse, or even for his boots. Likely some of the same stripe lurked in these hills. Living alone, the slain man had been an easy target. Duane knew it was his duty, even in the role of saddlebum, to report the killing to the law.

He closed the cabin door and headed for the shanty barn. Inside, he found the usual oddments of saddlery, a bridle, hackamore, and lash ropes. A pack saddle and kiacks were dumped in one corner, a half-used bale of hay in another. He lifted down the hackamore and picked out a rawhide lash rope.

The sun was arcing upward now, its fiery rays blasting the slopes. He slipped the hackamore over the mule's big ears, led it out. Sweat-soaked, he wrestled the dead weight of the stiffening corpse across the mule and roped it into place. Mounting Bullet, he pulled away from the scene of death, leading the mule with its grisly burden.

Dropping down into the valley, the little cavalcade wound its way through waves of rounded hills; left the hills behind and plugged over rolling swales that flowed across the valley floor. Ahead, chapparal bordering the creek made a verdant thread of green and in the distance rocky peaks were sharp-etched against the blue sweep of the sky.

Suddenly two riders came into view, bobbing up and down the swales as they cantered toward him from the direction of the ranch. When they drew closer, Buck Duane noted with interest that one was a girl. He checked his horse when they drew rein a dozen paces ahead and sat their saddles, wordlessly eyeing him.

The man, he guessed, was a cowman—a square-built, desert-eroded individual with features as weathered and expressionless as gray granite. Bleakly, he eyed first Duane, then the bloodied form roped across the mule.

But it was the girl who held Duane's attention. Vivid as a scarlet cactus, he thought, and likely as prickly. She was garbed in denim trousers, and a yellow silk shirt, open at the neck. A steeple-topped sombrero sat on a rippling mass of raven-black hair that flowed loose down her back. Her oval features were a delicate shade of brown, the texture of the skin flawless. Her red lips were willful and she sat the saddle with an unconscious air of arrogance. If she was aware of Buck Duane's intent, admiring gaze, she gave no sign of it.

"Who in hell are you, mister?" The cowman's voice was harshly challenging.

In no haste, Duane made a smoke, stuck it between his lips, plucked a match from his hatband and scraped it across the saddle. When he'd lit the cigarette, he replied, "Buck Duane, late of San Antone. And who might you be?"

"Cal Carson. I rod the CCC. I'm interested in knowing why you're crossing my range with a dead man."

Duane nodded toward the ugly seared-looking hills to the west. "Picked him up outside his cabin, back there. I had to take him into town or just leave him lying where he fell for the buzzards. I couldn't see myself doing that. Could you?"

"Who shot him?"

Duane raised his shoulders. "Your guess is as good as mine. Some jasper punched two holes in his chest with a Winchester."

"You pack a Winchester!" put in the girl. There was a subtle mockery in her eyes.

He eyed the butt of the rifle protruding from his saddle boot and smiled. "Since you make a point of it, ma'am, so does your—pard."

She turned to the granite-faced man beside her and commented, with amusement, "Next he'll be accusing you of shooting the man, Dad."

"Have you any idea who he is?" persisted the cowman, ignoring her.

"Wouldn't know him from Adam," confessed Duane.

"That's Jim Murdoch. He hung out in Wildcat Gulch."

"Surly as a bear with a sore head," added the girl. "He had a habit of taking after strangers with a shotgun."

Duane considered this new angle. Maybe Murdoch had loosed a load of buckshot at an unexpected visitor and the trespasser had become enraged and plugged him. But no, he reflected, the first two reports he'd heard had been those of a Winchester. Then there was the ransacked cabin.

"Everything points to robbery," he said. "The cabin's torn apart."

Unblinking, the cowman absorbed this. "You didn't get a glimpse of the killer then?"

Duane shook his head.

"Too bad!" said Carson. He touched his mount with the rowel and wheeled away. As she raised her reins to follow him, the girl's disdainful glance flicked over Duane's trail-stained clothes and he could have sworn she sniffed as the pony whirled around.

Finishing his smoke, Duane slacked in the saddle, staring after the receding riders as they cantered away across the plain. The girl had a touch of Spanish blood, he decided, and was likely as fiery as a mustang. But that didn't mean she wasn't pretty enough to turn the heads of nine men out of ten. He crushed his butt against a pants leg and heeled Bullet into motion again.

IV

The sun was beginning to slant westward when the buckskin's hooves drummed on the loose planks of a bridge that crossed the creek. Following the parallel ruts of a wagon road, Buck Duane emerged on a broad sandy widening of the trail that comprised Hertzburg's one and only street. On each side sat squat rock-and-adobe structures, with square-faced fronts, separated by alleys and weedgrown lots.

As Bullet jogged over the ruts, Duane's glance passed over a rambling general store, SIEGLER'S EMPORIUM lettered across its facade; a plank-and-adobe two-story structure, with rockers set upon a gallery that extended above the plankwalk, and whose weathered sign proclaimed it to be THE CROSSING HOUSE—ROOMS—ONE DOLLAR.

Life moved sluggishly in the heat of approaching noon and flies droned through the dry air. Here and there, saddlehorses lazily switched tails at the hitch rails. In shaded alleys, straw-hatted Mexicans squatted, drowsing or sucking cornhusk cigarettes, while a scattering of townsmen drifted along the plankwalks.

Drifting up street, he sighted a lean-to shack, propped against the side of the big rock-and-adobe Emporium. Above its doorway, a paint-peeling sign carried the words —EDWARD WELCH, TOWN MARSHAL.

Duane reined to the rail, dismounted and tied his animals. Townsmen began to gather, attracted by the mule's grisly burden.

When Duane stepped inside the shack the first thing that met his eyes were yellowing "Wanted" posters plastering the rear wall. A small pot-bellied heating stove and two straightback chairs filled most of the space. Ticketed rifles and handguns were heaped on a wide side shelf and a scratched oak desk was set under the front, and only window, a square of barn sash.

At the desk sat a sturdily built man, dehydrated down to bone and muscle. His faded gray eyes were set in a hawk-featured face, and a sun-bleached moustache drooped over his thin, humorless lips. His hair was iron-gray and thinning. He wore dark pants and a blue shirt, and a tarnished Town Marshal badge was pinned to his loose-hanging vest.

"I brought in a dead man," said Duane, and dropped onto a chair.

The marshal glanced out through the window, took in the body roped to the mule, and the curious townsmen and Mexicans clustering around it. His gaze came back to Duane, "That's Jim Murdoch!"

"So I hear?" said the Ranger.

"Did you kill him?"

Duane tautened, "Would I have brought him in if I had? I stumbled over the corpse outside his cabin, back in the hills," he went on, when the marshal continued to stare at him steadily. Then, remembering that Welch was only a town marshal, he added, "Maybe that's outside your jurisdiction?"

"Nope," rasped the other, "I'm deputized to handle anything within county limits." He dug the makin's from a pocket of his dangling vest. "Suppose you give me the lowdown. First, just who are you, mister?"

"Buck Duane, late of San Antone."

"Hold a job anyways around?"

Duane shook his head.

The marshal's faded eyes traveled over his visitor's worn denims, washed-out shirt, and cracked boots. "Saddle-bum?" he inquired abruptly.

"Let's just say tumbleweed," said Duane.

Welch grunted. Duane had a feeling he'd somehow gotten off to a bad start. The thought that suspicion for causing this Murdoch's death might fall on him had never entered his mind. Now he realized that he was a stranger, had no witnesses, no apparent proof he hadn't shot the man himself.

Carefully, he began to relate exactly how he had become involved. He wound up by describing the condition of the cabin and gave his opinion that the motive for the killing was robbery.

"What's more," Buck Duane concluded, "I picked these empties up about forty paces from the cabin behind a mesquite clump. There were tracks of riding boots, too." He fished out the two .44 shell cases and dropped them on the desk.

Throughout, Welch had listened in frowning silence, drawing on his smoke. He picked up the empty cases, weighing them on a leathery palm and eying them speculatively.

Again he looked out through the window and Duane knew he was focussing the butt of the rifle protruding from the boot strapped to the buckskin's saddle.

"So you pack a Winchester," he mused, "and you lack means of support. Murdoch was a surly old cuss. Who's to say you didn't brace him for a handout? He threatens you with his scattergun. You plug him, clean out the cabin, cache the loot and pack the body to town, figuring to run a blazer over the law." In sardonic challenge, his faded eyes probed Duane.

"All right, Marshal," Duane said. "I can prove my hands are clean."

"I'm waiting!" threw back Welch.

Fuming, Duane led the way outside, elbowed through the clutter of men eying Murdoch's limp remains. He lifted his rifle from its sheath, and walked down the alley beside the shack, dogged by the marshal.

They came out upon an open flat upon which outhouses were spaced like gaunt sentinels, amid a litter of boxes, barrels and bottles discarded by the stores that lined Main Street. Levering a cartridge into the breech, Duane slanted the rifle upward and squeezed the trigger. The sound of the report brought a surge of townsmen into the far end of the alley. Duane ejected the empty shell, gingerly picked up the hot metal case, and extended it to Welch.

"Check!" he said curtly.

Without speaking, the marshal compared its base with those of the two expended shells Duane had previously handed him. The indentation of the firing pin was practically in the center of the brass base. On the other two shells the pin had struck midway between center and rim.

The lawman looked up. "Guess that clears you," Welch admitted.

"That's sure a weight off my mind," said Duane stonily.

"Quite gritting your teeth," advised the marshal, the ghost of a grin flitting over his bleak features. "Now we got to figure out who did put the jasper's light out."

"We!" echoed Duane. "You rod the law around here, not me."

"Sure," agreed the marshal, "and I'm riding out at sun-up to give that cabin a once-over. You're a material witness, and you're riding, too." His tone hardened. "Stick around town!"

"What if I don't pack the price of a room?" protested Duane.

"I got a cell you can use," said Welch dryly.

The Texas Ranger shrugged, realizing the futility of protest. "See you at sun-up," he said over his shoulder.

Duane headed toward the livery, walked his mount over the loose planks of the barn and dismounted at an empty stall. No one seemed to be around. He guessed the liveryman had sauntered down the street to inspect the mortal remains of Jim Murdoch. Stripping off his horse's gear, he spread the damp saddle blanket and led Bullet to water.

Then Duane dipped a double measure of grain from a bin, dumped it into the feed box and, while the horse munched, worked on its coat with currycomb and brush. The dusty-flank look would come back quickly enough after a good grooming. Tied to town by the marshal's edict, he had little to do and plenty of time in which to do it.

If he hadn't poked his nose into something which was none of his business, he reflected with disgust, he'd be free to proceed with his mission.

Outside, the shadows lengthened and an emptiness beneath his belt reminded him that he hadn't eaten since sun-up. He stepped back to admire Bullet's coat, now smooth and shining. Satisfied, he dropped the brush into a box and hit for the street.

Drifting along the darkened plankwalk, Duane brushed aside a musty fly curtain that draped the doorway of the restaurant, The Ritz, slapped his hat on a peg and slid onto a stool at the counter.

Thirty minutes later, feeling well content, a thick steak with all the trimmin's beneath his belt, the Ranger stepped outside. Yellow light from the oil lamps of the saloon opposite washed over ponies tied at the rail, and the narrow windows of the hotel made bright oblongs against the night.

Silhouetted against the steamy window of the hash-house, Duane paused to make a smoke and decide whether to drop into the saloon, The Bull Pen, or head back to the livery and spread his soogans on the straw pile.

Flame lanced suddenly from the black mouth of an alley beside the saloon. He felt the breath of a bullet that droned past his cheek, heard the sharp snick as it perforated the window behind him. Duane spun around in startled surprise and eyed a neat circular hole drilled through the glass, surrounded by a spiderweb of cracks. The roar of the explosion was ringing in his ears when he realized that, but for Lady Luck, that slug would have scattered his brains.

Again the gun spilled flame and thunder. More glass splintered. Duane jumped for the hitch-rail, ducked under it and zigzagged across the hoof-pocked street, jerking his .45 as he dodged over the ruts.

V

Buck Duane was aware of men spilling out of the saloon, attracted by the sound of the shooting, as he dove into the dark canyon of the alley from which fire had spurted. Toward the far end, he glimpsed the vague outline of a moving form and loosed a shot. A gun thundered in return. The slug, deflected by a rock-and-adobe wall, hurtled past in screaming richochet.

Crouching, Duane raced in pursuit, reached the end of the alley and paused, his lungs heaving, his eyes searching the night. To his right rose a stack of empty cases piled in the rear of the saloon, and ahead lay a trash-littered lot. To the left bulked deserted loading platforms and the square rear ends of stores.

Nothing moved. The would-be bushwhacker, he reflected, had had ample time to make a getaway. He could have ducked up another alley and by now was probably mingling with other citizens on Main Street. But the thought that someone was gunning for him wasn't comforting. The Ranger dropped the ivory-butted .45 back into leather and began to retrace his footsteps.

When Buck Duane reached the mouth of the alley he found it blocked with milling, shouting men. Across the street more were gathered, around the shattered window of The Ritz. Welch came up at a run, buckling on his gunbelt. "What's the trouble?" he demanded, thrusting through the throng.

"Some bushwhacking bastard took a couple of shots at me and hotfooted down this alley," Duane told him. "Seems one of Murdoch's pards had the same notion you did. He must have figured I'd downed the maverick and aimed to even things up."

"Murdoch never had no pards," said the marshal. "The old coot was as popular as a skunk at a picnic. Could be," he added thoughtfully, "that was Murdoch's killer, figuring you could read his brand." His tone sharpened, "Maybe he figured right."

"All I know about that killer is that he left two .44 shell cases behind," said Duane forcefully.

"Seems he got different ideas," said Welch. "Well, see you at sun-up."

"Don't gamble on it," said Duane, with wry emphasis.

The marshal chuckled dryly and slapped him on the shoulder. "If you're born to be hanged, you sure won't be shot." Welch either had a peculiar sense of humor, or was intimating obliquely that he wasn't altogether convinced of his innocence. Duane turned away with a shrug and headed for the livery.

A stable lamp, turned low, hooked onto an upright, spread a sicky aura of light in the big barn. From the gloomy recesses came the stomp of a restless horse, the rattle of a halter rope. Duane picked up his spooled roll and hastened toward the straw pile, enveloped in darkness. The gloom was comforting with a would-be killer on the loose. As he yanked off his boots, he damned a certain braying mule for the dozenth time.

The growing light of a new day stained the horizon crimson and Duane was polishing off the last of a stack of flapjacks in the hash house when Welch jingled in. The marshal paused only to swallow a mug of coffee. Duane hastily cleaned up his plate and followed the lawman outside.

Shadows were still thick under the canopies of the plankwalks and the town slept, except for a grizzled old Mexican topping off the water barrels set along store fronts from a huge cask mounted on two creaking wheels and hauled by a bony mule.

The town marshal turned north when they crossed the plank bridge, following a trail that clung to the cutbanks of the sandy creek. It was pleasant riding in the freshness of early morning. Cottonwoods and willows made an umbrella of cool greenery; a squirrel scampered along a branch; cottontails bobbed through the brush; a coyote slunk across the plain with a stealthy backward glance. To make talk, Duane inquired, "This Murdoch been around long?"

"Most a year."

"Prospector?"

Welch eased in the saddle, brought out tobacco and papers. "Hell, no," he said. "The hombre's a retired mine superintendent from Hillsboro. His ticker went bad on him and he quit."

Duane remembered the girl of the tintype. "Any relatives around?"

The marshal yawned, and scratched a match. "He never said. But then, Murdoch always did keep his mouth cinched as tight as a miser's purse."

"Kind of fancied his own company?"

"That's right!" agreed the lawman emphatically. "The old moseyhorn wanted no truck with no one. He rode that doggoned mule into town every Saturday regular, picked up his chuck at Siegler's, ducked into The Bull Pen for two bottles of Kentucky Dew, and beat it back to the hills again. The old wart hog acted as sullen as a sore-headed dog. Once he ran some hunters off his place with a shotgun; and all they wanted was a dip of water from his ola."

Duane and Welch left the coolness of the shadowed creek and began angling across the flats toward the chaos of spiny hills and broken arroyos that lay to the west, already simmering beneath the searing rays of the rising sun.

"Carson, the CCC boss, braced me when I was bringing the corpse in," said Buck Duane.

"Another tarantula—so tough he has practically grown horns and is haired over."

"Which sure don't apply to his daughter."

"Part Mex. Pretty as a painted wagon, prickly as a procupine," agreed Welch. After which talk died between them.

When they dismounted outside Murdoch's cabin nothing seemed changed. A flock of plumed quail, dusting in the sand around the well, whirled away; and magpies chattered from the roof of the barn. As they walked toward the cabin door, Duane checked suddenly, gazing at the ground.

"There's been digging since I left," he announced abruptly, and pointed to freshly turned earth.

"You dead sure?" inquired Welch, squinting at the loose, sandy soil.

"Stake my saddle on it," Duane said. His glance traveled over the surrounding ground, patched with weeds and rank grass. "There's more! Some hombre's been gophering around."

They moved from one filled-in excavation to another, each about two feet square, its outline plain to the eye.

"Murdoch had something someone craved bad enough to kill him," Duane said. "Couldn't be it didn't come to light in the cabin so the killer skipped back after I left and got busy with a shovel."

"Any idea as to what it might be?" inquired Welch off-hand.

"Your guess is as good as mine," Duane said. "You claim Murdoch was a mining man. Could be he was prospecting on the side, located another Eldorado and squirreled up a slew of gold nuggets."

"Not in the Aridos Hills," declared the marshal emphatically. "They been raked over, never yielded an ounce of gold. Let's take a look at the cabin."

Welch stepped up to the door, levered it open and paused, eying the interior. Then he moved inside, bent and picked up two of the books scattered over the floor.

"*Chemical Minerology* and *Metalliferous Ores*," he read aloud. "Murdoch spent too much time just reading," he growled and threw them aside.

They looked over the bedroom and the leanto kitchen, then returned to the living room. The marshal dropped down into the leather upholstered rocker, reached for the half-empty bottle of Bourton set on the hearth, took a long pull and passed it to Duane.

"I will say," he said, smacking his lips, "Murdoch had an educated taste—this is choice liquor."

Idly, Buck Duane stirred the litter of books on the floor with a boot. A fat envelope slid out of one. He picked it up, tossed it to Welch. "Maybe," he said, "that's the answer."

Marshal Welch slid a wad of greenbacks from the envelope, tallied them with blunt fingers. Three hundred and sixty dollars," he announced.

Instantly Duane was on his knees, shaking out other books, but nothing more came to light. "What do you make of it?" he asked, coming to his feet.

"Take your pick," said Welch, and reached for the bottle. "Robbery, or an old feud."

"Maybe the girl can help us."

"Girl?"

Duane stepped into the bedroom, returned with the tintype. The lawman squinted at it. "Never knew she existed."

"Could be there are letters around," said Duane.

Together, they sifted through the contents of the bureau and the brassbound trunk in the bedroom. But not a letter, or a scrap of written material came to light.

"Maybe Ma Purdy could help," said Welch, dusting off his pants knees.

"Just who is Ma Purdy?" Duane asked.

The deputy's black features creased into a grin. "A widow woman with a prying disposition," he said. "She's postmistress of Hertzburg. What Ma don't know about other folks business isn't worth the knowing. I gamble she reads every postcard that goes through the mail. I wouldn't even put it beyond her to steam open a letter occasionally —if it looked interesting. Come, let's go back to town."

It was midday when they reached town. A tinkling bell signalized their entry into Siegler's Emporium. The Emporium, considered Duane, glancing around, seemed to stock almost everything a man could desire. Merchandise-laden shelves lined the walls and showcases packed with cheap jewelry, knives, watches, and patent medicines crowded the floor. Foodstuff spilled out of boxes and barrels; rakes, hoes, buckets were suspended from the rafters. A pleasant aroma of cinnamon and ground coffee permeated the air.

A skinny woman, in a plain black dress, sorted mail behind a wicket in the rear, over which a sign carried the words, *United States Post Office*.

At their approach, her head jerked up and her eyes, bright and beady as a sparrow's, focused on Welch's weathered features. "So you been out to Murdoch's place. I reckon you're the first who ever got near the door without a buckshot greeting."

Even her chirpy tone was birdlike, and flat as a raven's squawk. Her glance darted from one to the other. "Well, what treasure was he guarding?"

"You're barking up the wrong tree, Ma," the marshal said shortly. "There's no treasure. Murdoch just craved to be left alone."

"To do what!" she sniffed. "Swill rotgut? Fiddlesticks! Why was he scared of peekers? He never even invited that good-looking niece of his in Tucson to visit him."

"Now just what would you know about that niece, Ma?" inquired Welch persuasively.

"She teaches school and she has great expectations," replied Mrs. Purdy.

"Expectations of what?"

The widow raised thin shoulders. "When he wrote the girl at Christmas—" she cut off abruptly, compressing her thin lips.

The marshal glanced meaningfully at Duane. "Well?" he prompted.

"Well," said Mrs. Purdy, "it's my impression he left her plenty."

"There are nothing but rocks and rattlesnakes in Wildcat Gulch."

"That's what you think," snapped Ma. "Maybe Si Leeson, the lawyer, knows different. He made up Murdoch's will."

"Guess we'll drop in on Si," decided Welch. "I'm sure thanking you, Ma. I'm thinking we've got a real smart postmistress."

"Happy to oblige, Frosty," she said, looking flattered, "although you know how I hate to pry into other folks' business."

VI

There was nothing that he liked, Buck Duane decided, about Silas Leeson, attorney-at law. The room that Leeson used as his office, off the lobby of The Crossing House, was little larger than an oversized closet. When Duane entered at the heels of the marshal he saw a corpulent individual, garbed in a seedy Prince Albert coat and baggy striped pants. His soiled white shirt was brought together at the neck by a faded silk cravat and the buttons of a brocaded vest were loosened to accommodate the contour of a bulging belly.

Duane was reminded of an overripe melon going to seed —an impression that was enhanced by the lawyer's pudgy features and a bulbous nose etched red with tiny broken veins.

The small office was already crowded by the ancient roll-top desk at which the lawyer's form lumped, a bookcase packed with musty yellow tomes and two straightback chairs.

At their entry, Leeson abruptly thrust a bottle into a desk drawer and became busy shuffling papers.

"Good day to you, gentlemen!" he said. Despite physical decay, the lawyer's tone still held a certain depth and resonance. "I assume your visit pertains to the corpus delecti."

"You guessed right!" Welch dropped into a chair, and lifted tobacco and papers from a vest pocket. "I hear Murdoch made a will."

"And entrusted it to the keeping of his legal advisor, to wit, myself," boomed Leeson.

"He have anything to leave, beyond that cabin and quarter-section?"

The lawyer laced fat fingers across the swell of his paunch. "A client's communications to his lawyer are as sacred as those of a patient to a medical practitioner," he said smugly.

"Quite going legal on me," barked Welch. "I've got a murder on my hands and I'm hunting motive. What did Murdoch own that would justify a killing?"

Duane could have sworn that amusement, maybe derision, sparked in Leeson's watery eyes. "Nothing," he returned smoothly, "beyond said quarter-section and the appurtenances thereto."

"Who's heir?"

"A niece. She resides in Tucson and her profession is that of school teacher."

His forehead furrowed, the marshal busied himself making a cigarette.

"You will have an opportunity to interrogate the lady later," said Leeson. "I have already sent a telegraphic message from the depot to Tucson. She should arrive in ample time for the funeral."

"There'll be an inquest, too," said Welch and rose. "Well, I guess we'll hold our hosses."

Outside, Duane commented, "Leeson didn't help any. All wind and bombast."

The marshal spat. "Si's as slick as a greased hog. He had a big reputation, back east, before he hit the booze." He shrugged, "Well, maybe we'll get a lead from the girl."

Railway service on the branch line that terminated at Hertzburg was confined to a mixed passenger-freight twice weekly. At ten in the morning, two days later, Duane hunkered against the clapboards of the squat little depot, watching the distant black smoke that plumed across the flats. The girl was entitled to some sort of a reception committee, he reflected, even if it consisted of only one man. Welch was busy rounding up jurors for the inquest.

Through an open window behind him came the intermittent clatter of a telegraph key.

Ten minutes later, with a hiss of steam, the big-funneled engine rolled into the station, its bell tolling solemnly. Coupled behind it were a wood-headed tender, solitary passenger coach, two box cars, express car and caboose.

Duane came to his feet as passengers began spilling from the coach—a robust ranch wife, two drummers, and a waspy little man in a shiny serge suit. Finally—a slender-waisted girl in her early twenties. That tintype sure hadn't lied, Duane told himself.

With a confident stride, a carpet bag swinging from one hand, and a big purse looped on the other, the girl moved toward the depot. She wore a severely-cut black bodice, fastened high in the neck with a plain silver brooch, while the hem of a dark skirt brushed the tops of her high-button shoes. A neat bonnet was set upon a mass of auburn hair and her eyes—green as jade—hinted at cool self-possession.

Duane stepped out to intercept her. "Miss Stokes?" he inquired, removing his hat.

The girl stopped walking and her green eyes appraised him. "Who are you?" she inquired.

"The name's Duane—Buck Duane. I was the one who found your uncle's body." He reached and relieved her of her carpet bag. "Guess you need to freshen up. It's only a short distance to the hotel."

"Have the caught the man who killed Uncle?" she asked, dropping into step beside him.

Duane shook his head. "They will," he said.

Too quickly for his liking, they reached the hotel. Miss Stokes registered and retrieved her carpet bag. She flashed a brief smile. "Thanks so much for your help," she said and swung away.

Somewhat taken aback by so abrupt a dismissal, Duane headed for the inquest.

His testimony was soon over, and the verdict was, predictably, "Murder by person or persons unknown."

"What next?" Duane asked the marshal.

"Have you seen the girl around?"

"Sure, she's at the hotel."

"We may as well have a talk with her—right now."

They found Mildred Stokes seated in one of the well-worn leather rockers that lined the hotel lobby, listening—with obvious distaste—to Silas H. Leeson, who sat lumped in an adjoining rocker.

At their appearance, the lawyer rose, bowed ponderously to the girl and told Welch in sonorous tones, "I have informed this charming young lady as to the nature of her legacy and expressed the opinion that, since there is so little possibility of its being contested, I can see no reason why she shouldn't enjoy the full use of the property forthwith."

Leeson waddled away. Welch dropped into his vacated rocker and Duane sank down on the other side of the girl.

Mildred Stokes stared with displeasure at the rotund lawyer's receding back. "That man has been drinking," she announced forcefully. "He positively reeks of liquor. Furthermore, I don't trust him."

"Do you have any reason for mistrusting him ma'am, apart from that?" inquired Welch.

"I certainly have. I am the sole surviving relative. Uncle Jim gave me to understand that when he passed on I would be a wealthy woman—that I would never have to work again. This—alcoholic—insists that the estate consists merely of a scrubby quarter-section of land, practically worthless, with a small cabin attached to it." Her voice quivered with indignation.

"I'm afraid he's right," Duane pointed out. "I'd say the land wouldn't bring a dollar an acre. The cabin—" He raised his shoulders. "A hundred dollars, at most."

The girl stared at him tight-lipped, her green eyes flaming with anger.

"What gave you the idea the property was valuable?" Welch asked.

"His letters. He used such phrases as 'Fortune has rewarded me to an unbelievable extent' and 'I am now a wealthy man and this wealth will be yours.'" She paused an instant, then went on with cold exasperation, "This Leeson person insists there is not one dollar in real money. He claims I am actually liable for the expense of interment, *his* fees, and certain other legal charges." She laughed without humor. "On a school teacher's salary!"

Welch brought a wad of currency out of a back pocket. "Maybe this will help," he said. "Over three hundred dollars in greenbacks. Duane found the money in the cabin, hidden in a book."

Miss Mildred Stokes took the bills in grim silence, and thrust them into her purse. "Thank you!" she said.

"You'd better keep the find to yourself," cautioned the marshal. "Leeson will otherwise claim it's part of the estate. Once his grubhooks fasten on greenbacks you can usually kiss them goodbye."

"You can depend upon me, Marshal Welch," she assured him composedly. "Well, I suppose I better prepare for the funeral." She smiled quickly, rose and headed for the stairway.

"It's kind of curious, Murdoch peddling that kind of talk," murmured Welch, building a smoke.

"You forgot the digging?" said Duane.

From the moment when he'd stumbled on Murdoch's body just the fact that the slain man lived near the town where he'd gone to see if he could pry some vital information out of Welch had stirred a vague puzzlement in his mind. How many dark secrets did the town hold, and did such killings occur often there?

Could it possibly have some remote connection with the looted gold? But now, in view of what he had since heard, and the fact that Murdoch had been a newcomer to the region his puzzlement had sharply increased, and suspicion had taken a firmer hold on his mind.

VII

The marshal came to his feet. "That digging has me buffaloed," he admitted. "Well, I guess there's no point in hobbling you. You are free to leave town—any time you want to go back to saddlebumming again."

"That's mighty comforting," drawled Duane.

The Texas Ranger considered his next move. It was clear to him that he had better get busy on the job that had brought him to Hertzburg—locating close to a ton of looted gold. Curious he should stumble over a possibly related mystery. The murdered recluse had promised his niece wealth, and had apparently left her nothing but a barren quarter-section. And why the digging? And the shot that had been aimed at him in town? Wasn't that plain proof that someone, likely the killer, had reason to believe that there was more than rock and scrub on Murdoch's holding?

Captain MacNelly would say it was no skin off his nose. Duane had an important assignment and local crime was the business of the county sheriff.

A bland-featured man, balding and draped in a rusty frock coat, slid quietly into the lobby. He had the long, acquisitive nose and guileless eyes of the born trader, and his lips were as tight-locked as a rattrap.

The newcomer sank into a rocker and sat with an air of patient resignation, nursing a plug hat on his lap.

The Ranger drifted across to the desk. "Who's the frock-coated hombre?" he inquired.

"Mr. Siegler," the clerk tol him, low-voiced. "Owns the Emporium, this hotel, the saloon and most of what's left of the town," he went on. "Acts as undertaker and rents out the hearse. I gamble they don't plant their stiffs more handsome in San Antone than we do right here in Hertzburg."

In no amiable mood, Buck Duane entered The Ritz the next morning for breakfast. The shattered window of the hash house had been boarded up and the yellow light of a dangling oil lamp bathed the form of a solitary patron at the far end of the counter.

Duane slapped his hat on a peg and became aware, with a start, that the diner was Mildred Stokes. Well, he reflected, she hadn't shown any great desire for his company and he wasn't thrusting it upon her now. Sliding onto a stool as far distant from her as possible, he gave an order for flapjacks and coffee to the impassive Chinese behind the counter.

His head swiveled at the sound of her voice, tinged with amusement. "Did you really think, Mr. Duane, that I'd sell my uncle's place to you, or anyone else, for a mere pittance?"

"I wouldn't take it as a gift," he replied gruffly.

"Yet there are folks who would pay up to fifteen hundred dollars."

"Maybe they've been out in the sun too long," he countered.

She raised her shoulders. "They seem like hard-headed business men to me. One, a Mr. Carson, offered me a thousand cash. Another, who goes by the name of Connors, was willing to pay fifteen hundred, if I'd accept a down payment of five hundred."

"I'd say the gents are out of their minds," retorted

Duane, striving to strain the interest out of his voice. "The value just isn't there. They give any reasons?"

"Mr. Carson, a cowman, claims he wishes to demolish the cabin. He says it is likely to harbor rustlers."

"Makes sense," admitted Duane, "but not a thousand dollars' worth."

"Mr. Connors raises horses. He plans to use the cabin as a hunting camp."

"A mighty expensive hunting camp!" Duane said derisively. It was plain, he thought, that he was not alone in believing that Murdoch had cached something worthwhile on that quarter. "There's something smells about both deals."

Mildred Stokes' green eyes appraised him calmly. "I think the smell, as you term it, emanates from a different source—from the direction of a drunken lawyer and—a few other people I could mention."

"You take a look at that quarter section, and you'll change your mind," Duane assured her. "I could take my pick of ten thousand acres out in the hills, homestead a quarter for two bits an acre and throw up a cabin for fifty dollars. Being a schoolma'am, you can figure out how small the outlay would come to."

"Those men are not fools!"

"Maybe they figure they're buying more than just land."

"What, for instance?" she demanded sharply.

"I just wouldn't know," he admitted slowly, spilling molasses on his flapjacks. He began to eat. The girl, preoccupied, munched buttered home-made bread.

"I'd like to see Uncle's place for myself," she announced suddenly. "I can't leave Hertzburg for two days anyway."

"You ride?" he inquired, between mouthfuls.

"A little."

He glanced at her voluminous skirt. "In that?"

"I imagine the store stocks overalls."

"It would be a pleasure to take you out there," he said.

The sun was high when they left town. Miss Mildred Stokes straddled a hack rented from the livery. An oversize pair of bib overalls, stiff with newness, covered most of her, except the top of a white blouse. From the way she bumped leather and latched firmly onto the saddlehorn, Duane guessed her riding experience was strictly limited. But they jogged along the trail that followed the curves of Dead Horse Creek without mishap.

Before pulling away from the welcome shade of the chapparal that clothed the creek, he called a halt. Mildred Stokes dismounted stiffly, ruefully easing cramped limbs.

"Is it much further?" she inquired.

The Ranger hated to tell her that they had scarcely started and the worst lay ahead—the long drag across glaring flats, and a tedious climb up into the hills.

"Not so far," he replied evasively, and busied himself slacking cinches and rocking saddles.

Flayed by the sun, wreathed by a halo of dust stirred up by the horses' hooves, the two dragged across the parched expanse of the valley floor, while the silhouettes of sullen hills ahead seemed to recede rather than to draw closer. There was no talk between them.

The girl, Duane guessed, was suffering torment, galled raw by the saddle. Her lips remained tight set, and she stared fixedly ahead from beneath the side brim of a felt hat. Whatever Mildred Stokes lacked, Duane thought, it wasn't spunk.

Shadows had begun to slant eastward when they rode into the clearing and halted by the shany barn. Miss Stokes slumped in the saddle, her eyes closed, obviously exhausted. Buck Duane lifted her down and packed her limp form into the shade of the barn. Heading for the cabin, he routed out a towel and a bucket, and hit for the well.

A great deal of hard toil had gone into the digging of that well, he reflected, dropping down the wooden bucket suspended by a rope from the windlass. It was square and a good three feet across, its top rimmed by a coping of adobe bricks. Duane heard the bucket splash, and wound it up, slopping water.

Her body sagging against the warped clapboards of the barn, the girl wearily opened her eyes at his approach. Her white blouse was now a dirty gray, and the neat coils of her braided hair had loosened and straggled in disorder over her ears. But it was plain she was beyond fretting about her appearance.

Duane set the bucket of water beside her, and dropped the towel into her lap. "Dampen your face, and rest awhile," he said. Few women unaccustomed to the saddle, he knew, could have made that ride.

He looked around for more evidence of digging, and found plenty. It was as if a gopher had moved in—a human gopher. Some of the earth had been so freshly turned that the sound of their approach could have scared the digger off.

When Mildred Stokes hobbled stiffly around the angle of the cabin, he was still looking down at the pitted ground. Her hair was again arranged in neat coils and she had washed the grime from her face, and beaten the dust off her overalls.

She entered the cabin.

"Well, what do you think?" Duane inquired, when she reappeared.

The girl shrugged and said nothing.

"Now take a look around," he suggested, with a sweep of his arm.

She stood staring at the grim hills, etched with protruding rock and the scrubby brush. Then her gaze returned to the desolate cabin.

"What you figure the place is actually worth?" he asked.

"Ten cents!" she said and smiled tiredly. "I think I'll accept the thousand dollars Mr. Carson offered, before he changes his mind."

"The land isn't worth a third of that," he agreed. "It's what's hidden under it."

"I don't understand."

"There wasn't a spadeful of earth turned over when I found your uncle. Now look!" He indicated the numerous mounds of earth that specked the ground. "Someone's hunting something—and it's not just a mouldy saddle overgrown with weeds."

"You mean, you think Uncle buried his—his wealth?"

"Murdoch promised to leave you plenty. Why would he lie? Why was he shot? Why all this digging?"

"But I can't stay out in these desolate hills and guard the place," she protested. "I have to return to Tucson. I have to teach."

There was an almost pleading look in her green eyes. Duane fingered his chin. "I suppose," he said, "I could stick around, for a week or so."

And there'd be hell to pay, he thought, if Captain MacNelly ever thought I was letting myself in for helping out a lady tenderfoot—and neglecting my job!

VIII

Wearily, Mildred Stokes turned to the Ranger. "I really can't afford to pay for your time," she said, a look of defeat in her eyes.

Buck Duane raised his shoulders. "I'll donate the time," he assured her offhand. "There's chuck enough in the kitchen to feed me for a month."

"It's very kind of you," she said and her relieved smile was sufficient recompense.

"Forget it!" he returned gruffly. He eyed the sinking sun. "I guess we'd better hit the trail back to Hertzburg now."

She ran her hands down her buttocks with a wry grimace. "Couldn't we wait until it's—just a little cooler? I can't face that heat again."

Buck Duane agreed promptly. Mildred Stokes appeared

to be in a more amiable mood and the prospect of spending a few extra hours in her company was not displeasing to him. He carried out the upholstered rocker, set it in the shade of the porch and padded it with a blanket. With a sigh, the auburn haired girl sank gratefully into it.

The gulch was etched with shadow and the hills faded behind purpling veils when they pulled out. A sage-scented breeze whispered through the brush and brightening stars powdered the heavens. Dust fogged thick around them but, somehow, it didn't seem so bad.

When they jogged down the dim canyon of Hertzburg's Main Street the town was asleep and darkened, except in the vicinity of The Bull Pen and the lighted windows of the hotel. Outside The Crossing House they pulled to the rail. Mildred Stokes slid slackly out of leather and stood slumped against her mount, grasping the saddlehorn for support.

"You'd better let me help you inside," Duane said, eying her sympathetically.

"No!" she retorted, with a touch of spirit, and began limping across the plankwalk. Midway, she paused and turned. "Thank you—for everything, Buck," she said softly.

He raised a hand in farewell and reached for the dangling reins of her rented mount. Kneeing the buckskin, he hit for the livery.

There was no sign of Mildred Stokes when he downed breakfast in The Ritz the following morning. With hope that she'd appear, he hung around the hotel lobby until midmorning, then decided that she'd be likely to spend the day in bed, recuperating from the ride.

While he was loitering in town, he reflected, odds were that the unknown digger was gophering back in the hills. She was banking on him to protect her interests. His place was at the cabin. With no great enthusiasm, he rigged Bullet and pulled out.

In no haste, he was jogging across the flats when the thud of fast-moving hooves on the sun-baked ground brought his head around. Wreathed in dust, a buckboard whirled toward him, hauled by two half-broken broncs. There was no mistaking the driver. Dark hair streaming, sombrero bumping her back, was Carson's dark-eyed daughter, Rosita.

When the rig drew abreast, she hauled the sweat-plastered broncs to a halt. Duane, spitting dust, eyed her irately.

"Do you have to run the bejabbers out of those horses?" he demanded.

"How I handle my team is none of your business," she flared. "You misplaced your whey-faced school-ma'am?"

"Maybe you should stop nosing into my business," he said.

"Like inquiring if you two had a good time in the cabin last night?" taunted the girl.

"We were not at the cabin."

Rosita's long, unbound hair rippled as she tossed her head. "Stop spilling windies," she threw back. "I watched you two heading for the hills through dad's spyglass. You never rode back."

"Since you've got eyes like a cat, you should know better," he threw back with amusement.

"You calling me a cat?" she flamed.

Some impish impulse led Duane to prod this fiery girl further. He gravely eyed the hot color that tinged her cheeks, and the resentful twist of her red lips. His flat-planed features creased into a grin. "I'd say you were a ringtailed bobcat, fit for nothing but clawing."

In a spurt of temper, she swung at him wildly with the lash of her braided quirt, dangling by its loop from her right wrist. The leather thong whistled through the air. He ducked, an arm instinctively raised to protect his face, and she swung again.

The lash struck his forearm, coiled around it like an angry serpent—and bit like a red-hot branding iron. He kicked free of the oxbow stirrups, slid off his horse and grabbed the taut thong with his free hand. He hauled. The loop biting into her wrist, Rosita fought to retrieve her quirt. Duane reached, grasped her extended arm, and yanked her off the seat of the buckboard.

Rosita teetered, lost balance, and dropped into his arms, her legs flailing and fingers clawing. A furious panting bundle of feminity, she fought to break free as he grabbed her, striving to curb her clawing fingers without using undue force. Sharp nails raked his neck and his temper rose.

He spun her around, jerked the quirt free of her wrist and flung it aside. Then he crooked a knee and held her, writhing, across it. The flat of his right hand descended upon the taut seat of her jeans, again and again.

"Maybe a sound walloping will teach you to think twice before you use a quirt on me again."

Finally, he set Rosita down on her feet. Her breast rising and falling, she stood glaring at him. Her eyes were blazing cauldrons.

"You beast!" she choked. "If I had a shotgun, I'd shoot you dead."

"You're not to be trusted with a peashooter, much less a gun," he said.

"I hate you!"

"Too bad!" he said. "Now head back home before I beat some more dust out of the seat of your pants."

"You wouldn't dare!"

With the ghost of a grin, Duane moved toward her. She hastily spun around, scrambled up onto the seat of the buckboard and grabbed the lines. The restive broncs took off with a rush, scattering dust.

Duane stood watching the rig bounce away over the swales. Miss Rosita Carson, he decided, fingering his lacerated neck, was a regular spitfire. He was about to mount when he glimpsed her quirt lying in the dust. Picking it up, he looped it on the saddlehorn.

Nothing seemed changed when he dismounted at Murdoch's place near the pole corral. Quail still dusted themselves beyond the well, and the magpies, handsome with their white markings, skittered around the cabin roof. He stripped the gear off Bullet, watered the animal and loosed it in the corral. Smiling faintly, he eyed Rosita's quirt, then hung it from a nail in the barn.

Next he gave attention to the cabin. Here a clean-up job seemed in order. He gathered up the volumes scattering over the living room floor and slid back onto the shelves of the oak bookcase. After which he started restoring a semblance of order to the bedroom, replacing the contents of the bureau drawers.

A folded newspaper lay on the bottom of the lowest drawer. He saw that it was a copy of *The Hillsboro Herald* and the date showed it to be over a year old. Curious, he opened it up. Just why, he wondered, would James Murdoch have treasured a year-old newspaper?

The pages crackled with dryness as he idly rifled through them. Suddenly, his attention quickened. One news item was roughly circled with a pencil mark. It was headed: OUTLAWS LOOT GOLD SHIPMENT. With growing interest, he read:

Four guards were killed and a teamster wounded when a shipment of gold ingots from the Consolidated Mining Company, valued at over $750,000, was held up on the Logan Grade, about ten miles north of Hertzburg, Texas. The ingots were en route to Austin, Texas.

According to James Mullen, the wounded teamster, at least four men were involved in the outrage. Mullen states that the wagon carrying the gold was laboring up the rocky grade when there was a sudden burst of gunfire. A slug struck him in the neck, knocking him to the ground. Despite pain from the wound, he lay motionless, playing dead, and saw four masked men ride up to the wagon.

One dismounted, climbed up to the driving seat, picked up the lines and drove away, while his pards dropped in behind. The whole affair was over in minutes and had obviously been carefully planned.

It was not until late afternoon, seven hours later, that a prospector, heading into town for supplies, came across the bullet-riddled corpses of the guards and the wounded teamster, who was delirious with pain. Before nightfall, the teamster recovered sufficiently to gasp out the story of the holdup.

At time of publication, no trace of either the looted ingots or the renegades has been found, although posses are scouring the country.

Jack Curtis, manager of Consolidated, states that no effort will be spared to recover the gold and bring the outlaws to justice. In order to foil such holdups, he said, shipments were made at irregular intervals and the dates of departure were known only to office personnel. Because of this and the fact that a gold shipment has never before run into trouble, four armed guards were deemed sufficient.

Conscious of rising excitement, Buck Duane stared at the yellowing sheet. Was this the key to Murdoch's murder and the mysterious digging in the vicinity of the cabin? Town Marshal Welch had said that the dead man had been superintendent of the Little Sheba Mine, at Hillsboro, New Mexico, who had "retired" and had been living in the cabin for about a year. Could he have been a member of the gang, keeping cases on the cached gold? Were the looted ingots lying somewhere around, buried until an opportunity arose to move them down into Mexico? Could the wealth Murdoch had promised his niece be his share of the loot?

There must have been a reason for Murdoch's bushwhacking, the search of the cabin, the digging. The sensible thing to do would be to head into Hertzburg and hash it over with Welch. He had put off doing that too long.

IX

The town marshal looked up when Buck Duane jingled into his office. "What brings you back? Figured you'd shed the dust of Camino County."

The Ranger ignored the question. "What you know about this?" he asked, and plunked the aging copy of *The Hillsboro Herald*, in front of the lawman, indicating the penciled item.

Welch scanned the account of the hold-up silently, looked up. "How did you come to latch onto this?" he wanted to know.

Duane scraped up a chair, dropped into it and told of his deal with the schoolma'am to keep an eye on her property and his discovery of the news sheet when he was straightening up the cabin. He checked an impulse, which he had controlled from to first, to reveal his identity to Welch. Maybe he'd get further, he thought, if he stuck to his role of saddlebum.

"That looted shipment ever recovered?" he inquired.

Welch shook his head.

"Could be it's cached," Duane said. "Right there on Murdoch's quarter-section."

"Just what put that notion into your head?" The marshal asked, eying the Ranger with amusement.

"The sign points that way. Murdoch quit his job in Hillsboro near the time of the holdup. He locates within a short day's ride of the scene. He promises his niece he'll leave her well-fixed. He's bushwhacked and some hombre starts digging. What more do you need?"

"Plenty," threw back Welch and fingered for the makin's. "You seem to be weaving a whole blanket out of one oddment of wool. Murdoch was clean as a hound's tooth. Likely, some loco prospector got a notion the old carrion crow was wallowing in velvet. He beefs the hombre, searches the cabin, but overlooks the wad you located. You bull in and scare him off. He ducks back whenever chance offers and digs like crazy, hugging the idea he'll turn up aces. I'd say it's as simple as that."

"Could be," agreed Duane doubtfully. "How far did the law get clearing up the case?"

"No further than you could throw a posthole," admitted the marshal placidly.

"Why was that?"

Welch, a deliberate man, touched a match to his smoke. "Not one clue," he said, "outside the abandoned wagon, found in the hills beyond the grade. I scoured the Aridos with a posse. Sheriff Harrigan, down at Cochrane, threw in a slew of deputies. I'm pretty sure every waterhole and trail from here to the Border was watched. Consolidated even brung in Pinkertons. When the dust settled, all we'd come up with was that abandoned wagon."

"You figure the gold was cached?"

"Nope!" returned the marshal promptly. "I figure it was halfway to the Border before the sheriff started spreading his dragnet. Them ingots weigh twenty-seven pounds apiece. A mule could pack six—more at a pinch. A twenty-mule train could handle a ton and a half of gold— and move fast. Hombres smart enough to pull off that hold-up would be slick enough to plan their getaway."

"Just supposing the ingots were cached. Why not Murdoch's place?" persisted Duane.

"Why Murdoch's?" retorted Welch with patient resignation. "Ain't there ten thousand other likely spots? Why drag Murdoch in? Hell, he was a big shot in Hillsboro, superintendent of the Little Sheba Mine for most ten years. What's more, he was a sick man—his ticker was acting up. He'd just got back from a long spell in some eastern hospital. He warn't even around when the gang hit. He was taking it easy back in the hills.

"And, if he was tied in with the renegades there'd be no call for them to dig all over creation. They'd know just where they'd planted the loot, and exactly where to dig." He snorted. "I'd stake my saddle that gold crossed the Border less than twenty-four hours after it was lifted."

Duane sat rubbing his chin, considering this. "You're wrong, Welch," he said finally. "My gamble is that the gold's lying out at Murdoch's place right now. Here's the way I've got it figured. Murdoch's health forced him to quit. He was flat broke, on account of the high-priced eastern doctoring.

"So he planned the robbery. He picks up the hideaway in the hills, spreads it around he's retiring. Being on the inside, he knows when big shipments go out. He hunts up three, four hardcases and lays out the holdup plan. It goes off like clockwork. The ingots are cached on his place and the gang sits back to wait—until the searching posses cool off."

"The hardcases get impatient, shoot Murdoch—and

then forget where they planted the ingots!" put in the marshal, amusement flickering in his faded eyes.

The Ranger shook his head. "Murdoch keeps cases on the cache. I've an idea he was real shrewd that way. He begins to ask himself why he should split with three or four gun dummies. He'd figured everything. He was the brains and they were just tools. He's living alone, with time to kill. All he has to do is move the ingots to another spot, and tell the dummies to go plumb to hell. But he outsmarts himself. They get sore, kill him, and comb the cabin for a clue as to where he's moved the loot. Finding none, they start digging. Now," he challenged, with a faint smile. "Pick that to pieces!"

"A gent with your arguing talent is wasting time drifting saddle-loose around the country," declared Welch gravely. "You'd make a mint as a range lawyer."

"I doubt that," smiled Duane. "It seems you're not convinced."

"Not enough to plow up Murdoch's hundred and sixty acres," commented the marshal dryly.

When Duane left the law shack he paused on the plankwalk, fashioning a smoke and mentally debating whether or not to acquaint Mildred Stokes with his theory about the looted ingots. Probably she wouldn't take kindly to the thought that her uncle had been involved in the theft of a gold shipment. But his discovery of that newspaper had changed his whole set-up. If his idea held water, the week he had proposed to spend out at the cabin would be wasted time.

Murdoch's tough sidekicks would simply outwait him, then jump in when he rode off and dig at leisure. He had to stick around until his theory was proved or disproved. Miss Stokes was debating selling to Carson or this horse raiser. He had to persuade her to hold on.

When he arrived at the hotel, the sun was low in the sky and Main Street was bisected by long banners of slowly reddening radiance.

Mildred Stokes was slumped on one of the shabby rockers in the lobby of The Crossing House, plainly still suffering from the effects of her ride, and plainly bored by the attentions of a florid-face drummer.

A look of relief came into her eyes when she saw the Texan. She rose quickly and moved across the faded carpet toward him.

"You appear to be a mite saddlesore," commented Duane. "It happens to everyone at times."

"A mite!" she repeated wryly. "I have a feeling I'll never sit down in comfort again."

"It will pass," Duane assured her and steered her to a nearby seat. "Read this!" he said. He pulled out the creased copy of *The Hillsboro Herald* and passed it to her, indicating the marked account of the hold-up.

"Well?" she inquired, when she had read it slowly and carefully.

"I've got a crazy notion that gold may be buried on your quarter-section."

The young teacher's eyes opened wide with surprise. "Whatever gave you that idea?" she exclaimed.

He hesitated. "It's never been proved. But there are some ugly rumors floating about that your uncle was tied in with that robbery."

Her smooth forehead furrowed. "You make me more curious than ever," she said. She did not appear to be as shocked—or outraged—by what he had said as he had feared she might be.

"Well, this is how I figure it." Again, he outlined his theory concerning the holdup, and her uncle's possible part in it. To his further surprise, she heard him out without protest.

When he was through, she said thoughtfully, "Mother always believed that the Murdochs were never overly scrupulous. It seems she may have been right. So that's why those men were so anxious to buy!"

"I'm far from convinced of that," Duane told her. "Carson could have had a half-dozen reasons for wanting it. I hear the CCC's plagued with rustlers and that cabin could serve as a base for their operations. As for Conners, possibly he figured Murdoch chased visitors away because there was something he'd discovered about the property he didn't want anyone to know about. Something that made it valuable, perhaps, but not necessarily hidden gold."

"Well," she demanded, with a touch of irritation, "what action do you suggest I take?"

"Let me stick around, and see if I can locate the gold. Maybe I've been tilting at windmills. With luck, we could pocket a hundred fifty thousand dollars in bounty money for finding those ingots."

"That large a sum!" she breathed. "It seems incrdible!"

"Seventy-five thousand apiece."

Her green eyes questioned him sharply.

"A fifty-fifty split," he said. As a Ranger, he knew that he could not share in the reward—but it would be out of character for a "tumbleweed" not to insist on sharing in it.

"Yes," she said slowly, "I suppose that would be fair."

Duane stood up. "Since we seem to be in complete agreement I may as well head back to the hills." He smiled. "I guess that gold has gotten under my skin. I mean, just the possibility that it may actually be there. I'd hate to leave the place wide open."

When the jingle of his spur chains died, Mildred Stokes sat deep in thought, her small chin cradled on the palm of one hand. The drummer, lighting a fresh cigar, lumbered across the threadbare carpet to renew their acquaintance. Ignoring him, Mildred rose and headed for the street. The creased copy of *The Hillsboro Herald* lay on the floor beside her rocker where she had dropped it accidentally.

Town marshal Welch, deep sunk in thought, glanced up with surprise when the door opened and Mildred Stokes walked in. Hastily, he rose and pulled a chair forward.

She glanced at the hard wooden seat and repressed a shudder. "I prefer to stand," she told him.

Welch chuckled. "Saddle sores? Duane should have known a city girl can't bump leather for hours without raising blisters." He perched on a corner of the old oak desk. "Well, ma'am, what's on your mind?"

"Duane has just been in to see me," she began, without preamble. "It seems he's almost sure that stolen gold ingots, valued at perhaps three-quarters of a million dollars, are buried on the property my uncle left."

The marshal nodded, his faded eyes weighing her. "That's right," he said. "He was in here about an hour ago, trying to convince me."

"Do you believe he could *possibly* be right?"

"I'd say he's been smoking loco weed."

"Assuming the ingots did come to light," she asked, ignoring his comment, "your duty would be to take possession of them in the name of the law, wouldn't it?"

"I'm afraid so, ma'am," the marshall said.

"Isn't there a possibility that he might—decamp?"

"You mean run off with the gold?" Welch grinned. "Not a chance. It could weigh a ton and a half, supposing it's there—which I seriously doubt.

"You could be mistaken," she insisted. "Someone should keep a close watch on him. I'll be hundreds of miles away, in Tucson. My interests should be protected. I think that obligations devolves upon you."

"So you don't trust Duane?" he mused.

"I would trust anyone where three-quarters of a million in gold, or a hundred-fifty-thousand-dollar bounty, was involved," she retorted coolly.

X

When the Ranger jogged into the holding deep in the hills it was past midnight. A segment of moon laid a spectral sheen over bouldery slopes, while the discordant howling of a coyote pack floated across the barren ridges.

Duane stripped off Bullet's gear, turned the horse into the corral and headed for the cabin, packing his Winchester. Scarcely had he yanked off his boots in the boxy bedroom when the first shot shattered the brittle gypsum window pane, and buried itself in the timbered wall on the far side of the room.

Buck Duane dove for the kerosene lamp set on the bureau and doused the light. Ducking low, he moved quickly to the shattered window and peered out, his eyes level with the sill. Nothing moved. Wan moonlight washed over the dim outlines of hills and ridges; his horse made a lumpy blur in the corral and a startled bird fluttered through the night. A tiny tongue of flame licked through the obscurity.

Duane's head jerked down as the whipcrack of a second rifle shot reached his ears. He heard a thud as the bullet slapped into the timbers of the cabin. Groping, he found his Winchester and moved out into the living room. Here he hunkered by the fireplace, nursing the rifle, waiting and watching.

Lead continued to drone steadily into the timbered flank of the cabin. The marksman was apparently firing from a low ridge that paralleled the holding to the south, Duane told himself. It was long-range for a Winchester, which was probably why he couldn't find the window again, not without a light inside the shack to guide him. Just what did the coyote think he was gaining by random shooting?

It was difficult to resist the temptation to slip out and scout around. There had been four men in the hold-up gang, he reminded himself. They could all be lurking out in the night, ready to cut him down the instant he emerged. Thick log walls made the cabin practically bullet-proof. It would be smart to wait for dawn before poking around.

He began to nod. It had been a long and wearying day. Sleepily, he stretched out on the floor, the rifle beside him in case there was trouble.

In the early morn the squawking of magpies aroused him. He sat up, blinking drowsily around. Day had dawned. A broad shaft of sunlight speared through the window. Remembrance of the shooting flowed into his mind. He came quickly to his feet, stepped to the window and peered out.

It would have been hard to conceive of a more peaceful scene. The plumed quail were back, happily dusting beyond the well. Jewelled humming birds darted through the clear air and a sparrow hawk circled high overhead.

Opening the door, Duane slid outside, rifle slanted, brace for trouble. But nothing disturbed the serenity of the new day. Bullet stood hipshot in the corral, the quail arose with a whirl of wings, and the ridge from which a rifle had spat lead during the night lay bare and barren, bathed in early morning sunlight.

The Ranger packed a bucket of water from the well, started a fire in the sheetiron stove and filled the coffee pot. Waiting for the coffee to boil, he mulled over the shooting, and decided it could have but one object—to scare him off the place. If the rifleman had felt an urge to kill, he could have ghosted close and fired point-blank through a window. Duane made a mental note to drape those windows.

Even though his brain was well pickled in alcohol, Silas H. Leeson was possessed of considerable acumen and a complete lack of scruple. Despite this, he was perpetually in a state of financial insolvency. There was little legal business in Hertzburg and what there was came mainly from Julius Siegler. Siegler, a past master in the art of squeezing a dollar, considered that a room in The Crossing House, plus office space, amply compensated his legal aide for services rendered. This arrangement frequently left Silas short of funds to assuage a gnawing thirst.

He was in this aggravating condition when he wandered into the hotel lobby and plunked down into a rocker, running his tongue over dry lips. This was Saturday, the one day in the week when Hertzburg came alive. Ranchers, punchers, homesteaders from all over the valley headed for town, to meet and mingle, visit the stores and trade talk. The Bull Pen invariably did a land office business but Silas' credit had long run out.

Tortured by enticing visions of smooth Bourbon and jovial conviviality, the corpulent lawyer sat and suffered.

Incuriously, he picked up a newspaper lying on the floor beside the rocker, sighted an item outlined in pencil and became absorbed. Then inspiration dawned.

Julius Siegler was busy with his books in the rear of The Emporium when Leeson waddled down an aisle, a folded newspaper under one arm. At sight of the fleshy form bulking in the office doorway, Siegler growled, "No advances!" and continued figuring.

"Julius," remonstrated his visitor, "you totally miscomprehend the object of my visit."

"Never knew a time when you didn't need money," snapped the storekeeper. "What else could bring you here?"

Leeson chuckled with hearty goodwill. "At this time my financial affairs are of no consequence. What would you say if I offered to enrich you to the tune of some hundred thousand dollars?"

"I'd say you were drunk—as usual," grunted Siegler.

"You do me an injustice, a gross injustice," protested the pudgy lawyer. "Here, sir, is my proof!" He folded the newspaper to display the marked item, and tossed it on the storekeeper's desk.

Siegler sighed, pushed a ledger aside, picked up the yellowed sheet and perused it swiftly. "Well?" he demanded, looking up.

"Those looted ingots have never been recovered."

"Just what are you getting at?"

"At the present moment they're buried on a quarter-section bequeathed to a Miss Mildred Stokes. The bounty for their recovery, my dear sir, is one hundred and fifty thousand dollars."

"Murdoch's place!" Siegler pushed up his green eye-shade, leaned back in his chair, and laced bony fingers across a lean middle. He eyed the fleshy lawyer shrewdly. "So that's why there's been talk of digging up there," he murmured. Leeson noted, with elation, that the tone of his voice registered rising interest.

"The magnet's three-quarters of a million in ingots," asserted the lawyer. "With an absentee owner, interlopers have a free hand. This is a golden opportunity, Julius."

"To pack a spade up into the Aridos, chasing a will-o'-the-wisp?" The storekeeper's tone was dryly ironic.

"To acquire the property, run off trespassers and explore at leisure."

Siegler eyed his flabby legal adviser closely. "Just what gives you the notion that those ingots are cached on Murdoch's place?"

Leeson's slack features creased into a sly smile. "Certain significant statements made by James Murdoch at the time he made his will." He knew he was embroidering the truth, but who was to prove otherwise? Murdoch couldn't argue, he was dead. When he'd drawn the will, he'd been surprised when the recluse had listed only one rocky quarter-section as assets. Plainly, the crusty ex-mine superintendent had more.

A reasonable assumption was that he had converted his real assets into gold and what was more logical than to assume he'd buried the gold. It had been a happy inspiration to transform that presumably existing gold into looted ingots. Who would disprove the allegation?

"And just what were those significant statements?" inquired Siegler, with a frowning glance.

"Professional ethics forbid me to repeat them," said Leeson smugly. "I will say, under a seal of strict confidence, they indicated Murdoch was involved in the robbery."

Musing, Siegler eyed the paper. He looked up, his eyes as sharp as dagger points. "You're not giving me a run around, Si?"

"Why, Julius!" The lawyer's voice quivered in stricken protest.

"Just why haven't *you* grabbed these ingots—and the bounty?"

"They have yet to be located first," explained the lawyer patiently. "The right to search demands ownership. Could I afford to buy?"

Musing, the storekeeper abstracted a wooden toothpick from his vest pocket, and worried his front teeth. "Can the girl sell?" he demanded, abruptly.

"She can assign," said Leeson promptly. "Then, immediately probate proceedings are completed, the assignee will assume title."

"*Would* she sell?"

"Give me one reason why a sensible woman would hang on to a worthless quarter-section," chuckled the lawyer. "Providing, of course, she was offered a satisfactory financial inducement."

"Get Miss Stokes' best cash price," snapped Siegler, "and move fast."

"Indeed I will, Julius," Leeson assured him quickly. "That will involve a trip to Tucson," he said smoothly. "Personal persuasion is imperative. A small advance—"

"How much?" demanded the storekeeper, frowning irately.

"A hundred dollars."

Siegler slid open a drawer of his desk, lifted out a metal cash book, and carefully counted out five gold eagles. "Fifty dollars!" he rasped. "Not a cent more."

"If you say so," agreed the lawyer, striving to cloak his exhilaration. Siegler counted the coins in his eager palm.

In high good humor, Silas H. Leeson pushed through the batwings of The Bull Pen. His strategem had worked. No longer were his pockets empty. He'd outslickered Siegler, and that old skinflint was as slick as a greased hog. Probably there wasn't a dollar buried on that barren quarter-section. But who was to prove it?

The five gold eagles burning his pants pocket were a mere trifle in comparison to the honorarium he would add to whatever price the girl set. Siegler would buy. He had no doubt of it. The old tightwad had swallowed the bait, even if forking over the gold eagles had stuck for a moment in his gullet.

The saloon was crowded. Punchers from the CCC, Diamond, Currycomb, Running W., and townsmen, occupied all of the tables, with a sprinkling of cattle buyers, drummers and itinerants. At one end of the bar, cowmen bunched, trading cattle talk. At the other, Town Marshal Welch nursed a bottle of beer. The air pulsed with the steady drone of men's voices, punctuated by the clink of glasses. Blue clouds of tobacco smoke eddied and swirled.

Clutching a full bottle of Bourbon in one hand and a glass in the other, Leeson found space at a table and settled down. Six drinks later he was telling himself he was undoubtedly the smartest man in Hertzburg, if not in the entire state of Texas. He deserved to be treated with dignity and respect, and not like a legal "has been" just one notch above a saddlebum. Well, he would impress upon these yammering clods that Silas Leeson was a man of stature, that his acute mind had solved a mystery that had baffled the town marshal, the sheriff, even Pinkerton's.

"Gentlemen!" His rich, round tones boomed above the rumble of talk. "I have an announcement to make."

Talk cut off abruptly. Heads swiveled and patrons focused on Leeson's inflamed features, and bleary eyes.

"He's as drunk as a fiddler's clerk," grinned a puncher seated nearby.

Leeson weaved to his feet, clutching the edge of the table for support. "You will be happy to learn," the lawyer said, staring around him, "that the location of certain gold ingots, to the value of three-quarters of a million dollars, plundered over a year ago, is now known to your humble servant, Silas H. Leeson." He attempted to bow, staggered, and almost fell.

"You don't say! Where's the gold cached?" inquired the puncher, dropping a wink around his table.

"That sir," replied the lawyer, with drunken gravity, "is a confidential matter that must remain locked up here." He solemnly tapped his forehead. "I will, however, drop a hint—a certain quarter-section is involved." That he was close to blind drunk was clearly evident, but that he was unaware of what a spectacle he was making of himself was just as apparent.

Well pleased by the attention he had attracted, Leeson tilted his bottle, sank down in his chair and most inelegantly flopped across the table, amid roars of laughter. Talk broke out again and Silas H. Leeson, Hertzburg's prize drunk, was forgotten. That didn't bother Silas—he had sunk deep into booze-sodden slumber.

At dawn a swamper stumbled over Leeson's stiffening form in the alley beside the saloon. The lawyer was not a pretty sight. His skull had been smashed by repeated blows inflicted by a heavy weapon. It could have been the barrel of a Colt .45.

XI

Back in the hills, Buck Duane inched around the lonely holding, debating on his next move, and uncomfortably aware that he was a sitting duck for any lurking bushwhacker. There was little doubt in his mind now that the looted ingots were cached somewhere on Murdoch's quarter-section. The shooting of the previous night had provided ample proof that at least one member of the renegade gang was hanging around, resenting his presence enough to open fire on the shack.

They had probably gambled that Murdoch's killing would be laid to a feud, or a quarrel with some half-crazed prospector, and the place abandoned, leaving them with a free hand to search for the hidden gold. In their eyes he was an unexpected obstacle—a wandering saddlebum who had blundered blindly into their business. If they failed to scare him off, what would their next move be?

An hour later Duane was back in town. Slacked in his chair, the town marshal listened without comment when Duane told of the rifle shots. "It should be plain to a blind mule," the Ranger concluded, "that the hombre, or hombres, who beefed Murdoch are hellbent to scare me off. If you can come up with any good reason, outside of those looted ingots, I wish you'd spell it out."

"Maybe you got it figured," agreed Welch, adding

another butt to the litter around the stove.

"So you've finally seen the light!" said Duane ironically.

"Si Leeson was picked up in the alley beside the saloon this morning," Welch told him.

"Drunk?"

"Dead—his skull busted."

Despite his startlement Duane found himself wondering why Welch had so abruptly switched the subject. "Leeson get tangled in a fracas?" he asked.

"Could be, but I doubt it."

In response to Duane's questioning glance, the lawman informed him of the lawyer's drunken announcement in The Bull Pen the previous night. "Si was liquored up," he ended. "Quite possibly someone thought he knew too much and talked too much."

"You mean—you think one of Murdoch's pards was listening in?"

"It's a strong possibility, I would say."

"Well, what more proof do you need?"

"Just a little more might help," Welch said. "But I'm beginning to see it your way. Everyone in and out of town was tanking up in the saloon last night," he went on glumly. "No one was anywhere near the alley." His eroded features creased into a humorless grin, "You got the brains of a canary bird, you'll go hightailing it out of town before you join Si in boothill."

"Guess I've got a streak of mule in me," said Duane. "I'm sticking."

"All right. I've no objection to having someone around I can talk to now and then—when bullets start hitting people in crazy ways. You have a few ideas about it, and that's more than can be said for just anybody."

Duane rode back to the hills in the heat of midday. To his surprise, two saddlehorses were tied to the rail of the corral. One glance told him they were Carson's dun and a bay mare the cowman's daughter straddled. He wondered wryly if Rosita's father had ridden out to demand an accounting for the spanking. His cogitations were interrupted by the appearance of the girl. Nonchalantly she strolled out of the barn, idly twitching her quirt.

"Are you accustomed to making yourself at home in other folks' premises?" he asked.

"Only when they're concealing stolen property," she retorted. She flicked the quirt, and stood looking at him with lofty disdain.

"I don't see that flat-chested schoolteacher around," she said mockingly. "Don't tell me you've been using my quirt to scare her away."

"Miss Stokes is a lady, and behaves like one." Duane's voice had a snap to it.

"And you are as blind as the bats we have to smoke out of the bunkhouses to be taken in by her," she flung back at him.

He fingered the healing scratches on his neck inflicted by her raking nails. "A man's hardly blind when he prefers a woman who doesn't claw like a wildcat."

"I should have clawed your eyes out!" the girl said.

"I knew you were fully capable of doing just that—or trying to," he informed her, stepping out of leather. "What brought you up here?"

"We heard shooting," Duane spun around at the sound of Carson's harsh accents. The stocky cowman had just rounded the angle of the barn, and had clearly caught a part of the angry exchange of insults. "My boys been riding nights, on account of brand-blotchers," added the rancher. "They reported hearing gunfire up here. Figured I'd better look into it."

Carson's voice hardened. "Guess you and me had better have a little talk."

"Any time!" Duane told him, and began stripping off Bullet's gear. "Someone loosed some shots at me last night. I haven't the least idea why."

The girl wandered away. Carson sank on his heels against the barn, watching Duane water his mount and loose it in the corral. The Ranger dropped down beside him, began building a smoke, and inquired, "What's on your mind?"

"You!" barked Carson. "Just why are you sticking around?"

"It could be I'm watching the place for Miss Stokes."

Carson eyed him narrowly. "What needs watching—the sagebrush?"

Duane said nothing.

"You wouldn't be tied in with the coyotes who are rustling me blind?"

"Ask Welch whether he thinks I'm a rustler or not," Duane said. "You'll get an answer that will make you drop that idea pronto."

"So you claim," rasped Carson. "If I thought this place was likely to become a rustlers' hideaway—I'd burn it to the ground."

"Maybe that's why I'm staying—to make sure nothing like that happens to Miss Stokes' property. Brace her if you want to buy."

"I already braced her," Carson said, "and drew a blank."

"How do you know she doesn't plan to settle here?"

The rancher snorted. "A schoolma'am—alone! You must be loco."

Duane shrugged. "Whatever she decides to do—it's none of my business."

"Listen," grunted Carson. "I'll pay you to make it your business." He pulled a roll of greenbacks from a back pocket, and peeled off five bills. "Stick this hundred dollars in your jeans, then hit for Tucson. Make her see the light and I'll add another hundred."

"Not interested!" said Duane shortly.

"Buck me and you'll get gored," bristled the rancher.

Duane came to his feet. "I'm sticking right here."

"I got other ideas," fumed Carson. He straightened and strode, stiff-legged, toward his saddlehorse.

Carson's daughter had been drifting around close by and Duane guessed that she hadn't missed much of the talk. Thumbs hooked in his gunbelt, he watched the infuriated rancher loose his pony and swing into the saddle. Indolently Rosito followed suit, trailing her father as he pulled out. When her bay passed Duane, she checked the animal and called out, "Stubborn as a steer!"

"I can prod, too," he threw back.

"But you can still be corraled!" she taunted, challenge flashing in her dark eyes. Before he could feel he had evened the score with a suitable reply she roweled the bay and cantered out of earshot.

He stood watching father and daughter as their mounts wound through brush and boulders down gulch. If it wasn't enough to have the mysterious marksman gunning for him, he now had Carson on his neck.

When he turned and started back toward the cabin, he saw that the door was ajar. So Carson's daughter, and maybe her father, had gone inside. He had no sooner passed through the door and stepped into the bedroom then he came to an abrupt halt, quick anger sparkling in his eyes. The tintype of Mildred Stokes lay on the floor, the sheet of glass behind which it was framed, ground into small fragments. It could have been crushed by a small heel.

XII

As the setting sun reddened the upthrust peaks of the distant mountains, sending long, duncolored shadows wavering across the clearing Buck Duane's thoughts reverted to the shooting of the previous night. Would the unseen marksman be back with darkness, plonking lead at the cabin again?

When the hills finally faded behind thickening veils of purple, he draped the windows. Then he lit the lamp and prepared supper. By the time he'd cleaned up a mess of fried beans and bacon, darkness clothed the gulch. He slipped outside into a dim shadowland.

Picking his path carefully through the obscurity, the Ranger legged toward the ridge that overshadowed the holding to the south. He reached its flank and began slowly working up the rock-etched incline. Sweating, slipping on loose shale, he continued persistently upward, using his hands now to grab the stunted brush that scabbed the slope for support as the grade became steeper.

When finally he approached the crest, he bellied down, worming between outcroppings of rock. Breathing hard, he turned his head and looked back into the gulch—a chasm of darkness in which a small square gleamed faintly, a covered side window of the cabin. Around him, vague in the uncertain light, fragments of rock and patches of scrubby brush splotched the hogback. If the sharp-shooting jasper paid a return visit, he reflected with satisfaction, he'd be there to give him more than he bargained for.

He settled himself to wait, stretched out and relaxed, staring up at the silent legions of stars blinking overhead, through which, like a fiery spark, an occasional tiny meteorite flashed and died. Unbroken by quiet lay on the solitudes, broken abruptly by the flat unmistakable sprang of a Winchester further down ridge. He jerked to a sitting position, staring through the night. A segment of moon floated serenely above the ridges, its wan light laying a tracery shadow over the brush, and loose rock botched around. But he could detect no sign of movement.

Again, the whiplike crack of a rifleshot punched into his ears. Slowly, he began crawling in the direction of the sound, easing around misshapen fragments of rock, and skirting thorny mesquite. Once he pulled back hastily at the sound of a disturbed diamondback's warning rattle.

A third gunshot shattered the silence, very close now. He froze, then flattened out and slithered ahead. Not more than a few paces distant he glimpsed the form of a man—vague in the night—stretched out, Winchester cuddled to shoulder.

The rifle belched fire. By the powder flash he saw that the marksman was compactly built, broad-shouldered, and clad in rider's garb. Metal tinkled as the stranger ejected the empty shell and it dropped upon rock.

Nerves tight, Duane wormed closer. The rifle stabbed

fire again. The sound of movement muffled by the report, the Ranger jerked to his feet, took one long step and flung himself upon the outstretched form. He groped for the other's throat and—found he had a tiger by the tail. The chunky marksman was as hard-muscled and quick-moving as a mustang. He gasped at the impact of Duane's rangy form, then hunched his back.

Duane clung like a cougar, fingers digging into the muscular neck. With ease, it seemed, the other rolled, throwing him off balance. A knee pistoned into Duane's groin like a hard-driven wagon pole, and the other wrenched free as Duane grunted with agony, and slackened his grip.

The two men grappled, threshing over the ground, their legs flailing. Hooked fingers groped for Duane's eyes. He latched onto the fingers, levered them backward, and pressed his face against the stocky rider's shirted chest. His free fist bunched and smashed at his opponent's features, no more than a blur in the night.

Gulping air in sobbing gasps, the stranger latched onto the Ranger's hair, wrenching his head back, fighting desperately to break free. Still struggling with silent ferocity, they rolled downward over the rough ground interlocked, their writhing bodies cannoning into a boulder. Grunting and gasping, the frantic rider found Duane's windpipe, and his hard fingers compressed like the steel jaws of a trap.

Half-throttled now, blood salty on his lips, the Ranger fought to break the hold, conscious of a roaring in his ears, a red curtain clouding his eyes. Choking, he smashed at his assailant's features with savage short-arm jabs, experiencing a sudden, bitter exhilaration as the grip on his throat loosened and he felt the other's muscles relax.

Sucking air into his straining lungs, he continued blindly pounding with bloodied fists until, like a thunderclap, a crushing blow descended upon the back of his head. Consciousness left him in a blinding flash of light. He sprawled senselss over the slack form beneath him.

Long ages later, Duane groaned and stirred. His eyes

blinked open and he stared, uncomprehending, at a spread of stars. His brain fogged, he struggled to a sitting position, groaned again and clapped both hands to the back of his head as waves of pain surged over him. For a while he sat unmoving, nursing his bruised skull, striving to think coherently. Gradually, remembrance seeped back —the gunshots, the fight, the blow.

As the waves of pain subsided, his fingers, gingerly exploring, touched a swelling through his hair that seemed as big as a watermelon. There must have been a second man on the ridge he reflected—a man who'd ducked into the picture just as he'd mastered the chunky marksman, and clouted him with a gun butt.

He had just started to struggle to his feet when the glint of moonlight on metal caught his eye. Duane reached out and picked up the brass shell of an expended cartridge. A second and a third lay close to where they had been ejected from a Winchester. He gathered them up, stuffed them into a pants pocket. A moment later he was crossing the uneven terrain, swaying unsteadily. When at last he stumbled into the cabin he flopped gratefully onto the bed, and lay exhausted. Finally he sank into an uneasy sleep that was half stupor.

The sun was high and magpies clattered cheerfully around the eaves when the Ranger awoke the next morning. His throat felt as though he had been swallowing ashes, his head throbbed persistently and it seemed every muscle in his bruised body made aching complaint. Half-dazed, he blundered into the kitchen, stripped off his shirt and sloshed cold water over his head and torso.

Two steaming mugs of black coffee helped to clarify his thoughts. Duane remembered the empties he had picked up on the ridge. Fishing them out, he examined the bases. On each, the firing pin had struck practically on center. The two empties he had picked up at the scene of Murdoch's killing carried the indents off-center, which indicated the man he had battled the previous night wasn't Murdoch's bushwhacker. At least, he considered, that disposed of Welch's theory—there was more than one half-crazed prospector interested in the quarter-section.

XIII

There was no shooting that night or the next, and Buck Duane began to feel that his unknown assailants had decided he wouldn't scare. It was plain that they had really wanted to do no more than scare him. The hombre who had laid what was in all likelihood a steel barrel across his skull could have finished him right then and there, which strongly suggested they had no desire for the Murdoch place to become the focus of attention again because of another killing.

They had apparently just wanted him out of the way and a chance to continue digging. He would have gotten busy with a shovel himself. But he was restrained by the thought that Murdoch was too slick to move the ingots to a spot where they could be turned up by random digging.

There were a hundred spots in the rugged terrain within a mile of the cabin where buried gold would elude discovery until Doomsday. It was curious the ex-mine superintendent hadn't given his niece a clue to their location, knowing his associates were the type who would kill without a glimmer of a scruple. Murdoch had probably figured they'd never rub him out and forfeit a chance of locating the loot as long as he alone knew where it was hidden. And that, of course, had been a tragic miscalculation.

The soreness from the Ranger's own rough-and-tumble with the rider on the ridge had worn off, and the only reminder of the fracas was a slowly shrinking lump on the back of his head. It was still painful and he was in no amiable frame of mind when three riders jogged in—the town marshal, the granite-faced Carson and a tall rider with lean, leathery features and pale eyes bleak as lava knobs.

What now, wondered Duane, remembering the cowman's last visit. He sauntered forward to meet them as they peeled out of leather by the corral.

"Guess you're acquainted with these gents," said Welch. "Jim Carson rods the CCC, Lanky Larn'er his foreman."

Duane nodded at the two, who stood eying him impassively. "Well," he inquired, "what brought you up here?"

Welch looked uncomfortable. "Carson's having trouble with rustlers and—" he paused to clear his throat.

"Don't beat around the bush, Frosty," put in the cowman, with harsh impatience. "Tell this maverick I got a notion he's packing a sticky rope."

"Just hearing you say it is enough," Duane said, his anger rising. "It's a damned lie."

"Hold on now," exclaimed Welch quickly. "We can settle this peacefully. Carson filed a complaint and it's my duty to follow through. I've got no choice he claims his boys found sign of rustled stock, right in this gulch."

"Maybe he never heard of strays."

"I figured strays, but Carson's dead set on bracing you." Welch eyed the cowman. "All right, it's your move. Lay proof on the line, or withdraw your complaint."

"I'm sure we'll find proof," growled the rancher. He nodded to his foreman. "Poke around, Lanky. Maybe you'll turn up something."

Fuming, Duane watched the tall foreman stroll around the barn, eyes searching, kicking aside moldering pieces of equipment junked through the years. What was he expecting to find, wondered the Ranger—a freshskinned hide or a sacked side of beef? Carson was on unsure ground—and knew it. Just what did the tough old moseyhorn have in mind, filing a loco charge and dragging the marshal up into the hills?

Welch made a cigarette, his glance following the foreman. The rancher just stood unmoving, as though carved from rock.

The foreman finished his leisurely inspection and

ducked into the barn. The heads of the three men waiting outside swiveled when he backed out dragging two hides, so fresh that they hadn't began to stiffen. Duane glanced at Welch and saw that there was a look of dawning amazement in his eyes. Carson chuckled.

Without speaking, the tall foreman spread the hides, hair side up, then turned to his boss. "Rolled up," he said, "and stuck behind a bale of hay. The saddlebum is as guilty as hell."

With tight anger, Duane stared at the hides, each with the neat "CCC" brand burned through the hair. It was plain enough now. Carson had known all along the hides were there. He'd either had them planted or had been told they were hidden in the barn. On his previous visit, he'd warned that he always got what he wanted. Carson wanted him—Duane—off the Murdoch place and he was the type to whom the end always justified the means.

The Ranger had difficulty in restraining himself from rabbing Carson by the shoulders, forcing him to his knees, and beating the truth out of him.

"Those hides were planted!" he said quietly.

"I expected you to say that," retorted Carson, the ghost of a grin flitting around his tight lips. "Well, I guess that clears everything up, Frosty."

The marshal nodded grimly. Yanking a pair of handcuffs from a back pocket, he clamped them on Duane's wrists.

Lanky Larner rolled up the hides. "You'll need these for evidence," he drawled, and secured the cumbersome bundle behind the cantle of Welch's saddlehorse.

Carson walked up to the prisoner. "Maybe I should have brought a bunch of the boys and strung you up," he rasped.

"All right," Welch said. "That's enough. Taking him back to town is my job." He waited with his hands planted on his hips until Carson and his men mounted and rode off. Then when the sound of their horses' hoof-beats died, Welch fished out a key, unlocked the cuffs and dropped them into his pocket.

"Aren't you taking chances with a dangerous rustler?" said Duane, with dreary humor.

"Not when I got your gun," returned the lawman. "Let's chew this over."

They both hunkered against the barn.

"I hope you realize it was a frameup!" declared the Ranger. "Two steers! Could I eat the meat? If not, where would I peddle it?"

"Carson rods the biggest spread in the valley," said Welch. "Why would he frame you?"

"To get me off this place," Duane said. He related the story of Carson's former visit, the cowmen's offer of a handsome bonus if Miss Stokes could be persuaded to sell, and his rage at being turned down.

Then the Ranger told Welch about the shooting from the ridge and the midnight fracas. "I've got a bump as big as a camel's hump on the back of my head to prove it," he concluded. "Apparently there's two outfits hellbent to run me off—Carson's CCC and the bunch who beefed Murdoch."

"Talk of buried gold is percolating all over now," Welch said, his voice tinged with resentment. "Mrs. Purdy claims Siegler's dickering with the schoolma'am." He snorted. "All acting as crazy as popcorn on a hot stove."

"Why the shooting?" said Duane.

"Carson's punchers roostering you. That old moseyhorn's sure on the prod." He came back to his feet. "I guess we'd better start back."

"Do you intend to jug me!" Duane was unable to keep anger out of his voice.

"What choice have I got?" said Welch. "Carson's filed a complaint and dug up evidence." He nodded at the bulky bundle roped behind his cantle and wrinkled his nose. "Mighty odorous evidence, too. Failing bail, the sheriff holds you for the circuit judge. But the odds are you'll never face trial. Carson saw me clamp handcuffs on you and I'm pretty sure the old wart hog's satisfied. He doesn't think you'll come back here. When the case comes up I'll stake my saddle he won't prosecute."

XIV

Sheriff Harrigan was proud of his jail, mainly because it provided concrete evidence of the voters' wisdom in electing him to office—and presented a solid argument for reelection. A long, low adobe, it sat behind the courthouse in Cochrane. Its walls were four feet thick and its steel-barred cells escape-proof, and it hadn't cost the taxpayers one red cent, beyond materials, due to the sheriff's happy inspiration to use prison labor in its construction.

Before the week was out, Buck Duane had an unexpected visitor—the unctuous, bland-featured Julius Siegler. The gaunt-looking storekeeper was garbed in the rusty frock coat, dark pants and plug hat he usually reserved for such ceremonial occasions as funerals.

When he padded unobtrusively down the jail corridor, darting apprehensive glances into the cells, he reminded the prisoner of nothing so much as an itinerant preacher slipping into a house of ill-fame. Reaching Duane's cell, he paused, peering between the bars.

"So you've fallen on evil days, young man," he observed.

"I would be the last to deny that," Duane said, regarding the storekeeper curiously. "But I hope you didn't come here just to remind me of it. I'm not ready to be planted."

Siegler's smooth features contorted into a melancholy smile. "When that time arrives," he said, "may I suggest that nowhere would the ceremonies be handled more efficiently than at Hertzburg."

"That's a pleasant thought," rejoined the Ranger, his puzzlement increasing. "But don't tell me you dropped in to drum up business."

"No." Siegler's countenance twisted into a wintry smile. "I came to arrange for your release—on bail."

Duane stared at him incredulously. What possible reason could the old carrion crow have for helping him out of jail? "You'll go bail—for me?"

"Under certain conditions," Siegler said.

"What conditions?" Duane asked suspiciously. It was difficult to imagine Julius Siegler doing a stranger—or anyone, for that matter—a favor without prospect of personal profit.

"Perfectly reasonable conditions." The storekeeper laced long fingers across his middle and his guileless eyes dwelt mediatively upon the man behind the bars. "I am dickering with Miss Stokes for purchase of the Murdoch place. It has come to my knowledge that several men—quite illegally—are digging on the property. It is essential that they be closely watched."

Duane thought fast. It was plain that the old moneybags had somehow obtained knowledge of the hidden gold and was scared that it might be removed before he obtained possession of the quarter-section. "You know why they're digging?" he said.

"I have a notion," admitted the storekeeper cautiously.

"I see. Have you any objections to spelling it out for me?"

"I've reason to believe there's something valuable buried there," returned the other quickly. "I wish to explore the possibility."

"Why brace me?"

"You are the only person who is well acquainted with the property. Furthermore, it is necessary to cross the CCC range to reach it. Carson, who owns the ranch is a belligerent type. He persists in regarding all interlopers as rustlers. Various persons I have hired have been fired upon in the past and run off."

"So you ran out of volunteers and got the notion that if you bailed me out I might be willing to risk getting riddled with lead. Is that it?"

Siegler frowned, ignoring the question. "I need a trustworthy man," he went on, "who will advise me immediately if anything unusual transpires."

"It's a deal!" said Duane promptly. Anything, he thought, to get out of this hole.

"Excellent!" Relief showed plain in the storekeeper's

tone. He was clearly tortured by the thought that someone would get to that gold first and ace him out of a $150,000 bounty, reflected Duane, as his gaze followed Siegler's decorous exit. Now he was due to sweat awhile himself, waiting to see if the storekeeper went through with the deal.

Hours passed, and it was early afternoon before the jailer reappeared, a ring of keys jingling on his belt. In no haste, he fitted one to the cell gate, swung it open. "Rattle your hocks," he growled. "Sheriff craves a word with you."

He steered his prisoner out of the jail, along a covered dog-trot, and through a rear door of the courthouse. Their footsteps echoed down a wide corridor, along which closed doors were spaced, each neatly lettered with the name of a county official. The last, near the glass-panelled front doors, carried the words, WALTER HARRIGAN, *County Sheriff*.

The beefy jailer turned the handle and nudged his prisoner inside. Buck found himself in a high-ceilinged room. Four straightback chairs were line up against the far wall. A rack, beyond them, held a row of lethal-looking shot guns. The opposite wall was plastered with "Wanted" notices. At the end of the room, by two narrow front windows, a bull of a man sat hunched at a rolltop desk, a stogie stuck between his lips. At the prisoner's entrance he swung around.

Sheriff Harrigan was graying and going to fat. His florid features reflected the meaningless affability of the elected official and his belly lapped over his belt. But a strong sweet of jaw was plain beneath the flesh jowls.

"Well, Duane," he drawled, reaching for a sheet lying on the desk, "you're in luck." He eyed the sheet, intoned, "Order for the release of Buck Duane, signed by Judge Nabors. Bail set at two hundred fifty dollars, furnished by Julius Siegler, Hertzburg." Benevolently, he added, "Now keep out of trouble!"

"I never was in trouble," retorted the prisoner. "I was framed."

The sheriff smiled resignedly. "Sure," he said. "All you got to do is convince a jury."

XV

A quick trip to the old Murdoch place showed Duane that several men—he guessed at least three—had been digging extensively on the property.

Since Siegler had eased him out of jail for the express purpose of keeping cases on the Murdoch place, Buck Duane felt the storekeeper was at least entitled to some kind of an immediate report, even if Siegler would not like the news. He decided to head right back to The Emporium.

The Siegler he found enthroned in his office, amid accounts, catalogs and cash books, was very different from the self-affacing, benevolent funeral director. There was little guilelessness in Siegler's sharp eyes and an edge to his greeting.

Duane swept some price lists off a chair by the desk, dropped onto it and told him of the digging.

Pulling abstractedly at his long nose, Siegler listened to the story with frowning attention. He appeared pleased, rather than annoyed, by news of the continued digging. "That certainly confirms Silas Leeson's claim," he murmured.

"Leeson's claim?" questioned Duane.

"Silas suspected there might be something of worth buried on the quarter-section," he explained hastily. "I meant to tell you that when we had our talk."

Just how much did the storekeeper really know, wondered Duane. Aloud, he asked, "Is it your idea I should get back out there?"

Worrying the end of a pencil with sharp teeth, Siegler thought it over. "Perhaps you had better remain in town," he finally decided. "The interlopers—have apparently taken flight and I expect to learn, any day, that Miss

Stokes has accepted the very generous officer I made for the property. Immediately I assume possession, I intend to hire as many men as I can round up—to dig. You will supervise their efforts."

Playing up to his role of saddlebum, Duane reminded his new "boss," "I've got to eat—and sleep. You forgot the county stopped supplying me with board and lodging?"

"I'll instruct the hotel clerk to allot a room and Ah Wang at the restaurant to provide meals." The storekeeper's tone held obvious reluctance.

The old tightwad certainly hated to pay out, thought Duane and, from sheer perversity, decided to prod further, "A man gets thirsty," he observed pointedly.

"A wise man drinks water—Nature's nectar," said Siegler, with a wintry smile. "In Hertzburg there is no lack of water. If you are dissatisfied, young man, I can always revoke the bail bond."

The old fellow didn't have him over the barrel exactly. But going back to jail would not have helped him. He smiled tightly and rose. "Well—it's all right with me if you want me to drink your health in water," he observed, and headed for the street.

Three days passed and no further word came from the storekeeper. Duane was sitting in a relaxed position in one of the shabby rockers that decorated the hotel lobby, killing time, when he heard the distant shriek of an engine whistle. Hat tilted over his eyes, he continued to half-doze, aware that the deep tolling of an engine bell from the direction of the railway depot meant that the mixed passenger-freight had arrived.

From beneath the hatbrim, he glimpsed not long afterwards the flirt of skirts. Duane straightened in his seat and blinked with surprise. Mildred Stokes, composed and correct as always, was crossing the lobby with a brisk, decisive stride. At her heels tagged a plump Mexican girl in red skirt and white camiso, a filmy rebozo swathed around head and shoulders. Both girls packed traveling bags.

Duane rose quickly, stepped forward and intercepted the school ma'am. "Welcome back, Miss Stokes," he said. "If I had known—"

She stopped and stared at him in surprise. "I thought you were watching my property," she said, her voice accusing.

"There's been trouble out there."

"But you gave me to understand you wouldn't leave the place unguarded—no matter how much trouble you had to contend with."

It was plain, Duane reflected, that she knew nothing of what had transpired on the lonely quarter-section.

"There's a great deal that needs to be explained," he said. "There are times when a man has no choice."

"There's no need for explanations," she assured him sharply. She tried to push past him, but he blocked her path.

"You sold—to Siegler?"

"No!" she snapped. "Not that he hasn't been pestering me to sell. Pinkerton's, the detective agency, have also been plaguing me—for permission to dig on the property." Her prim lips tightened. "You told me yourself that—well, that you were almost sure my uncle, had hidden gold there. The newspaper you showed me—"

"I'm more sure than ever now. If you'll just listen—"

"I intend to investigate personally, and I need no assistance," she told him stiffly. "Come, Juana!"

"You're not going into the hills alone," said the Ranger.

"I have a companion!"

"You'll both be heading straight into trouble—big trouble."

"Poppycock!" she cried. "I am quite capable of taking care of myself. Now perhaps you will excuse me."

Baffled, Buck Duane returned to his chair and sat watching the schoolma'am and her Mexican friend—or servant, he couldn't guess which—book a room and head for the stairway.

He could not be sure, of course. But the possibility could

not be ruled out that gold fever had infected Murdoch's niece. Siegler's efforts to buy the quarter-section and Pinkerton's eagerness to dig had perhaps convinced her that wealth awaited the first person to get busy with a shovel. What seemed just as likely, however, was the simple fact that there were women who could go into a sudden rage when they had the mistaken idea that a man should never disappoint them, even when he had no choice. His cogitations were interrupted by the reappearance of Mildred Stokes on the stairs. She hurried down and moved purposefully toward him.

"We need a guide to the property," she said, her voice still a trifle brusque, but no longer angrily accusing. "Are you available?"

"Yes—but only because I couldn't go on respecting myself if I let *any* two women go out there alone."

"Then please rent two saddlehorses and a pack animal, to carry supplies. Then meet us at the store."

Within the hour, they pulled out—Duane ahead, leading a well-laden pack mule; Mildred Stokes, enveloped in overalls, tailing him and Juana in the rear, her bare legs dangling on each side of her mount. They'd scarcely hit the river trail when dust smoked ahead and a buckboard came into view, bumping and bouncing behind a team stretched out at full gallop. Duane didn't have to guess who held the lines.

Rosita Carson hauled the sweatplastered broncs to a halt when the vehicle drew close. Her red lips curved with amusement as she sat quietly watching the riders file past.

"So now you have a harem!" she taunted Duane, ignoring Miss Stokes' first startled, then enraged look. Concealing his irritation, the Ranger stared straight ahead.

Dead and deserted, Murdoch's place lay sweltering in the sun when they rode in. Trail-stained and saddlesore, the girls wearily dragged into the cabin and close the door behind them. Duane busied himself unloading the pack mule, stacking supplies on the porch. Among the schoolma'am's purchases was a double-barrelled shotgun.

He chuckled, thinking she was the type who would use it. When he was through, he knuckled the door. Mildred Stokes, now spruce in white blouse and dark skirt, opened it.

"Would you like me to pack in water and wood?" he inquired.

"No," she informed him crisply. "But I suggest you loose the pack in the corral." She opened the handbag dangling from a wrist, extracted a leather purse and carefully counted out five silver dollars. "That, I believe, is the agreed amount for your services. That should take care of it."

Duane stood very still, eying the lengthening shadows and wondering how many pairs of eyes were casing them through the gathering gloom. "Won't cost you a dollar, ma'am," he said, with mock humility in his voice.

Then, one by one, he spun the coins in the sagebrush a few feet from where they were standing. He had a sudden impulse to take her firmly by the shoulders and shake her, then bring his lips down hard on hers. But he restrained himself.

Sudden anger flamed in Mildred Stokes' eyes. "I insist that you leave at once. Juana and I are quite capable of looking after ourselves. And, remember, we have a shotgun."

So did Murdoch,, thought the Ranger, but it didn't help any. Mildred raised the gun and trained it on him. "I'm very serious about what I just said. I want you to go, at once."

Jogging through the thickening darkness back to town, Duane couldn't keep his thoughts off the irrationally impulsive green-eyed girl he'd left back in the hills with her plump Mexican companion. Common sense told him there was less chance of chasing the desperados who had held up the gold shipment away from Murdoch's place than scaring bees away from honey.

They'd killed at least five men to get that gold and it was a sure thing they wouldn't quit as long as a chance of retrieving it remained. Mildred Stokes was sitting on a powder keg. But Duane realized she had no intention of returning to town where he might shake some sense into her.

He returned the rented saddlehorses, ate in The Ritz—at Siegler's expense—and decided to let one night go by, feeling convinced Mildred was in considerably less danger than a man would have been. The gold-seekers would see in her no real obstacle to their plans, and would not try to scare her off immediately. And they'd know that if they harmed her the whole town would be in an uproar and a dozen posses would be after them with as many nooses.

When he awoke the next morning, the sun already rimmed the eastern horizon. He'd omitted to pull down the window shade and a broad white shaft spanned the hotel room, patching the far wall.

Sluiced off and shaved, Buck Duane dropped down the creaky treads of the stairway and headed for the hash-house. Little activity showed on Main Street, beyond a store clerk or two sweeping off fronts and washing windows, and the wrinkled Mexican, the zanzero, refilling water barrels set along the plankwalk. He saw Welch, always an early riser, step out of the eating house, building a smoke.

The frenzied beat of hooves on the plank bridge that spanned the creek reached his ears, like the tattoo on a distant drum. Someone in an all-fired hurry, he thought, then tensed with surprise at sight of the pack mule he had left with the girls. Stretched out at full gallop, it came down the wide, sandy street, neck outstretched, tail streaming.

Riding bareback was the Mexican girl, clutching its flying mane with one hand, belaboring it with a switch with the other. Her long hair in disorder, her rumpled red skirt displaying bare brown legs, she frantically lashed the mule, her features contorted with terror.

Welch ran out into the street as she allowed the mule to halt. It stood gaunted and trembling, blowing hard with lowered head. Duane, dashing up behind the marshal, saw that the girl's bare legs were scratched and scoured by brush.

"They shoot! They keel!" gasped the girl. Then she fainted, dropping slack across the mule's withers.

XVI

Between them, the town marshal and Buck Duane eased the slumped Mexican girl off the jaded mule, and carried her into the lobby of the hotel.

"We'll need a doctor," Duane said, when they lowered her into a rocker, and she fell back limply on the shabby cushions.

"There's no doctor closer than Cochrane," Welch said, his face set in tight lines. The girl's eyes were closed and her dark hair straggled in disorder over her swarthy face.

"I'd better get Ma Purday," Welch decided. "She'll know what to do."

He was gone barely five minutes when the widow hustled in with a rustle of skirts. Ma Purdy's quick glance strayed over Juana's grumpled garb, and the lacerations on her brown legs. She picked up a limp wrist and checked the girl's pulse. Then her beady eyes fixed on Duane. "You took her out to Murdoch's, with Miss Stokes?" It was more accusation than question.

Duane nodded.

"If there's anything to the talk that's floating around, that's no place for a woman."

"Miss Stokes was determined to take over the cabin," Duane said. "She forced me to leave at the point of a gun. I wouldn't be telling you this if I wasn't twenty times as concerned as you are."

Ma Purdy spoke to the clerk, who had left the desk and was standing at Welch's side. "We need a room, George, and a crock of hot water. Now you," she turned to Duane, "pack her upstairs."

The Ranger gathered up the unconscious girl in his arms and followed Ma's stringy form up the stairway. She consulted a key tab and threw open the door of a room on the second floor. Duane deposited Juana on the bed, and remained for a moment staring down at her, hoping she would open her eyes and begin to talk. But when that seemed unlikely he strode out of the room.

In the lobby he rejoined Marshal Welch. "She may not be able to speak for an hour or more. We've got to get to the cabin fast."

"I know. I'll swear in a posse, and—"

"That'll take time."

"A half hour I'm afraid."

"And Miss Stokes may not even be alive. Hell, I'm riding, right now."

"Makes sense," said Welch. "Let's get started."

Nothing seemed amiss when they jogged into the holding. Magpies still chattered among the weeds sprouting from the cabin roof, and humming birds darted the dapple sunlight for flashing jewels. They peeled out of leather in front of the cabin and Duane saw that the door was closed. Fearful of what lay behind it, he hurried inside. Everything appeared to be in order—the Rochester lamp stood exactly in the center of the table, the two chairs with laced rawhide seats were drawn up precisely on either side, and the bookcase was no longer grayed by a thick layer of dust.

He stepped quickly into the bedroom. The bed was neatly made. A flannel nightgown lay carefully folded on a chair beside it and a pair of furry slippers was set underneath.

There appeared to be nothing amiss in the kitchen, either. Perplexed, he moved outside. Welch, hunkered against an upright of the porch, was drawing on a cigarette.

"I can't understand it!" Duane exclaimed. "You'd think she had just stepped out for a moment."

The marshal said nothing, just pointed. Following the direction of his finger, Duane glimpsed an overalled form busily digging beyond a clumb of mesquite, two hundred paces or more beyond the well. "I'll be damned!" he muttered.

At their approach, Mildred Stokes straightened, brushing back wisps of auburn hair from her damp forehead. "Well?" she challenged.

"We thought we might find you lying here dead," said Duane.

"Dead!" the schoolma'am seemed amused. "That fool Juana, I suppose. There was firing during the night and some bullets hit the cabin. She became hysterical and rode off. I shouted after her, begging her to be sensible, but she paid no attention."

"Weren't you frightened, too, ma'am?" inquired Welch.

"I'm certainly not going to be driven off my property by a few random shots," she replied.

"Not when you're searching for buried treasure," put in Duane deadpan.

"Is that a crime?" Miss Stokes bristled. "This is my property and I have every right to dig wherever and whenever I please."

"Ma'am," put in the marshal bleakly, "maybe you should think twice about that. The shots could have been intended as a warning. Next time this night-shooting hombre may feel the same way about you as he did about your uncle. He may shoot to kill. This is no place for a woman—alone."

"That's for me to decide," she cried. "Right now, you're trespassing. I'll thank you to leave." The two men exchanged glances. Welch raised his shoulders in a fatalistic gesture. The stubborn Mildred Stokes strode away, stopped at a sandy spot and began turning the earth over again.

"I never saw a stubborner woman!" breathed Welch, with soft vehemence.

"What do you think should be done about it?" said Duane, watching the girl as she awkwardly wielded the heavy shovel.

"Nothing!" barked the marshal.

"We can't just leave her here now. You know that as well as I do."

"We sure can't run her off," Welch said. "This is her property."

Disgust written plain on his face, he began trudging back to the cabin. Duane followed him.

When they reached their horses, the marshal stepped into leather. Duane made no effort to mount.

"Who's stepping on your shirttail?" inquired Welch irately.

"I'm sticking around."

"For what?"

"Maybe I can make her change her mind."

"You sure got my good wishes," growled the lawman, and raised his reins.

Buck Duane stood watching Welch pull away. The marshal, he considered, was certainly very angry. But perhaps he couldn't be blamed for feeling the way he did. They'd pushed their ponies hard, through a long, tiring ride, not knowing what they would find at its end, and the only thanks they'd received for their efforts had been a slap in the face.

The school ma'am had a mind of her own, all right. But the Ranger had to admit she was spunky, too. Few women—or men for that matter—would stick it out, alone, in an isolated cabin, menaced by unseen enemies throwing lead in the night.

The Ranger stripped the gear off his mount, watered Bullet and loosed him in the corral. Later he hunkered in the shade of the porch, smoking and eying the quite mad girl as she toiled out in the sunglare.

Near noon, she walked back to the cabin. She looked hot, tired and annoyed. It was not until she'd disgustedly thrown the shovel aside that she became aware of Duane's presence.

"What are you doing here?" Mildred Stokes demanded.

"I just thought I'd stick around."

"I don't need you—or any man—around."

"I'm afraid you've got no choice," he said.

With an exasperated glance, she brushed past him and entered the cabin, firmly closing the door. He heard the bar drop into place.

After awhile, Duane came to his feet, drifted around to the barn, found a patch of shade and stretched out in siesta.

When he awoke, the sun was beginning to arc toward the west. He saw a moving form, out amid the waste of scrub and rock. Mildred Stokes, he reflected, was certainly dead-set on locating the buried ingots.

When she dragged in toward sundown he had the coffee pot bubbling on the stove and chuck sizzling in a frying pan. Beyond an angrily contemptuous glance, the girl ignored him. Plainly sore-muscled from digging, she sank into a chair and accepted in frigid silence the plate of bacon and beans he placed before her. Setting the steaming coffee pot on the table, he pulled up a chair and began eating his own supper.

Her plate emptied, Mildred Stokes sipped her coffee, looking at the Ranger with angry green eyes. "Mr. Duane," she said forcefully. "You must realize that you can't stay—overnight."

"Why not?" he inquired, between mouthfuls.

"It certainly wouldn't be proper."

"I took a couple of blankets out into the barn."

"Don't you realize," she flung back at him, "that I prefer to be *alone*—that is, if you don't mind?"

"And don't you realize," he mimicked tolerantly, "that the hombres who stole those ingots are still ghosting around. As Welch said, if they can't scare you off, they may decide to shoot you."

"Nonsense!" she snapped.

Duane shrugged. It was plain that the girl was obsessed by a golden vision. She could think of nothing but buried ingots—and the fortune that awaited her if she could uncover them.

Throughout the evening she endured his presence with chilled indifference. With darkness, he wandered out to the barn and squatted against its clapboards, smoking.

Gradually the gloom thickened, and a chill breeze soughed across the ridges and rustled dead brush, and a night bird circled with harsh chittering.

Duane came erect, fingered his way inside the darkened barn and found his blankets. At a thought, he moved outside again and slid his Winchester out of the boot. Trouble was brewing, he could feel it in his bones. The distant spang of a rifle shot stirred him into wakefulness. He sat up, fumbling for his boots. From somewhere out in the night, another, and another gunshot spluttered like firecrackers. Grabbing the Winchester, Duane slid outside.

From the ridge to the south, a lance of flame licked through the darkness. He heard the drone of a slug that plonked into the timbers of the cabin. A second gun opened up, from the west. Crouching, he ran around to the front of the cabin. The door was firmly secured. He hammered it frantically with a fist. It opened hesitantly. Dim in the starlight, he saw Mildred Stokes, a robe wrapt around her. The remaining window shattered, the bullet buzzing across the room like an angry hornet.

"We've got trouble," he called out, and stepped inside. Slamming the door, he dropped the bar into place.

"They're only trying to scare us," insisted the girl, now invisible in the darkened cabin. But he detected a quaver in her tone.

"They might just prefer to kill us," he snapped, and ducked instinctively as another slug whined through the broken window. "Get down!"

A chair clattered as he stumbled over it, moving to a spot from which he could watch both windows. Beyond the bedroom window, a flicker of red caught his eye. He sniffed. There was the scent of burning on the air. He ran into the bedroom and glanced out through the window frame, still edged with ragged fragments of gypsum.

"Good Lord!" he exclaimed. "The barn's afire."

XVII

Quickly, Buck Duane smashed splinters of gypsum projecting from the frame flat with the barrel of his Winchester, and squeezed through. When he hurried around the angle of the cabin, the barn came into full view. Burning wood crackled and yellow-red tongues of flame licked up the heat-shrunk clapboards. Snorting in terror, Bullet raced around the corral. Dim in the shadows beyond, Duane glimpsed the form of a moving man. Without pausing, he levered a shell into the breech and swung the Winchester to his shoulder. He squeezed the trigger, ejected the empty shell, fired again.

The barn was doomed. One glance made that plain. Already, the fire had taken hold with a deep-throated, menacing roar. Waves of heat beat at him as flames began to curl high above the roof. The Ranger quashed an impulse to run for water, knowing that the few buckets he could have packed from the well would be useless.

First he had to get Bullet out of danger. He ran for the corral. By the pole gate, the horse's rig lay on the ground. He snatched up the bridle, ducked inside, slipped it over the terrified animal's ears, secured the throat latch, and let it out.

The horse out of harm's way, Duane stood watching the conflagration, frustrated at his own impotence. Sparks showered as the roof crashed, dragging the blazing walls down with it. A column of fire now shot skyward, smoke ballooning above it like a vast mushroom, obscuring the stars. Suddenly, he became aware that Mildred Stokes was standing beside him, still wrapped in her robe, the shotgun grasped in both hands. The garish light of the fire reflected in her green eyes as she stared absorbed at the blazing barn.

"Was it deliberately set?" There was no tremor in her clear voice.

"I'm sure it was," he replied. "I threw a couple of shots at the jasper who put a torch to it."

As sparks showered high, she threw an apprehensive glance at the cabin behind them. "Is it going to spread?"

"I don't think so!" he assured her. "There's not much to burn, outside the cabin, and that's roofed with six inches of soddy."

They stood in silence, watching the flames gradually die down. The old shanty barn had been nothing more than a shell, considered Duane—just walls and roof. Soon it was reduced to a square of glowing debris, amidst which smoldering timbers still crackled. The air was thick with floating ash and rank with the acrid stench of burning. Then Duane noticed that the desultory firing from the night had died away, too.

"Guess we better get back inside," he said. "Well, they made it plain."

"That they want me out," returned Mildred bleakly. "Well, they won't get rid of me so easily."

"Talking that way makes no sense at all," the Ranger said with tight exasperation. He took her arm and began steering her back to the cabin.

Inside, he routed out an old slicker, tore it in half and covered the two smashed windows. This done, he lit the Rochester lamp. "You can go back to bed," he told her. "They'll probably leave us in peace—until tomorrow night."

"And you?" She eyed him uncertainly.

"I'm staying—right here!"

She bit back a protest and stepped into the bedroom, still packing the shotgun. He chuckled silently when he heard the sound of a chair back being jammed beneath a door knob, and sank into the upholstered rocker. Yawning, he reached and turned out the lamp, dozed off—and awoke in darkness. Moving to the window, he yanked down the oilskin shading it. Outside, dawn showed wan and gray. Tenuous fingers of light wavered across the sky, erasing the stars.

His muscles stiff, Duane drifted into the kitchen, stuffed kindling into the stove and spilled water from a bucket into the coffee pot. He was mixing flapjack batter and the coffee had begun to perk when Mildred Stokes walked in, a picture of spruceness, from the smoothly-coiled plaits of her auburn hair, through white blouse and dark skirt, down to button shoes. No one, he thought, would have guessed that she had spent half the night dodging lead.

She favored him with a cool nod and sat down in a chair by the window.

"Well," he asked, "did you have any second thoughts about sticking around?"

"Why should I?"

He shrugged. "You've forgotten the shooting, the burning barn? If you weren't so blind to all reason you'd pull out."

"And give those bandits a free hand? Never!"

"They'll be back!"

"And I'll be ready! Remember, I have a gun, too."

"I'm very much afraid," he told her soberly, "you'd never have a chance to use it."

Breakfast over, Buck Duane left the dishes for her to wash and wandered outside. He wanted to be alone, to figure out a course of action. It was plain that the obdurate Mildred Stokes could never be pried away from the Murdoch place as long as hope remained of recovering the looted ingots—and it was equally plain that their mysterious assailants would never stop for the same reason. And there were indications that the attackers were losing patience. At first they'd contented themselves with random shooting. Now they'd burned down the barn. Would the cabin be next?

Duane drifted around to where the barn had stood. Now all that remained was a sooted square, cumbered by a few half-consumed timbers, from which tiny tendrils of smoke still curled. He remembered the skulking form at which he had thrown lead, and probably missed! For no good reason, he wandered past the smoking debris, over ground cumbered with loose rock and stunted brush. Suddenly he jerked back on his heels at sight of a form in puncher garb, sprawled unmoving, face downward on the rugged ground.

The dead rider was tall and stringy. He was clad in gray shirt and corduroys, the bottoms thrust into spurred high boots. A broad gunbelt was buckled around his waist and a dented can lay by one limp hand. Easing closer, Duane saw that the shirt, between the dead man's shoulder blades, was stiff with dried blood, and a neat hole gaped where a bullet had punched through. So, by a streak of luck, he'd tagged the firebug. Bending, he picked up the can, sniffed. Coal oil. That banished all doubt. He rolled the body over, and almost gasped with surprise as he stared down at the slack features of Lanky Larner, the CCC foreman.

He had been wrong all the time, he mused. It was the CCC, not the looters, that was hellbent to clear all interlopers off the Murdoch place. Why? Could Carson, the cowman be on the track of the ingots, too? Following Murdoch's killing, and the discovery of Si Leeson's battered body in the alley beside the saloon, loose talk had been circulating all over town regarding buried treasure on the quarter-section. Likely, it had reached Carson's ears, and the rancher had decided to bull his way into the gold hunt.

It was more than puzzling, but one thing was sure—he had to get down to Hertzburg and inform the marshal. Welch would probably know how to handle it. He'd better leave the corpse where it was. There was no spare pony on which to bring it to town, and Mildred Stokes would just have to stomach a dead body lying around. He felt that she was tough enough to take it.

When Duane headed back to the cabin, she was just emerging, overall-clad.

"You're getting your wish," he told her. "There's something important I've got to see about in town. I'll be back before sundown."

"Don't hurry on my account," Mildred told him unconcernedly. She picked up the shovel.

Seated at his scarred desk, Town Marshal Welch listened impassively while Buck Duane told of the firing of the barn, the shooting in the night, and his discovery of the CCC foreman's body with the empty coal oil can.

When he was through, Welch grunted irritably, "That girl's sure stirring up a peck of trouble."

"She's simply standing up for her rights!" said Duane. "Carson's the troublemaker, I'd say. You should slap an arson charge on him."

"You figure I could make it stick?" The marshal's face was grim, but there was a trace of sardonic humor in his voice. "Cal's the biggest cowman in the valley. He heads the Cattlemen's Protective."

"That hardly gives him the right to fire a neighbor's barn?" Buck Duane pointed out. "Hell, you could make a try at it."

"I guess I'll have to. In view of what you've told me, I'm dutybound to brace the old buffalo," agreed the marshal, with scant enthusiasm.

When the buildings of the CCC came into view beneath the cottonwoods that flanked them like lofty sentinels the spread gave Duane the impression of being as big as Hertzburg. The ranchhouse, a long, rambling rock-and-adobe, was built around a central patio. Slit windows, barred with Spanish grillwork, and a low parapet that bordered the flat roof, gave the impression of a fort. Maybe a fort had been needed when Carson first drove a herd into the valley, thought Duane. Around the house lay a blotch of buildings —a long adobe bunkhouse, with lean-to cookshack, a big barn, a blacksmith shop, a stable and a wagon shed. A windmill clunked and whirled fitfully.

The big spread seemed empty when the two rode into the yard. A fat man, in singlet and greasy pants, emptied a bucket of water through the cookhouse door; a solitary puncher mucked out the stable. No one else appeared to be around, until Duane saw Carson's chunky form, slacked in an old rocker, set on the gallery that fronted the house. Nearby, his daughter, in crisp ginghams, occupied another rocker. She was busily knitting. The sight of the fiery Rosita engaged in such a humdrum household task caused the Ranger to smile to himself. So there was another, more domestic side, to her character.

They dismounted at the water trough, tied their mounts, with the spare pony Welch had brought alone to pack Lanky's body to town.

The weathered old rancher watched them poker-faced as they plowed through the dust of the yard.

"Howdy, Cal," greeted the marshal.

Carson nodded brusquely, then turned to Duane. "How is it you ain't in jail?" he asked.

"Out on bail," the Ranger grinned at him. "I never belonged there, as you well know."

Carson snorted. "I'll forget how I feel about it for a moment—or try to. Rest your legs anyway." He switched his attention to the lawman. "What brought you out here, Frosty?"

"A killing!" replied the marshal. "Lanky, your foreman, was beefed last night, firing the Murdoch barn."

Carson stared at him for a moment in stunned disbelief, too appalled by the new to say anything in reply.

"The law calls it arson," put in Duane. "There was shooting, too—at a girl."

Rosita recovered from the shock faster than her father.

"Not the green-eyed one, the schoolma'am?" she asked.

"Just what do you know about that burning, Cal?" asked Welch.

"Lanky knew I wanted that gulch cleared. Murdoch ran off tresspassers with a shotgun. Now he's buzzard bait, rustler scum skulk around there like coyotes around a carcase."

"So Lanky overplayed his hand?" persisted the marshal.

"And you hope to pin it on me!" Carson shrugged.

"Go right ahead! A cowman has got a right to keep his range clean."

"Guess I'll chew it over with the sheriff," said Welch, and rose. Duane saw that he wasn't over-anxious to antagonize the rancher.

"When you see the sheriff, tell him to quash charges

against Duane." The heads of the three men swivelled at the sound of Rosita's voice.

"You plumb crazy, girl?" spluttered her father.

"Not too crazy to watch Lanky and Willis beef two prime steers and skin them out, down by the creek," she retorted. "Or to wonder why Willis packed the hides up to the hills."

"You been chewing loco weed," snorted Cal Carson.

"I can lead you to the carcasses, or what's left of them," the dark-haired girl said coolly to her perplexed father.

XVIII

It was near noon. A blazing sun flayed Wildcat Gulch and the surrounding hills simmered under its blasting rays, the ridges quivering through undulating heat waves. Frosty Welch had picked up the body of the CCC foreman and headed back to town.

Buck Duane squatted in the shade of the porch, watching Mildred Stokes moving about among clumped mesquite with her shovel. Queer what a fever for gold could do, he mused. Even a steer had sense enough to seek shelter from the sun at midday, but here was a girl, unused to hard labor, slaving like a convict on a rock pile, with blistered hands and aching bach. Chasing ghost gold.

One hundred and fourteen ingots, scaling twenty-seven pounds apiece, a ton and a half of metal. The renegades must have discovered that burying that much gold was quite a chore, even for four men. And it would have been a tougher chore for Murdoch, alone, to move the loot to another cache. He would have been compelled to handle the job under cover of darkness. Daylight would have revealed his trickery to his partners, probably keeping cases on him from the hills around. Dig another hole in the rocky ground, move almost a ton dead weight, bury it and cover it, all between dusk and dawn. An almost impossible chore for one man.

Possibly, reflected Duane, Murdoch hadn't reburied the ingots. Possibly he'd just moved them. But that didn't make sense either. They would have been discovered if they had been left above ground. The quarter-section now had been pretty well combed over—one hundred and fourteen gold bricks would stand out like a boil on a bald head. Murdoch had been shrewd—smart enough to outfox them all.

Mildred was moving in, and he could see by her dragging steps that she was tuckered out. She dropped the shovel by the porch, wearily mounted the wooden steps and dipped a drink from the ola. Then she sagged down against the front of the cabin. For the first time she looked at Duane with what seemed a bid for sympathy in her eyes.

"It's curious your uncle didn't give you *some* notion as to where you'd find the gold," the Ranger commented.

She raised her shoulders hopelessly. Her eyes held a new expression of warmth now. "He was always vague," she said. "He never went beyond hinting at great wealth, enough to keep me in luxury for the rest of my life. Actually, he wrote very seldom and I never met him in person. He wrote mostly about his ranch. Ranch!" She laughed with bitter scorn. "A waste of rocks and scrub!"

"Did he ever mention any special features of the ranch?" prompted Duane.

"No," she returned thoughtfully, "except perhaps the well. He seemed awfully proud of his well. He said he had the sweetest water in Camino County and that when I inherited the place I was to be sure and clean it out regularly—as though I would know how!"

The Ranger listened to each word Mildred Stokes said. As she finished talking an idea hit Duane with the impact of a thunderbolt. What better hiding place for a load of looted ingots than the bottom of a well? What easier spot to store them? All Murdoch would have to do was toss the bricks down a hole. No digging, no covering up, no laborious packing to some inaccessible spot.

Buck Duane, his eyes sober, rose slowly to his feet.

"What's wrong?" said Mildred Stokes.

"I'm going down the well."

"You're—what?" she gasped.

"I just got a fool notion. You'd better go into the house. I'll need to strip to my underwear."

"But you'll dirty the water," she protested. "Are you crazy?"

"I don't think so," Duane said. "We'll see."

With an incredulous glance, Mildred struggled to her feet, hurried into the cabin and firmly closed the door. Quite clearly she had decided she wanted no part in so wild an undertaking.

Duane collected his coiled rope and headed for the well. Carefully, he checked the capstan from which the wooden water bucket was lowered. It seemed solid. The handle whirled when he dropped the bucket down and he heard a splash below. Next he knotted his own rope, spacing the knots a foot or so apart. This done, he secured one end around the capstan and tossed the remainder after the bucket. Two ropes, he considered, would carry his weight without strain.

The Ranger stripped and straddled the low brick parapet, latched onto the doubled rope and began easing down, hand-over-hand.

The well was not so deep as he'd thought. Duane quickly felt the chill of water on his feet, creeping up to his knees, his thighs, his chest. After the searing heat atop the well it seemed cold, icy cold, biting into the marrow of his bones. His feet sank into soft mud.

Cautiously, water lapping around his chest, Duane quested with the toes of one foot. His pulse jumped with excitement as he explored the dark depths. The bottom of the well was studded with bricklike shapes, bedded in mud. Loosing his grip of the ropes, he drew a deep breath, ducked, fingered in sticky sediment and fastened onto one of the bricks. It came reluctantly out of the slimy ooze like a boot out of gumbo. Grasping it with both hands, Duane came erect, and stood clasping the brick to his chest, gasping.

It was as heavy as solid granite and by the faint light that filtered down through the mouth of the well he saw that it was black and slimy. Quickly, he tied it to the end of his dangling rope and dropped it, then began to climb up toward the square of bright sunlight above.

He soon discovered that while it had been a cinch dropping down, climbing was another matter. His wet fingers were numb with cold and slipped on the ropes. His arm and shoulder muscles protesting, the Ranger slowly hauled his chilled body upward.

Breathing hard, Duane struggled over the parapet, and began to haul up the brick suspended at the end of his reata. By the time he'd gotten it up, warmth was again seeping into his body.

He pulled on his pants, dug a stock knife out of a pocket, flicked the blade open, and began eagerly scraping slime off the black brick. It glinted dull yellow.

In his excitement, Duane almost ran to the cabin.

Mildred Stokes' features, plainly puzzled, were framed in a window.

"We found it!" Duane said, smiling. "The gold's at the bottom of the well."

Stunned disbelief, slowly dissolving doubt, then joy, registered in quick succession on the girl's face. She disappeared for an instant. Then the door of the cabin was flung open and the schoolma'am hurried out.

Duane handed her the brick, dripping slime. "Scrape it!" he said. "It's the only way of making sure."

Cuddling his find, Mildred Stokes hurried back into the cabin. Duane followed with his face set in tight lines. Dumping the heavy brick on the table in the leanto kitchen, Mildred Stokes reflected a knife from a shelf and began paring off sticky black scale.

"Gold!" she breathed, as shining yellow showed through.

"And there's plenty more bricks where that one came from," Duane said.

"So that's why Uncle suggested I clean out the well," exclaimed Mildred, her green eyes shining. "Oh, how dense can a person be!" She turned to Duane. "Can we salvage the others?"

He fingered his chin. "We can," he said. "After sundown. There are too many eyes in these hills to set to work now."

It was midnight before Duane quit, chilled and boneweary. Fifteen bricklike ingots, dripping black slime, were stacked beside the well. "The rest are down there," he said. "I'm sure of that now. We'll take these inside the cabin and hide them. The rest are safer where they are for the moment." Now that the excitement was wearing off, Duane felt boneweary and grateful for a needed rest.

He turned to Mildred Stokes. "You get some sleep, ma'am," he told her. "I'll carry these ingots inside and then bed down here for the rest of the night."

"Do you think I could sleep *now*?" she said.

Duane was too tired to argue. After he'd carried the ingots inside the cabin he started a fire in the stove and dried off his sodden pants. Then he wrapped himself in a couple of blankets and stretched out on the porch. While he slept, Mildred Stokes patroled restlessly from cabin to well. Not a single rifleshot disturbed the silence of the night.

With dawn Buck Duane awoke. Mildred, haggard with fatigue, sat on the porch steps.

"You need to rest!" he told her gently.

"I'll never rest until that gold is safe," she said, with a drawn smile. "I'm more grateful to you than I can say—Buck." It was the first time she had ever addressed him by his first name.

"I'll get Welch," the Ranger told her. "But first, we'd both better have some hot coffee."

Not even the prospect of a warming drink could wrench Mildred Stokes from the square pile of grimy bricks. When Duane saddled up and pulled away, he left her still hovering around the treasure.

Jogging across the valley flats, Duane thought of her keeping solitary vigil, and battled growing misgivings. It was a sure thing, he reflected, that the renegades, or CCC, maybe both, were still keeping a sharp watch on Murdoch's place. The night had been so dark he doubted that they could have seen him strip and descend the well. But still the remote possibility gnawed at him.

When the Ranger reached town, he tied up outside the law shack—and found it vacant. Emerging almost at a run, he was buttonholed by the beady-eyed Ma Purdy.

"I heard Cal Carson is withdrawing the rustling charge!" she fired at him in her flat, dry tone.

"Yes, ma'am," he said. "Have you seen Welch around?"

"Haven't seen Frosty since yesterday noon," she declared. "You still working for Miss Stokes out at Murdoch's?"

He nodded, and was relieved when she asked him no more questions. Striding up street, he met Julius Siegler.

"I've been looking for you!" the storekeeper said. "What's this I hear about your tying up with Miss Stokes? Why do you think I went your bail?"

Duane was his affable self. "Simmer down!" he advised. "I've been working on the girl. Would you pay a thousand for that quarter-section?"

"Why—why, of course," stammered Siegler, remembering Mildred Stokes had been cold to a two thousand offer.

"You tender a thousand dollars next time she comes to town, and I'm sure she'll take it," said Duane, and strode away.

Inquiries at the saloon, the barber shop, the livery, yielded no news of the town marshal. The barkeep at The Bull Pen pointed out that it wasn't uncommon for Frosty Welch to be out of town, since his bailiwack took in the entire valley and recently rustlers had been a nuisance.

Torn between anxiety for Mildred Stokes' welfare and the importance of locating the marshal, Duane fretted around town for an hour or more. Finally, he left word for

Welch to meet him at the Murdoch cabin. Then he headed back to the hills.

XIX

It was quiet when Buck Duane jogged into Murdoch's place—much too quiet. When Bullet rounded the cabin, his eyes sought the well. He thought Mildred Stokes might be standing guard there. She was nowhere in sight. Restraining a growing premonition, he stepped down from his horse and walked toward the cabin looking for the girl.

When he'd pulled out to go to town, something must have happened he was reluctant to let himself think about.

The sound of muffled groaning from the closed cabin spun him into action. Two quick steps took him across the porch. He threw the door open. Bound hand and foot, a bandana muffling her mouth, Mildred Stokes was writhing on the floor, baffled anger in her green eyes.

In a flash Duane was down on his knees beside her, ripping off her bonds. She came to a sitting position, ruefully rubbing her slim wrists, wealed and reddened by rawhide rope.

"That crooked marshal!" Mildred exclaimed. There was no panic in her flat tone, just bitter vexation.

"Frosty Welch—crooked?" Duane stared at her incredulously.

"Crooked as a rattlesnake," she said back, tight with anger.

"What gave you that idea?" Duane asked.

"Just after you left, he rode in with some mules," she said. "I wondered how he got out here so quickly, but before I could speak he grabbed me, wrenched my arms behind my back, tied me hand and foot. Then he bound and gagged me and dumped me in the cabin."

Duane stood frowning, trying to assimilate the girl's amazing charge. So Welch had gone bad! It seemed unbelievable. While supposedly out trailing rustlers he must have gone down into the well and made off with the gold which had not been removed. But where had he rounded up the mules? And where was he packing the loot?

There seemed to be but one answer—the Border. Mexico was the best place for a renegade lawman, where he'd be safe from posses and pursuit.

"I'm taking off," Duane told the girl quietly. "I'm going after Welch."

"You'll never catch up with him," she said, with flat hopelessness. "He's been gone for hours. And who knows where?"

"I think I know," said Duane as he headed for the door.

He filled his waterbag, hung it on the horn and started off. Hour after hour, Bullet jogged southward. The grass-carpeted valley flats lay far behind and the ragged silhouette of the Aristos had long faded into the heat haze in the rider's rear. Bullet's hooves rang upon heat-hardened earth, patched with thorny growth.

Westward, the shapes of distant ranges floated blue above the horizon, but ahead lay nothing but arid desert, its surface a monotony of cactus, sand and eroded rock. Into this, the horse plodded, a mite crawling through an infinity of space. Dust-mantled, eyes slitted against the sunglare, its rider gazed across the arid expanse, seeking some sign that his quarry lay ahead—and finding none.

Seemed, Duane considered, he was gambling on a busted flush. The terrain was strange to him. He was ignorant of its trails and waterholes. Likely he'd ride blindly ahead until his mount quit, gaunted. Meanwhile, Welch, to whom the terrain was as familiar as the palm of his hand, made his leisurely way toward the Border by another route.

Shadows lengthened as the sun dropped westward. A rattler slithered from beneath a rock, dust devils whirled across the waste, the buckskin's steady pace faltered. Duane drew rein and stepped down. He drank briefly from the sagging waterbag, spilled what remained into his hand

and held it to Bullet's dustcrusted muzzle.

Then he slacked cinches and rocked the saddle. Building a smoke, he surveyed the darkening waste around. The sun, a glowing ball of red, was sinking behind a mountain chain far to the west. A myriad of shadows patched the desert. Seemed he'd have to forget Welch, he reflected, and give all his thought to survival. Bullet was jaded, he'd used up his water, he had no more chance of recovering those ingots than a wax cat had of surviving in hell.

Across the plain, beams of the dying sun touched the tip of a finger of rock, projecting from the maw of the desert, gilding it golden. A half-forgotten memory stirred in Duane's mind. He'd once heard a puncher speak of Pinnacle Wells. Maybe he'd stumbled across the Wells. If so, it would be a life-saver, and provide a good spot to spend the night.

The stars flamed overhead when the Ranger approached the dim bulk of the pinnacle. The terrain had broken up into a jumble of sundered rock. Threading between boulders, Duane steered his weary pony toward its base. Through the night gleamed a dull red glow, pricking like an oversized cigarette tip through the darkness. A camp fire, he thought, and checked his mount. Tautly alert now, he slid out of the saddle, trailed his reins and lifted his Winchester out of the boot.

Afoot, he began scrambling ahead, worming through a chaos of heaped rock. The moon, near full, floated from behind slow-drifting masses of cottony cloud and its pale light bathed the pinnacle. Not a hundred paces from the campfire now, squirming between boulders, Duane glimpsed mules and a horse, bunched beyond the fire. Kiacks and rigging were stacked nearby, part-covered by a tarp.

Like a dark mirror, an irregular sheet of water pooled in a rocky basin, reflecting the stars. A bedroll lay spread by the fire, but there was no sign of life, beyond the animals. Luck had sure dealt aces, considered the Ranger, with surging triumph.

Cautiously, Duane crawled ahead, reached a sandy

stretch, sparcely dotted with huge fragments of talus. Suddenly a bullet screeched off a nearby rock in shrill ricochet. He flattened, the report of a Winchester ringing in his ears. Silence again enveloped the waterhole. Again, he began worming ahead. The report of a second gunshot punched into his ears. Flying grit blinded him as the slug bedded in sand, almost in his face. He cried out, as though in agony, rolled and lay sprawled behind a misshapen chunk of rock.

It was an old trick, he reflected, simulating death in order to draw an enemy out of cover, and likely it wouldn't fool an oldtimer like Frosty Welch. Anyway, from the gunflash, he'd located the source of the shooting—a nest of boulders beyond the pool.

For awhile the Range lay waiting, but the unseen marksman gave no further sign of his presence. Stealthily, Duane began to pull back, sticking to the shadows. When he figured he was beyond sight of his opponent, he began to circle, working toward the flank of the nested boulders.

Bedded down, Duane watched the boulders, silvered by moonlight. Silence shrouded the scene. He had no option but to wait it out, he decided—either until the marshal became convinced he had tagged his pursuer and emerged from cover, or day dawned. Daylight should give him an edge.

Time dragged. A meteor flashed across the sky, and was consumed. Feathery talus dust floated down from the pinnacle towering above like fine rain. A hoof clicked on rock as a mule changed position.

Stretched out behind cover, Duane fought an overwhelming urge to sleep. He'd been in the saddle since sunup. He was bone-weary, and his eyelids seemed loaded with lead. Once or twice, he snapped up his drooping head.

Drowsily, he became aware that dawn was breaking. The mules, the ashes of the dead fire, and the stacked gear took shape through wan gray light. Overhead, the heavens began to lighten and the stars to dim. Suddenly, like a jack-in-the-box, a man's head and shoulders showed above the clutter of boulders. Duane shook off his drowsiness, cuddled the Winchester to a shoulder. Tensed, with his finger hooked on the trigger, he lay watching.

For a full minute, the marshal stood unmoving, except for his head as it swiveled while he searched the shadows. Then, his rifle slanted under one arm, he stepped out into the open.

Duane called out the marshal's name. The renegade lawman pivoted, quick as a teased cat, and swung up the barrel of his Winchester. Duane's rifle barked just once. Welch jackknifed, dropping the Winchester, clutching at his stomach. Bunched up, he fell forward, lay twisting spasmodically.

Muscles cramped, Duane came slowly to his feet, moved cautiously toward the wounded man, his rifle leveled. Closing up, he saw there was no fight left in the gasping, squirming lawman. He kicked the rifle out of reach, bent and slid Welch's sixgun out of its holster and placed it beneath his own waistband. Blood, bright scarlet, seeped around the marshal's belt buckle.

"You played out of luck, Frosty," Duane said, eying the twisting form.

Welch rolled onto his back, knees doubled up. "Did you have to tag me in the guts?" he gasped.

Duane said nothing, hunkering beside the mortally wounded man.

"A smoke!" begged the marshal.

Duane rolled a cigarette, placed it between the dying man's lips and touched a match to the tip. In a spasm of agony, Welch bit it off. Duane flicked the glowing end into the sand.

The marshal lay tensed, thin lips compressed, fingers digging into his stomach, bleak eyes fastened on Duane.

"You fooled me," he muttered hoarsely. "Figured I'd tagged you with that second shot." His eroded features twisted into a humorless grin, "Well, I almost made it!"

Duane fashioned a smoke for himself. "So you saw a chance and took it!"

"Chance! Hell, I organized the hold-up, figured it out

with Murdoch, and cut three hardcases in to lend a hand."

Duane looked reflectively at the dying lawman. Carefully the Ranger reached for the other's rifle, squeezed trigger, ejected the empty and eyed its base. "Murdoch crossed you, and you fed him two slugs, with this Winchester," he said.

"It was a pleasure!"

Then your hardcases got busy digging," said Duane. "How is it they're not around?"

"I sent them on ahead, to San Pereto across the Border, to wait for their cut."

"So you were heading for San Pereto?"

Welch's teeth locked against pain, then he returned hoarsely, "Nope—El Quito."

"Isn't that pueblo forty miles east of San Pereto?"

"Sure!" Cold humor sparked in the marshal's pale eyes. "I just didn't figure on a divvy."

"You sure are a prime double-crosser," said Duane with disgust.

He rose, sauntered over to the stacked gear. As he expected, the mules' kiacks were heavy with the black bricks. Welch, he considered, would never survive the ride back to Hertzburg. At the most, he'd never last more than three days—three days of agony. Returning to the wounded man, the Ranger stood looking down at him.

"I'm going to leave you, and bring back a doctor," he said. "You'd never survive the ride back to town."

Another spasm of pain contorted Welch's thin features. "No sawbones can help me—not with a slug in my belly," he whispered hoarsely. "You just leave my sixgun."

Duane lifted the Colt from beneath his waistband, set it carefully beside the doomed man and backed away, hand on the butt of his own ivory-butted .45. Welch, he reflected, was no more to be trusted than a dying rattlesnake.

Out of range, the Ranger began to pick his way between scattered rock toward his saddlehorse.

The deep boom of a .45 reverberated in his ears.

XX

Then Buck Duane came riding into San Antonio for the second time in—How long had it been actually? Two decades, a century and a half? He no longer felt like a stranger to himself. He would feel that way again before long, he was sure of that. But now at least he felt like a whole man, complete in every aspect of himself.

The dark stranger would always be with him, the killer from his ancestral past. But he had drawn that killer's claws this time with a vengeance, for though he had been fast on the trigger and brought a scheming, hypocritical scoundrel to justice, he had felt, even as his gun flamed and roared that it was a Texas Ranger who was doing the shooting, and not an ancestral ghost skulking in shadows with his passion for slaying out of control.

Duane wondered just what MacNelly was going to say to him. Though he had received a telegram of congratulation a few hours after he'd wired his superior a full report, nothing could take the place of a face-to-face meeting.

Duane didn't think MacNelly was going to pin medals on him. But he was looking forward to a reception that would cheer and warm him a little, and give him a justified feeling of pride.

Ten minutes after he'd entered the outskirts of town Duane was tying Bullet to a hitching rack in front of the Buckhorn Hotel where he'd had his previous talk with the Captain. Then in a few minutes Buck Duane was shaking hands with MacNelly. The two dilapidated rocking chairs were at his back, standing in almost the same place where the earlier chairs had been.

MacNelly had risen instantly on catching sight of Duane. The Captain's handclasp was warm and firm.

Then they both sat down and Duane waited for the man-to-man congratulations to come pouring out of the Captain. Instead, MacNelly took two telegrams out of his pocket and handed them to Duane without saying a word.

The Ranger tore the first one open and read: "Tell Mr.

Duane all is forgiven. Tell him, please, that I will be waiting for him to tell me that he was very foolish to threaten to put me across his knee and spank me as if I were a little girl. I am not a little girl. Tell him, please, that I am waiting to prove to him that I am a woman." It was signed—"Rosita."

The second one he read with just as much astonishment. "I feel that it is my duty to inform you that Mr. Duane has performed the task assigned to him with exemplary courage and single-minded dedication. Please assure him that I will never cease to be grateful to him." It was signed "Mildred Stokes."

"You're quite a hand with the women, aren't you?" MacNelly said, looking at him with a broad grin on his face.

"A Ranger has to be able to deal with anything that comes up," Duane said solemnly, "bad men, wild cards, and good women. And I'm not saying which is the most trouble!"

HIGH VALLEY RIVER

I

At the crowded San Antonio Hotel bar the big man was as alone as if still riding the range in his high, West Texas home. His brow was furrowed by thought, and his weathered face set in lines of increasing determination. Suddenly he set his half emptied glass on the bar and turned away towards the door to the street.

It was all over in an instant. The big fellow pushed open the swinging doors and stepped into the street. It was as if he'd walked head on into an invisible barrier. The force of the heavy, forty-five caliber slug stopped him in his tracks and stiffened every nerve and muscle with shock. His six-foot body slammed back against the door frame and then fell, half over the sill.

In the howling hullabaloo of a San Antonio Saturday night few people even heard the shot. No one noticed who had fired.

Three or four of the more responsible business men in the hotel bar left their drinking and ran over to where the shot man lay, still paralyzed by the shock of his wound.

"He's not dead yet," one of them said. "Sam, you run see if Doc Willis is in his office."

"He'll be dead soon," Sam replied, "but I'll go anyhow." He ran out the door.

The wounded man had been shot through the stomach. Given the terrible smashing power of a forty-five and the still primitive medical techniques of the late nineteenth century frontier, he hadn't a chance to survive. They knew it even as they tried to make him more comfortable.

It was obvious, as the shock wore off a little, that he knew it too.

"Rangers," he said in a hoarse, feeble voice. "I got to talk to Rangers."

"Take it easy, man," somebody said. "Save your strength. The doc'll be here quick." They were wadding bar towels to try to stanch the terrible wounds, front and back of his body. It wasn't much use.

"Doc h—" the man said weakly. "Too late for a doc. Ranger. . .Ranger. . ."

A short wiry man with the look of command in his keen, intelligent grey eyes pushed through the crowd in the doorway.

"Give me room," he said, and men fell back instinctively. "It's all right, mister," he said. "It's okay. I'm a Ranger. MacNelly's my name. You can tell me whatever is it."

"Thank God," the man gasped, "but alone."

"Move him into one of the ground floor rooms," Captain MacNelly commanded. "Send in the doc when he gets here—and hurry up. Time's running fast for this man."

Men who owned their own ranches and stores jumped to obey the little man. They knew authority when they met it face to face.

"He died all right," Captain MacNelly said the next morning in his sparsely furnished office in the San Antonio Ranger barracks.

"He died hard though, and it gave him time to talk. He wasn't afraid any more, so he said all he could."

"I know," the man sitting in the plain kitchen chair in front of the bare oak table which served the Captain for a desk said slowly. "When a man sees old-skull-and-bones in the door it will unlock his tongue. I suppose it's a job for us."

"A job for you, Buck," MacNelly said. "He told enough for me to know there's something badly wrong up in his country, but not enough for me to know exactly what. Towards the end there his mind was wandering, and some of the things he said weren't exactly clear. Some of them sounded downright crazy."

"You want me to take in a squad and find out?" Buck Duane asked.

"I want you to take yourself in, Buck. No squad, no badge even. The dead man was mighty emphatic about that. If a Texas Ranger even shows himself up that way, he told me, why then it's all up with his friends."

"What would happen then?" Buck Duane asked.

"You won't believe me, but I'll give it to you in his own words. Just about his last words they were too. Mr. Smith will kill the river, he said. Just like that—Mr. Smith will kill the river."

"If he can kill a river," Duane said, "this Smith must ride mighty tall in the saddle. You're right, Captain. It doesn't make sense."

"It had better make sense," MacNelly said, "when you come out of High Valley City, Buck. Somebody up there has the town in his hand and the ranchers in fear of death. After last night I can see how come they're scared. Murder and all, it's Ranger business. After I tell you what I know I want you to go up there and find Mr. Smith and what he's up to and bring him out."

There was silence in the room for a moment. Then MacNelly scratched a big sulphur match on his boot sole and lit a long black cigar.

"Finding a Smith ought to be easy," Duane said with a grin. "First and last there's more hombres calling themselves Smith in Texas than in the whole rest of the States. Always has been a popular name with gents racing some sheriff from back home. Only how do I know which is the right Smith, Cap? Am I looking for a lame Mr. Smith, or a gotch-eared Smith or a Mr. Bob Smith or what?"

"You're looking for a Mr. Smith who can sit five hundred miles away in High Valley and kill a man in the

Austin Hotel in San Antonio in just two minutes after that man decides to come see the Rangers," MacNelly said. "That's the kind of Mr. Smith you're looking for, and that's all I know. Near as the dead man could say, there ain't nobody in High Valley has even seen Mr. Smith. They know he's there all right, because he kills anybody don't take his orders meek as a lamb—but nobody sees him."

"I'm one lamb ain't quite that meek," Duane said. "If he's alive, I'll bring in Mr. Smith for you."

"Now that's the kind of talk I like to hear," MacNelly said. "I knew I could count on you, Buck. Now listen close while I tell you all I can. In the morning you can ride."

"In the morning I ride," Buck Duane said. He pulled his chair closer to the table.

II

High noon found Buck Duane and his mount Bullet well on the roads that led west and north from San Antonio into the high country of West Texas. The big man sat his saddle easily with the air born of a lifetime on horseback. He wore no badge except the two big guns holstered low and tied down by rawhide thongs around the worn woolen trouser legs and the Winchester in its saddle boot.

The pack horse he led bore no official brand. Only an observer who noted the beautiful grace of his steel-muscled body and his air of unwavering alertness to all about him would have guessed that this was a man who had ridden the outlaw trails for a decade before joining the Rangers. Only one who had looked into his steel grey eyes could know what sort of man Buck Duane really was.

He pushed his horse steadily onwards, sleeping in hospitable ranch houses, small town hotels or under the clean, high-riding stars, depending upon where the evening found him.

As he rode his mind was busy weighing and considering the few facts which Captain MacNelly had been able to give him concerning his mission.

Buck Duane had never been to High Valley City. His outlaw days had been spent in the country further south and nearer to the Rio Grande.

He'd heard of the place, of course, as sooner or later the verbal grapevine of the frontier brought him news of all sorts of places and people.

The town was young, even for the raw frontier of Texas. It had been settled largely in the past five or six years. Men spoke well of the country in which it lay. The valley was called high, but actually it was in a range of rolling hills at the edge of a much higher escarpment.

The land was said to be good, carpeted with prairie and buffalo grass and watered by the High Valley River, which came down from the loftier hills to the west. There was cottonwood along the river and evergreens further up. It should have been—and as far as anyone in San Antonio knew—it was an ideal ranching country.

The papers on the dead man identified him as William Bass, rancher in the valley and owner of the registered W-B brand. Duane's ostensible errand was to carry news of the man's death, return his valuables to any survivors and report his burial in San Antonio.

He'd decided to pass himself off as a potential buyer of a ranch of his own. It would give him a perfectly logical "cover" for as long as he wanted to remain in the Valley, ride over the land and ask questions.

It should also provide a position of standing that a mere saddlebum or a fugitive from justice would lack.

He'd use his own name, talk to as many ranchers as he could reach, and keep alert for any sign of the mysterious Mr. Smith.

Later on, when he knew what it was that Bass had feared so greatly and what "killing a river" actually meant, he could either reveal his true identity as a Ranger or send for Captain MacNelly and a troop if he felt that any help would be needed.

In any case, he'd start out as a prospective land and cattle buyer and play it by ear from there on in.

The last night before reaching High Valley City Buck Duane made a dry camp in a clump of cottonwoods along the bank of the High Valley River itself. It was a peaceful summer night with the tall grass blowing and the leaves of the trees shifting and whispering in the wind. The sun-warmed ground was firm under his blankets and the high-riding moon showered the prairie with silver light so bright a man could have read fine print if he'd had a book with him.

Duane did not. He lay on top of his blanket with his head pillowed on Bullet's saddle and thought about the job ahead. Duane knew himself competent to handle just about any situation that might arise. Long years on the owlhoot trail had taught him things that most men never knew. His wits and his guns had been the match for enemies before, yet he knew enough never to indulge in the luxury of overconfidence.

Someone, not far away, had woven a net of evil. There was a body under a plain wooden cross in San Antonio to prove how deadly that menace could be and how far its murderous reach extended. The same danger would be directed against Buck Duane if he made the slightest slip in judgment or in action—and well he knew no man was proof against a murderer's bullet.

More shaking than anything else was the element of mystery involved. A Texas Ranger was used to going against long odds. He lived by danger as another man did by bread. But this was against known enemies and odds that could be calculated in advance, long as they might prove to be.

"An enemy understood is already half beaten," had been one of Buck Duane's personal sayings for as long as he could remember. He'd learned it at the knee of his father, that legendary gunslinger whose name still made men pause in fear and who had been a name to conjure with before the guns of ambush cut him down.

Tomorrow though, Duane would ride against an unknown enemy and odds which he could not name. Instead of a man of flesh and blood it was a shadow which he chased this time. He couldn't plan against a faceless, formless evil. He could only wait and maintain ceaseless vigilance.

At last Duane closed his eyes and slept. It is a measure of the man that no nightmare haunted his rest and that he woke refreshed at the first lark call of daybreak.

The town, when he first spotted it from a slight rise of the road, showed nothing to indicate the presence of a lurking menace of any sort.

There was the usual half mile of one story false-fronted frame buildings: stores, saloons and the few professional offices needed to serve a cattle town. Back of this, small frame homes clustered along the river bank under cottonwood trees which cut the sun's heat.

There were a few larger buildings on higher ground to house the leading citizens. There was the white wooden spire of a church—and a little way out of town a building that just had to be the familiar one room school with a big iron triangle hanging from posts in the yard to summon students in place of a bell. That was all.

The river ran close by the town. It was a good hundred feet wide, flowing fast over a rocky bed and with what looked like a deep channel in the center. There was no bridge, so it had to be fordable by horse or wagon.

Duane headed straight for a building which proclaimed *Restaurant* in bright red paint on a newly made sign. He knew well enough what sort of meal he'd have to make do with if he took the only other choice of eating place and stopped at the saloon.

A motherly looking woman at the restaurant served him boiled hominy with redeye gravy, fried eggs, country ham and gossip, all in heaping portions. She also tried to question him on news of the world outside.

Between mouthfuls of the savory food Buck Duane gave

her news from the East, being careful to omit any references to the murder of the late Mr. Bass.

She told him herself that "Bill Bass went on to San Antone to buy supplies." His ranch, it seemed, was north and west of town towards Sweetwater Gap where the river comes down.

"Yes—there was a lawyer in town. Warn't likely he'd wake up till noon though. No, she didn't know of any ranch for sale."

In all of her talk there was no mention of anyone by the name of Smith, or any indication of menace hanging over the area. Of course she was new in town herself—the paint hardly dry on her business sign—and that might account for it.

After eating Duane went up the street to the office of "Judge" Gowanus, the town's single attorney at law. The legal eagle had just risen from the couch in his office where he slept and opened the door clad only in a suit of dirty cotton "long john" underwear.

Sight of a client, or at least a stranger who might turn out to be a client, worked miracles in a matter of minutes. After a long snort of whiskey and a short one from the water pitcher, Gowanus climbed into a reasonably clean shirt and pants, got his boots on and offered Duane a drink and a chair.

The first thing Buck Duane did was to offer to turn over the small packet of Bass's personal possessions which "the San Antone authorities asked me to bring on up, since I was coming along anyway."

"Old Bill Bass dead?" Gowanus looked considerably startled. "What happened? Get himself in a fight?"

"No fight," Duane said. "At least that ain't what I heard. Wasn't there myself of course. Seems like somebody unknown just shot him down in cold blood when he was leaving his hotel. Wouldn't know if he had any enemies down there, would you?"

"Who, me?" Gowanus looked scared to death himself. "How would I know about anything that far off? What do you want to know fer anyway?"

"No reason," Duane said easily. "Just curiosity."

The lawyer poured out what was left in the whiskey bottle. It filled the one tumbler halfway, and he drank it down at one gulp. It didn't seem to steady him much.

"Well, don't get so curious," he snapped at Duane. "Feller gets killed, it's best leave it alone less'n you're a sheriff or som'at."

"Not me," Buck Duane said.

"Okay then. Leave it be. Terrible thing though. Nice feller like Bill. Goes off on a business trip and next thing you bring back his wallet. He live long after the shooting?" He shot a sly glance at Duane and then fumbled in a desk drawer and brought up another bottle.

"I wouldn't know," Duane said. "I told you I wasn't there."

"Oh, so you did. So you did. Now look here, friend, whyn't you carry that stuff out to the W-B yourself? His widow'll likely have questions and you know more about it than I do. Sides, I hate riding in the hot sun. Anybody in town kin direct you."

"Since you suggest it," Duane said, "I'll do just that. Now for my own business—I'm thinking of buying a ranch up this way. You know about anything available?"

Gowanus gave himself time for another drink before answering. The liquor was beginning to take effect. He gave Duane a long, owlish stare.

"Want to buy a ranch," he inquired. "Well you ain't the first to say that, nor yet the last to regret it. Look like a handy sort of chap with those guns though, so why shouldn't you buy a ranch?"

"I asked about land," Duane said.

"So you did. So you did, mister. Well, for the matter of that there's plenty land. Plenty government land for a man to take up. Land and water." He laughed to himself and cocked his head at Duane. "On the other hand, if you really want land, why then the man to see is Ace Holden. Yes, you go see Ace."

"Why him?"

"Because I said so," Gowanus said. "You do or you don't—I can't care less. Now go on get out of here and let a man drink his breakfast in peace. Go on, I said."

Buck Duane left. "He knows more about Bass' killing than he wants to let on," he told himself. "He's scared by it, and I'd like to know why."

The only hotel in town was also the saloon and gambling house. *Ace Holden, Prop.* the sign outside said. Duane knew there'd be little rest or sleep for anyone taking a room there. The bar would be open all night.

Down at the far end of the street he found a neat white clapboard two-story house with a sign that said simply *Rooms*.

The landlady was a handsome woman in her forties with warm brown eyes and her hair tied back in a bun. She gave the handsome, lean muscled rider an appreciative glance and showed him to a clean, comfortable room in the ground floor rear not far from the kitchen.

"Three dollars a week," she said. "You want board, it'll be three more."

Buck Duane sniffed the odor of biscuits coming from the kitchen and his face warmed with a rare smile.

"I'll want board," he said.

The woman smiled back and made to close the door. Then she remembered.

"In advance," she said.

Duane gave her six dollars. He left his saddle bags in the room and took both horses down the street to the one livery stable.

"Keep the pack beast here," he told the owner. "Just feed and water the big roan. I'm riding out a ways this afternoon, but I'll bring him back tonight."

III

While Bullet was being cared for Buck Duane went down the street to Ace Holden's combined hotel, bar and gambling house.

He stood up to the forty-foot long mahogany bar and ordered beer. The bar was expensive and the big mirror on the wall behind it must have cost a fortune to haul this far west.

"Nice place," he told the bartender.

"You can bet on that," the man said. "Ace—he's the owner—he likes to do things right. Yessiree. Nothing but the best for Ace."

"Sounds like a real sport," Buck Duane said.

"You can bet on it," the bartender said. "Even got a pool table in the back room. Real ivory balls. Come all the way from Afrikee, they did. And say, mister. You come back tonight when the girls has got their paint on and come downstairs. You just do that. Fanciest girls in a thousand miles, Ace says. They knows tricks you never even heard of. Just you see." He wiped the bar with his rag and went to another customer.

Buck Duane took his time over the beer, but no one who might have been Ace Holden came into the room. He decided to ride on out to the Bass ranch and see the gambler later.

It wasn't much of a ride. The ranch house was only a few miles north of town and close to the river. It sat comfortably under the shade of big cottonwoods.

Mrs. Bass herself, a matronly woman about the same age as the dead man, met Duane at the door of the house. When he began to work up to his errand she guessed it right away and asked him into the big, homey kitchen to sit down.

Buck Duane broke the news as kindly as he could.

"It was just one shot," he said. "He died right off. Possibly he never even knew he'd been hit."

He thought that might comfort her, and besides, MacNelly had warned him not to let on how much the man had talked.

She took it bravely with the innate courage and natural dignity which ennobled so many ranch wives and mothers on the far frontier. Her face set in a cruel mask of calm, but Duane could see the pulse beat quicken and throb at her throat as she fought to control any visible display of the emotion which wracked her within.

"It's easier that we had no children," she said, half to herself. "To lose a father would have made things so hard for them. A woman alone can manage—."

Duane couldn't help asking: "Just what do you plan to do, Mrs. Bass?"

"I'll manage," she said. "William had a little money in the San Antonio bank. That's why he went all that way to do business. It'll be enough to take me back to Ohio. I've a married sister there; and perhaps a little restaurant or sewing to help out—" Her voice trailed off.

"You've got a fine ranch here," Buck Duane said. "I couldn't help but notice as I rode in. Surely, even if you don't care to stay on, it'll fetch a good price for you. Enough to put into a good business back east?"

Mrs. Bass gave him a level look.

"Oh, no," she said. "But of course you're a stranger and don't know. It isn't that easy here in High Valley. I can sell, but not at my price. But now—I don't mean to impose upon your kindness in coming to see me. Let me fix a pot of coffee, Mr. Duane."

"You aren't imposing, though I will accept the coffee. What you just said interests me for another reason. I've just come into a bit of money myself. The real reason I came out to this part of Texas in the first place was to look for a small ranch for myself. If you do decide to sell—and your spread here proves out as good as it looks to me now —you might not have to depend on finding a local buyer."

Mrs. Bass was bustling about the stove, and kept her face averted from his eyes.

"That's real nice of you to say, Mr. Duane. If things were different I might maybe talk business with you. But there's special things here in the valley. Please just take my word for it."

"I wish you'd explain," Duane said. When she kept stubbornly silent he went on, "I really do like the looks of this valley. If you don't sell me your land, I'm sure I can find somebody else that will. I'm willing to pay a fair price."

She took down two large, blue willow-pattern cups and saucers and set them on the table. Next to the cups went a small plate holding a brown cone of sugar to be dipped in the hot drink and a crock of thick cream.

"I think," Buck Duane said, "it'd only be fair if you told me what you meant just now. I'm honestly interested."

"Maybe you are," she said. "I kind of like you and I think you could be honest, but you're a stranger. In this place we don't talk open like to strangers. It ain't healthy."

She caught a sob in her throat and Duane knew she was thinking of her husband. In a moment she had control of herself again.

"No. It ain't always healthy, Mr. Duane. If you insist on staying round here long, you'll find out for yourself. I wish you'd just ride on while you can. I truly do. I'll make out all right."

Buck Duane said: "You owe me more explanation than that, Mrs. Bass. I am a stranger, just like you say. If there's something I'll find out anyway, don't you think it better I should hear it from friendly lips first—and know what it is I'll be up against?"

She poured the coffee for them both and set out cold biscuits, fresh sweet butter and a glass of homemade jelly. Her resolve seemed to be weakening.

"I don't know," she said. "I honestly don't know."

Duane pushed his advantage. "I'm a man grown, Mrs. Bass. When I know the facts I can make a decision what to do. But not before I know. I'm a free man and I can take care of myself."

He realized right away that had been the wrong thing to say.

Her control broke completely for the first time. She put both elbows down on the table, buried her face in her hands and shook with great sobs.

"Oh, Mr. Duane," she managed finally, "I'm sorry. Truly I'm sorry. It's just that my Bill always used to say that. He could take care of himself. He was so proud of that. And now—"

Buck Duane had to fight down the impulse to say to her: "He did take care of you. He lived to say enough to bring me here." He knew it would be a comfort, but he dared not talk as yet. Perhaps, later on if she came to trust him. . .But first he had to know she had summoned up the courage to defy the nameless menace that hung over this beautiful valley. To talk too soon would be to betray the mission upon which Captain MacNelly had sent him.

All he could say was: "I'm sorry."

"I know you are," she said. "Somehow I feel it. Maybe later on, when I've had time to think, when the shock of hearing about Mr. Bass has worn off. Like I say, maybe then." She couldn't finish.

Duane got to his feet. "I'm sorry, Mrs. Bass. I should have remembered how you must feel. I'll ride along now. I am really interested in this ranch though, if you do decide to sell. Later on, when you feel better, I'll stop by again and talk to you about it. Meantime, if you change your mind, I've taken a room at Mrs. Burke's in town. You can reach me there."

She wiped her eyes. "At Sally Burke's? That's good. She runs a nice clean house and the meals'll stick to your ribs."

She walked to the door with him. Just as he was about to leave she put a hand on his elbow. "Mr. Duane, maybe I shouldn't say anything at all more right now. I just can't help it though. You've been so considerate. A real gentleman. I've said too much already as it is. Still, you just remember this one thing.

"To buy or sell land in High Valley. It don't matter either way. There's just one man you have to see. One man only. You mark what I say now—and I just hope I'm not saying too much. But I feel like somehow I owed it to you—"

She paused.

"Yes, Mrs. Bass," Duane said.

"You got to go see that man." She paused again and then seemed to gather her courage. "It's Ace Holden," she said. "You want to stay in town more'n overnight you make your peace with Ace Holden. Nobody buys or sells without he gives the word. That's all."

Buck Duane bowed and went down the two steps to the hardpacked, clean-swept yard.

"Thank you, Mrs. Bass," he said. "I'll remember. Thank you again for telling me."

His mind was full of other questions as he rode slowly back towards the river. Why Ace Holden? Didn't the ranchers own their land? What about "Mr. Smith"? Was Holden just another name for Smith? Nobody's mentioned that name yet. What could Ace Holden do to Mrs. Bass if she sold against his will? There were a lot of answers Buck Duane needed to know.

Some of the Bass cattle were grazing near the ranchhouse itself. They looked well fed and healthy. They all bore the W-B brand, but some of the other and older steers bore an additional brand. That was normal enough when a man had bought grown steers. He'd naturally add his own brand.

What was unusual to Duane's trained and experienced eye was that some of the original brands had obviously been changed and reworked with a hot iron. He rode as close as he could to the grazing steers to make sure his eyes hadn't betrayed him. They hadn't.

"Those brands have been changed," Duane told Bullet and patted the big horse's neck. "Bass wouldn't do that.

He might cross out the old brand with a swipe of the iron before putting on his W Bar B. Lots of men do that, but only a rustler reworks a brand. Now I'm sure Bass and his wife ain't rustlers, and they don't seem the sort to buy stolen stock from then that steals it."

He sat his horse for a while and watched the cattle move about.

"Some of them are Texas steers," he thought. "On the other hand some look like they was bred south of the Rio Grande. How would Mex steers get up this way?"

After a while he filed the questions in his mind and rode on into town.

IV

The dinner at Sally Burke's boarding house was as savory and good as Mrs. Bass had predicted. There were only three other boarders. One was a middle-aged spinster who taught at the town school. The second was a younger man who clerked in the drygoods store and the third a traveling whiskey salesman from St. Louis.

The drummer did most of the talking; answered mostly in monosyllables by the clerk and Mrs. Burke. The school teacher gave an occasional dissapproving sniff, but Buck Duane noticed she had an appetite like a man and really shoveled in the roast beef and potatoes that came to the table on heaped ironstone platters.

After eating, the teacher retired to her room and the three men took chairs on the long wooden porch that fronted the house. The other two lit cigars.

Buck Duane had learned not to smoke during his long years on the outlaw side of the law. Tobacco was hard to come by and an unsatisfied craving bad for a man alone. Besides the smell of smoke could give a man away to a pursuer. It was easier to chew, as some outlaws did, or not to smoke at all. He put his feet up on the rail, tipped back his chair and pretended to doze while the others talked.

For a time he could hear Mrs. Burke moving about and clattering dishes in the kitchen. When he judged by the sounds that her chores were nearly done he walked back through the house and drew himself a glass of water from the small pump at the sink.

"That was a fine meal," he said appreciatively.

Sally Burke untied her apron and hung it on a nail. Together they stepped out under the shade of the giant cottonwood tree in the rear yard. Dusk had fallen and a cool breeze blew up from the river. Fireflies made glowing spots of light. The moon had not yet climbed up over the eastern horizon. It was a quiet and friendly moment, and both of them savored it.

"You interest me, Buck Duane," she said. She was a tall woman and her head came a big higher than his shoulder. She wasn't looking at him as she spoke.

"Thank you," he said.

"Don't misunderstand me," she said then, still not looking directly at him. Her hair blew a little in the breeze where it had come loose from the bun. "Of course you interest me as a man does a woman alone. That wasn't what I meant."

Both of them were silent then.

"Aren't you going to ask me what I did mean?" she asked finally.

Duane laughed softly.

"I was just hoping you'd tell me without asking," he said.

She did turn and look at him then. In the dusk her face made an ivory oval.

"That's what I meant," she said. "Part of you I can understand just like I knew you'd say that before you did. The rest of you is harder to see into than a chunk of flint."

"What do you think you see?" he asked in a friendly voice.

"I see a man," she said. "Not like a braggart or a fool

but a riding man. I see eyes that mask a thinking man. I see two guns tied down in a very special way."

"Did your husband wear his guns like that?" Duane asked.

"My husband didn't tie down guns," she said. "He carried one gun, a musket, over his shoulder. We were children really when we married back in Tennessee and then he went away to war. My husband, Mr. Duane, left his bones in the mud at Bloody Shiloh Church when the Tennessee Infantry didn't quite push Grant into the river. The books all say it was a glorious battle and a great day for the South, but my husband never came home to me."

They stood silent for a long time.

"I've known other men," she said at last. It was both statement and invitation and required no immediate answer.

"You wear guns like a fighting man," Sally Burke said, "but you ride in town and eat at my table instead of Ace's place. You ride like a cattleman, but your hands aren't calloused from the rope. You wear boots of the finest leather I've ever seen, but there's no silver conchos on your saddle. Every way I look at you, Mr. Duane, you are and you aren't. It puzzles me."

"We're going to be friends," Buck Duane said. "In time I won't puzzle you any more."

"I wonder," she said. "I wonder if the woman lives who'll ever really know you like she could an ordinary man. I'll be glad to find out."

A bat went silently in and out of the cottonwood branches, filling its belly with insects snapped on the wing.

"It's this town that bothers me," Duane said then. "What's wrong with this place, Sally?"

"So you sense it already," she said. "Try to find out for yourself, Buck. Then come and ask me again. I won't lie to you but I think it's better you form your own opinion first. You won't do that here under my big tree though."

"I know," Duane said. "I know. I'll go down to Ace Holden's place presently. That's where the action is.

Everybody and everything in this town points to Ace Holden. I've been told that twice today."

"Isn't that your answer then?"

"I don't think so," Buck Duane said. "I get the idea all the fingers point to Ace Holden because it's the easy thing to do. I haven't seen Ace yet, but I wonder what I'll find when I do. Will he really be man enough for everybody to be afraid of? What's what I wonder."

"Don't wonder aloud to anybody but me," she said. "Maybe it isn't even safe to talk to me. That bat might be listening. You're a smart man, Mr. Buck Duane, and now I wonder something else. I wonder if you're as good with those guns as you are with wondering."

"I try to be," he said.

"It seems to me I've heard you were," she said. "I've heard of a Duane. I don't know where or when. It isn't important anyway. You and I are friends."

Sally Burke turned to face him, and on a sudden impulse they shook hands there in the dusk. Her hand was soft and warm, but her grip was steady like a man's.

Buck Duane went back in the house and belted on his guns. He spun the cylinders and settled them in the holsters exactly to his taste. It was a warm evening so he left his long-tailed coat in the room and wore only a vest over a clean white shirt. He took off the rider's neckerchief he wore by day and left the shirt open at the throat. From that moment on at least one of his hands was never more than inches from the butt of a holstered Colt.

Buck Duane was a fighting man with those guns. He'd shot the head off a striking rattler in a draw that was already one of the legends of the West. He lived by the things his gunman father had taught him as a boy.

"Don't ever wear a gun unless you're willing to use it," the elder Duane had said.

"Don't touch it till you start to draw."

"When you draw a gun kill your man. Don't ever bluff a man, boy. Kill him or let him be."

Whenever he prepared for a possible fight Duane could

hear his father's voice again, just as clear as if the man were there in the room and he was just a boy again.

The father had killed by choice. Buck Duane never did. His worst nightmare was the remembered face of the first man he'd had to kill. That first shooting was in self defense, and so were all the others. The gunsels who feared Duane would never have dreamed it of course, but he hated to kill. He always felt sick, body and soul, after a shoot-out.

It was only a half mile from Sally Burke's boarding house to Ace Holden's place, but Buck Duane wouldn't have dreamed of walking the distance. His pack horse was still at the Livery Stable, but Bullet was in the pasture back of Sally's barn. He came to Duane's call and let himself be saddled.

It wasn't only that no Texan would willingly walk across the street if he could ride. Depending on what happened in the saloon, Duane might have to ride for his life. A horse half a mile away wouldn't have been much use to him then.

The front of the saloon was a blaze of light that spilled out across the street. Buck Duane could see men going in and out. As he came closer he could hear the mixed and compounded blast of sound that always came from these places when there was a crowd. Mixed into the other noises he could hear a piano and a fiddle being played.

Duane tied Bullet at the near end of the hitching rail and stepped up on the wooden walkway fronting the gambling hall. He noticed that the windows fronting the place had been painted over with whitewash. Light spilled through, but no one on the sidewalk as he was could see inside except by going right up to the door. It was a common practice with bars where the patrons were likely to be men on the run. They didn't have to worry so much about who might be at their backs.

Buck Duane pushed right through the swinging doors without hesitation but managed to sweep the barroom with a quick glance before he got far inside. To his relief there was no one in the room who he could recognize from the outlaw years. Recognition was a risk he took on every job he undertook for Captain MacNelly and the Rangers.

The room wasn't crowded. It was only a Thursday night, and the big play would wait until Saturday in a town as small as this one. There were a dozen men and half a dozen women at the bar. They seemed to be trying to make up for their small number by the amount of noise they could make.

A couple of the men looked like merchants. Most of the rest were riders from the nearby ranches. Off by themselves were three men whom Buck Duane spotted instantly for professional gun-hands.

There was a poker table going at one end of the room and five men seated there playing strict attention to their cards. Only one of them really caught Duane's attention. He was tall and slender, not skinny but gracefully lean. His age could have been anything from forty-five to sixty, but was probably about halfway between. His black hair was beginning to thin and show streaks of grey. He wore a grey frock coat and trousers, expensive boots, and a spotless white linen shirt. There was a diamond ring on the third finger of his right hand and a very heavy gold watch chain across his vest.

Ordinarily Duane would have pegged the man as a gambler, but somehow this one didn't fit the role. The hand which held his cards carelessly over the table was sunbrowned as a professional gambler's never is. His face was tanned also, but it was the face of an educated and cultivated man of the world. His lips smiled easily as he said something to the other players, but Duane had an instant realization that this could be a very dangerous man. If he was armed, the weapons were concealed by his long coat.

As Duane came into the room this man raised his head and for an instant looked right at the Ranger. It was just a glance but Buck Duane felt as if he'd been examined, classified, and stored in the man's memory file.

"Eyes like that," he thought, "could look right through

and count the joints in my backbone."

The feeling of uneasiness was so strong, that he almost, but not quite broke step and turned to face the man. He managed to control himself and walked on to the bar.

"I'd like to talk to Ace," he told the bartender after he'd ordered a beer.

"It don't work quite that way," the man said with a trace of insolence that hadn't showed in his manner earlier in the day. "If Ace wants to talk to you, he sends for you. Did he send for you mister?"

Duane fixed the bartender with a cold grey eye.

"You tell him it's Buck Duane," he said. "When you say it, it's Mister Duane. You tell him I want to talk business."

The barkeep didn't like the look or the tone, but he still hesitated. Duane's left hand shot out and caught the man's shirt front above the apron he wore. He yanked the fellow forward with enough force so his fat paunch slammed against the bar and the wind was jolted out of him.

"Tell Ace," he said. "Now."

His arm straightened and shoved the man back against the counter under the mirror. A couple of bottles tottered to the floor and smashed. The man didn't even wait to clean up the mess. He crab-walked along behind the bar, keeping his face turned to Duane, until he came to a door at the end of the mirror and bolted through.

Buck Duane didn't turn his head, but the mirror showed him that the men and women at the bar had seen the byplay and were watching him out of the corner of their eyes. The three gunsels off to his left pushed back their chairs and stood up, but made no move to come closer to him. Only the poker players seemed totally wrapped up in their game.

The bartender came out of the door again. Ace Holden was with him.

Holden was a big man, maybe six-foot-two or three in his tooled leather boots, and broad across the shoulders. He was heavy with the fat of good living and had a paunch that bulged out over his gunbelt. The holster was empty. There were rings with flashing red and green stones on both hands, and diamond buttons to his vest. His face was red and sweat had stained his shirt and the armholes of his black frock coat. The eyes looking out of the beefy face were small and mean and vicious.

"You Duane?" he asked needlessly. "What makes you think I want to talk business this time of night?"

"Whenever I try to talk it with anyone else around here," Duane said, "somehow or other your name comes up. Seems to me if I'm going to talk at all, it'd have to be with you."

"Well now," Holden said expansively. "Well now, that might or mightn't be the case. All depends on what sort of business you got in mind. Ain't plannin' on opening another saloon, are you?"

"Not that," Duane said.

"Well then, come on and let's go back and set where we can talk."

Instead of taking Duane through the door which presumably led to his office Holden led the way to a table far enough from the bar itself so they couldn't be overheard. He took the chair that put his back to the wall. That left Duane to sit with his back to the three gunslingers.

Duane wasn't buying. He picked the chair up and moved it so that he faced the room also and sat beside Ace Holden instead of across the table.

"You're mighty carefuly for a business man," Holden said.

Buck Duane said nothing.

"I'm a mite careful too," Ace Holden continued. "Way we are now neither of us could put a gun on the other 'thout my friends seeing it."

"You're too careful," Duane said. "I'm not riding gun hand. Not this trip. I heard tell this was good sweetwater country, and I came to see about starting a spread here myself. Nothing raunchy about it. I got money to pay in a draft on a San Antone bank. All fair and square."

"That ain't the point," Ace Holden said. "You only been here less'n a day now. Suppose there was land to sell, and suppose—just to suppose—I might mebbe influence the seller to make you a deal, how do we know you be the sort of man to fit into our community here? You come riding in with tied down guns and your head in the air like you was Frank Younger or Jesse James hisself. This here's a peaceful town. Everybody sort of makes it a point to get along."

"I'm a peaceful man," Duane said. "I don't push anybody. What's that got to do with ranching?"

"It ain't so much the ranching it's got to do with. Round here let's just say it's to do with the living." He threw back his head and roared with laughter. One of his big hands slapped the table twice, palm down.

Buck Duane saw that the gunmen were watching. He took the table slapping for a signal of some sort to them, but they didn't move.

"All right, Mr. Holden," he said. "It ain't all that funny. I figure to go on living, here or any place. You ain't answered my question about land to sell."

"I ain't made up my mind yet," Holden said.

"I suppose there's government land for the homesteading?" Duane said. His inference was plain enough. He could buy direct.

Ace Holden went on laughing but the mean little eyes narrowed. There wasn't any humor in his expression when he spoke again.

"You're a stranger here," he said, "and that there idea just proves it for sure. There's homestead land all right, but it ain't healthy land. Them as gets it is short of water, short of feed, short of supplies. You might even say they was short of time. Yessiree, that's about it. Them homesteaders is short-lived people."

"So, if I want land, I wait for you to make up your mind," Duane said. "No offense meant. Like you say I'm a stranger in these parts."

"Now you're seeing the light," Ace Holden said.

"That's just about right. You wait for me to make up my mind about how you fit into our homey little community. When I make it up, I'll let you know one way or t'other. Meantimes, if you get impatient, a man's always free to ride out the way he rode in."

Holden got to his feet and so did Duane. Ace Holden made no effort to shake hands. He turned and walked back towards the bar. As he did, one of the thin-faced gunmen stepped out to talk to him.

Ace Holden stopped walking. His back was to Buck Duane and his broad shoulders and massive body hid the gunman from sight. The way the two of them stood a clump of bar patrons kept them from being reflected in the mirror.

Buck Duane felt the old familiar icy knot of tension form in the pit of his stomach. It was always that way just before he had to fight for his life. He never wanted to kill, but he knew the time had come again. His fingers hung close to the butt of the heavy black forty-five.

When the action came it was lightning fast.

Ace Holden took two fast steps to his own right. It took him out of the line of fire and exposed the man who had been hidden from Duane's line of sight.

The gunman had no delusions about chivalry. Like all his kind he murdered for cash and never gave his victim a chance when it could be helped. His gun was already out when Holden stepped aside, and his left hand was sweeping down and in to fan the hammer for a burst.

Buck Duane went down on his right knee and his own gun seemed almost to jump out of the holster into his hand. With the perfect timing achieved by years of endless practice his thumb cocked the hammer as the muzzle came up and his trigger finger tightened so that the shot crashed exactly as the weapon came level. He aimed his whole body rather than just the gun. The whole thing was so fast that no spectator managed to follow it.

The wiry gunman was fast. He got off his first shot so that it merged with the report of Duane's gun. The trouble with fanning, though, was that it was never aimed fire. The fanner relied on a quick burst to bracket and flatten his man.

This one had no time for a burst. His first shot went over Duane's shoulder where the Ranger had dropped to his knee. Then Duane's shot took him and killed him.

That the man got off a second shot at all was a tribute to his speed. It was instinct or reflex or the paralyzing shock of the forty-five slug that moved his hand. He was dead on his feet when the hammer fell.

It was pure accident, but the bullet hit Duane's left arm just below the shoulder. If it had struck bone, he would have been crippled for life. As it was, the shock of the ragged flesh wound swung him partly around, twisting his body to the left, and temporarily putting that arm out of commission.

Only a powerful man with a will of iron could have kept himself under control. Buck Duane managed it. The smoking muzzle of his big Colts swung back to cover Holden and his two other gun hands. The gunsels made no move at all.

Ace Holden put his hands up shoulder high.

"I ain't armed," he yelled. "Everybody witness! I got no gun. He'll murder me."

"Somebody give him a gun," Duane said. His voice was pitched low, but in the sudden silence that followed the crashing shots it carried to all parts of the room.

Blood was soaking Duane's shirt sleeve and dripping from the hanging fingers of his left hand, but the big Ranger didn't seem to notice. His eyes were icy cold and the hand holding his gun never wavered.

"Give him a gun," he said again.

"For God's sake no!" Ace Holden yelled. "I got no quarrel with you, Duane. It was Sam's idea. He thought he knew you from some place. I swear it. I won't fight you."

Buck Duane knew perfectly well that if their roles had been reversed Ace Holden would have shot him dead in his tracks. He knew that the big man would never forgive him for the humilitation of having had to beg for his life. As long as Ace Holden lived he, Buck Duane, could expect a bullet in the back the first moment his guard was relaxed in the slightest.

Holden's man would never have fired on him without orders. Every man and woman in the room knew it.

Even so, Duane couldn't bring himself to pull trigger on an unarmed man who kept his hands up. To his last day he'd never know why, but Buck Duane had never killed except in self defense. He hated taking the life of another man. Once attacked, he could be a smoothly coordinated, lightning fast killing machine, but he could not or would not kill except to preserve his own life.

After a moment he dropped his gun back in its holster.

V

There was a long sigh of relief from the people in the bar. Then the silence was broken by an entirely new voice from the doorway which led into the hotel lobby.

"If you'd murdered him, Mister, I'd have had to shoot you down. I'm glad you didn't, because I'd have hated to do it."

It was a woman's voice, calm and collected and with the crisp accent and cultivated tone of an educated lady. As Buck Duane turned slowly he saw her in the doorway.

She stood straight and proud, although actually she was a small woman and lightly boned. For all of that she held the ivory handled derringer steady as a rock. She wore a dress of powder blue material with a skirt divided for riding like a man and soft leather boots showing under the trailing edge. Her eyes were black and her hair raven-wing dark and curling about a beautiful oval face. To Duane's eye she could have been any age, but of a surety she was all woman.

He recovered himself. "Why thank you, Miss. I'm glad too that you didn't shoot."

She made a simple gesture and the derringer vanished into a pocket of the dress.

"All's well that ends well," she said in a lighter tone. "Now, sir, it's time something was done about that wound of yours. You're bleeding on the floor." She raised her voice: "Dan, get your bag."

"Yes, my dear." It was the distinguished looking man at the poker table who answered. He reached down to the floor beside his chair and straightened up holding a black leather doctor's bag with heavy Mexican silver fittings.

"Come over here, man," he said easily. "I'll put a ligature around that arm for now, and then we'll all go and get the wound properly dressed."

"I'll be obliged," Duane said. "No man can make blood as fast as it runs out." He walked over to the table and sat down.

"Something of a philosopher as well?" the doctor said. "Good man. This won't take a minute."

He deftly slit the sleeve of Duane's shirt to expose the wound, applied a wad of cotton and gauze and twisted a tourniquet above the cut so that the bleeding stopped.

"That should do it for now," he said. "We'll go on to my office for a real dressing. You can ride, I think?"

"I can ride," the Ranger said. He thought of many rides for life he'd made with wounds far worse than this. "But first I'll buy the house a drink."

Ace Holden had vanished into his office and his two remaining gunmen with him. A couple of swampers had carried out the dead man and thrown sand to cover the pool of blood on the floor. Now the customers crowded up to the bar.

Buck Duane poured himself a good four fingers from the whiskey bottle that was brought to the table and drank it down all at once. The burning warmth of the raw spirits began to melt the cold knot in his stomach.

Buck Duane, the doctor and the small woman rode out

of town up the hill to where the big houses of the well-to-do stood under the shade of live oak and cottonwood trees. It was only about a mile to go.

The doctor and his sister Ann—he'd introduced himself as Daniel Mills—lived in the biggest house of all. There was a butler to meet them at the door and a scurry of Mexican maids to take their hats and bring drinks.

The doctor's office was in the ground floor rear, and he took Duane there at once for a highly professional cleaning and dressing of the wound. Duane noticed that he washed his hands and instruments in liquid from a big jug of grain alcohol before starting to work on the wound.

"A newfangled notion," Doctor Mills said wryly. "Read about it in a journal from the University at Edinburgh in Scotland. Some of my colleagues laugh at it, but I get many fewer infected wounds since I began its use."

Mills cleaned Duane's wound carefully and bound it up.

"Should be right as rain in a few days for a healthy chap like yourself," he said. "You're lucky the bone wasn't even nicked. Clean wound is always best, I say."

They went back into the big front parlor where Ann Mills was waiting for them, and the servants had brought cold meat and cakes and wine.

"Sit down and rest a bit," Ann said. "It's late, but there's still time to talk. Why on earth did that man ever draw on you, Mr. Duane? Had he really known you somewhere else?"

"Not to my knowledge, Miss Mills," Duane said, and helped himself to food and drink. "I think he drew because Ace Holden told him to."

"I think so too," the doctor said, "but why would Ace do that? Had you just quarreled with him? I saw you talking."

"It puzzles me," Duane said. "No, we didn't quarrel. I'd just told him I was thinking of buying a ranch in this beautiful valley. For some reason or other he didn't seem to like the idea, but there wasn't any actual quarrel. Certainly nothing was said that I'd have thought worth killing a man for."

"Did you defy Ace?" Ann asked. "He's a most arbitrary man and used to lording it over the people here. If his temper was bad tonight anyway, he might take offense where another man wouldn't."

"No," Duane said. "Not even defiance, though I might have done just that had the talk gone on much further. That isn't all that puzzles me either, ma'am. What makes everybody around here so afraid of Ace Holden?"

"I'm not afraid of him," she said with spirit.

"I believe you aren't," Duane said. "That isn't what I meant. But in just one day I've talked to other folk who were. If I wanted to buy land, they say, I must see Ace. I never heard of a set-up like this any place in Texas before. Does he own this town, or what?"

"Not exactly own," the doctor said. "No, you couldn't really say he owns High Valley. Not in the sense of bought and paid for anyway."

"In another sense you might say he did," Ann Mills said. "It is sort of an unusual thing for Texas. He has a mortgage on the valley. That mortgage is fear."

"What Ann means," her brother said, "is you aren't the first man around here Ace Holden took a dislike to who's had to fight for his life. I'll admit though that you're the first of the lot to come out of the fight alive. Those boys of Ace's don't usually miss."

"That one didn't exactly miss," Duane said. "He was just a mite slower than he should have been. It's an edge the gun fanner ought never to give the other man. Because he don't aim, he's got to be a lot quicker getting the shots off."

"Ahem," Mills chucked and then said, "For Sam that's only an academic point by now. The question remains, just what are you going to do, Mr. Duane? You don't seem to share the general fear of Ace and his boys."

"I just reckon to take care of myself," Duane said. "If the other fellow starts a ruckus, I finish it."

"So you do—and most effectively, I must say. By the

way, if it's any help to you, Sam Huie was the fastest of those three."

"That's right," Ann added. "Since you took Sam, you could take the other two as long as they stand up to you like he did."

"Or they could backshoot me, you mean. That's been tried before, Miss Mills. I'm a Texan and so I'm a stubborn and independent man. I can take care of myself."

"Seems to me someone else around here used to say that," the doctor said over his wine glass. "It was Bill Bass, if I remember rightly."

There was meaning behind the remark which Duane couldn't fathom. It wasn't quite a threat, nor yet a question. More like a test thrown out to see how he'd react.

Duane decided to appear perfectly open and candid. "Bass? That's the feller whose papers I brought back with me from San Antone. Got himself killed down there, and they figured at the Bank since I was coming right up here anyway it'd be faster than the mail." He stopped and laughed. "Maybe save postage too, I guess."

Neither of his hearers seemed overly surprised.

"You weren't by chance there when he was killed?" Doctor Mills asked. "No last words for his widow or anything like that?"

"Not that I know of," Duane said. "Nobody said anything about his living long enough to talk, and I wasn't there myself."

"Oh yes, of course." There was a sudden feeling of relaxed tension in the room.

Buck Duane didn't like it. Somehow they'd been hanging on the answer to that one question. What did they think he'd say? More to the point, was it something they were afraid they'd hear? He decided he needed to know a lot more about this couple.

"I'm most grateful to you both," he said, getting to his feet, "but it's been a right long day. What with loss of blood and all, I'd best be on my way."

They urged him to spend the night, but he refused. The doctor laughed at the idea of payment for dressing the wound.

"Just watching that marvelous draw of yours was payment enough," he protested. "I really didn't do anything."

Buck Duane watched the shadows as he rode back to Sally Burke's place, but there were no threats or lurking figures. He put Bullet in the barn, and walked up to the house and to his room. Nobody else was up and about.

Duane was asleep almost as soon as he hit the bed. That is most of him slept. One tiny corner of his mind listened for any unusual sound or presence. A man who's been hunted for years can never really sleep as sound as other men. His life has for too long depended upon unending alertness to any variant from the norm. Had anyone even come close to the window, Duane would have been instantly awake and reaching for his gun without any conscious awareness of what had roused him.

That was what happened in the morning. He woke—became totally awake, and gun in hand—all in an instant. Without knowing how he knew, he was aware of someone standing in the hall outside his door.

He was right. There was a soft tap on the door and then Sally's voice: "Are you all right, Buck? Don't get up unless you feel like it. I heard abut last night. But if you're hungry, I've saved some breakfast and the rest have gone out."

"I'll be with you in a minute," he called back. "Thanks a lot."

Sally Burke gave him a big platter of bacon and fried eggs, biscuits and honey, fried potatoes and a slab of leftover canned peach pie with a lighter crust than the best San Antonio chef had ever made. He ate heartily and then they sat with china mugs of hot boiled coffee so thick the spoon would almost stand erect.

It was only then that she tried to talk.

"They tell me you shot Sam Huie last night, Buck. Does

that mean you got the answer to your questions?"

"Not exactly," Duane said, "I met Ace Holden and we didn't like each other worth shucks. It wasn't enough for him to tell me to get out of town. He had to tell his man to help me on my way. If you heard the story, you know it was no stand-up fight. More like backshooting me, except that Sam wasn't quite as good as he thought he was.

"When that was over I met Doctor Mills and his sister and they took me home for wine and to tell me in their own way to get out of town. They weren't quite as blunt about it as Ace had been, but in the end it all added up to the same thing. Every living soul I've seen in High Valley wants me gone except you, Sally."

"Since you're stubborn enough to stay around anyway," she said, "I might as well tell you what I can. This High Valley range is a rather special type of place. We're more or less cut off from the rest of the state up here. It's wonderful grazing land and the river gives plenty of water, but it's only been settled about ten years. We're out ahead of most people and the real law hasn't caught up with us yet.

"That makes a perfect set-up for somebody like Ace Holden. As far as this valley is concerned he just took over as the law."

"How could he do that?"

"He did it because he made everybody afraid of him," she said. "Right at first a couple of ranchers told him where to go when he started pushing them around. I can show you their neat wooden crosses in the graveyard back of the church."

"As raw as that?" Buck Duane asked.

"Not quite." Sally poured him more coffee. "Ace didn't shoot anybody himself that we know of. One of the men got into a fight with his gun hands over cards. The other was found bushwhacked with two Winchester slugs in his back. Then there was Willis Tremacher, who has the big hardware store in town. He was all for getting up a citizens' committee and hiring a marshal. Right then was when two wagon loads of goods he'd ordered and paid for were raided by bandits. The drivers were killed."

"I see," Duane said quietly. "Now nobody else wants to be first to stand on the spot marked X. That's all very fine, but isn't it dangerous for Ace too? Suppose somebody hired a killer to take him out of the picture? Or suppose I'd shot him last night like maybe I ought to have when he was under my gun? Wouldn't that solve the problem all in one neat little package?"

She gave a short, bitter laugh. "Oh, don't fool yourself that hasn't been thought of. It has. More than once. Only I guess whoever's back of all the trouble must have thought of it first. You see Ace doesn't claim to give orders in his own name. He claims to be acting for somebody else, that the killings are ordered by somebody else."

"Who?" Buck Duane felt he was hitting paydirt now.

Sally shook her head. "That's the devil of it. Nobody knows. The only name used is Mr. Smith. Mr. Smith wants this. Mr. Smith has so-and-so killed. Only nobody ever saw Mr. Smith. There's all sorts of yarns. He's Reeder the Renegade. He's one of the Youngers. He's a Mexican hidalgo with connections this side of the border. The story that makes most sense to me is he has an outlaw and rustler stronghold somewhere West of here in the hills back of the Rainbow Ranch—that's the big spread at the head of the valley. Only thing wrong with that theory is he never rustles steers in here. His men aren't seen. Somebody gets killed, that's all, and Ace Holden issues orders."

"What kind of orders?" Duane asked. "Surely that ought to indicate something?"

"See what you can make of it then. Of course I don't know the whole story. For one thing anybody borrows money here gets it from the High Valley Bank. The owner of record of that bank is Ace Holden. Anybody wants a loan gets one, with lots of fine print in the papers he signs. So everybody owes Ace, and back of Ace is this Mr. Smith. Only rancher around here dared bank outside was Bill Bass, and don't think folks aren't saying that's why he's dead.

"Ranchers have to buy their stock from Ace Holden, on credit with easy terms and high interest. Where does Ace get the beef critters to sell? They're driven down from the Rainbow. Some of them are Spanish cattle, which is where the Mexican hidalgo story got started. Nobody knows. They're good steers and this range makes them better, but everybody's in debt to Ace and whoever backs Ace. Then when they sell the cattle it has to be to Ace. The Rainbow hands drive all stock out of here to the market in one big herd. The men know they could get a better price if they made their own drives to railhead, but they just don't dare."

"I can see one thing plain enough," Duane said. "This Smith hombre, whoever he is, can take over the valley for his personal ranch any time he wants. All he has to do is foreclose all the notes and mortgages people signed at a time when he's already fixed it so they can't pay, like refusing to buy their cattle. Meantime, he's got everybody stocking range and making improvements at their own expense while he sits back and skims the cream. Sooner or later he'll grab the whole cow, if he isn't stopped."

"Can't the law stop him, Buck?" she asked suddenly. "Oh, I don't mean that drunken fool Judge Gowanus. I mean Texas law. Why can't somebody like you ride out of here and report all this to the Governor or the Rangers or somebody?"

"I could do that easy," Buck Duane said, "only I know just enough about the law to tell you it wouldn't do one bit of good. You can't arrest a man nobody ever saw and who maybe doesn't even exist. Besides he hasn't done anything."

"Ace has," she said. "Why don't they arrest Ace?"

"Because they wouldn't have any proof he done one thing that was criminal. That's why not," Duane said. "It's no crime to have people scared of you. Outslickering the borrower with fine print in a loan paper's not criminal either. The law says a man's supposed to know what he signs. And if all the cattlemen sell to the same person, there ain't a law on the books that makes a criminal of that buyer. He's just a smart business man.

"Now it would be different, let's say, if somebody came forth with some legal evidence that could stand up in a court of law. Say there was a witness with proof who did the bushwacking, or somebody could produce a threat to his life in writing. It might even do if a couple of ranchers would stand up and swear they were made to sell their cattle under pain of death. You reckon any of them might do that?"

"You know better," Sally said. "You know darn good and well they wouldn't dare."

"That sort of makes it a Mexican stand-off," Duane said. "Seems a shame too. Specially since it must be exactly what this Smith feller must have figured on right from the first. Of course there's just one other thing. The folks here might all get together and run Ace out or kill him if they had to, fight off this Smith and his gang if they came, sell their cattle for top price and some way pay off those loans. Course it wouldn't be easy, any of it."

"Some folks have been nigh desperate enough to try against any odds," Sally said, "except for one thing I didn't mention, because I can hardly believe it myself, let alone repeat it to a stranger like you.

"This Mr. Smith, he has an ace in the hole nobody could fight, even if they knew for sure what it was."

"Tell me," Duane said. "Maybe it might help."

"Well, promise me now you won't just say I've gone clean out of my wits.

"The word is that, if Mr. Smith is crossed, if he ever chooses, he can kill the river."

"Kill the river?" Duane said. "High Valley River? Now how in the name of all that's holy does anybody kill a river?

"A river's a think of nature like a mountain. Like the sun or a rainstorm."

"I don't know," she said. "If anybody's been told how, they haven't passed it on to me. All I know is that the ranchers believe he can do what he says. He's done everything else he said, hasn't he? Bill Bass sort of hinted he'd talk in San Antonio, and Bill's dead. Ten to one somebody from Ace followed and shot him down. And without the river this valley couldn't be worth a wooden nutmeg to anything bigger'n jackrabbits.

"Save for Stover's well down south of here it's the only sweet water for sixty-seventy miles in any direction. Cattle need water, and folks are no different than their cow critters. Truth is, nobody dares take a chance Smith is right. That's just exactly how buffaloed he's got them all."

"He hasn't got me scared," Duane said. "Not yet he hasn't anyhow."

"What can you do?" Sally asked. "If all the other folks can't do anything, what makes you think you can? Just one man and all? How can you?"

"I'm not the rest of your folks," the Ranger said. "I'm Buck Duane and I don't like being pushed around by man or ghost or anybody hides behind the name of Smith. The first thing I'll do is go look at this river of yours. If it can be killed I'll find out. I figure I'll see it fast as this Smith could. Anyway, when I get back you'll know about the river and if there's a gang holed up in the hills."

"You'd really do that?"

"Sure I would. It'll take me out of town for a few days till this arm heals anyway. Time I get back I'll likely need two hands to shoot with."

VI

Buck Duane saddled Bullet and got his pack horse from the livery stable, loaded all his gear, and went by the saloon. The bartender wasn't happy to see him, but he put up a beer. Duane drank it down and said nothing.

"You leaving town?" the bartender asked.

"What else you think I loaded my stuff for?" Duane

said in a surly tone. He wanted it assumed he was giving up and moving on for good. "I'm riding out aways, but that don't mean I won't be back."

"Sure," the bartender said and wiped the bar. His expression was scornful. "Sure, fella. Anything you say."

I fooled that one, Duane thought as he mounted up. Maybe even Ace will believe him. He'll want to because he can claim he scared me out. Make up a little for the way he had to crawl last night. He'll want to think I'm running.

This Mr. Smith now—if there really is a Mr. Smith—he might not be fooled so easy. He's got to be smarter than Ace Holden, or Ace wouldn't work for him. It'd be the other way around. He'll be worried about me after last night, and he'll likely try to think of what he'd do if he was me. Once he figures out I wouldn't likely just up and run, the rest of it'll come to him fast enough.

Duane remembered something Captain MacNelly used to tell his men.

"If you can out-think the man you're after," the veteran Ranger officer would say, "you've got him. Sooner or later you've got him. Sometimes you come up against one you can't out-think, and when you do, outrun him. Keep just a jump ahead of where he's sure you are. Then you'll have him too before it's over."

One of the Confederate cavalry commanders in the late war had said much the same thing. "Get thar fustest with the mostest."

This was a case where Buck Duane knew he'd have to do just that. If there really was an outlaw gang in the hills, and they caught him in the open, it was all up with Buck Duane. He'd been an outlaw himself for enough years to have a proper respect for the fighting ability of the owlhoot fraternity. They had to be either good with their guns or dead. On their own ground and against a single man they were very, very good indeed.

Duane had to move fast and far. Swing a wide loop, as the ranchers would say.

He headed out of the valley to begin with, then swung

away from the river and the road which bordered it. He'd rather have waited for nightfall, but had a persistent feeling that speed was of the greatest importance.

Heading back up the valley, he stayed almost in the shadow of the western hills. That meant he couldn't be seen by anyone in or near the town even if they used a powerful telescope. The valley was anywhere from twenty to thirty miles broad throughout most of its length, only narrowing where the river came out of the hills. It was roughly forty miles in length.

It was a real prize that Mr. Smith was grasping for, Buck Duane thought as he rode and looked about him. It was a kingdom in miniature, richer and fairer than many a European or Asiatic principality.

To an outland visitor the grasslands would have been as monotonous as a placid sea except that the color was green or splashed with the hues of grass flowers in season. In places the waving tips reached saddle-high on a mounted man, particularly where, as in High Valley, there was water and sun to spare.

Within the grass plains themselves there is endless, merciless warfare between species. Grasses are long-lived, can reproduce by seed or root, and are all equally at home on the prairies. The different sorts struggle without cease for light and water and nutrients.

The root systems of different grasses grow at varying levels in the soil. Each species, as it tries to expand, must battle with the others. Sometimes a minor factor makes the different between success and failure. Big bluestem flourishes on the fat soils of the moist lower slopes such as the ground where Duane rode.

The little bluestem, only half the height of its cousin grass, becomes dominant as the slopes increase. Its root system is more efficient at gathering and storing water, and that gives it a real advantage on the higher plains.

The true prairie is a mixture of living plants whose roots go down to different levels, some shallow, some probing many feet into the soil. Together they bind the earth in a carpet so thick and tough and hard that again and again the iron plows of the homesteaders broke before they could turn a furrow.

Violet, ground plum, wood sorrel and cat's paw flower in early spring and then lie shaded by the summer grass. Other flowers like the hawkweed stake out their claim by growing a tight rosette of leaves to shade the soil. As the grasses grow higher the hawkweed's stem grows with them to keep its crowning rosette in the sun.

Through all of these plants and more Duane rode north and west. Under the cover of wavering grasses, the rodents and birds and insects at home in the grass hurried to get out of his path. The fragrance of sun on grass, spiced by the cool wind off the hills tingled his nostrils and freshened his blood like a strange and wonderful wine.

Far in the distance lay the silver ribbon of High Valley River, fringed by live oak and cottonwood. Where it widened into placid pools the westering sun struck blinding corruscations of reflected light.

Most of the ranch houses he saw were near the river and the road. He stayed well back of them so as to attract no attention that could be avoided. He couldn't be sure of course that some rider wouldn't see him at a distance, but he hoped that no thought would be given to his passing, particularly if he was too far off to be recognized.

He camped in the grass that night and ate cold food that Sally Burke had packed into his saddle bags. It was cold after the heat of the day, but he risked not even the smallest fire. Piled grasses made his bed, and it was far softer than—any that Duane had known in the years gone by.

Soon after starting out in the morning Duane came to a place whre the valley narrowed to only about five miles in width and the hills steepened and straightened to a wall. Above this point the hills fell back again and the slopes decreased, but this narrow gap marked the commencement of the Rainbow Ranch. To make double sure, the whole gap had been fenced across with the new and expensive barbed wire just now beginning to be imported from Chicago, St. Louis and Kansas City.

Like most riders of the open range Buck Duane hated and despised the wire as a cruel and inhuman trap for beasts of all sorts. On this particular morning he disliked it even more than usual.

Its presence meant that he'd have to get out of the valley in order to continue in the direction he wanted to go. It was too high for Bullet, let alone the burdened pack horse, to have jumped.

He carried wire cutters in his bags as a matter of course, and could have made a breach in a minute's time. The trouble was that, even if he tried to twist the cut ends of the wire together the first line rider along the fence would have known someone had gone through. If Ace's people were looking for him that would give them a hot trail to follow. Accordingly he pushed off to the left, where a notch cut into the low bluff on his side of the fence.

About a mile from the notch natural caution, strengthened by long years on the run, halted him. He got a pair of powerful army-type field glasses out of his saddle bags and carefully inspected the ground ahead. Nothing unusual showed. The grassy hills rose in easy swells on both sides of the notch, growing steeper and steeper as the land rose away from the prairie. There were no rock piles behind which a bushwacker could hide and no trees. The fast growing, deep rooted grasses preempted all water and ground which might have nourished larger growth.

Buck Duane decided it was safe to use the pass, but he never for an instant relaxed his alertness as he rode in.

It was well that he did not. The two men had lain in ambush in the tall grass back of a slight hollow on the side of the nearest hill. They'd taken the trouble to throw and hobble their horses back of the crown of the hill.

Nothing at all showed except waving grass till the men got partly upright and prepared to aim their Winchesters. That made a wrong ripple in the even flow of grass before the wind.

Duane couldn't see into the grass, but the wrongness triggered him to instant action. He was over the far side of Bullet, hanging on by saddle horn and stirrup like an Indian, and pounding his mount in a dead run around the flank of the hill on the other side of the notch. He dropped the rein of the packhorse, but that animal, lightly loaded and actually brought as a spare mount in case of a long endurance chase, sensed danger and came racing at Bullet's heels.

Duane actually widened the gap by fifty yards before the first shot crashed out. The bushwackers, like most saddle men, were far more used to pistol than to rifle. The man-high grass made it hard to aim and the sudden dash of their intended victim threw them off balance.

At least a dozen shots were fired before Duane got out of effective range of the black-powder rifles. Only one came close and that nicked the pack horse's ear and sent him into a frenzied gallop.

Duane pulled Bullet to a halt. He considered going back and trying to capture and question one of the men, but decided against it when he saw them mount in haste and ride back towards the Rainbow spread.

That was Mr. Smith, he thought to himself. Maybe he had somebody posted to see if he'd really left the valley. Maybe he just played a hunch. He knew Duane was a stranger here, who'd come to the fence and decided not to cut it. That notch was a natural trap to toll a rider in, so he put his killers there. Ace Holden wasn't that smart. Not by a country mile he wasn't.

Again, he remembered Captain MacNelly's voice: "If you can't outthink them, you've got to out-run 'em."

Duane pushed rapidly into the hills, but avoided making the wide, sweeping arc to avoid passing near Rainbow Range that the ordinary man would have done.

They wouldn't expect him to stay close, so they'd run fast into the hills, expecting to cut his trail five or ten miles back in. Likely enough they'd miss his track completely, what with being in a hurry and not looking for it so close.

Ordinarily rustlers and gunmen weren't much good at tracking anything smaller than a herd of steers.

His experience as a lone outlaw who often had to hunt and kill wild game for food had taught Buck Duane the art of tracking and a supreme contempt for those who had never learned.

He kept just off the skyline back of the first low ridge of hills bordering the valley. At regular intervals he'd dismount, go to the ridge and glass the area. He not only wanted to spot pursuit, but also to see and memorize the lay of the land back of that Rainbow fence.

He saw the two bushwackers riding hard up the river road to the cluster of ranch buildings. Once they reached it, however, no knot of riders came out and headed for the hills. He needn't worry about immediate pursuit.

Curiously enough that bothered him more than if he'd seen a posse on his track. Smith had been one jump ahead of him at the fence. What did he have up his sleeve now?

Except for the nature of his errand the Ranger would have been fascinated by the vista which stretched out before him. A line of green trees and sparkles of reflected sun marked High Valley River wind-up the middle of the valley. Stretching to the hills on both sides was a sweep of tall grass like a green-gold sea, dotted by islands of feeding cattle. There were probably two or three thousand steers in sight, more than he'd expected to see by far.

If they were as thick further up, even a rich range like this one would be overgrazed. Where, he wondered, did they get such a herd, and what was the point of building it to unwieldy size?

There was only one logical answer. The Rainbow riders were either rustlers themselves or closely leagued to one of the big outlaw bands. The herds he saw were stolen, from the look of them, many from the big Mexican haciendas below the Rio Grande.

Anyone who knew the hills could drive them in a back entrance to the valley through the wild country running straight to the border. Once on the Rainbow range they could be fattened for another drive to market, and the brands doctored at leisure.

He'd been told that the valley ranchers bought Rainbow stock. Also other steers could be mixed into the one big market drive that went out of the valley each year. The big herd, all Rainbow owned but containing cattle with the varied brands of the small ranchers, made a perfect cover for disposal of the stolen stock.

Here was something that would certainly justify calling in MacNelly and a troop of Rangers to clear up the whole dirty situation in the Valley. Threats and unknown bushwackers were one thing. A major rustling headquarters with very probable international complications was something else again.

Buck Duane knew that he still had things to do before riding out of there however. He had to find an entrance by which the herds could be brought out of the hills onto Rainbow range. That should be easy enough.

He had also to determine if there were actually rustlers holed up in the hills and scout their hide-out so the Rangers would know how to take it. Actually Duane rather doubted if he'd find such a place. The Rainbow itself could offer safe and comfortable shelter to any number of riders as long as they came and went by the back door. There'd be no reason for the High Valley people to even suspect their presence.

Before making any drastic move Duane also needed to know what, if anything, was meant by the strange threat to "kill the river." He figured it was all a bluff but didn't quite dare to discount a man as smart as Mr. Smith had already shown himself to be. If there was a way to stop the water, there'd be no sense in attacking the ranch and having the whole valley ruined at the same time.

On the other hand, if Buck Duane could discover how the damage could be done, then the Rangers could think of a way to prevent it.

Last, but certainly not least of the tasks ahead, he had to learn the identity of Mr. Smith himself. He might be Ace

Holden of course, or whoever ramrodded the Rainbow lying there in the distance. He might be the chief of an outlaw band, possibly Reeder the Renegade himself, or a business man a thousand miles off to the East who pulled the strings to make the valley people dance like marionettes. He might be anybody in the valley, maybe even a woman. Maybe Sally Burke herself. It was as tantalizing as trying to find the shadow of one tree in a wood on a moonless night.

Whoever he was he had a veritable gold mine in High Valley. He could use it as safe base for rustling, storage of stolen or pillaged goods or hide-out for his men. He could make the people buy his steers and pay him interest on his loans. In time, when the march of settlement caught up to the valley and rustling would no longer be possible, he could take over the whole magnificent range for his own and make another fortune as an honest rancher. Stranger things had happened, and would again, in the incredibly rich Western country.

So far the only fly in this golden ointment, Buck Duane thought wryly, was himself. At the moment that was all he was, a minor inconvenience to be swatted and obliterated. That was the reason for the ambush. Later on, especially if Mr. Smith should realize Duane wasn't just a loan rancher looking for a spread but a Texas Ranger, the hunt would be on in earnest.

They'd know they had to kill him then. Every man and every gun at Mr. Smith's command would be mobilized to hunt him down. When that happened he knew he'd have to both outrun and outthink them all. Even then the odds against his getting safely back to the captain with his report would be long indeed.

He had to move now, and move fast while he still had a little leeway.

Duane rode back into the hills. He'd liked to have stayed and scouted the ranch buildings more closely, but he didn't dare take the time. Even at the distance he'd glassed the place from, he could see that it was a regular settlement, almost a village in itself.

The ranch house was big and rambling. There were outbuildings and sheds, barns, cookhouses, a smithy and bunkhouses as big as the barracks he'd seen at army posts. There were two big horse corrals and another where a few cattle were being held, probably waiting to have their stolen brands worked over.

The Ranger had decided on a long horseshoe loop through the hills that closed in the head of High Valley. He'd be sure to find the back way in.

He was lucky. It was barely four in the afternoon when he crossed what looked like a regular road leading towards the ranch. Thousands of cattle must have been driven this way over a long period of time to make such a beaten track.

Duane began to realize the size of the operation he was up against. This was no gang of outlaws and misfits, making hit-and-run cattle raids whenever they ran out of money. It was a big business, a very big business indeed. There'd have to be a big man back of it all. Somebody who had brains and money and talent and specialized knowledge to organize and then to keep things running smoothly.

For the first time Duane began to wonder if a single Ranger could possibly pit himself against such a set-up with any chance of coming out alive.

He didn't bother to follow the cattle trail into the point where it entered High Valley. That would be easy enough whenever the Rangers were ready to strike. Besides, if he followed it in he might run into guards or more bushwackers. There was no point in taking the risk.

He did ride onto the road as if he were going towards the valley, then turned his horses and backtracked for at least half a mile. Nobody in the area could have picked out his tracks in that trampled and hard-beaten strip.

Then he left the road where an outcropping of rock would hide his tracks and angled across country in search of a camping spot.

He had climbed high enough now so that the short upland grass was being challenged by clumps of trees, mostly the ubiquitous firs of the western uplands. He circled one such forest clump which covered a couple of acres of slope and found himself looking into the muzzle of an ancient Hawken buffalo rifle at a range of about three feet. At that range it looked bigger than the barrel of a shotgun. It looked a lot more like a cannon.

VII

The man back of the Hawken was old enough to be Buck Duane's grandfather or maybe even his grandfather's grandfather. "Older than sin and tougher than time," Captain MacNelly would have said. For all of that the hand that held the rifle was as steady as a rock, and the eyes that looked Duane over were keen and alive.

"Just set steady fer a minute," the patriarch said. "I been expectin' ye fer a long spell now."

"Put the gun down," Duane said, recovering himself. "There's no reason a couple of reasonable men can't talk things over."

"Hah," the oldster said. His long white beard jumped when he said it. He wore a dirty leather shirt that had once been fringed, woolen pants and high moccasins bound round the legs instead of boots. A flop-brimmed black felt hat, long since devitalized by usage and held together by thick grease, covered his head.

"Hah. What makes you think me a reasonable man, bub? How do ye know I ain't just aimin' to shoot you off the back of that there horse animal and take you stuff fer my own? Answer me that."

It was a long time since anyone had called Buck Duane "bub." It amused him and he began to relax.

"I know it easy enough," he said. "Anybody that could

make me walk right under his gun without my knowing he was alive could have shot me out of the saddle with no trouble at all. That's what he would have done too instead of risking my pulling one of my Colts before you could shoot."

The muzzle of the rifle lowered. "Durned ef I don't think ye'd have tried it too, if'n I really meant ye harm. Well, light and set. I been expectin' ye too long a while to waste good time with useless jawclabber now."

"What do you mean expected me?" Duane asked. "You been trailin me?"

"Kept ye in sight ever since ye run round those two tarnation fools at the pass. Could have nailed ye any time, but that there ain't my meaning. I been expectin you with my mind fer five years now. Sooner or later somebody had to come pokin' round about what goes on down there. Just had to. Now light and set easy. I got things to say."

Buck Duane swung down off Bullet's back.

"Just why do you think I'm poking around?" he asked. "Mightn't I be just another saddlebum going through?"

The old man gave a snort that might have been either laughter or contempt, or perhaps a little of each and some other emotion for good measure. Duane couldn't tell.

"You ain't no saddlebum," he said, "nor neither are ye one of the wild bunch, though there's much the same stamp on you that outlaws have. Give me odds and I'll bet right here that ye're one a' them Texas Rangers. Am I right?"

"You're right," Duane said, "but how you did it is way out beyond me."

"Easy as he knew I wouldn't shoot," the other said, and spat tobacco juice in the dust, automatically burying it in the dirt with a flick of one foot to keep a tracker from seeing it. "I knew someday or other the folks outside would begin to wonder 'bout this valley. Mebbe one a them poor fools down thar writ a letter out. Anyway, when they wondered, they'd send somebody to see and report.

"Now who would they be most likely to send in? The

Governor? A Yankee school-marm? General William Tecumsah Sherman? Shecks no. Thar's only just one likely feller to drap by, and that would be a Texas Ranger. Right?"

"Right," Duane told him. "Are we safe to just sit here and jaw?"

"Safe as if we was perched up on the moon," the old man said. "I'm Lefty Wilder, mountain man." He said the last with pride. "I'm wilder than most by nature and by name. I trapped with Deef Smith when I were a mere lunker, and been in the mountains all my life."

"Glad to know you, Lefty," Duane said. "I'm Buck Duane, and like you figured, I'm a Ranger. You're the only person in High Valley that knows it except me."

"I ain't in High Valley nor want to be," the old man said. "So it's still your secret. I live up in the hills here. More comfortable that way, though they's mighty small hills to the Rockies where I trapped. Don't feel too comfortable with too many folks close by."

"I see that. Do you still trap?"

"Just when I want a skin fer myself. No market. 'Stead o' that I pan a leetle gold late years. Ain't much of the stuff in here, but enough to keep an old man like me in coffee and salt. Now you found the rustler's road, you going out again?"

"Not quite yet, old-timer," Duane said. "Two more things I need to know first, and I'd take kindly to any help you could give.

"Firstly, what is really back of the thing all the valley folk are so scared of? I mean what is this talk about killing the river?

"And last, but for sure not least, just who is this Mister Smith I hear talk of?"

Lefty Wilder scuffed the ground with the toe of his moccasin and chewed reflectively on a twig. "Fust question I know the answer to," he said then. "Camp with me tonight, and in the morning I'll take and show ye. As fer the second, that I don't rightly know any better'n them chicken-hearted ranchers do. You have to find that out fer yerself."

"I'd hoped you'd know," Duane said. "You must have seen the rustler's herds driven in and then ride out." He knew the old fellow's curiosity would have made that a cinch. "Who leads them?"

"Sometimes Neal Rogers rides," Lefty Wilder said, "he's the one ramrods the Rainbow for Ace. That is supposing that Ace Holden owns the Rainbow, which I don't think is so myself. A big, tough man—prob'ly overdue fer hanging in three-four places."

"He is that," Buck Duane agreed. "The Rangers have a wanted notice on that name."

"Well, he's the one. Fast with a gun and damn-your-eyes in general. Ace never rides. Once er twice there was a feller with them might just be the one you want. Tall but not heavy, slim almost like a woman in man's clothes. City bought clothes. Always wore a neckerchief tied around his face. I thought it were to keep dust out of his nose, but it could just as well be a disguise."

"Ever see him anywhere else?" Duane asked. "Would you recognize him if you did?"

"No to both questions," Lefty Wilder said. "I ain't never heard his voice nor seen him off a horse. Might know him if he rode by with his mask on, but nary other way. Let's go now, bub. Camp's still a ways farther on."

Buck Duane left it at that. He mounted Bullet. Lefty Wilder whistled and a small shaggy mustang pony came out of the trees where he'd been feeding. He had a blanket cinched around his middle for a saddle and no stirrups. A rangy, long-haired mongrel dog as big as a wolf came with him and bared his fangs in a ritual snarl at Duane.

"Won't bite lessen I tells him," Lefty Wilder said. "Come on."

Duane fed the old man his storebought rations that night and in the morning. Wilder drank a whole pot of strong, boiled coffee sweetened with condensed milk.

After that they left the camp and rode north and east for

some miles. With difficulty Duane restrained himself from asking the old fellow where they were going. He was content to know that the mystery of killing the river was shortly to be solved.

At mid-morning they rested their horses on a ridge of land. The river lay before them, coming down from the north and making a slow bend eastward towards the valley.

"This is where a river might be killed," Lefty Wilder said and pointed. "Not rightly killed as a river, but just as good as fer the valley folks. Look for yourself."

At this point Duane could look down on the ground below well enough so that he presently noticed what the old trapper wanted him to see.

The river was neither as wide nor as placid here as farther down its course, but still carried a good spate of water. It came out of a rather steep-walled canyon that ran almost due north-south.

Directly opposite the canyon mouth opened a rather broad valley split down the middle by the shelf of rock on which their horses rested. This height ran almost, but not quite to the mouth of the canyon. Canyon and the two branches of the valley thus formed a Y shaped figure, with the canyon for a tail. The river ran down the eastern arm of the Y.

Buck Duane saw however that the western pointing fell away more rapidly into the hills. At some time in the distant past an earthquake or other cataclysm of nature had broken the cliff where the river came out and tumbled masses of rock to block the root of the western arm. It was this barrier of fallen rock, rather than the natural lie of the land which determined that the river ran east instead of west from this point.

"Ye see it now, bub?" old Lefty Wilder asked.

"I see it," Duane said. "I ain't sure I believe it, but I see it. Somebody with money and a little engineering study could plant dynamite to blow through that ridge of loose rock and dirt."

"Pre-cisely," Wilder said. "Only need a small channel to get her started. The water 'ud cut the rest. Fust thing anybody knows in the valley there's trout flapping in the sun where their nice sweet water used ta be. Coupla small feeder streams might still keep a trickle going, but there wouldn't be nothing left you could rightly call a river. Nothing at all."

Buck Duane sat his horse and thought.

"Once done," he mused aloud, "it would take an army and a dam to put the water back in its present channel. As far as High Valley's concerned that river would sure enough be dead, and so would the town and the ranches around it. No wonder Ace has them scared if he even hints at being able to turn the water to the west."

"Right as rain," Lefty Wilder said. "Now that ye knows, bub, what'd you figure to do about all this?"

Duane didn't lose his aplomb.

"What I won't do," he said, "is monkey around down there or even go any closer. They may have sent somebody to watch it since they knew I was in the hills. Nothing could be done there anyhow."

"Right you are."

"So," Duane continued, "there's only one other thing I can do that could do any good at all. I've got to find this Mr. Smith. He's the top man, the hinge pin of this whole set-up. He's the one who'd give the order to blow that rock. Once I've got him under arrest, he'll have no reason to do that. His cover'll be blown and his game spoiled anyhow."

"So you just go and arrest him," Lefty Wilder said. "I heerd ye Rangers was a mite tetched, and now I believe it. Before ye go making arrests, wouldn't it be a smart idee to find yer man? How ye going to do that, bub?"

VIII

Buck Duane left sugar, flour, coffee and salt with old Lefty Wilder to eke out his mountain food, and headed back towards the valley. He actually had only a very general idea of what he meant to do when he got there. To say he'd arrest Mister Smith was one thing, but to do it was a horse of another color. First he had to find the man.

By now Duane was pretty sure that Smith wasn't off someplace in the East. The whole operation was too big and too complicated for an absentee-landlord set up. That was particularly true with men like Ace Holden for subordinates. Nobody as smart as Smith seemed to be would trust Ace Holden to make major decisions in a time of emergency. He'd have to be on hand himself for fast consultation if trouble came up. That meant Smith had to be somebody in the valley itself. There was no other settlement less than a couple of days' ride away.

It might be a smarter Ace Holden, using the blustering Ace role as a cover to hide his real abilities. Or if so, why not Judge Gowanus? Nobody would suspect him of brains enough to uncork one of his own bottles. Doctor Dan Mills had the education and presence to organize this rustler's paradise and to see the shock value implicit in a threat to cut off the water. On the other hand why would a man like that get involved with crime in the first place? Why risk position and fortune and professional status against exposure and arrest?

It could be one of the townsmen or ranchers leading a double life. Even Sally Burke herself had the brains and courage needed. "Slender like a woman," old Lefty Wilder had said. Duane hated to think that might be the case, but he had to consider it.

There was another possibility he wanted to check out first. Quite simply it was that the mystery man might be a mystery only because he stayed permanently out at the Rainbow spread ranch complex. If he never went further into the valley itself and arrived and left by the rear door, the rustler's road, of course none of the other ranchers would know him by sight.

The Rainbow fence had always been a boundary line. Riders from the big ranch might and did come into town on Saturday nights for the dubious diversions offered by Ace's place, but it was all one-way traffic. Nobody from outside was welcome to pass the fence going in. As a matter of fact nobody wanted to.

Duane wanted a look at the residents of the big, two-story, timber and stone ranchouse he'd so far seen only through his field glass.

Wanting and getting that look could be two very different propositions. As a rustler's hide-out the place would be closely guarded. There'd be more men staying there than were needed to look after the cattle and they'd be alert for trouble. Most of them would be gun hands and better at a fight than at regular ranch work.

People would be coming and going around the headquarters complex all day and far into the night. Chances were the only time he could get close enough to see an individual would be so late at night that everybody, including Smith, would be in bed. He couldn't identify a leader that way.

Well, there was no use in worrying about it in advance. Rangers were used to having to meet all sorts of sudden and extreme emergencies. On a wild and expanding frontier no officer of the law could operate by the book. Every situation had to be played by ear with the sole criterion that nothing was really impossible for a brave and determined man.

As it turned out Duane didn't have to solve that particular problem right away.

He took his time going back across the rustler's trail and scouting the country for the benefit of Captain MacNelly and his men. Lefty Wilder had told him the only good route into the Rainbow territory, except for the guarded rustler's pass, was on the west about three miles north of the ranch house. Here a good stand of trees offered cover from watchers and the shallow floor of an ancient, eroded down canyon, now just a long depression in the prairie, extended that cover until close to his objective. The old man had given him explicit directions as to the route he should follow, and he planned to arrive just before dark.

Duane spotted the improvised camp in a cluster of cottonwoods on the bank of a mere trickle of feeder stream, about five in the afternoon.

He could see that it had been carefully placed so that anyone coming in to the point he was heading for would have to see it. That made him wonder. A picket posted like the men at the notch to shoot him down would have gone to great pains to conceal a camp instead of putting it where he couldn't have missed it in case he came this way.

He took out his glass and carefully focused on the fire and the figure sitting by it. Then he saw that it was Ann Mills, the doctor's sister. That puzzled him even more. What was she doing out in the hills?

The idea came to him that she could have been put there solely as bait to lure him into a trap. He spent the next hour and a half making a wide circle around the campfire. He found her tracks, but only her tracks, leading into the little hollow where she was sitting. Duane was a competent tracker. If there was an ambush, then it was a one-woman affair.

He decided to ride on in to the fire. If she was waiting for him, he'd find out. If not, he could always keep her under observation till he decided what his next move ought to be.

She didn't even look up when she heard his horses coming in behind her. That meant either that she expected him or was dead sure anybody who might show up there would be a friend. He stopped Bullet only twenty feet or so from her back.

"It's Mr. Duane, isn't it?" she called out and then started to rise and turn in the same motion. "Light and set a spell, as you people out here say."

Natural caution made Duane scan the horizon once more even though he was sure there were no watchers. Then he dismounted.

"I saw your fire and recognized you," he said. "I thought I'd stop by and see if you needed anything."

"Of course you made doubly sure I was alone first," she said, and laughed as he tried to keep a poker face. "No, I didn't see you, if that makes any difference. I'm just sure a careful man like you would circle any camp before riding in—that is he would if he thought himself in hostile country."

Duane walked over and stood looking down at her. "And whyever would I think that, Miss Mills? Does Ace Holden's hand reach out this far?"

"Let's make it Ann and Buck," she said and sat down again. He sat beside her. "Leave the formality for my brother's drawing room, which is a stuffy place at best. To answer your question, Buck—yes, it reaches here and a lot further. I think you know that already, or you wouldn't be heading back towards the pass down to the Rainbow. Would you, now?"

Duane preferred to let her do all the answering.

"That's quite an assumption, Ann." He tried the name and found it good in his mouth. "What do you mean by it?"

"Oh," she said, "why can't we just be honest with each other? This one time at least—this one night? You really mean how much do I know about the doings at the Rainbow? I know a lot, kind sir. Maybe things that could help you."

She paused then and lit a thin, dark cigar, hardly larger than a cigarette, which she took from a silver-mounted leather case.

"Back East," she said, smiling, "women, even nice women, Buck, are allowed many privileges they aren't out here. Smoking alone or in the company of family or a close friend is sometimes one of them."

"Thank you," Duane said.

"For thinking of you as a friend? I have a feeling I don't quite understand that somehow I'm the one who should feel honored by it. I wish that I had met you sooner, Buck."

Duane thought of the long, lonely outlaw years.

"You wouldn't have liked me," was all he said.

"Don't be too sure of that, my friend," she said. "Don't be too sure at all. I might even have loved you as an outlaw, though I'm perfectly sure I'd have hated a life on the dodge. I'm not made for that sort of life."

"What makes you think I was ever an outlaw?"

"Oh, my dear," she said. "Haven't you realized yet that I know who Buck Duane is? I don't think my brother Dan realizes it yet, but I've heard of you. Half the West has. You were an outlaw because you killed a man, and now you're where you really belong. You're a Texas Ranger and defending the very law that tried so hard to bring you in to hang. It's no great secret."

"I wish it were," Duane said. "Who else in the valley knows?"

"I haven't gone around discussing it," she said. "I wanted to keep you all to myself. Seriously though, I don't really think anyone else knows. If Dan had recognized you, I think he would have mentioned it to me. The rest of our fellow citizens aren't overly bright. Or hadn't you noticed? If one of them knew, it would be all over town. Then you'd be in hostile territory for sure.

"So I think you and I are the only ones who really know. So far it's our secret, and I'm as ready as you to let it stay that way."

"You'll have to tell me why," Duane said. "I'd like to know where everybody stands."

"You mean why do I let you see how much I know?" she asked. "Of course you do. If I know so much about the Rainbow, doesn't that mean I'm one of them?"

"You can't really blame me," Duane said.

"Of course I don't blame you," she said. "You have to ask, and in good time I mean to answer. Not before we eat though. And don't tell me you're not hungry. I brought special things for us, and I'll taste them first so you'll know I haven't put poison in anything, not even the wine."

She actually had three bottles of good wine cooling in the little feeder stream. There was cold roasted chicken and smoked wild turkey and a ham and loaves of crusty homemade bread and cans and jars of other things Buck Duane hadn't tasted before.

As dusk fell, the fire shed a warm circle of light about the spot where they sat and the evening breeze of the high prairies murmured in the grass and riffled the high branches of the cottonwood trees. There was a moment of repletion and warmth and contentment for them both.

Then Ann Mills turned to him, her face serious in the flickering light of the sinking fire.

"Time to talk, Buck Duane," she said. "It's time for me to answer questions now. It's funny, I almost told you all this the other night after Dan tied up your arm, but then I thought you were going away out of all our lives anyway and there wouldn't be much point in it.

"Things would have been much simpler really if you had ridden on back to San Antonio or wherever it was they sent you from. Because you're still here some really nasty people are going to think they have to kill you. There's a lot of them, and they're tough. Good as you are with those big guns, I'm afraid they have a real chance of succeeding.

"How do I know all this? It's not any real mystery, and it doesn't mean I'm one of the gang. I'm not, you know. We found out, Dan and I, because he's a doctor. Soon after we came here he was called out to the Rainbow on more than one occasion. Always it was to treat men bad hurt with gunshot wounds.

"Dan is an intelligent man, and they couldn't blindfold him while he worked, could they? He saw enough to make a pretty good guess at what I'm sure you've already found out, that the Rainbow Ranch is really just a cover up for some big rustling operation. They in turn—oh, I suppose I might as well come right and say Ace Holden since I've said so much already—were also no fools. Ace knew Dan had been putting two and two together. They might have killed him then, as they killed others before and since, but they didn't.

"Dan is the only doctor within at least two hundred miles, and a rustler gang can certainly use a doctor to advantage. So instead of killing my brother they just set out to make sure that he would never give them away."

"How could they do that?" the Ranger asked. "A man like your brother—"

"I know," she said. "Dan is all you imply. Wealthy, cultivated, college trained, an Easterner and a respected professional man, and a wonderful person besides.

"The trouble is, Buck, everybody has an Achilles' heel. That means an area where he's vulnerable, where he can be reached. Dan's no exception. He is, and always has been an insane, inveterate gambler. Why do you think we took what we could of what used to be the family fortune and came and buried ourselves in a wilderness like this? It was because Dan was running away from staggering gambling debts back home.

"Ace Holden used his connections to find out about those debts. He went East and bought Dan's I.O.U.'s for a few cents on the dollar. They're locked in his safe now."

"That's one way to hold a gambler," Duane admitted.

"It's not the only one. They let him gamble any time he wants in Ace's place—on credit. In the time since we got here, he's lost almost thirty thousand dollars more than he wins. So you see why he does their medical work and keeps his mouth shut. He hates it. We both do, but he can't help himself."

Duane had his own opinion in regards to her last statement, but he decided to keep it to himself. Instead he asked another question.

"Suppose you tell me the one thing more I need to know," he said. "Just who is Mister Smith?"

She looked him right in the face and her own eyes in the

firelight were wide and guileless. Her voice had the ring of sincerity. "Buck, I honestly don't know. I'm terribly sorry. I'd tell you if I could. I'll say who I think it is, but that's all I can give you is my own opinion."

"All right," Duane said, hiding his disappointment, "then suppose you make your guess and tell me why you make it. That could be a help."

"I can't prove it," she said, "but I'm logically and morally sure Mister Smith is Ace Holden. Oh, I know Ace talks about getting instructions and waiting for orders, but it's just talk. Nobody's ever seen this mystery boss of his. At least no one ever admitted to it that I know. I think "Smith" is just somebody Ace made up so the valley people wouldn't hold him personally responsible for everything his men do. Like what the Old Testament would call a scapegoat—only in this case it isn't even a real scapegoat but just a shadow. Just something Ace made up to hide himself behind."

She didn't know it, but her words were convincing Buck Duane that some of his own thinking had been correct.

"All right, I think you may be right," he said. "Only one thing—you know Ace a lot better than I do. Has he got the brains to plan something like this and carry it through?"

"I think so," she said. "Ace is self educated, but crime is his specialty. He knows it inside out. He may not be an intelligent man in the same way that Dan is, but he's tricky and shrewd and used to living by his wits. Now is that all you have to ask me tonight?"

"No," Duane said. "There's the question you know I've got to ask. Why do you tell me all this, with your own brother involved at least as an accessory? Ace Holden can ruin you both, strip you of everything you own if he finds out. You still tell me all this. Why?"

"That was the question I waited for," Ann said. "I thought up answers that would make me look noble and honest and brave, but now that you're here, face to face like this, I can't lie to you. I'll tell it just the way it really is.

I've got a reason for telling you, a selfish reason, and I'm going to ask a price.

"You're probably guessed the reason. The only way I can see for Dan to get out from under this blackmail is to have the Rangers break up the gang and arrest or kill Ace Holden."

"I can guess the price, too," Duane said. "You want your testimony to buy your brother out." She nodded. "Maybe it can at that. It will certainly help, but I'm not the one who can promise you how much. I'm only a Ranger. What happens to your brother will be up to a judge. Had you thought about that?"

She put out her hand and took hold of his wrist. Even at that moment her touch was both strong and caressing. "Yes, I'd thought of that. So I want more than your promise to help. I want you to go with me tomorrow and get those I.O.U.'s out of Ace's safe. I know the combination. I stole a copy of it the night you had the gunfight, while Ace was talking to you and was careless. Didn't you wonder how I came to be in the hotel that night?

"I can get you into the safe, Buck. Anything else you find there, and there should be plenty, you can keep for evidence. Just let me take the markers, and forget about Dan when the arrests come. Will you do it, Buck? Will you, darling?"

The moon had risen and the fire was dying. The night was alive with the smell and rustle of living, growing things. There under the big trees by the little stream, it was cool and pleasant.

Duane sat quietly for a time before answering. Then he said: "Supposing the facts are what you say, and you can help me get enough evidence to expose and arrest the real Mr. Smith, then I reckon your brother's medical services don't have to be brought to anybody's attention."

She leaned over and kissed him. It wasn't a warm and grateful kiss, but the hot and passionate lips of a woman fully aroused that he felt. Involuntarily, his arms tightened about her. Later—much later—they rolled up in their separate blankets and slept.

IX

In the morning Buck Duane and Ann Mills talked over their plans for getting hold of the papers.

Duane had another question then. "If Ace really is the rustler king, why would he keep anything incriminating in town? Wouldn't he figure it'd be safer out at the Rainbow?"

Ann just laughed at him.

"Exactly the opposite," she said. "The last people in the world Ace Holden is going to trust with really important information or evidence about anything at all are his own men. He's probably cheating them on their share of the take anyway. And even if that's not so, look at the hold it would give them for blackmail.

"No, Buck, he'll have everything important right in the hotel safe where he spends most of his own time and where he can keep his eye on it personally."

Duane accepted that statement without argument. He was relieved that he didn't have to try sneaking into the heavily guarded ranch house.

They swung wide of the Rainbow land and came back into the valley a couple of miles the other side of the fence.

"Don't you think I should ask for help from some of the ranchers?" Duane asked. "These aren't big spreads, maybe two or three riding hands apiece, but if they'd back us, the job would be a simple one." He wanted to see what she'd say.

"You know better than that, darling," Ann said.

She was smoking one of her small cigars and her long hair blew in the wind. The stetson she wore was cocked at a rakish angle and her breasts strained the fabric of her linen blouse. She wore the long skirt split into two much oversized trouser legs and boots.

"If you think seeing just one Ranger here will put heart in those spineless sheep after six years of fear, you're making an awful mistake. The only time they'll come out in the open is after you've got Ace behind bars."

It was the answer he'd expected her to give—indeed the same he'd have had to give himself, if their roles had been reversed. He knew the valley ranchers had to protect their water at just about any cost.

If the rock slide was ever actually blown, or if Smith were to attempt a foreclosure of the whole valley at one time, they would probably rise in desperation. Now with the rationalizations of years still in their mouths and the widow Bass's tears still wet on her cheeks, the best he could hope for was an uneasy neutrality. Accordingly he and Ann stayed back from the river all day as they rode. As far as they could tell nobody saw them pass.

They planned to ride into town after dark but still early enough so the saloon might not be crowded. They'd go into the place by the back door, and put a gun in Ace's belly. If he refused to open the office door for them, Buck would break it down or shoot the lock off. Ann would use the safe combination to open it quickly.

With speed and luck they could be in and out, with Ace as a prisoner, before anyone else realized what the raid was all about.

"From there on, I'll take it," Duane said. "Once I get him in San Antone with evidence to convict, your troubles will be over."

They rode up to town in the full dark that follows a summer twilight before the moon gets over the horizon. They left their horses in a clump of brush near an old tumbledown shack and walked the last hundred yards to the rear of Ace's saloon.

"That's his office window," Ann pointed. "It's dark now, so he must still be out front at the bar."

The window had heavy iron bars bolted to its frame.

Otherwise Duane would have gained entrance to the office by that route.

Nobody saw them go into the back door. They tried the office door and found it locked.

"No help for it now," Duane said in a low tone. "We'll have to get him out of the bar."

"He knows me," she said. "I can get him to come back here easier than you can."

"Is he used to entertaining you in the office?" Duane asked. She shook her head indignantly. "Then I'm the one to fetch him back. I've got a couple of powerful arguments to convince Mister Ace he better come." He tapped his gun butts.

"All right," she said. "Don't fail. Oh, Buck, darling, don't fail me now." She spoke in a low tone and a burst of piano music from the big room almost drowned out her words.

Buck Duane walked the few steps up the narrow hall. A strange chill of premonition touched his spine and that old knot of twisted cold was in his stomach. The killing chill he called it and it always came when a gunfight was near.

He opened the door and went in. The room was full of light and the piano was tinkling and banging away, but there were only a few customers at the bar. At this early hour only one of the hotel girls had come downstairs. She was the first to see and recognize Duane.

She opened her mouth to scream.

Ace Holden was at the bar with his back to the door, talking to a customer. One of the two gunsels Buck had seen before was on his boss' other side tilting a glass of whiskey to his mouth.

The other gun Duane had seen was at the same table they'd used before, dealing himself a hand of solitaire.

The woman's scream froze everyone in the room and stopped the piano. It was as if a movie had suddenly stopped on a single frame, except that these were real people in a real place.

The gunman standing beside Ace Holden was the first

person in the big room to recover. He opened his hand, dropping the whiskey glass to smash on the floor, and dug for his gun. The need to stop and then reverse the direction of his hand slowed him down.

Duane out-drew the man easily and shot him through the upper right arm. The big bullet splintered the bone so he'd never use a gun with that hand again.

His partner got halfway up from the table. When he saw Duane's smoking gun swing his way, he put his hands up.

"Hold it!" Duane said. His voice carried clearly through every part of the room. "Next person makes a move Ace gets the top of his head shot off. I've no business with the rest of you. Stay quiet and you won't get hurt."

"He means it," Ace Holden yelled, his voice cracking on a high squeal of fright. "Nobody move, for God's sake." Then to Duane: "What do you want with me? I'm not armed. I wouldn't draw on you if I was."

"Ace Holden," Duane said icily. "In the name of the Law and of the State of Texas I place you under arrest on a charge of cattle rustling and murder. Come along peaceably or I take you anyway."

"Arrest me! Me? You're crazy. What authority have you to arrest anyone?"

"Full authority of the Law," Buck Duane said to the room at large. "I'm a Texas Ranger."

"Oh, my God." It was the woman's voice. "A Ranger."

"A Ranger?" someone in the back of the room said. "You know what that means, boys? Now God help us all."

Two men in the room stirred uneasily. One of them wearing the sweat-soiled shirt and high boots of a rancher called out then: "You, Ranger. Man, you don't know what you'll do to this whole valley if you take that man."

"Come on, Ace," Duane said. "Into your office."

There was a murmur from the men as Ace Holden still held back, and then confused voices. "We can't let him do it."

"Stop the Ranger."

"Rescue Ace."

"Move," Duane said to Holden, "or I'll kill you where you stand. Now." He gestured with his gun.

Ace Holden looked at the Ranger and knew then that he was seeing death itself. He started to move slowly towards the door. He said: "Don't shoot, boys. He means it." His voice was almost a bleat like that of a scared sheep. Whatever else Ace Holden may have been, he was surely no fighting man.

Buck Duane moved after him, trying to watch Holden and the whole room at the same time.

"You men don't interfere," he said at the door. "Obstruct an officer in the execution of his duty, and you'll have a full Ranger troop here in a week to hunt you down." That stopped them for the moment.

Ace Holden himself put up no fight at all. He went down the hall to the door of his office. When he saw Ann Mills standing there he went white as a sheet and his big mouth gulped air like a fish out of water. He looked as if he wanted to say something, but couldn't quite make it.

"Hello, Ace," she said. "It's my turn now, isn't it? Just keep your mouth shut and cooperate and hope you stay alive. Don't make any mistakes now. Get this door unlocked."

Ace Holden did as he was told and then gave Duane his ring of keys. Ann went to the safe, consulted a slip of paper from her pocket and spun the dial right and left. There was a confused murmur of voices from the hallway outside the closed door.

"What's going on?" they heard.

"He's got Ace in there. He's going to arrest him. Didn't you hear him say he was a Ranger?"

"Ranger? Then Smith will—Oh no."

Ann got the safe open. There were a couple of tin dispatch boxes inside. When she opened the first one it was full of money, mostly bills and ten and twenty dollar gold pieces. She just turned that out on the table to see if there were papers underneath. There weren't and she left the money where it had fallen.

The second box was locked, but one of Ace Holden's keys opened it. This one was full of legal papers, notebooks, envelopes, and the like. She started to dig into the pile.

"Better hurry up," Duane said. "I don't want that crowd to get any crazy ideas."

"They haven't got the guts, darling," Ann said. "Besides, it'll only take a minute to find what I want."

Buck Duane went to the door and cracked it open. The men in the hallway fell over each others' feet backing out of the hall into the bar again.

"You're making a mistake, Ranger," Ace Holden said behind Duane's back. "I'm not the one you want."

There was a sudden crashing shot that sounded like a cannon in the small office. Buck whirled to see Ace Holden standing with a dazed and uncomprehending look on his face while blood poured out to stain his shirt front over the heart. Ann had fired her big forty-four caliber derringer into him at a range of about two feet. He was dead before he hit the floor.

Ann Mills looked from the body to Duane.

"He went for his gun," Ann said. "When your back was turned. He grabbed for a hidden gun. At least I couldn't take a chance it was anything else. He'd have shot you in the back."

"I needed that man for a witness," Duane said. "Why couldn't you have just winged him?"

He knelt over Holden's body and searched. There was a pearl-handled thirty-two rimfire in a belt holster right at the small of his back. He could have decided to try for it, but Duane began to wonder. It wasn't like Ace Holden.

"We've got to hurry," Ann reminded him. She shoved the tin box of papers into his hand. "There's your evidence. Enough to hang the whole Rainbow crew. Believe me it's all there."

There were loud voices in the hall. Duane opened the

door wide enough to let Ann follow him through, but not enough so the men outside could see Ace Holden on the floor. He had the box in his left hand and his gun in his right.

With a show of calm Duane holstered his gun and shut and locked the door with his right hand. He was betting the men weren't worked to anything like a killing rage as yet. He was right. They hesitated and then started back towards the bar once more.

Ann and Duane walked down the hall in the opposite direction towards the rear door of the building.

There was a sudden thunder of fast running ponies in the main street of town, and a wild burst of yelling. It sounded to the Ranger as if at least a couple of dozen riders were coming hell bent for leather.

Ann tugged at his arm.

"He's done it," she yelled. "Oh, damn him, damn him, damn him. He's done it. Run."

"Done what?"

"Sent in the Rainbow riders. Run, darling. Run for the horses."

She dropped his arm and ran like a deer for the shed where their horses were tied.

She didn't make it. Most of the riders pulled up their horses in the street fronting the hotel and bar, but one, either bolder or smarter than the rest came right around into the yard behind. He rode with the reins in his teeth, guiding his pony with knee and spur and waving a big forty-five in each hand.

Ann's running figure caught his eye, and he started firing both guns as he came. She screamed and lurched and went down in the mud.

Buck Duane shot the man out of his saddle. The horse went on to circle the hotel and rejoin its mates in front.

Duane felt as if he was running slow-motion like something in a nightmare, but it was probable that he'd never in his life moved as fast as he did right then. When he got to Ann there was blood all over her linen blouse. All he could see was blood and mud and her face rigid with shock, the eyes wide open and blank.

He swung her up over his shoulder. She still held on to the two thick envelopes she'd taken from the tin box. He ran as fast as the highheeled boots would let him for the shelter of the shed. Once inside he set her down with infinite gentleness against the wall. He unfastened the buttons of the bloody shirt.

She'd been shot through the left side of the stomach. The bullet had gone on out the back without hitting bone, but God only knew what else had been torn up by its passage.

For the moment shock, mercifully was sparing her pain.

He took his neckerchief and hers and made a rude bandage; after first putting a pad made of strips torn from her shirt over each wound. It might stop the bleeding. For the moment it was all he could do.

The noise at the hotel had quieted down, and Duane knew this meant there'd be a rush in short order. The shed had been built a long time before as a crude stable. The rear and side walls were of heavy tree-nailed plank. There were wide doors in front which he left open; and in front of the place the fairly stout remains of a rail and pole fence. There was a growth of weed and new brush on the right and rear of the shack where the ground sloped down to the river. In front there was almost a clear reach of level ground to the hotel, one hundred yards away.

Duane had his own carbine and a near twin from Ann's saddle sheath. He checked that both were loaded and sat down to wait. There was a heavy wooden horse trough in the small corral space outside the shack and he used this as cover, figuring the rustlers would follow a natural inclination to shoot into the cabin through the open doors and overlook where he lay. The night left the cabin and its yard in shadow while the lights of the hotel and street would silhouette any attacker for his sights.

Within five minutes guns were firing at the shack from the windows in both floors of the hotel. Duane stayed quiet and made no reply. If they wanted to waste lead on the heavy timbers, he didn't care to stop them.

Shortly after that he saw the back door of the hotel out of which he and Ann had run begin to ease open. When it was fully open he fired into the doorway. A wild yell and the sudden slam of the door told him he'd made a hit.

At that the snipers in the windows opened up as fast as they could pump the levers of their Winchesters. A regular hail of lead harmlessly pelted the old shack. Duane held his fire.

As he expected they made a try to get him at the very peak of the fusillade. Two men came in sight around each corner of the hotel and the four made converging runs on the shack.

Duane's first two shots knocked down the men coming from his left. One of them got up and came on again. It took Duane two more shots to bring him down again.

By this time the two from the right were closing distance fast. If they hadn't made the twin mistakes of stopping to fire at him and trying to run in high-heeled boots, they'd have been right on top of him.

Duane shot the lead man at such close range the powder blast almost scorched his shirt.

That was too much for number four. He swung wide of the corral and ducked around the corner of the shack. Duane came after him at a crouching run, but the man was already hidden in the brush and crashing his way downslope to the river.

The Ranger pointed rather than aimed in the direction of the sound and fired. He heard the sodden "thunk" of the bullet hitting flesh and then a brief thrashing about, suddenly stilled.

For the moment, that was all. Even the men in the hotel stopped firing for lack of a real target to aim at. Just then the moon rose and shed silvery light across High Valley. With that light to aid Duane's already deadly shooting another rush on the shack would have been suicidal and everyone knew it.

Buck Duane slipped back into the shack. It was darker here, but he could see Ann still sitting where he'd left her, with her back propped against the wall. The shock was wearing off now, and pain was tearing at her all along the track of the wound. Her teeth bit into her lip, but she uttered no sound except for an occasional low moan.

"Good girl," Duane said. "Just hold on. We'll get out of this."

Ann shook her head and spoke with difficulty. "You will. Not me. I'm dying."

"No," Duane protested. "No. I'll parley with those men. They'll have to let your brother take you out of here and treat you. No man would refuse—"

She held up one hand to stop him. "They might let him, but. . .couldn't. . .make him come. . ."

"Oh God," Duane said beginning to lose his control. "What are you talking about? Your own brother."

"You don't understand darling. Dan is my husband, not my brother."

Duane took that news almost as if it were a wound. He flinched. Ann looked as if she was about to faint. A little blood ran from the corners of her mouth. He wiped it away with a cloth, and she looked at him and smiled.

"You see, darling. It's all over now. You can't fool me about dying. I'm too close. Dan won't save me if he could. Who do you think sent the riders in to kill us both? He did."

The horses, tethered inside the shack, shifted and stamped. It reminded Duane and he got his canteen off Bullet's saddle horn and offered her water.

She shook her head. "Not for stomach wound, darling. Must talk before I die. I'm sorry, Buck. It could have been wonderful for us, if only—"

"It still will be," he burst out desperately. "I don't care what you—"

"No," Ann interrupted. "Let me talk, dear. So little time. If I hadn't married Dan—He is your Mister Smith. Ace Holden just the front to mask us. Us. It was both our idea. After he fled debts in East.

"I told him I could meet you coming out and I give you papers involving Ace. Take. . .attention from us. Ace was beginning to blackmail us. Time to get rid of him."

Ann held up her hand and offered the envelopes to him. "I'd hold out papers involving us. Nobody knew except a couple of rustlers and Ace Holden.

"It would have worked except there was more to it than that. Last night I knew I loved you. More than I ever felt for Dan. For just a little while I thought I could go away with you. Foolish. Had to pay for everything I've done, like this. Guess I knew all along.

"Dan must have guessed or maybe just suspicious. He sent the Rainbow riders in to kill us both."

Suddenly Ann's eyes widened and her right hand flashed up with the derringer. She fired so close to Duane's face that he felt the powder burn. The man who had sneaked up to the shack door while Buck Duane was distracted took the bullet in his heart and fell backwards out the door.

The shock and action was too much for Ann Mills.

"Everybody gets a chance at one decent thing," she said.

Then her body heaved and a rush of blood came out of her mouth. Duane reached out to catch her, but she slipped sideways, utterly limp. In seconds he was holding only a lifeless body.

For a long moment there was absolute silence while Buck Duane looked at the pale, dead face of the woman who had loved him so briefly and so well.

Then the Ranger reloaded all his guns. He was going to get out of the shack and go up to the hotel and kill every man he found inside. For the first time, Buck Duane wanted to kill, to wipe out everyone who'd been a part of this terrible thing.

His own safety didn't matter any more, or his duty as a Ranger. "If I wait for them," he thought, "sooner or later they'll think to burn me out. They won't expect me to come up there. I'll go down through the brush and under cover of the river bank till I can cut up to the street. Half of them will die before they even know I'm there." It was the route he'd planned to use for escape from the valley before Ann was hit. Duane gathered himself for action.

It was then that the silence was shattered. There were riders pouring into town from the north and west. Rifle, pistol and shotgun fire broke out on the far side of the hotel from him. He could hear men yell and scream in pain, and then it was over.

A voice called out from the hotel: "You can come up, Ranger. The rustlers are dead or taken. Come up, and bring the woman with you."

Buck Duane brought her, lying limp and dead in his arms.

The new force were the valley ranchers and their hands. When the fighting started only one person in town had kept her head. That was Sally Burke. She'd saddled her horse and ridden for help. Most of the men were at a meeting in respect to the dead Bill Bass. The minister was holding services in the Bass ranch house only a few miles out of town.

When they heard the news, the men forgot their fears in a burst of desperate resolve and poured into town to rescue the Ranger and shoot it out with the rustlers regardless of the cost. They'd hardly dared to hope that Duane would still be alive.

"Where's Doctor Mills?" the Ranger asked, dry-eyed and hard.

"He rode out of town as we rode in," someone said. "He must have heard us coming. Kind of strange at that for a Doc to run from wounded men."

"He's your Mr. Smith," Duane said, "and he knows I've got the truth. I'll get him for you."

"He's gone to kill the river," said a voice that hushed the rest.

"He's riding to his death," Duane said. "Somebody fetch the horses up from the shack. I know where he's heading, and I'll bring him back. Don't worry about your river. He can't do the job alone. Just clean things up here, and wait for me."

Duane drove his horses without mercy all that night. At dawn he passed the Rainbow ranch without anyone trying to stop him. The men were dead or prisoners in town. The doctor had gone by a little before, a Mexican serving woman told him.

"He ride up big cow road."

That would be the rustler's trail.

Duane rode after him. He had three mounts, counting Ann's fine bay mare and he'd been shifting from one to the other all night. They were still fresh. He'd come up to Doctor Mills sometime that day, and when he did the doctor was a dead man. No trial for this one. No prison. No fast death by the spine-cracking hangman's rope. "I'll gut shoot him as she was shot," Duane told himself. "And then I'll stand and watch him die." Duane had never felt like this before. The old, cold knot in his guts was a flaming hot coal now. He burned with the need for vengeance in a way that it would frighten him to remember later on.

The morning sun came up, brassy hot, before Duane came to the rustler's pass. By its rays Duane saw horses and a standing figure right at the mouth of the pass. He took out his field glasses for a look. Then the figure which had been so tense relaxed and slumped in the saddle.

When he rode up, old Lefty Wilder was sitting on a rock smoking his stub of a pipe and watching his mustang pony graze with the doctor's big black stallion.

Doctor Dan Mills—Mister Smith—lay just where the bullet that pulverized his heart had knocked him out of the saddle. He did not look graceful or important or deadly any more.

"I kind of thought ye'd be along, bub," Lefty Wilder said and spat towards the corpse. "Been watching this place since we said good-by before."

Duane got off his horse and sat down.

"I wanted that one for myself," he said through dry

lips. "I needed that one."

"Better that I got him then," Lefty Wilder said. "Man gets no good from a personal shooting.

"I figgered ye and the young lady would stir up a mess down there when I seen ye together. After that somebody'd be along to blow the river or to save his own neck, and he'd be the one you'd want most of all. So I figgered to wait here and sort of persuade him to linger till you came. This feller tried for his gun."

Buck Duane got his canteen and drank some water. The canvas case showed a stain of Ann Mills' blood where he had held it gently to her mouth.

"The young lady's dead, old-timer," Duane said in a voice hoarse with emotion.

"Lucky fer this rider he saw me first," Lefty Wilder said with understanding. He got off the rock and whistled to his mustang. When the pony trotted over, the old man got on his back.

"I know," he said in farewell. "Sometimes a man just needs to be alone."

Lefty Wilder left Buck Duane with the body of the man Captain MacNelly had sent him to find.

THE LONG TRAIL TO NOWHERE

I

The Ranger captain's face was stern. "It's trouble, Buck," MacNelly said. "Bad trouble—like a wound that can bleed this whole State of Texas white, unless we manage to stop it in time."

Buck Duane had no doubt now of the importance of the mission he was being given.

The San Antonio office of the Texas Rangers was not an important-looking building. It was just another one-story adobe, not far from the historic Alamo on a street of saloons, gunsmiths' and saddlers' shops, wooden sidewalks and false fronts; all blanketed this day by searing Texas sun and all-pervading, wind-driven dust.

To a casual observer, MacNelly was as undistinguished-looking as the street itself. A wiry little man, all rawhide and spring steel, he wore no uniform or insignia of rank. His trousers were old and tucked into a pair of soft, high-heeled boots. He wore a leather jacket over a faded blue denim shirt and a knotted silk kerchief served both for tie and mask against trail dust and winter wind. The heavy revolvers belted around his waist were no different from those worn by a hundred casual passers-by in the street outside.

Only the eyes—keen, questing, intelligent, determined eyes—marked him as a leader among strong and passionate men. They were a sign of command far more meaningful than tailored cloth or epaulets could have been for a lesser man.

MacNelly sat behind a plain oak table upon which a map of West Texas had been spread out and pointed to it with one sun-browned hand.

"There it is," he said, and indicated a line that had been drawn in with ink. "That's the new cattle drive found and marked by Charlie Goodnight and Ollie Loving back in sixty-six. You notice how it swings south and west of the Llano Estacado to avoid the worst of the Indian war parties of those days, and then goes north roughly along the line of the Pecos River all the way to Colorado. Much of that route is in New Mexico Territory and no concern of ours, but the first few hundred miles from Port Concho are very much our business. That's where the trouble is."

"I see," Buck Duane said, leaning forward to follow the captain's finger.

Duane was a tall man and a quiet man, yet with the deadly quiet of a Vesuvius in the instant before eruption. His eyes matched the captain's, his frame was spare and powerful, his hands long fingered and graceful. This was a man forever tensed and ready for instant action, yet with the soft-spoken ease of one fully assured of his own ability to handle any crisis.

He wore the heavy shirt and woolen pants, the high boots and pointed, wide-brimmed Stetson hat of the frontiersman. His two guns hung low and were tied down to the leg to make possible a fast and deadly draw in emergency.

"Maybe you do see," Captain MacNelly said. "Let me go over it anyway. Rustlers have been raiding the ranchers near the start of the trail. Herds waiting to go north have been hit just before the start. Others have left Fort Concho and never been heard of again. It's rustling combined with raiding on a big scale—a very big scale. Unless we can stop it, that whole trail north will be unusable. The ranchers out there will be left with no market for their steers."

"Can't you cut off the market for the stolen stock and break up the whole operation that way?" Duane asked.

"We could," the Captain said, "except that we don't know where the market is. The stolen steers and horses go roughly south and west into some of the wildest country and the face of the earth. That much we know. What we don't know is where they come out again or who sells them on the other end. That's going to be your assignment this time, to find out."

Duane looked at the map. "That won't be much help," he said quizically. It was a statement of fact. Except for a few entries bracketed with question marks, that part of the map was a blank.

"You'll have to fill in most of those blanks for yourself and us," Captain MacNelly agreed. "Most of the area there was Commanche country—that and Comanchero. Up till the last few years no white man could keep his hair for a week in there unless he was Comanchero and renegade. The Indians and renegades brought their war parties east along the secret trails through the Staked Plains.

"They took their booty and captives back the same way to bases we haven't found to this day. Forty years ago it was big business. Caravans of booty and slave buyers came up from Mexico to buy and go South again. The Comancheros were white renegades who rode with the redskins."

"Could they be at the bottom of this?"

"Not likely, Buck. That was a long time ago. The army broke up the trade back before the War. Most of the Comancheros were killed then. A few took their money to Mexico. Some may have stayed with the Indians. I don't envy them. Most are dead by now."

"Yes," Duane said, "but I'll have to go into their country anyhow."

"That's right. I hate to ask you, and the Lord knows what you'll find there. We've suspected the old Comanchero trails were being used by this rustler outfit. The trouble is, we can't find any trace of herds that size appearing in Mexico. It's not a matter of a few moseyhorns. Steers by the thousand and horses too are going somewhere. There'd have to be a trace if it was into Northern Mexico."

"It seems likely, Captain. Well, there's just one way to find out. I'll have to join up with the rustlers and go with them on a drive. If I live—and I think I will—I'll get back to you."

"I know you will," the Ranger officer said. "Just try not to take too many chances this time out. In spite of what some people think, we're law officers first and last and not glory boys. Go through with the drive if you have to. Once we know the route and the market, we can break up this operation. It doesn't need a one-man stand."

Buck Duane's lips curled in one of his rare, warm smiles. "Right you are, Captain. You may remember I took all the long chances any man could ask for when I was on the other side of the badge. . .back when I was an outlaw, before you gave me a second chance to be a human and a citizen."

"It's a chance you've more than made good, Buck," the captain said. "You know I'll never regret the moment you shook my hand and joined the Rangers."

"Neither will I," Duane said. "No one will ever know how much it's meant to me. I'll do my level best to do this job for you."

II

A week later Buck Duane rode west across the endless, empty West Texas plains. Man and horse—his favorite mount, big Bullet—were like a single living entity, the glorious beast seemingly guided by the rider's very thought more than by rein or spur. The setting sun sent golden bands across a velvet carpet of prairie grass tall enough to brush the rider's heels and the horse's belly.

Duane rode at peace with the world and himself. His immediate goal was a cottonwood-fringed stream bank a couple of miles ahead where he would camp for the night. The eyes of his mind went further ahead than that, to the time when he would have earned the right to a ranch of his own—perhaps even a wife to love and a son to teach to ride and shoot and to bear himself like a man.

Buck Duane was the son of a gunslinger who had been a living legend in his day. Men said Duane had pulled trigger twice after a rival's bullet had torn his heart. His son had inherited the legend, the deadly skill with a gun, and the wild pride that had made him kill an enemy in turn and seek the endless exile that the outlaw gunman knows. Only a stubborn refusal to debase himself by a murder, rape and robbery and the faith of a Ranger officer had saved him from a lonely death as climax to a wasted life.

His thoughts went back long years to his first campfires on the outlaw trail when the ghost of the man he'd killed came back to make a horror of the dark.

Suddenly his attention was forcibly pulled back to the present by the sight of a thin whisp of smoke rising above the very grove of cottonwoods towards which he was riding. It was only a trace a less keen-eyed man might not have seen at all. Whoever built the fire had made it small, and used dry wood that would give out a minimum of smoke.

All the more reason for caution. Now that the Indians were mostly driven to the west and the frontier pushed on a hundred miles with them, an honest rider or settler was not afraid to show sign in these parts. A furtive fire meant furtive men—and furtive men were dangerous men. No one needed to tell that to Buck Duane.

He pulled his repeating Winchester rifle from its leather saddle scabbard, and circled Bullet so as to approach the camping spot from downwind, where no tethered mount or Indian dog would scent him and give warning.

Because of the cottonwoods and because the ground dipped down to the streambed, Duane couldn't see the campsite unless he rode right up to it. By the same token the people there could not see him, either, unless they'd thought to post a guard.

Apparently they hadn't, and this set Duane's mind more at ease. Outlaws or raiding Indians would have spotted him at once, but his trained eye and ear detected no sign of an alert. He finally decided the chances of an ambush were too slight to stop him from riding in, and pulled Bullet out of the tall grass onto what appeared to be a trail running close to the smoke. He deliberately let the bit and spurs jingle and his mount's shoes pound on harder ground.

As he had intended, the men around the fire heard him coming in time to look him over. When they showed themselves on higher ground, he realized they would not make a first hostile move. He grinned to himself. He wanted to contact men of the owlhoot trail who could guide him to the rustlers he sought.

The men who stood at the edge of the cottonwood grove seemed to fill the bill. There were only two of them and they were watching him warily as he rode up the trail. Their backs were to the westering sun, which gave them some advantage, but Duane was not afraid.

The elder and heavier of the pair was a typical frontier hardcase with a month's-long curl of black beard and a broken nose. His clothing was black and shiny from the undisturbed accumulation of grease, smoke and dirt. He wore a single holstered Colt and carried a double barreled, cap-fired shotgun sawed off for ease in handling. At short range this could be a deadly weapon against beast or man.

His companion was slender and much younger, in fact hardly more than a boy. He wore a broad brimmed, low crowned "farmer's" hat, a blue and white checked shirt, worn denim Levi's grown tight against his swelling thighs and an old pair of boots which must once have belonged to a bigger man. "He can take two steps before the boots move," Duane thought and grinned to himself.

The boy's gun was another matter. It was a beautiful weapon, carefully oiled, tied down with a rawhide thong, and with the plain wooden butt worn smooth from handling and notched like Duane's own. "He inherited that," the Ranger decided, "from a gunslinging pa. Just like I did my own."

He was close enough now that he pulled up his horse and held out both hands with palms open to show that he came in peace.

"Stop right thar, stranger, and git down," the older man called. "Who are you and where do you ride?"

The implied threat brought that old familiar fighting chill to Duane's body and mind. His muscles tensed as adrenalin poured into his blood. His arms and hands swung easily, ready to draw and fire. He knew he could kill both men without trouble, but some wild, hidden thing within him craved to put it to the test.

For the ten thousandth time he cursed that killer instinct in his brain and breast and brought it under iron control. He forced his teeth to part and his lips to smile.

"Let's all relax, boys," he called out. "I wear no badge and I carry no quarrel. The way you show smoke there, if I meant harm I could've crept round and bushwhacked the pair of you an hour ago."

The boy looked startled. The older man didn't. "Maybe you could," he said. "Maybe not. No man's done it yet, for sure." He let the muzzle of the shotgun drop to point at the ground.

"I come in peace," Duane said, and made an Indian sign well known among the badlands outlaws.

The fellow recognized it and relaxed. "Why didn't you say so?" he asked. "Ride in to the fire, then. We've meat and coffee but no sugar nor flour. Welcome to share."

"I've plenty of both," Duane said, "I left San Antone in a hurry but stocked up at a crossroads store on the way. Welcome to share."

He gave Bullet a meager ration of oats and then hobbled him to graze the tall, nutritious grasses. he left the saddle on his mount's back, but loosed the cinch a bit. He carried his rifle and saddlebags to the fire, got out flour and sourdough and made biscuits for them all.

All three fell to with good appetite, but the boy ate like a ravening wolf. Buck Duane figured he had been on the run long enough to find the days long and the rations short. His partner tried to slow him down.

"A meal's a meal and enough's enough," he said, half to the kid and half in apology to Duane. "No restaurant on tomorrow's trail."

"I didn't think." The boy pushed back his plate in embarrsssment. "I'll take less next time."

Buck Duane laughed. "I've enough for a day or so," he said. "Might as well eat. We're none of us headed for California this trip, I think."

"Oh, no," the boy said suddenly. "We'll find friends sooner than that."

His partner almost hit him. Duane moved to stop it. "I'm looking for friends myself," he said. "Friends with a loose rope and not too picky about the brand they drop it on. Had to leave the city a bit sudden-like, if you know what I mean. I'd aim to stay out of sight for a time and make some money while I did."

They all relaxed. "Ride with us if you like," the hardcase said. "Feller I know out here is calling in his friends—though I'd say it's guns he wants a mite more than ropes."

"I've guns at my belt," Duane said. "I'll ride along and see what pay he offers for them. Call me Buck," he added.

"I'm Bart," the older man said. "Just Bart. And this here—" he grinned when he said it—"is the Jackrabbit Kid."

"I'm not," the boy said hotly. "Jack's my name, but that's all. You're too free with your tongue, Bart."

"And you're too lippy with your betters, Kid," Bart said. "You run like a jack and eat like a horse. Your ears droop and your mouth never shuts. Now what's that but a jackrabbit?"

The boy sputtered wordless anger.

Buck Duane knew the hot anger and the nameless pride that surged within the youngster and would shortly force him to reach for the holstered gun at his side. If he did that, Bart would probably kill him—not because he wanted to, but because a confrontation had taken place between two armed males and neither would be able to think of an alternative answer.

"It's a name," Duane said, "and not a bad one at that. You might say it's original. There must be a dozen Pecos Kids, but this one means you and nobody else."

The boy was diverted as Duane had intended he would be. "But—Jackrabbit," he said. "Who wants to be called for a. . .?"

"Lop-eared, mangy, cactus-jumping varmint?" Duane laughed. "I suppose that's what you were going to say. On the other hand the jack's not so bad. He can outrun a horse and kick a rattler to death and his females love him. He's mean when he wants, but he minds his own business—and he's so tough you have to hit him with lightning to kill him. Not a bad name for a young man just starting out, I'd say."

Even Bart looked impressed. "By God, boy," he said, "I didn't rightly know what sort of a handle I was putting to you. I surely didn't."

The young fellow was obviously pleased and mollified. "The way you put it stranger, it don't sound so bad after all. Has to be hit with lightning to kill him. I never really thought of it that way before. What's your handle, Mister?"

"Buck," Duane said. "Just you calle me Buck."

"Don't you never learn, boy?" Bart reproved. "Out here you don't ask a man his name. Specially not a gunslinger."

The Kid looked at Duane with new respect.

Shortly after dark they smothered the fire and slept. It was summer, but each man put a blanket under him and slept fully dressed with his head on saddle or bedding roll and his weapons in easy reach.

Buck Duane lay on his back and saw the stars blaze like lanterns in the black immensity of sky above him. Far off a coyote yipped a call to its brothers, and rustlings in the grass told of mice and small creatures going to and fro. No larger animals moved so close to the smell man and cooked food and fire except for their own horses. Duane knew when Bullet came to the stream to drink.

After a while he thought again of the name, "Jackrabbit Kid" and smiled. With that smile on his face he fell asleep.

They were up at daybreak and eating cold biscuit and meat. By instinct neither Bart nor Duane would risk a fire for coffee. They saddled and rode north all through that day along the bank of the stream.

Around four in the afternoon they came upon an old man camped by the trickle that the stream had become. He was a dirty old man with a tobacco-stained beard and an odor ranker than a spring-wakened bear.

His teeth were broken and snagged and one boot showed toes through a rent. His only weapon was an ancient cap-and-ball buffalo gun with octagonal barrel and engraved lock plate. He called Bart by name and Bart called him Old Hank.

"Jerry left me here to p'int you fellers coming in," the ancient said importantly. "He's holding a herd by the spring in Old Comanche Draw. Ye're to lather them broncs going in, fer nobody late for the ruckus draws no pay."

Bart nodded. "I know the spot. How many has gone in, old Hairy Hank?"

The oldster ruffled. "Keep a civil tongue in your head, young Bart, er I'll tan your britches like I did yer daddy's long 'fore you was born. How should I know how many? This ain't the only road they riding in. You got any whiskey for an old man to warm his bones?" The question was directed to them all.

"I got no whiskey," Bart said. "Did I, I'd drink it myself."

"You want to trade for that gun?" Duane asked on

impulse. "Might be I could find whiskey then."

The old man's face lit up at the thought until a dozen years dropped off his shoulders. "Whiskey? How much whiskey?"

"How much is it worth to you?" Duane asked.

The old man shook his head. "I feared you'd ask that. No, I can't trade, son. Leastways not my buffler gun. This here's the last I've got. The last of my manhood I mean. Why, with this gun, I could shoot the eye out of a gopher, and name you the eye to boot. Ag'in the Cheyenne once. . ." His voice trailed off.

Buck Duane found a flask with only an inch of whiskey in the bottom in his saddle bags, and gave it to the old man.

The three of them rode west and then a little north of west. Bart had been to the rendezvous before, and showed them the way. Duane memorized the landmarks as they rode. It was wild country, only recently ceded by the Indians and still sheltering occasional raiding bands of Comanche and Apache.

The plains rolled endlessly to a horizon broken in the west and south by jagged peaks and long blue ranges of hills unmapped and unnamed. Jagged ravines, hidden draws and valleys invisible until a rider reached the rim, scarred the earth as if a titanic jaguar had clawed and rent the land. A thousand wild blooms and twisted cacti sheltered in the grass, from sweet wild strawberry to the sacred mushrooms of the medicine men.

There were still buffalo to be seen, but in a few short years this would be cattle range from end to end. At least it would be, Buck Duane reminded himself, if missions like his own were not frustrated by the wild and merciless outlaws of the border.

About noon, while crossing an apparently unbroken plain, they apparently came to the rim of a vast sunken draw which stretched away a good six miles to the west. The gash was a hundred feet below the level of the plains and a trail wound down a short way from where they halted.

There was a shine of water in the valley and green shade of cottonwood. The grass stretched deep and green, and Duane could see cattle grazing and two separate horse herds, or remudas, watched by riders.

There were men at the head of the trail down into the valley, at least half a dozen of them sitting at ease below the rim of the drop-off. Bart rode ahead to parley with them briefly and then waved his companions to come on. They spurred their mounts to join him.

Duane studied these fellows carefully without seeming to do so. It was always necessary for him to watch out for men who had known him during his outlaw days. The name of Buck Duane was a standing challenge to aspiring gunmen and established killers. To fight him and kill him would be a triumph that could make a man famous through the length and breadth of the West.

From long experience Duane knew that many would be unable to resist the challenge which he represented. He did not want to have to kill, but he wanted even less to fall before a backshooter's gun or that of a crazy kid inspired beyond his normal ability with a six-shooter.

He wanted even less to be recognized by someone who had known him as a Ranger. In that event every man in the valley would join in a crazy drive to shoot him down.

The outlaw, the killer, the gunman and the lawman alike lived only at the price of eternal vigilance.

Bart was similarly alert. The Kid was not. He rode with the careless innocence and friendly smile of a tail-wagging puppy.

Once down the narrow, winding trail to the valley floor they rode at once to the largest grove of cottonwoods. A rude corral of split saplings had been fenced off here and there were three or four rudely constructed log cabins. Evidently this was a more or less permanent headquarters base for the rustlers. The first part of Buck Duane's mission had been accomplished. He'd located, and was about to join one of the bands Captain MacNelly had mentioned. The hardest and most dangerous work was still ahead.

III

When they had put their horses into the corral and their saddles and bedrolls outside the fence, one of the rustlers took the three riders to a cook shack where they were given big tin plates of beef and beans, biscuit with blackstrap molasses, and cups of strong boiled coffee. They ate with healthy appetite—most especially the Jackrabbit Kid.

After they had cleaned the plates a tall, dark man in a fringed buckskin jacket, tooled leather boots and Mexican silver spurs came out of what appeared to be the headquarters cabin and walked over to them. His hat was an oversized Mex sombrero and the leather of his gun belt and holster was elaborately worked. He wore a close-cropped beard—not stubble but carefully trimmed—and his eyes were a curious light hazel shot with yellow like a cat's. Buck Duane knew him at once, but held his peace and gave no sign.

"My name's Jim Dancer," the man said. "I captain the guns in this crowd. This is Jerry Link's company, but right now the hiring's for guns—and I do it. Any objection?"

Nobody said a word.

"We don't ask a man questions here," Dancer said. "You might say we hire the gun and don't care who pulls the trigger. Only one thing. You take my money—then you take orders from me. Any man who doesn't, I tend to personally. Until I tell you so, you'll be my man and nobody else's."

He paused again.

"Be sure that's understood. Now as to pay. You get a hundred dollars in United States gold coin today. After that you share in all the money that this band will make—and I can promise you that will be plenty. Jerry Link takes twenty per cent off the top, and I take fifteen. The rest is share and share alike."

He shook hands with each of the three. "Go on into the cabin for your gold," he said to Bart and the Kid. When Buck Duane started to follow he held him back.

"I know you," he said quietly.

Duane looked him in the face. "Hello, Jim. It's been a long time."

"So it has," Dancer said. "Six years at least. I've been south of the Line most of that time. You hired to me, Duane. How much will you be my man?"

Duane thought it over. "How do you mean that, Jim?"

"I can't tell you now." Dancer's face and manner were eager. "Something big in the wind, and I need men like you that I can trust. Walk away from the fire tonight. I'll find you and tell you then. If anything starts, look for me. There's plenty in it for you."

Duane just nodded, but kept a serene poker face. When Dancer left him, he walked on into the cabin after his two friends.

Jerry Link was inside, seated behind a table counting gold ten-dollar pieces out of a buckskin bag for Bart and the Kid. He looked up when Duane came through the door, and stopped what he was doing while he gave the Ranger a long looking over. Link could tell a real professional from a rough like Bart, and the new man interested him.

The rustler chief was a big man himself—as tall as Duane but broader and heavier. Men said he could straighten a horseshoe with his hands, and he looked it. His clothes were made by a San Antonio tailor. He was shaved and powdered as if a barber had been after him and there were pearl studs in the front of his not-overly-clean linen shirt.

His eyes were more intelligent than Bart's, but there was a curiously strained quality about them. They were the eyes of the unscrupulous and successful businessman of all times and places.

"Hello," he said to the room in general, "now who is this?"

Duane just looked at him. "Call me Buck," he said.

"Call you Buck—George, Henry or Robert E. Lee," Jerry Link said. "I'll call you whatever you please, but I wish I knew who you are. You're not like the rest of these gunnies for sure. You're a man whose name I'd know if I heard it. I'll swear to that. You want to tell me?"

"Just Buck will do," Duane said.

"You must be real fast with that gun to take it so easy-like," Link said, with a halfway challenge in his eye and voice.

Duane's face became an unmoving mask out of which the eyes looked bleakly. His right hand came to rest only an inch or so from the notched butt of the gun his father had worn before him. Deep inside him something cold and deadly came to life.

"There's just one way to find out, Mister," he said so softly that his lips scarcely moved. Nonetheless, every men in the room heard the words and sensed the thing that spoke.

Jerry Link had no intention of fighting then. His face smiled broadly, though his eyes were cold. He kept both hands in sight and busy with the bag of gold coins on the table.

"Hold on," he said in a jovial tone. "No offense meant at all. Buck it is, as long as you say so. I'm here to hire men, not to quarrel with them."

Duane allowed the tension to hold just a second longer before he smiled and the whole roomful of men relaxed. Then he picked up his coins off the table and turned away.

Outside in the fresh air the Kid looked at him with a new respect. "I don't know who you are, Mister," he said impulsively, "and I'm not about to ask. That fellow in there was afraid of you. He didn't want it to show, but I could tell. You must be somebody like Doc Holliday or Curly Bill for him to be afraid. I'm proud to ride with you."

Duane looked at him. "A man should only be proud to ride with himself," he said.

"I can trust you, can't I?" the Kid asked.

Duane gave him a long, grave look. "Out here this side of the law," he said, "you mustn't ever take any man's word for that. You've got to make up your own mind to it. You have to learn to do that fast. You have to judge every man you let stand behind you."

"Well," the Kid said, "I trust you, Buck, whoever you are. This is all new to me. I was raised in Galveston on the Gulf of Mexico. I wouldn't be here except I killed a man." He saw Duane look at him. "Oh—not what you might think. It wasn't murder. He—he insulted my sister. You understand I had to call him for that."

"I understand." Buck Duane's mind was back across the years to the boy that he had been. Again he buckled on his father's gun and walked downtown to seek a man. Again he saw a body in the dust.

He shook his head to drive the memories away. "It had to be, I suppose," he said, "but still I'm sorry, Jack." For fear of saying too much too soon, he walked away.

Men in the camp rested or drank or gambled through the afternoon. Before dusk another big meal was served and each man got a tin cup of coffee and whiskey—half and half. There was more liquor for those who wanted to pay for it. Voices rose until there was a rowdy clamor about the fires. These were desperate and reckless men, and there was tension in the air.

When darkness fell Duane walked away from the fires out to the edge of the grove on the side away from the corral. It wasn't long before he heard footsteps and made out Jim Dancer's figure coming towards him. The gunman had taken off his Mexican spurs and wore a low-crowned Stetson instead of the elaborate sombrero which he usually favored. In the darkness Duane recognized him mainly by the familiar tones of his voice.

"What's on your mind, Jim?" Duane asked.

"Give me time," Dancer said. "I won't say I wasn't surprised to see you here—but I will say I'm glad. I heard how you called Jerry's bluff, Buck, so I guess I won't have to explain to you the sort of man he is."

"Mean and cruel," Duane said. "Greedy above all, and sometimes too greedy to be smart."

"That's it," Dancer said. "That's purely it. Right now he's fixing to try something real stupid. He's going to tackle the Old Man himself—the rustler king—the one who makes the profits possible. He can't win, Buck. He can't."

"That all depends on how and what he does, don't it—Jim," Buck said in his usual mild tones.

"This time he's dead before he pulls trigger," Dancer said. "He and any ranny as sides him will be coyote bait this time tomorrow night."

"So soon?"

"And how do I know? That's what you're asking, Buck. The Old Man knows. Don't ask me how. He knows and he won't talk into no bushwhack any more than Tuanah Parker and his red devils would. I know he knows, and he'll cut Jerry Link to worm food all for sure. Him and those who hold close to him. I'm giving you the chance to step out of that. I'll not offer it again."

"You're asking me to side with you against Link and with this Old Man of yours," Buck Duane said. He heard a whisper of sound where a third man stood behind him to be sure he never left the spot alive unless he joined with Dancer.

"First tell your man behind me to go away, Jim," he said. "I don't have to draw. I've had a derringer in my left hand pointed at your belly since before you spoke first. It's a .44 rimfire, Jim. Your guts won't stand it."

Dancer grunted, and Duane heard the man behind him walk away. "Don't worry, Jim," he said. "I'll join with you. This Link is nothing but a mouth to me."

"Then why the derringer?" Dancer said in relief.

"I just didn't want you to think any man could backshoot Buck Duane," the Ranger said. "I wanted you to remember just who I really am. It's best for us both that you do. Now I'll join with you in this fight. Not only that, but I'll speak for the two men who rode in with me today. Now tell me all you know and what you plan."

They talked for over an hour longer before going back into the grove to bed down for the night.

IV

Before dawn the camp was awake and the men moving according to Jerry Link's orders for the day. The rustlers who made up Link's original group were busy rounding up the herds of stolen cattle and horses and driving them up the hidden valley to its southwest end. Here there was a more gradual rise of land and another cleft in the walls through which stock could be driven up to the level of the plains.

The herds would be driven through this gap and over the plains to the west until intercepted by the drovers personally responsible to the "Old Man," who would take over the job. At this time also Jerry Link would be paid for the stolen stock at a rate previously agreed upon.

There was never any precisely appointed place of rendezvous. As Dancer had explained the night before. "That Old Man, he's a regular old gray wolf for smartness. If he named one spot to meet, somebody could lay an ambush there. So all he says is he'll meet on such and such a trail. You see?"

Jerry Link's plan was to attack the Old Man's band as soon as it appeared. For this purpose he infiltrated several of his hired gunmen among the drovers, trusting to the dust and confusion of a trail herd on the move to conceal their presence.

The rest of the gunmen, under the command of Jim Dancer, were to stay just over the rise of ground on the flank where the Old Man would not see them. At the first sound of shots they would ride in at a run to strike the enemy in flank and rear and complete their rout.

Strategically and tactically it was a good plan. The only fault lay in the fact that Dancer had sold out to the enemy before the first shot was to be fired. He had ten men with him, including Duane, Bart and the Kid, and all of them were in on the secret. On top of that, the main body of the Old Man's people were forewarned and on the alert.

Dancer kept his men much closer to the trail herd than had been originally planned. He saw the compact knot of strangers riding hard, not from the road ahead where Link expected them, but from the rear where they had watched the herd pass.

Caught by surprise, Link made a bold try. A spatter of rifle shots from his rearguard riders opened the battle. After that he could only fight.

The new riders came up with a whoop and stampeded the herd right through and over the Link riders. It was impossible to make a stand, and Link's men were run over or shot down in ones or twos almost before they knew what had hit them.

The hard knot of gunmen riding under the rustler's direct eye were another matter. Knowing they could expect no mercy, these fellows resolved to die hard. By desperate spurring about half of them got clear of the stampede just in time to find themselves in the path of Dancer's oncoming riders.

Someone in Dancer's party fired a shot and then both groups were galloping at each other like two Indian war bands, and firing as they came. Wounded horses screamed with pain. Men dropped the reins and slammed to the ground dead or wounded.

Duane held his fire. Gunman without equal as he was, he was still not a killer by preference. Link's riders were beaten. There was nothing to be gained by killing them, or by being killed by them in a senseless melee. If he could have spotted the rustler captain himself, it would have been another matter.

Link would remember the betrayal—and the name of every man involved. He would make it his business to hunt them down, and he'd remember the face of the mysterious "Buck—just Buck." As long as he lived, Link would represent a danger.

In the first wild charge, Duane did not see the rustler. Men from both bands fell. Others swept through. Duane whirled his horse in pursuit. It was then that he saw Link.

The rustler had almost gotten away. About two hundred yards behind the fighting line his horse had broken its foreleg in an old gopher hole.

Link was on his feet, glaring wildly and defiantly around. His Winchester had been torn from his hand by the fall, but both ornately decorated .45s were still in their holster.

Buck Duane swung Bullet around, and at the same moment saw that the Kid had spotted Link. "Get back," Duane yelled. He was sure the inexperienced boy would get himself killed. The Kid didn't hear him, but Link did.

Duane swung out of the saddle and ran forward on foot. "Fair fight!" he shouted. "Get back, Kid. This man's mine. Get back all of you. Fair fight and winner take all."

The other rustlers caught his meaning. He wanted a man-to-man shootout. If Link won, he'd go free. The idea appealed to their reckless minds. Two masters would meet and fight it out and a new legend of the owlhoot trail would be born.

To show his nerve, Duane swung Bullet's head so that when he dismounted he would have his back to the rustler for a few seconds. Ordinarily such a move would be suicide, and every man present knew it—but this was no longer a battle. For the two men it had become a ritual duel like the combat between Hector and Achilles under Trojan walls in the dim, barbaric past. If either man violated the unwritten frontier code, the watchers would shoot him down without mercy.

Buck Duane turned to face his enemy. They were on a level expanse of prairie overgrown with knee-high grass and surrounded by a rough circle of armed men. He and Link were about sixty yards apart. Neither would want to risk a shot at that distance.

Duane took the initiative at once by starting a slow, implacable walk towards the rustler. All emotion had gone out of him except for the cold, terrible will to slay. This man must be killed, not for Duane's own sake, but for all that he and the Rangers stood for in the world. Link was at once the enemy of Buck Duane and of all decent men and women everywhere.

To the watchers his walk might have seemed casual, but it was not. He was sure each lightly placed foot felt solid ground before he put his weight on it. His hands, which appeared to swing easily, were never more than an inch or two from the butts of his two guns. His eyes never wavered for an instant from the face of his enemy.

A lesser gunman might have watched his opponent's hands. Duane knew that the eyes would give first signal of the draw.

Closer and closer he came. He saw sweat burst and bead on the rustler's brow. He saw the man struggle to make himself walk forward in turn—and fail. Link's eyes became desperate.

In that precise instant, Duane knew himself the winner. He had won the battle to impose his strength on the other, and the thin, imponderable "edge" that spelled victory was his.

Link braced his spread feet in the ground. To run was suicide. He had no choice but to stand and draw at the tall, spare figure which came remorselessly on.

Duane watched the rustler's face. He saw the lips skin back, the left eye close and the right bore suddenly at his face. Without hesitation his own hand dropped and gripped the notched butt of the .45 his father had worn. His thumb pulled the hammer back as the gun cleared leather. His trigger finger tightened and he fired precisely as the muzzle came level.

He never saw Link draw, but he heard the man's gun fire a split second behind his own. The shot sprayed dirt where it struck wild.

Duane's bullet struck Link exactly over the heart. The impact of the heavy slug was like a blow from a driven piledriver in force and effect. The man's arms and legs jerked wildly like those of a puppet. His body went back in a sort of awkward hop and then fell lifeless to the ground. Duane slid his own gun back into its holster and turned to walk back to the waiting Bullet.

He heard the wild yell of applause from the ring of sweating, dust-grimed men. He saw the Kid waving his hat and shouting with wide-open mouth. He felt a little sick.

By the time Duane was halfway to his horse, he was surrounded by a respectful ring of rustlers and outlaws. They'd seen—and so been part of—a shootout that would be remembered as long as men rode the West, and they knew it.

"I never saw his hand move," one man said. "I swear I never even saw him draw. It was like the bullet came from the palm of his hand. That's what it was."

"That Link was fast," another said. "I seen him kill three men myself, but against this one he was like a child with a toy gun. He never had a chance."

"My Lord, Buck," Jim Dancer called out. "That was the finest draw I ever saw—bar none. The finest and the smoothest."

"You know him?" said a voice. "Who is he?" Others echoed the question.

Dancer hesitated. "Hold on boys. He might not want to say. Ask and see if he'll tell you.

"He'll tell me," said a new voice quietly, and a rider brought his horse into the center of the ring.

Duane knew the tone of deserved command when he heard it. He turned slowly and found he had to look up at the man who sat a big gray stallion with the ease and flair of another J.E.B. Stuart. He wore a plain black suit, a theatrical black cloak and a broad-rimmed black hat that looked as if it ought to sport a plume, but didn't. His boots were unornamented but of the finest leather. He wore one gun, belted high under his long cloak and black coat. It wasn't a quick-draw rig.

There was no doubt at all that this was the legendary Old Man, the king of the badlands outlaws. His face and manner showed command in spite of the white hair and the smooth cheeks of age. His blue eyes were restless in the calm face, but they looked down at Duane without fear or hesitation.

"You'll tell me your name," he said in statement and not in question.

"I will," Duane said without hesitation. Then he let it drop. He let suspense build until the men about him were quiet and held their horses still—until he and the Old Man were alone in a circle of waiting and of silence. Then: "I'm Buck Duane."

"I thought so," the Old Man said. "I saw your father kill a man with that same style."

It was impossible to tell whether the Old Man was speaking truly, but the very statement gave him standing with his men. It restored the balance Duane had moved with his announcement. Duane's respect for the ability and intelligence of this man increased.

"Ride out a ways with me," the outlaw said. "I'd like to talk with you, Buck."

They rode to the top of a small rise in the prairie where Bullet and the gray could graze side by side and where the outlaw chief could watch everything that went on.

The fighting was ended and men were busy rounding up and bringing back the stampeded beasts. The bodies of the dead were left unburied on the ground to be eaten by wolf and coyote or by the buzzards circling overhead.

The Ranger hoped, in the back of his mind, that the Kid noticed the bodies. It was a careless and disreputable end to a dozen outlaw trails that had begun as human lives. These had been men—and their fellows left them for meat to feed the big, stinking birds. They were as unmissed and unmourned as so many lizards trampled by the horses.

"You're thinking," the Old Man said. "It's not a usual thing for a man to do out here."

"Sometimes I forget myself," Duane said.

"You're not a usual man, Buck," the outlaw said. "You don't have to pretend with me. I know a fine sense of the dramatic when I see one. I am where I am and what I am today, Mr. Duane, because I have a natural and cultivated gift for reading men as others read books. Now there's a riddle I must read from you—the riddle of just what you are doing here."

Duane hesitated, searching his mind for the right answer to give this strange old man.

"Oh, I know in general why you're with these people," the Old Man said. "A man of your sort is forever on the run in the very nature of things. What I want is a good deal more specific than that. Why with Link's band instead of any other? Why did you side with me instead of with Link at the showdown? And finally why that dramatic duel back there? Much may depend on your answers, Buck." The frost-cold blue eyes fixed on the Ranger.

Duane looked him right in the eye. "That's a lot of questions, sir. I'll try to give you honest answers—not because I fear you, but because it's my nature. Actually one phrase will answer most of what you asked. I wanted to meet you and work for you—to ride with you, that is. I sought out Link because I heard he sold to you. It was pure luck I heard of his intentions. Jim Dancer knew me and wanted me on his side. I joined because it gave me a reason to ask to stay with you—and because I never for a minute thought Link could beat you."

The Old Man was smiling. "You tell a good story, Duane; but what about the killing of Link? Was that for me, too?"

"I wouldn't pretend to you it was only that," Duane said. "It was better for Jerry Link to die than to live and hate me and perhaps strike me in the future. That was part of it. It was a chance to win the respect of you and your men. That was another part."

He didn't mention his third reason—the desire to keep Link from killing the Jackrabbit Kid. The Old Man might understand that reason, but he was unlikely to respect it. More likely he would count it a sign of weakness in Duane.

The outlaw had been looking out over the plains. Now he turned back to Duane. "I believe you," he said. "You speak well. I've lost some men in this fight in spite of the outcome never being in doubt. I'll need to replace them. You can be one of those to ride with me. In fact, you and

Dancer can pick the others. I'll be glad to have you with me, Buck."

"Thank you," Duane said.

The second major step of his mission had been accomplished just as Captain MacNelly had foreseen that it would be. The hardest part was still ahead.

V

Once in control of the field, the outlaws moved with a speed and businesslike precision which put to shame the efforts of Jerry Link's men. Cattle and horses which had stampeded over miles of prairie were rounded up and brought back at a fast clip. They were then split again into a total of four smaller herds which could each be managed by a few riders.

The first of these trail herds moved out as soon as it had been formed. The others were each only an hour or so behind. To avoid the later groups finding scant forage, the herds did not follow in each other's tracks but fanned out on roughly parallel routes. A rear guard of picked gunmen stayed behind to detect and deal with any possible pursuit either by a posse or an Indian band which might have picked up the trail.

If pursuit had materialized, a single rider could have alerted the nearest herd which, in turn, would warn the others. By day a signal fire could do the job instead of a rider. Meanwhile the attacker would be ambushed by some of the most deadly fighters in the West.

Buck Duane found himself held with this picked cadre of gunfighters. It was a compliment, for these were all hardened frontier guerrilla fighters and gunslingers, and it kept him out of the dust and confusion of the herds—not to speak of the work of driving, feeding and herding cattle and horses.

On the other hand, it cut him off from contact with his only possible allies and friends. After the shooting of Jerry Link, Bart and the Jackrabbit Kid had attached themselves to Duane. They shared in the prestige of having ridden into camp with him, felt unbounded confidence in his skill with revolver, and firmly proclaimed themselves his friends and followers. Both had, however, been assigned to go with the second of the four trail herds.

Jim Dancer, who might have sided Duane if he felt it to be his own advantage, had been assigned as captain of the third of the four herds.

Each of these smaller units was handled by a captain who answered directly to the Old Man and six riders. Unlike a regular trail herd, there were no regular cooks or horse herders with these groups. The outlaws took turns at these jobs, and Buck Duane was sure that even a coyote would turn up his nose at some of the resultant meals. There was plenty of food, though no chuck wagons. Flour and other supplies moved on pack horses.

The Chief's picked group fared otherwise, and much to their advantage. Besides the Old Man himself there were nine gunslingers, of whom Duane was one. In addition there were two big tough men. After the first day Duane assumed they had been personal bodyguards to the Chief back in the East. At least they were blindly loyal to him, and to him alone. One served as cook, producing menus that included such luxuries as canned corn, tomatoes and peaches as well as a glass of whiskey for each man. The other was a horse wrangler and herded the remuda of spare mounts.

After a week of generally westerly movement, the habitual caution of the rear guard was considerably relaxed. They were now a couple of hundred miles from the nearest really settled country in which a sizable posse could have been raised and far beyond even an outlying ranch. No one came this way but Indians and men of their own stripe or an occasional lonely trapper. They kept an eye out, of course. It would have been impossible for such men not to have done so, but there was no real expectation of danger.

About noon of the eighth day the trail of the herds they had been following all turned due south instead of west. It was the first indication the Ranger had had of the direction in which their market really lay. No one had talked around the camp fires, and he hadn't dared ask any questions.

Their route so far had skirted the southern limits of the wild and empty Llano Estacado. Now it turned south and headed towards the spot where the town of Marathon, Texas, would one day be built. The land began to rise through a tangle of rugged hills and gorges.

Ahead of them Duane saw the looming ridges of what he knew must be the Santiago Mountains. He'd heard of this country in his outlaw days, though never riding this far himself. It was reputed to be savage country, "Man-killer mountains and wild beasts to eat your bones." If there were safe passes through, he hadn't heard of them, although the outlaw grapevine of hunted men would usually pass along all such information.

The Old Man seemed to know where he was going, however.

On the first day after the turn south he called together Duane and two of the other riders. Both of them were men making their first trip with him.

"Take a spare horse apiece and load a pack horse with four days' rations," he ordered. "We're making a special run ahead of everybody. The herds and the rest of your fellows will catch up to us at rendezvous."

The four of them circled the herds and went slightly west of south at a pace that brought out the best in their horses. The Chief kept in the lead. To Duane there was no trace of a trail, let alone a road, but the man went as surely and as steadily as if following a heavily traveled turnpike. It was obvious that he'd been this way many times before.

The rode straight for the mountains which reared an apparently unbroken wall. From a distance the mountains were purple spires marching together as if to bar mankind forever from some secret treasure to the south.

"We ain't going over them things," a rider called Louman said incredulously. "One of them old mountain men like Jim Bridger would be hard put to do it on foot, let alone man and horse. For a herd of beef critters, it'd be purely impossible."

The Old Man reined to a halt and spoke to them all. "For the first and last time I'm telling you," he said. "Whatever I ask you to do is possible. We don't climb those mountains—though I think it might be done. There's a pass only I and the Indians know, Persimmon Gap I call it, because there's wild fruit growing there. Fruit and sweet water and an easy grade to take the steers across. We'll camp there in the morning at as pretty a spot as ever one of you has seen. That's where we meet the guide who'll take us the rest of the way."

"The rest of the way?" one of the men asked. "Where's that?"

The Chief was in a good humor. Instead of letting his temper rise, he just chuckled. "You ask no fool questions," he said, "and I won't have to give fool answers. Where we go is nobody's business but mine just so long as I take you there and bring you back with your pockets full of heavy gold eagles.

"Now is it? Of course not. So all I'll say is we go through some of the worst country Satan ever made as slick as a hot knife cutting butter. We go places nobody on earth could follow us, and we ride easy all the way."

"It sound okay to me, Chief."

"It had better, boy. It just had better."

"Is this guide one of ours?" That was Louman.

The Chief pondered. "You'll have to know soon or late, so best I tell you now. Our guide is nobody's man—matter of fact, no man at all. To be honest she's a woman. Not only that but a young and handsome woman—and a lady, if any of you know what that is."

Buck Duane and the other two looked their incredulity.

"You'll see," the Old Man said with satisfaction. "Just one thing, though. I tell it so you remember. I said this is a lady. No man of mine can put hand to her—not the tip of a finger nor the breath of a word from his mouth. She's to be as safe in this crew as an angel in heaven. There'll be no whiskey issued while she rides with us. No chancy talk. No gambling round the fires at night. The men will wash, and call her Ma'am. Whoever breaks the rules I'll kill myself."

"What's so holy about this one? Ain't a woman a woman?"

"If you could understand the answer to that," the outlaw said, "you wouldn't have to ask the question. Two reasons, then. She's the guide. If she rides away we're lost—every man jack of us. And if we could find a way out, she's got friends in those mountains to see that we don't."

"Comanches?" Buck Duane asked.

The chief nodded. "And Apaches, boys. Crueller than buzzards and deadlier than snakes. Men who'd eat us for the salt in our meat. We'll be watched every step past the Gap, and if they turn hostile not even a memory of us will ever get out of here."

After that the men rode wrapped in their own thoughts. Duane was particularly busy trying to think out the mystery. A woman who knew this country and was guarded by the wild Indians of the mountains had to be an Indian herself, or somebody who lived with the tribes.

Yet the Chief has used the word "lady" and had obviously used it in the sense with which he'd been familiar in his original home. Duane had decided some time earlier that the outlaw had to be a product of the old pre-war Cotton South. Men of that stripe used "lady" in a special connotation that meant far more than "female" or "woman."

It was obvious also that this lady guide was the key to answer all the questions which had baffled Captain MacNelly and the Rangers. The stolen herds disappeared from sight of lawmen because they went through country considered absolutely impassable by the frontiersmen, and accordingly unknown to them. They could do so only because there was a guide available.

On the other hand the stolen stock couldn't stay in such a wilderness. Roving bands of Stone Age savages don't buy beef for gold. Somewhere or other the ponies and beeves had to come out again. At the end of this trip, if all went well, he'd know where and how. He already had one invaluable fact. Persimmon Gap was on Texas soil. A few Rangers could ambush the future herds there. Of course there were probably other passes going south. Without knowledge of the final destination, nothing could really be accomplished.

He'd hoped that by joining the band he'd overhear enough talk from the men to find out what he had to know. The Old Man had proved smarter than he thought. Apparently only he—and possibly a few trusted lieutenants—knew where they were going. The rest just rode where they were told. The men who knew the truth kept closed mouths.

There was no help for it. Duane had to go every step of the way with his band. He tried to think what he'd heard about the territory they were headed for. There had been vague talk of a range of mountains. The Chisos, he thought they were called. "Peaks that would kill a curly horn sheep," an old mountain trapper had said. "No roads, no water, no buffler, no beaver. Just rock all the way into the clouds. Nothing lives there. Even the buzzards don't fly over. They'd starve on them hills."

It wasn't an encouraging prospect. However, the old trappers were notorious for embroidering every tale. If the country was really that bad, no herd could get through—and the Chief had used this route often, by the way he talked. Well, he'd soon find out what sort of lady came from country "that would starve ary buzzard."

The campsite at the entrance to Persimmon Gap was everything the Chief had promised—ripe fruit, sweet water, grass and trees. The men, including Duane, ate heartily and slept well.

In the morning, when Duane opened his eyes, the guide had come into camp so silently as not to awaken any of the men. She was drinking coffee by the fire with the Chief.

The first impression Duane got was a slender, rounded female body seen from the rear. She was dressed in buckskin jacket and loose trousers that at once concealed and revealed her womanhood. Her hair was bound round by a blue silk kerchief, but raven locks escaped at the neck and over the ears. Her back was towards him and they were talking in voices too low to overhear.

A little to her right and rear an old Apache squatted on his heels. At first sight he was a bundle of filthy, shapeless rags gripping an ancient double-barreled Hawken-made buffalo gun in one brown claw. He had heard the slight sounds Duane made on waking, and was regarding the Ranger out of beady black eyes. The rest of his face was hidden by loose rags hanging from the filthy turban that both concealed and protected his ancient head.

The old Indian said something under his breath—or perhaps just hissed softly like a viper at rest. In any case the woman heard and turned her head.

Eyes bluer than a summer sky met Buck Duane's. He saw youth and warmth and the pink of blood under sun-browned cheeks. He saw white teeth and a high, broad brow and a firm, determined chin above the soft white column of throat. There was a spark of something intangible that leaped between them and needed no words.

Then: "Good morning, rider," she said. "Come and have some coffee with us."

VI

It was two days more before the first of the trail herds reached Persimmon Gap. The others were right on its heels. The riders rested another day before any attempt was made to push on. The beasts were rested, fed and watered, to be ready for what all believed would be the difficult stretch ahead.

In those days Buck Duane was constantly near Juana—it was the only name she gave. The Old Man had taken him aside the first morning.

"Seems like she's taken a shine to you, Duane," he'd said. "You stay right close to her. I can't exactly appoint you Captain of the Royal Guard, so to speak, but you stay just as close as if that's what I'd done. She fears nobody—and that old Indian is supposed to be her guard. You know what that amounts to. There's men here would sooner backshoot an Apache than spit. There's others too stupid not to take the girl into the trees by force if they had to. I don't have to tell you what men will do to a girl out here."

"No," Duane said, "you don't. Anybody tries it, I'll stop him."

"You do it boy. You do just that. Anything happens to that girl, we're all dead—every man of us. Dead and our skulls bleaching on a stick outside a 'Pache hogan. There's men up there—" he gestured vaguely to the south—"that worship the ground she walks on."

"I'll manage," Duane said. "I'll remember."

"See that you do. Kill a man if you have to, but I misdoubt you will. They saw you bring down Jerry Link and I don't reckon there's a man here to face you lessen he's drunk or crazy. If you have to shoot one, though, I'll back you all the way. My word on it, Buck."

Duane was sure that he meant it.

Staying close to the girl kept him busy. She insisted on inspecting every head of stock that was driven into camp, to "make sure that it can stand the drive." She spoke to the men of the need to stay close to the herd, not straggle, and leave all decisions to the Old Man and herself.

"Mind your own business if you want to get through alive," she told each group in turn. "If you see anything being stolen—even your own saddle, mind—you come tell me. It will be returned. If you go after the thief, somebody will be hurt and maybe even a war started."

"I ain't afraid of no Injuns," one rider had growled under his breath.

Juana heard, and turned on him with eyes blazing. "Then you're a fool, rider," she said. "Then you're a simple fool. There's proud and deadly men watching this herd and every man and beast in it all the way. The tribes in there fear nothing—and with cause. Offend them, and they'll swallow every man and beast of you like a ripe persimmon off the tree there."

The outlaw only spat. Buck Duane moved a step forward. "Take your hat off when you walk to a lady," he said.

That brought the rough up short. Duane's voice was gentle—but it had been just as gentle when he spoke to Jerry Link. The rider lowered his eyes and took off his wide-brimmed hat.

"That's better," Duane said easily. "Now listen, all of you. Any man don't heed what Miss Juana says to him, had better hope the warriors get to him before me and the Old Man do. They'll be ministering angels compared to what the Chief will do to him, and every man can bet on that."

There was no more open defiance.

Now that all the herds were reunited, Bart and the Kid had once more attached themselves to Duane. The three of them shared a campfire and put down their bedrolls together close to Juana's own camp. In this way one or the other of them was always awake and alert to guard against danger to her.

During the day the old Indian, whom she called Poco—Spanish for little man—was always at her heels. At night he melted into the dark, but Duane was sure he was never far away. The old Apache did not seem a very formidable guard. Even the top of his turban only reached to a height of five feet two, and he looked like nothing more than an ambulatory bundle of rags with two black eyes peering out.

Duane knew better. A man like this would have developed incredible endurance and cunning. "He can walk an antelope till it dies of weariness, steal the food from a wolf's mouth, and hide behind a blade of grass," Buck Duane told the Kid. "That gun of his is a Hawken, one of the most accurate ever made. It throws a two-ounce slug that'll paralyze a charging buffalo, and he can hit a sparrow with it as far as he can see one. What you think is a poor old man, Kid, is more like a one-man army—and don't you ever forget it."

The Kid only nodded. These were rough days for him. He was torn between an adolescent passion for Juana and a chivalrous resolve to respect what he obviously considered to be Duane's prior right to her. Duane knew how he felt, but there was nothing to say that wouldn't just make him feel worse.

The more Duane watched the boy, the more he saw his own youth over again and the more he regretted the Kid's presence in the camp. This was an outlaw band.

The men who made it up could never again return to the civilized world behind the frontier. Their lives were as certain as those of the inarticulate wild beasts with which they shared the wastelands of the outer frontier.

They had no pasts to be proud of, no futures to look forward to. Each night's lonely fire might be the last to warm their bones. They lived in fear and rage and unspoken loneliness, and they died by violence to the thunder of guns or the swift jerking of a hangman's noose.

He tried to point this out to the boy more than once, but without success.

"I killed a man," the Jackrabbit Kid said with a stubborn set to his jaw. "Whether or not I like it I can't go back. I can't let them hang me. I don't have any choice. I'm an outlaw just like you are, Buck."

It was the last sentence that twisted into Duane just like a knife. The boy wanted to be like him—or rather like what he believed Duane to be. In his friend he saw the model of the gunman, the calm and deadly slayer of men, the hero of the bank. Duane could not reveal the truth without jeopardizing his whole mission and breaking his faith as a Texas Ranger.

Juana saw the struggle within him and divined its basis. "The Kid is a good boy," she said one day. "I don't think he'll stay with these men or become like them. The West is wide. In California they will not know what he has done or care. He can go there and make a life."

"You know California?" Duane was surprised.

She laughed a delighted golden laugh. "I went to school there for, years. Surely, Buck, you didn't think Poco taught me to speak English! You can't have thought I was only a mountain Indian girl? They don't read and write, you know. They don't lead men or wear a revolver as I do."

She paused for a moment. "Some of them are very lovely, though, Buck. Perhaps there are times when I envy Poco's granddaughters the simplicity of the lives they live."

"Who . . . ?" Buck Duane began and hesitated.

"Who am I? What am I doing here? Don't ask me now, Buck. There's a secret, but it isn't mine to give away. Not now is isn't. I've taken an oath—a very solemn oath. My lips are sealed."

She looked at him with mute appeal, her face more serious than he had ever seen it.

"I understand," Duane said. "At least I do about the oath. I've taken one, too, about some things. I want to know about you, Juana, but I won't press you now or ever till you're ready to tell me yourself of your own free will."

They stood together looking down the length of the meadow where the stolen horses had been gathered. Beyond were the clean, high, sweeping curves of the mountains.

He looked at her and saw her breasts curve like the hills and the wind blowing strands of raven hair about her cheeks. He saw the long, sweet oval of her face and the incredibly blue eyes like chips of lapis lazuli, and feelings he had thought long lost rose up within him.

She smiled a special smile for him. "Thank you, dear Buck," she said.

The Old Man called Duane to his fire that night to talk to him alone. He poured himself a shot of whiskey in the silver cap of a leather-bound flask. Then he poured again and handed the cap to Duane.

Duane sniffed the whiskey appreciatively and then emptied the small silver cup into the fire. The flames bit the alcohol and danced a blue flicker where it fell.

"You made a rule," he told the Chief. "You can break it for yourself, but I can't. No drinking in this camp, you said."

"I knew it," the outlaw said. "I knew it from the first."

He waited for Duane to answer, but the Ranger only sat quietly. Experience had taught him not to talk when another man was probing or testing him. When someone tried to look into his mind it was better to say as little as possible.

"You're no more a run-of-the-mill thief and scoundrel than I am," the Chief said at last. "There's few can equal you with a gun. I've seen them all, and if you're not the best, the best is still not safe from you. Yet you're not a killer for the love of it. I know you're an outlaw, but something inside tells me you don't fit the role. What are you, Buck Duane?"

"I'm your hired gun."

The Old Man moved in anger. He wore his long, black old-fashioned frock coat buttoned around him against the evening chill, but under it Duane could see a clean linen shirt with golden studs. The Old Man's hands were clean and almost frail but somehow cruel like the claws of a hawk.

"Duane . . . Duane," he said at last, "I'd like to be your friend, but how can I when you make sport of me?"

Buck Duane still sat silent.

"When I was your age," the Chief said, "I owned broad acres in the Delta and five hundred slaves. I had a great white house and women, white or black, for every night in the year. I rode with Nathan Forrest before I commanded a rabble like this. I drank my whiskey from cut crystal, and I shall again. A man like you could go a long way in my service."

"I mean to do just that," Duane said.

"Good. Good. I'd hoped you'd say just that. But remember, Duane, and don't make sport of me. Don't mock me and don't betray me. Don't try to play your hand and mine. We play my hand and it's good enough to win for us all. I do the thinking, Mr. Duane, and all is well."

Duane gave him a long, level look across the fire. "You have a particular point in mind, of course."

"You see that, do you?" The outlaw brushed a hand across his shaggy white eyebrows. "It's the girl. The Indian Queen." He laughed. "It's Juana. I put you to guard her and she likes you. She'll have no one else. But she's not yours, Duane. She's mine. Oh, I don't mean to bed with. I'm old for that. Take her into the bushes if you like and she'll go . . . but never forget she's mine to guide my herds. Don't ask her to guide for you, or you're dead and your bones white, man.

"And don't look at me with your frosty eyes. I'm no Jerry Link to stand against you on the open prairie with fifty fools to gape. I've forty men to shoot you in the back. I've a cook to slip death in your coffee cup. Cross me, Duane, and you won't ever have a second chance."

"Now hold on," Duane said. "If I was the man you picture there you'd be dead by now. Or I could kill you were we sit. Oh, I now your bodyguards are out there in the dark with buckshot loads to cut me down. They'd never see my hand move or know a thing till you fell forward and the fire burned off your beard."

"And so?" The outlaw chief was calm enough.

"I'm your man." Duane said, "but never from fear. You've got something here that a man has to have if he wants to go out of the badlands. The name of it is Organization. I need it and can't make it for myself, because I never ran a plantation or commanded a regiment. As long as you have that you can turn your back to me as safe as if you had a sheet of steel under that fancy coat of yours."

It was a long gamble, and Buck Duane realized it perfectly well. He'd revealed himself as a thinking man, and if the Chief didn't believe in his loyalty, he was marked for death. No outlaw captain dares to tolerate a thinking man in the band unless he can be absolutely sure of his loyalty.

They sat for a time and watched the fire. Then the Chief took two cigars from the silver case and offered one to Duane. "Light up," he said. "I made no rule about these. I'm glad we talked man. I could tell there was something in your mind that made you different from the rest of them out there. Some of them are herd dogs and some are fighting pit bulls, but you, Duane, you're a man. Not only a man but a thinking man."

"Thank you," Duane said. "You're a thinking man yourself."

"Both of us know the key to success is this business," the Chief went on as if he hadn't heard. "It has to be organized. I set up my market first. I can pay the rustlers better than any market near to them. I handle stock in wholesale lots, as a merchant would say. I have a market and I have a way to reach that market where I can't be followed."

"Do you really need the girl?" Duane asked.

"You mean why don't I just drive through by myself?" the outlaw said. "You're a thinker, man. You tell me."

"Because she keeps the Indians off you?"

"That's one reason. Maybe it's the biggest one. I don't know how many Indians there are out there or how well armed. Still, I can't risk being cut off in those mountains.

"The other reason is she never guides us by exactly the same route. As many times as I've been through I can't be absolutely sure I could make it on my own. You'll see for yourself shortly. Well now, Mister Buck Duane, do you want to be my man?"

This time Duane didn't hesitate in his answer. "Yes, I do. I'd be a fool not to hold to a man who can do what you're doing."

"You'll not regret it. I'm generous to my men. You'll live well and die in your bed in a mansion looking down on whatever city you choose. You'll have children to mourn you and a bishop to pray over your tomb. Believe me, man, I can make you rich and I will because I need men like yoiu as much as you need me. Now go on back and find some sleep. We move out in the morning."

Duane lay in his blankets that night and thought of his talk with the Chief. Above him the stars blazed like lamps in the clear air as they swung their magnificent slow minuet about the sleeping earth. The air he breathed came clear and cold over thousands of miles of prairie and mountain and bore with it all the life essence of that journey. He could sense the slow breathing of a million sleeping buffalo and the quickened heartbeats of gopher and mouse and small scurrying creatures.

He knew the hunger of the questing lobo wolf and the exaltation of the mountain goat looking down over hundreds of miles of moon-washed foothill and plain. In the wind he smelled pine and oak and cottonwood and the acrid mesquite. For a moment he was part of the land and the land was part of him.

It was all of this that he was being asked to sell for a promise of gold and women and a fever of greed. He thought of the Old Man in his broadcloth coat and linen shirt, his diamond rings and hidden derringer. He thought of the mind twisted by greed for gold and power, and by the endless fear that walked in the shadows of both.

He thought—but he did not envy the Chief.

VII

The long column of men and beasts got under way in the clear, chill light of the next morning's dawn with a great sound of hoofs and rattling horns, and lowing of cattle and the neigh and whinning of hundreds of horses, and the shouts and whoops of the rustlers as they started the herd. This time they were going through as a single herd—all under the control of the mysterious girl who had ridden in out of nowhere.

Juana and the Old Man, with Buck Duane and a half dozen of the gunslingers, rode point to show the way and keep out of the dust and confusion of the herds.

The girl's horse was a magnificent beast of a breed which Duane had never seen before. Its body was a shimmering color just off true gold while the flowing mane and tail shone silver white in the sun. She had told him that it was called a palomino and was bred by the haughty Mexican landholders in the southern part of California. It was a spirited animal, much given to prancing and the caracole, and Juana was a beautiful and inspiring sight as she headed the long column up the pass.

The pace was easy. The Chief wanted to bring every beast to market in prime condition so that it would bring a higher price. Besides, with no remaining danger of pursuit, there was no real reason to hurry.

They came over the spine of the pass late on the following day and had their first glimpse of the country to the south through which the drive must go. Directly ahead, at a distance of about thirty miles, they saw the looming bulk of the Chisos Mountains rising like a monumental blue-green pyramid against the clear blue sky.

From that distance they seemed to be piled arrows of naked rock, though the outlines were softened and the peaks blanketed by more than a thousand varieties of growing plant from the spined, scarlet-bloomed strawberry cactus of the flats to ancient, wind-twisted Douglas fir at the peaks.

The flat plain under the mountain loom looked unbroken—but this was illusion. Unseen to the watchers, arroyos and steep canyons, many of them awesomely deep, slashed the sands and gave a home to mule deer, cougar, and other beasts. Antelope flashed their white rumps as they bounded away across the plains, and rattlesnakes and lizards uncounted sheltered from the heat under cactus or piled stone.

Some miles ahead and a little to their left a line of green from tree and brush showed the presence of water—the nameless stream that men would later call Tornillo Creek. It skirted the hills and poured its water down to empty in the Rio Grande.

At first Buck Duane thought that this must be the route they would take. An easy drive, he thought. Follow that creek and push the herds across to Mexico. Buyers could wait safely on the other side.

He realized then that this would be far too easy. It didn't check out at all with the need for a guide or with the elaborate preparations already made for crossing the roughest sort of country. More than that, it was sure that the entry of large herds into Mexico at this point would be known to the government officials there and they would have passed along the information to the Texas authorities and so to Captain MacNelly.

Sure enough, the drive stopped at the headwaters of the creek just long enough to rest and water the stock, and make an overnight camp.

At this point two bands of Indians came into camp under safeguard promised by the Chief. Apparently one was composed of Apaches and the second and larger group of Comanches. There was a ceremonial pow-wow with the Old Man and Juana in the evening with feasting, pipe smoking and speeches. In the morning each band was allowed to cut out a small herd of cattle and horses and drive it away. By an hour after dawn they were gone.

"What does it mean?" the Jackrabbit Kid asked Duane. "I thought all Indians out this far were hostiles."

"They are," Duane told him. "You can bet your hair on it. If anyone of those jolly riders out there caught you alone this side of the pass, he'd bushwhack you before you knew it. This is where the Old Man pays them off for safe passage through the rest of their country. If he didn't they'd be killing riders and stealing stock every foot of the way from here on out. Believe me, it's a lot safer and cheaper to do it this way."

"Miss Juana lives with them?" the Kid asked again. "I don't understand it. She's so sweet and all and like a lady from back home."

"I don't understand it either," Duane said. "She hasn't told me anything."

The Kid sensed the tension back of that answer and decided to change the subject. "Watch this draw," he said. "I been practicing. Ain't it good?" His hand flashed down to pull the big gun out of its holster.

"It's a good draw," Duane said, "for an East Texas kid your age. That's all. It's fast, but not sure. You couldn't do it like that with a stampede coming up behind and your pony going end over end from fright. You couldn't do it with a man in front and one off to your left both drawing on you at once. You're a showman with that gun, Kid. Out here that's not enough. You have to be better than that."

"I practice every day," the Kid said. "How long before I'll be good enough?"

"Never," Duane said. "Before you're good enough with that thing you'll be dead. You'll go up against a killer, boy, and that'll be it. You'll be a trick shot and an artist with the gun and a real killer will cut you down while you're still making up your mind to draw. It's not speed that gives a man the edge, or skill or fancy shots. The thing that means the edge is the desire to kill. The man who has it'll get you every time."

The Kid's face fell. He scuffed the sand with one boot toe in dejection.

"Don't take it that way, Kid," Duane said. "Outside of killing, the real gunman isn't worth a damn. He just goes on killing and killing until somebody a little better or a little luckier kills him. He never sleeps more than minutes at a time and never twice in the same place for fear of being killed. He puts his back to the wall all his life because he can't trust anyone he sees. He eats wild meat without salt and drinks alkali water and he's never clean because sand isn't soap. If he dies in the open air nobody bothers to bury him.

"You can go home. You have it in you to be a real man and walk the streets with your head up. You can make a life like a man and not like a lobo skulking on the high plains. Don't you see that, boy?"

"But Buck, if all that's really so . . . ? I mean, why didn't you? I mean—you are a gunslinger, aren't you?"

It was an unforgivable question, and the Kid realized it almost at once. His face reddened with embarrassment and regret.

Duane didn't respond with anger. "Suppose I told you, Kid," he said, "that when I needed somebody to talk to me like I just did to you he wasn't there? Suppose I said I thought I was trapped with no way out until after a while I really was? Sometimes a man gets a chance to make a choice just once. If he misses that chance, it may never come again."

It wasn't the whole truth about Buck Duane, but it was close enough. It was all he could say.

The herd moved out again the next morning, moving just to the east of the foothills of the Chisos mountains. It was far from a straight route, as frequent detours around the deep arroyos had to be made as well as bends to bring the beasts past the comparatively few supplies of clean water.

After two days Juana, in response to some sign known only to herself, ordered a turn due west. This aimed them right at the highest and loftiest peaks of the mountains.

As soon as the herd straightened out on this new route, Duane could see smoke signals rising in the highest peaks ahead. The Old Man saw it too, and questioned Juana.

"Don't worry," she told him. "Those are Apache fires. They're made by Poco's people. They just give the news of our coming and the word that we come in peace."

Later, when they were riding alone, she told Buck, "In the raiding days—not so long past at that—the Apaches lived in the high mountains. The Commanches were the stronger tribe and held the plains where we ride now. Comanche war bands going into Mexico to raid or to sell Texas booty circled the mountains to the east or west. Sometimes the tribes were at war and there were desperate battles. Usually the Apaches would try to cut off a Comanche party who had finished a raid and had guns, prisoners or horses with them. Sometimes they won. That's how Poco got his gun."

"You seem to be equally at home with both tribes," Duane said.

"I am," she admitted. "I have good friends among both and can go and come perfectly freely. They will not harm me." She sensed the intensity of his unspoken curiosity and added with a smile, "I'll tell you why. It's because I never tell the secrets of one tribe to the other. Because of that they both trust me. Besides, I bring presents to my friends , and I arrange for this outlaw we ride with to pay for his passage in meat and in trade goods that they need."

"Including guns?" Duane asked bitterly.

"Of course," she said. "These people must hunt and defend themselves just like anybody else. Just like your Texans do. These tribes don't go out to raid any more since the army posts were built north and west of them. If an American is ever killed with those guns, it's because he came in here looking for trouble."

The answer did not really satisfy either of them, so they dropped the subject. Bullet and the beautiful, strange palomino horse paced side by side so that the two riders could talk in low tones without danger of anyone overhearing.

"Buck," she said suddenly, "do you have a woman of

your own some place back there in Texas? I mean a wife? Do you have children?"

"No," he said without any further explanation, but she wouldn't let it rest at that.

"I don't understand it," she said. "Among the tribes a man like you would have been married long ago. The chiefs would have wanted to give you their daughters. The girls would have made advances to you till you could not help yourself. I think that even in California they would have caught you and made you a married man. So what is the matter with the women of Texas?"

"Nothing is the matter with them," Duane said. "Besides, don't be so lofty about Texas. These mountains of yours are within the boundaries of that state. That's why I'v—"

"That's why what?"

He had meant to say, "That's why I'm here at all," and had caught himself just in time. Now he changed it to. "That's why you mustn't say it that way. You're a Texan yourself."

"Oh, no," she said. "I'm a woman of this whole wide, beautiful free land men call the West. No one state is wide enough to bound me. I belong to them all, just as I am not bound by any one of the tribes or clans of the people here."

They rode for a while in silence, savoring the hot, spiced wind that blew over the plains. She was a woman though, and could not let the subject drop.

"You dodged my question, Buck. Have you ever loved and been loved? Be honest now."

He said only, "Yes."

"Do you still love her? I must know."

"No," he said. "There is no woman back there to whom I am bound in any way. How could there be? I was an outlaw before my twentieth year. Every man's hand turned against me. I slept in the rocks like a coyote. I was named a killer and it was a test of men's courage to try to kill me.

What woman could stand that?"

"Any woman who loved you," she said simply.

They looked at each other as they rode, and there were many things unspoken except in their eyes. When they talked again it was of matters connected with the drive.

The cattle entered the foothills, moving due west. Before them towered the great bulk of the central Chisos, black and purple and overwhelming—looking ready to let slip a landslide or tumble a single peak to swallow men and beasts in one vast gulp.

Juana led them through valleys and draws and along the suddenly easy slopes of mountains. At least once each day there was water for man or beast.

"Why through here?" Duane asked her one day. "If we're heading west, isn't there a trail from the north down that side of these peaks? Why go through? Or couldn't we have just gone on south to he Rio Grande by the road we were on?"

"If there is a trail to the west," she answered, "and I'm not saying there is or isn't, the Indians close it. No herd is allowed to go that way. As far as the Rio Grande is concerned, it runs through a gorge where you would want to cross. Both banks are hundreds of feet high, and no cattle ford anywhere. Besides that part of Mexico isn't where the Old Man is going."

It was the nearest anyone had come to telling him the things Captain MacNelly and the Rangers had to know.

One crisp mountain dawn a band of Indians appeared directly ahead on the trail. By their size and the size of their horses and the way they wore feathers and paint Duane recognized them as Comanches. These fiercest riders of the plains sat their horses as if man and beast were a single entity. The horses were the magnificent result of more than a century of raising and breeding.

By contrast the Apaches used scrub ponies—rode them to death and then ate them.

Juana insisted on going alone to parley with this band. From her manner Duane reckoned she had not expected the visit. The Chief came up to wait with him at the point, and he too seemed anxious and disturbed. Behind them the restless herds milled and gave tongue to their impatience to get on with it. The rustlers herding the beasts were hard put to it to keep them under control.

The girl was gone for almost two hours—and when she returned her face and eyes were both grave. After her fashion, she got right to the point with the Old Man.

"There will be a delay," she said. "I hadn't expected it his trip, but it can't be helped. There's plenty of grass and water in the valley where we camped last night. You'll have to hold the herds there for a few days.

"And why do I have to do any such thing?"

"Because the Comanches won't let you move out," she said flatly. "There's enough of them around you here on the high ground to wipe you out and your men any time they feel like it. And believe me, they feel like it. Only a promise to me keeps the hair on your heads right this minute. As long as you stay in that valley, nothing will happen—but you'd better believe what I say and stay where I tell you."

"I've a right to know what this is all about." For the first time Duane could remember, the Old Man had lost his air of easy command. His old cheeks were flushed with concealed anger and impatience.

"In these hills," Juana said, "only those who live here have any rights at all. You don't live here. I'll tell you only this. I have to go into the mountains to see someone. It's a matter of much great importance than you and your herds. I'll be gone only a few days, but in the meantime you have to wait here for me. Either that or be eaten by the tribes. You've no other choice at all."

The outlaw fought hard for self-control. "Well, if it's only a few days."

"Better that than forever," Juana assured him. "One more thing. I'm taking Poco with me. Also I want Buck Duane and the Jackrabbit Kid. You go get him, Buck—and both of you bring your bedrolls and grub for a couple of days. Take an extra sack of white flour and coffee and sugar. Get on with it, now."

"Look here!" the Chief protested. "I don't want my men going off into those hills, with or without you. If anybody goes, it will be me."

"It will be who I say it is." For the first time there was anger in her voice. "You aren't wanted where I'm going. Go ahead, Buck. Don't waste any more time."

As Duane rode off he heard the Chief talking heatedly. The Old Man was angry. Duane would learn more of the secrets of the mountains than the Old Man wanted him to know. Juana was firm, however. When Duane and the Kid rode back, she was still refusing to even discuss the matter further.

When Poco brought up her personal things, the four of them rode off at once for the head of the valley and the waiting party of Comanche braves.

VIII

Somewhat to Buck Duane's surprise, the Indians left them as soon as the trail twisted into the woods out of sight of the men in the valley.

"We don't need them," Juana explained. "I know perfectly well where I'm going. The rest of you are as safe with me as if you were home in your own beds."

Duane rode side by side with Juana. The Kid and Poco had dropped a little way behind. "Can you tell me where you're going and why?" Duane asked.

"Of course," she said. Her face was still grave. "The Comanches brought me word I've been afraid of getting for a long time now. My father has been ill. Now he's dying and has sent for me. There's not much time, and I must go to him as fast as I can. The drive must wait."

"Of course you must," Duane said. "But why do you take me and the Kid along? We would have been safe enough back there—that is, we would unless you've reason to think the Indians will attack."

"They won't attack unless the Old Man's a bigger fool than he looks. They'll take some beef and look haughty about it, but that's all. That isn't the reason I brought you, Buck. Father knew I was guiding a drive. He sent word that if there was a white man with the riders whom I could trust, I was to bring him with me. I can trust you, Buck."

"Yes," Duane said. "Thank you for the compliment. I won't abuse your faith. What about the Kid, though?"

"I know what you're trying to do for the Kid, Buck. Maybe this trip will help. I asked you to bring him on the chance that it would help."

"Which brings us around to you again," Duane said seriously. "I can't press you, but isn't it about time you told me who you are—and who this father of yours is? What you're doing up here in the first place? I know you're not a Comanche or Apache."

"Not yet," she said. "I can't tell you anything yet. Oh, please, Buck, don't make it any harder for me right now by trying to insist. It can't do any good. You'll know everything you've been wondering about before very long now. I promise you that I won't hold anything back when the time comes. Not a thing. Right now isn't the time, though. We have to press on as fast as we can, and just pray that I get home in time. There may not be very much time left, Buck. This has been a long while coming, but when a man reaches *lecho de muerte* he can't bargain or delay."

There was nothing more that Buck Duane could do or say.

The pace Juana set forced the horses to the limit of their endurance. The trail wound south and west and climbed higher and higher into the mountains. Sometimes it narrowed so that they had to dismount and lead their horses on a narrow shelf bordering ravines that fell away into dizzying gulfs below them.

There was no regularly marked trail—in fact, nothing in the way of evidence of prior travel that Duane could make out—and his eyes were trained by years of hunted, outlaw living in the past. Juana and Poco however moved as surely as if the way was paved and railed for every foot.

They made a dry camp that night with only the water from the canteens for themselves and their weary horses. After dark Poco made a tiny fire of long-dead twigs and branches deep in a cleft of the mountainside where it could not possibly be seen by anyone more than a few yards away.

Over this improbably small blaze he cooked their supper of fried meat and a sort of thick pancake cooked in a grease, and boiled a single small pot of coffee. They spread their bedrolls on a floor of solid rock, but in spite of this the men were weary enough to fall into deep and dreamless sleep.

Duane awoke once, well on into the night towards dawn. Juane was standing, wrapped in a heavy blanket, leaning against the wall of rock and gazing out into the gulf of darkness roofed by stars. He watched for some minutes but she did not move, and he soon fell asleep again. When he awoke once more the first gray of dawn was in the sky.

They were moving again before full daylight, and kept on hour after hour without any pause except to refill their canteens and drink the clean, icy water of a mountain rill. Horses and men began to show the strain but, young as she was, Juane was apparently tireless.

There was neither inclination nor breath for talk. Even the usually ebullient Jackrabbit Kid rode in silence, overawed by the situation in which he found himself.

Higher and higher they climbed on the flank of the great peak which Juane called "el Casa Grande"—the great house. The way she said the words they might have meant "the house of God."

At last, in early afternoon, they rounded a jagged mass of rock and found themselves upon a broad, flat shelf from the other end of which the path at last turned down instead of continuing its awesome climb.

For the first time all day Juana reined her magnificent

palomino, its mane and tail blowing in the cold mountain wind, and gave them time to rest and look out at the fantastic panorama spread out below their eyes.

As long as Buck Duane had lived and ridden through the West, he had to catch his breath at the view that spread before them. The Jackrabbit Kid forgot his role as outlaw and gunman, and openly gaped with his eyes round and wide and his jaw hanging open.

Even the usually masklike face of the Apache Poco showed traces of emotions which Duane could translate as love and pride. Only Juana looked out through tired and halfclosed eyes that hid whatever things her heart might feel.

They were on the rim of a vast natural bowl, as if God himself had scooped a shovelful of the heart of the mountain to take away for his pleasure. The ground fell away before them for at least two thousand feet, and the opposite edge of the great depression was at least three miles away.

All round the rim the jagged peaks of native rock rose up like the stone fangs of an old Aztec sword edge. It was as if each pinnacle of stone tried to lift up its tooth above its fellows in an awful content of savage pride.

Below the slopes grew gentler and the mantle of green vegetation came to clothe the rock and warm the view to something a little less savage than a crater on the moon. The shadows marched indigo and purple, Prussian blue and black into the depths as the westering sun dropped down behind the peaks.

Far, far down in the heart of this great, silent pool of savage beauty there was a shine of water where a lake bottomed the otherwise unfloored gulf. Duane thought he could make out buildings on its shore and the rise of a plume of smoke that came up straight to meet the winds that blew it instantly to nothingless.

Juane moved her horse a step or two until they were side by side. Her hand touched his briefly. "There is my home," she said.

"It's beautiful," Duane said.

"More than beautiful, Buck. It's home . . . home! We must hurry now. Don't worry. The trail's all downhill now and wide and clearly marked."

She was right. From this point on there was a pleasant riding path looping down the slopes in long easy grades. In places there were signs that rock had been cut or blasted away and grades built up and filled.

"Your father made this road?" Duane asked.

"Not by himself," she said. "When he first came here he had helpers. They made the road—with him of course—and the hacienda, the buildings down by the lake. That was a long while ago, many years before I was born. They're all dead now, but after they died he taught the Indians to keep things up after a fashion."

"Indians?"

"Oh yes, there's an Apache clan living in here. Poco's own people, to be exact. That's why we don't have any sort of regular guard at the top of the trail. Not even a snake could slithere over there without the Apaches knowing it. Though there's no danger of anyone coming up the mountain by accident. At least nobody has in all the years. He'd have to get by the Comanches and Apaches and then find that trail we came up today. I guess you could say that this is the safest place to live in all the West."

"Why did your father come here in the first place?"

"That's one of the things he'll tell you himself," she said. "That is, if he's still alive when we get home. I think he is. One of the Apaches would have met us at the rim to break the news if he'd died. They're very careful about such things. Careful and considerate among themselves in spite of what people think."

In another hour they were close enough to the lake for Duane to see the buildings Juana had referred to as the hacienda. There were several of them; some built of stone chinked with clay and others of the logs of the trees which grew in profusion on the inner slopes of the great natural bowl. All were surrounded by a breast-high wall of smaller stones and clay. There was a gate flanked by two tall cairns of stone.

The main building sat on a low elevation facing the lake and fronted by a broad verandah roofed by an extension of the main roof to the house. It looked as if it contained at least seven or eight fair-sized rooms. Immediately to the rear and joined by a roofed passage was a cookhouse. Smoke rose from the chimney in the quiet evening air.

"Poco's wife is getting us some dinner," Juana said.

There was a stable, and back of it a corral in which Duane could see two or three of the beautiful cream-and-gold palomino horses like the one Juana rode. There was no sign of the camp of the other Apaches she had spoken of.

When they were still half a mile from the gates Juana put her tired horse to a run and quickly vanished inside the big house. The Jackrabbit Kid would have followed at once but Duane held him back.

"Don't be pushy, Kid. She has a right to see her father without us crowding right at her heels. She'll tell us when we're wanted, you can be sure."

For the remaining distance they kept their horses at a slow walk, and indeed the weary beasts seemed glad enough to rest after their hard climb over the rough mountain trails earlier in the day.

After entering the unwatched gates they all, including Poco, put their horses in the big corral and saw that they had feed and water. Only when that was done did the old Apache motion them to bring their bedrolls and supplies up to the big house. An equally ancient Indian woman came out of the cookhouse and took over the supplies they'd brought.

She was probably Poco's wife, but neither of them showed the least emotion of being reunited.

"She looks happier to see the sugar and coffee than her man," the Kid said in a low voice.

"They tell me lots of wives are like that," Duane answered him with a smile. "It takes all kinds to make a world."

Just at this moment Juana came out on the broad verandah, which Duane observed was floored with slabs of native stone, and motioned them on.

"Thank you for being so considerate," she said in a low, sweet tone. "He's still alive, though very weak. He wants to see you both right after you've eaten."

"If time's that short, we can wait till later to eat," Duane said to her.

"Oh no. That won't be necessary. He wants you to be comfortable before he sees you, and he's sure he'll live until early morning at least. He says a man so close to death can't help but know. Sarah has been cooking for us ever since we were first seen coming in, so everything is ready now."

They entered the house through a forty-by-twenty-foot living room furnished richly. Some of the furnishings, crude but strong and comfortable, had obviously been made right here in the valley. Other pieces, incongruously, showed the craft of the Eastern or even European cabinetmaker. The same incongruity recurred throughout the whole house. A gilded and scrolled mirror of the Spanish type hung over a chest of mountain oak. Fine French and English porcelain was used to serve the dinner.

It set Duane to wondering. No mountain recluse could have chosen and assembled these things, much less brought them in over the incredible mountain trails. There was a fortune in fine furnishings here, even to his untrained eye. Duane had never before seen—let alone priced—such furniture and works of art and yet he knew instinctively that Texas held nothing to match some of them, even in the homes of the great ranchers or the Governor's mansion in Austin.

His mind found only one answer—yet he hesitated to admit it even to himself. Time enough, he thought, after he'd met the owner of these things and heard the story told by his own lips in whatever way he wished to tell it.

The food was simple, but deliciously cooked. With it

was served a bottle of mellow, golden Spanish wine. A fire was crackling on the broad hearth at their backs, and all three ate with good appetite after the journey of the day.

By the time they finished full night had come to the valley behind its mighty walls of stone. Here and there flickers of light upon the wooded slopes showed the location of Apache fires, and the stars hung like immense, radiant globes in the black velvet dome of sky.

Juana vanished down a long hallway while Duane smoked a fine, dark Havana cigar and the Jackrabbit Kid looked as if he'd like to try one of the same but hesitated for fear of making a coughing, spluttering fool of himself.

"What is this place, Buck?" he asked. "How on earth did it ever get here in the middle of the back of beyond? Or am I just dreaming?"

"I know as little as you do," Duane said. "We'll find out soon enough, I think. Till then it's silly to go making wild guesses. I'm happy just to feel this good food putting strength back in my limbs. That's something you have to learn when you ride the outlaw trail, boy. Never rate anything higher than a good hot meal. You'll know that for yourself when you've roasted grasshoppers and snake meat without salt, or made a dinner of raw lizard because you daren't light a fire. It's not all riding with the Old Man's drives, you know."

The girl came back along the hallway and beckoned to them. "He wants to see you now."

They followed Juana to a great square room with floor of polished oak and windows draped in velvet to shut out the night. The light was from a fire flickering upon the hearth and candles burning in heavy Mexican silver candlesticks before a shrine which held a massive golden crucifix.

A very old Indian man squatted on his heels by the hearth and watched them with black eyes. By the paint smeared on face and body, the feathers in his hair and the medicine bags and rattles hung about his neck over the naked chest, Duane knew that this was the Apache medicine man.

The room was dominated by an immense four-poster bed carved from ebony and teak and shrouded by a tester of priceless purple velvet and brocade of gold and silver thread. In the dim light it was possible to see that an old man lay there, his body covered by soft-woven Navaho blankets, and his emaciated, almost skull-like face resting on piled pillows. Only the eyes, as blue and as bright as Juana's own, marked this as a man and not a mummy from a thousand-year-old grave.

There were chairs beside the bed and they all three sat down.

"You are welcome," a remarkably strong and melodious voice said in slightly accented English. "To the home of Don Francisco Jesus Alvarez y Luno O'Brien."

The voice ceased and the dying man waited until the pause stretched out and out. "You do not recognize the name," he said at last. "Perhaps that is as well. Let it die with me and be forgotten as I wish that I might be forgotten and . . ."

"No, Father. No," Juana said with deep emotion. "I will never forget you. Never."

For the first time since Duane had seen her she seemed on the brink of tears.

"Better you should forget," the old voice said. "After tonight you will wish to forget."

"Not I," she said. "It is time to tell you, Father. I know who you are. Did you think it could be kept from me all these years? I know all your secrets and I do not care."

"Not all," the man said firmly. "No one can know all but I. That is why you are here tonight, and why I asked that you bring with you these men. You must hear my story and so must others so that it may stand forever as warning to all who would err as I have erred, and sin as I have sinned."

He paused and his eyes looked at Duane. "I'm sure that Senor Duane at least is old enough to have heard my other name. Senor, you know of Captain Oberon? Of Captain

Diablo Oberon? Aha. I see you do indeed."

Try as he might Duane had not been able to suppress a sudden start of horror and repulsion as he remembered half-understood tales of his childhood. There was no Texan in those days who had not heard of the Captain Oberon, most merciless and deadly of all the white chiefs of the renegade Comancheros. No one, it was said, had seen his face as captive or enemy and returned to tell the tale.

This was the legendary master of evil who had become a faceless horror riding out of the Staked Plains at the head of a wild band of red and white fiends to raid and burn and kill. For year after year his name had struck terror to Mexican vaquero and Texan borderer alike. In the end he had vanished in some horrible and nameless fashion that had made men say, "His master the Devil came and took him away."

This, then, was the old man who lay so still upon the great carved bed? This was Juana's beloved father? Buck Duane did not know what to do or say.

"You will listen, then, Senores," the dying man said. "There is no padre here to shrive my soul, but I must speak it out at last. You will listen—and if you cannot understand or pardon, I will not blame you."

THE COMANCHERO'S STORY

I was born, Senores, a grandee of Spain and Mexico. There is no better nor more noble blood than flows in my dear daughter's veins. How then do I come here?

I was born also with a taint of pride and cruelty that came to dominate the rest of me to such an extent that all the decent and human impulses were shut out. At an early age my sins had become so well known in Spain that the King banished me to our family estates in Mexico for life. My father wept to see me go, but spoke no word to protest a sentence which he well knew to be just.

It was not long before even the frontier republic of Mexico became too hot to hold me. Our family holdings there were extensive, but not rich. There had been a silver mine, long since worked out. The life of a ranchero was too tame for me. I gambled, blustered and dueled until my enemies were too many and too powerful for me to show my face in the Valley of Mexico.

Greed and arrogance drove me to the frontier and to the wild, mad lands beyond. I was taken and tortured by Comanches. I laughed in their faces, challenged their chief to combat and slew him with my naked hands.

The bloody warriors admired such exploits and recognized me as one of their own in spirit if not in the flesh. I was adopted into the tribe and soon gained the fame and status of a war band chief. Wild spirits—Indian, Mexican, and a few American—flocked to my command, drawn by the greed of gold and the legend of my invincibility.

In the war of Texan Independence I was Santa Anna's ally. When the Americans fought Mexico, I raided both armies alike. Neither Texan ranch and homestead nor Mexican ranchero, mine and village were safe from my raids after that. I sold captives into slavery, burned and slew. There was no crime or sin I scorned.

I used the paths through these mountains to raid and to bring home my loot. The torture fires of my braves burned where this house now stands. In my arrogance and sinful pride I cursed the name of God. Because of my education and knowledge of the outside world I became business agent for the Comancheros of other bands. I had allies among the merchants of Mexico and of Peru and England and Spain. I had business associates in Havana and New Orleans, New York and Lisbon and London. I was known and feared under a dozen names in the capitals of the world.

Yet always greed and lust and the demonic cruelty within me drew me back to this wild, God-cursed frontier of savagery, rapine and death. Or perhaps it was God himself who knew that I had grown too evil for the world without.

I thought that I had grown invulnerable—but, alas, no man is that. My last and bloodiest raid was over thirty years ago.

I had struck deep into the Texas settlements, and my band was rich with slaves and cattle, fine horses, weapons and trade goods. We came south and west of this very peak and crossed into Mexico at a point close to the place where the Rio Grande plunges into its wild ravines.

It was there that disaster struck. The Mexican authorities had been alerted by a traitor in my band. Their cavalry struck us in force when half our train was still in the river ford. American cavalry working with the Mexicans came down on the rear of our column. It was not a battle but a wild and bloody rout.

Some of my warriors, a band of captives, and a herd of stolen horses alone broke free. I led them in wild flight into the high mountains of northern Mexico. At first the Federales were close on our heels and there were bloody rear-guard actions in which the last of our wagons of loot were lost.

It was then that still more terrible foes appeared to harry the remnant of our band. The Yaqui Indians, sworn enemy to Comanche and Apache, came down upon us in force. We fought them off with heavy losses to both sides and fled ever deeper into the wild and trackless peaks. They came hot on our heels. The Mexican cavalry dared not follow where we went, but the clans of the Yaqui gathered for the kill.

Winter was on us then—and in those barren piles of naked rocks its cold and terror was magnified a hundred times.

We found a valley with water and wood. It was really just a mighty knife cut in the hills, but there was only one narrow pass to let men in and out. The Yaqui watched one end and we the other. This was journey's end.

We ate the few deer in the desolate valley—and the horses we had driven in. We ate our horses and the bark of trees.

Among the captives was a young and beautiful American girl who had been captured on her way to marry a frontier preacher in Texas. She nursed us like a saint and cared for us. She was alive only because I had saved her for my own vile purposes.

In the end there was nothing more to eat—except ourselves!

Shrink back in horror if you will, young men. There is an awful time of decision in which the lust to live will overrule all things. I do not seek to excuse, only to tell what we did.

In a frenzy of madness we ate first the prisoners, all except the woman captive, who was to become your mother, and then the weakest ones of our own band. I would not let them eat your mother and I was still the strongest of them all. They looked on me with superstitious fear. El Captain Diablo was devil indeed in those awful weeks.

Of us all, only your mother-to-be would not eat human flesh. She lived on mosses and small creeping things caught with incredible patience, and the boiled leather of harness and shoes. She grew thin as a skeleton, and never really recovered from those times.

At last, creeping among the rocks in search of food, she found a way to scale the canyon cliffs. Those of us who lived still—and we were few—followed that precarious way to freedom and fled north across the terrible and barren peaks. Some sickened on the way, and we left them where they fell to die. In the Spring, the Yaquis found the bodies in the canyon and decided devils must have come to carry off the rest of us. That place is still forbidden ground.

In the end a few of us won back to this place, and here you, Juana, were born. The Apaches befriended us and kept our secret well. I sent you out to be educated and brought you here at other times. You know the rest and can tell the Senores at leisure.

The old man's face was livid. His breath came in gasps, and he seemed on the point of death. One claw-like hand reached forth.

"You must forgive me, my child, so that I may die. Forgiveness of man I cannot expect. That of God I dare not even ask, but yours I must have."

"You had it long ago, my father," she said in heartfelt tones.

"No, no. You could not forgive what you did not yet know. My child, you are not the child of love. Your mother could not love me though I sought to win her. At last I took her for my own by force, and from that hellish union you became the fruit. It was at your birth she died."

"I forgive you, Father," the girl said.

"Observe, Senores," The old man went on, "the end of pride and arrogance and lust and greed. Observe strength drained and skill made useless and all violence brought down to nothing on this bed.

"For year upon year I lived on here while all my comrades died before my eyes. In all those years I longed above anything else to return to the world I had so carelessly cast aside in the days of my youth. I could not even hope to go weep upon my blessed mother's grave. I could seek no help from priest or church. I was forever outlawed and forever damned and this valley only a special hell that God had made to hold me. There is treasure here to rouse the envy of a king, and at any moment I would have given it all—to the last scudo—for a chance to walk a city's streets again as a man among men. But I could never go forth. This valley was my tomb. I was forever and ever cut off from all humanity.

"Go now, when I have died, and let my story be told. Take my dear Juana with you if she wishes to go. This house and this retreat and all that I have gathered here is hers. Do not seek to take anything hence for yourselves. The Apaches will stop you.

"One last thing, Senores. If ever it is in your hearts, speak to a priest for me and say I beg his prayers. Say that

I seek only a prayer for a soul that is forever damned."

It was all that he could say. The skull-like head fell back upon the pillow, and, though life remained, its light now flickered only dimly in his breast.

The Indian shaman pressed a cup of some dark and stinking liquid to the thin lips and the old man swallowed a few drops. Juane was weeping and her body shook with uncontrollable sobs.

IX

The Jackrabbit Kid sat as if paralyzed by what he had heard. Duane got to his feet and shook the Kid's shoulders until he had attracted his attention. They went out together and closed the door softly on that room of horror and of sadness.

Back in the big living room the fire had been built up to last the night. There were comfortable chairs and bottles of whiskey, brandy and wine set out, and a silver box of the good Havana cigars. The old Comanchero had lacked for no luxury in all his years of exile. The things that he needed had been bought abroad by agents of Juana and passed from hand to hand, from Mexican to Indian and at last to this hidden place.

Buck Duane would have preferred to be alone with his thoughts, but the Jackrabbit Kid wouldn't have it that way.

"Lord, Buck," he said, "do you think that old man really did all the things he said?"

"He said so, boy. Why else do you suppose he did that unless they're true? Dying men don't play games."

"If he did, I'm not sorry for him. All that killing and evil and eating his own men. I don't understand how a human being could . . ." The boy's voice trailed off in sheer horror.

"You better understand," Duane said suddenly and with an intensity that brought the boy up in his chair. "Don't you get it, Kid? Don't you see? You wear that gun and you ride big with rustlers and killers. You say you're an outlaw, and you want to stay an outlaw? Don't you?"

"I've got to, Buck. I killed a man."

"Got to, nothing. You killed a man nobody heard of in a town ain't even on the map. In self-defense too. What does that do—make you Jesse James? Not unless you want it to, it doesn't. You got your eyes full of stars and your head full of adventure. That's why you've got, isn't it?"

"But, Buck . . . you . . . I mean . . . Here I am and . . ."

"And a fine fool you're making of yourself, Kid, sitting here acting shocked by what that man says. Don't you know who he is? He's yourself, Kid, in another sixty years if you get to the top of the road you've picked for yourself. That's no two-bit rustler like Jerry Link, nor no business operator like the Old Man. In there on that bed lies the king of them all. That's el Captain Diablo, the devil's brother-in-law, the man whose name the murdering hill 'Paches use to scare their kids with. He's got treasure to buy St. Louis if he wants it. No man dared go against him when he rode, and now he's dying in his bed."

"But, Buck—eating his own men!"

"You want to be a real outlaw, Kid? Then you better be ready to eat your own mother if need be. You better be ready to anything that a man did and more—not for treasure and a castle like this, but just to stay alive. Just to hide in the rocks like a snake, boy, and freeze in the winter like a sore-legged mangy coyote. Just to know that no man on earth will hesitate to kill you if he can. You think about all that, Kid, before and go condemning an old man lying in their waiting for Satan to come pluck him off his deathbed. You hear me, now."

After a long pause. "You sound like you liked him, Buck."

"No, Kid," Duane said. "I don't like him. I hate his guts. His and Billy Bonney's, and Jeff Harpe's, and Jesse

James's and the rest. I hate them because the put glamour on the gun and a youngster like you don't see it till too late. I hate them for that, but as to that old man, I do something else. I understand him."

One of the big logs on the fire cracked like a gunshot and sent a golden shower of sparks dancing up the flue.

"I understand him, Kid. You think about that. It could be me on that bed in there. It could be you, less'n we both die in the rocks. You think it out."

They both sat for a long while watching the fire burn low and busy with their own thoughts. Sometimes Duane dozed, but he knew that the alertness cultivated through long years of living as a hunted man would rouse him at the slightest unusual sound.

So it was. In the time of deepest sleep, just before the flash of dawn ran over the rim of this hidden valley, he heard the girl's light step at th e far end of the passage and came full awake.

She paused in the doorway and looked at the. She had been weeping, but now her eyes were dry. She held her head up with a curious mixture of mature pride and childish defiance.

Duane came to his feet. Behind him the Kid slept on with his head on the back of the chair and his mouth open.

Juane put out her hand and then let it drop at her side. "It's over," she said. "A few minutes ago. He struggled terribly for life at the end, but he did not cry out."

She paused and looked at the Ranger with a mixture of doubt, perplexity and fear in her beautiful eyes. "I suppose," she said. "I mean, now, after what you heard, you'll think . . ."

"You mean," Duane said, "that maybe I'll condemn him and shrink away from his daughter. That was his life, Juana. You and I mightn't want to copy him, but I can understand it. It has nothing to do with you."

He took her in his arms and kissed her very gently on the forehead. It was all the moment allowed, and it was enough. She clung to his tall figure and wept against his shoulder.

Behind them the Kid slept on.

Late in the morning all three ate a breakfast of steaks, eggs and corn cakes washed down with coffee strong enough to stand a spoon in.

The old Comanchero's body had been taken up into the hills by the Apaches to be buried in a secret place.

"It was his wish," Juana explained. "Even I am not to know exactly where he is. For years he's been afraid that the descendants of the people he wronged long ago would find his body and desecrate the grave. To me this whole valley will always be his home—living or dead."

A transformed Poco in ceremonial paint and a white buckskin jacket beaded with sacred symbols had led the warriors who took the corpse away. At first the men had hardly recognized him when he passed.

"Who is Poco?" the Kid asked.

"That's only the name we use for him when we got out of the mountains," Juana said. "His real name is Vibora and he was the first of father's war chiefs."

Duane knew the name as that of the boldest, cruelest and most famous of the old-time terrors of the frontier. "I called him a one-man army once," he said. "I guess I was right, for sure."

"Have you always lived here?" Duane said after the Kid had gone out to the corral to look at the palominos. "I mean, what are your plans now? How will you manage?"

"That will be easy enough," she answered. "Father never wanted me to grow up as an Indian. You know I was educated in California. Besides that I've gone in and out of here for years. Years ago Father established bank accounts and business agents in Europe and New York and New Orleans. He has treasure here, buried somewhere.

"I suppose Poco will show me later on. It was only the least of his fortune. He established me as his heir and business representative some while ago. The truth is, Buck,

I can live anywhere in the world I really want to."

"Then why? I don't mean why come back here, but why act as guide for a rustler band?"

"It was Father's idea. The years had changed him, but he was still a bandit and a greedy one at heart. When the Old Man first got the idea of running his herds this way, the Comanches brought us the news. They wanted to wipe him out, but Father said no. He sent me with the war chief to make a bargain. We'd give him safe passage and guard him and guide him out again. In return he gave beef and guns to the Indians and brought in supplies to us.

"It appealed both to Father's greed and his sense of humor. Besides it supplied the Indians with things they wanted and helped keep them from raiding and drawing attention to this place. If we'd kept the Old Man out completely, others might have come after him and found out the secret of the Chisos."

"Where does he take the beef?"

This was the question that had led Captain MacNelly to send Buck Duane into the badlands in the first place. He held his breath waiting for the answer. When it came his heart sank again, for it took him not one step further.

"I honestly don't know, Buck. Oh, I take him out to the west over the old Comanchero trails. I know them all, and I try to double him around and confuse him as much as I can every trip. In the end I take him out of the badlands onto fairly open ground somewhere between the Pecos and the Rio Grande. I know he has buyers who meet him there after I leave, but whether they're Mexican or American and where they take the stock I don't know. There must be a changing of brands, but after that the beef could go north, west or south. It's never been any of my affair, so I haven't troubled to find out."

"What are you going to do now?" Duane asked to hide his disappointment.

"Go on back and take him through, I guess," she answered. "I don't really want to, of course, but I can't see any way out. I don't even dare leave the drive where it is more than another day or so. They'd be sure to pick a quarrel with the Comanche, and if they did, not a man of them would ever get out of the trap they're in. No—I'll see them through this time, but not again."

"Won't the Comanche be upset at losing their beef and the rest of the toll the rustlers pay?"

"If they are, they can guide him through themselves. Anyway that's what I'll tell the Old Man."

"He won't be happy about it," Duane said. "By the way, who is he, really?"

"I know that," she said. "I found out from some of my outside business connections soon after this whole thing started. His name, though he's used a lot of them in his time, is really Virgil Dawson. He was a cotton broker in New Orleans before the War, a blockade runner and then crooked contractor and scalawag under the Reconstruction government. When his deals began to smell too high for the city, he came west. No matter what he touches, he gets rich. Buck, I'm going to have to ask you and the Kid not to tell him anything of what you've seen and heard of this trip."

"I'll answer for both of us," Duane said.

"Thanks. I hope it won't make trouble for you."

"No more than I have anyway," Duane said. "I'm sure a mind like Dawson's will suspect you and me of all sorts of double dealing on this trip. I'll try to convince him it was just a sort of honeymoon, if you'll forgive me."

"That's what I wish it had been," she said forthrightly, "and well you know it. But all that can wait. My father isn't buried yet."

He took her hand and held it and a current of life and desire ran hot between them.

X

The following morning Poco came back out of the hills in his usual ragged garb, and the four of them left the hidden valley of the Chisos range. The ride was all downhill this time, and much easier on the horses. They could have made Dawson's camp by late evening, but preferred to camp on the trail so as to come in after daylight.

It was that night that Juana and Buck Duane opened their hearts to each other blazing Western stars.

Toward morning he told her his story—his whole story including the outlaw years and his present status as a member of Captain MacNelly's company of Texas Rangers. He assured her that it was only the Old Man and his buyers to the west who would be turned in to the law.

"Once he's taken and the rustling broken up," Duane said, "there'll be no reason to interfere with the Indian's life in this secluded valley."

When she understood, Juana was frankly delighted. "Oh Buck," she said. "Somehow I knew you were too fine a man—too strong and decent—to be an outlaw and a hunted man. Now I can truly love you."

When they rode out of the cover of the trees in the morning and saw the trail camp with breakfast fires smoking and the herds grazing in the valley, Buck Duane was ready for whatever might come. He knew that the Chief would never believe that he and Juana had not been plotting to take the secret route away from him. His mind simply would not credit that they had not.

Duane's death—"execution" the Chief would probably call it—must have been already decided upon. The only question in Duane's mind was when and how the attempt would be made. That it would be was as certain as that night follows day.

The way Duane saw it, the Old Man wouldn't try anything right away. He would figure Duane and Juana were in cahoots. If he killed one—unless, of course, he could make it look like an accident—he would have to kill the other, too. That would leave him without a guide.

Of course, he might figure he could find his way out without the girl. It was possible he could—except for the Comanches and Apaches. If their friend were killed, the tribes would come down on the herd like wolves.

For all these reasons Duane felt he would be reasonably safe until the herds were in open country and close to Dawson's rendezvous with his buyers. That is, except for the possibility of an "accident" or an uncontrollable rage on Dawson's part.

He had told a little of this to Juana when they were alone the night before—not that he was certain the attack would be made, but only enough to alert her. He didn't want her bringing down the Indians before he'd managed to get the facts the Rangers needed.

As soon as they were sighted a rider broke away from the herds and came up at a gallop. It proved to be Bart.

"Am I glad to see you, Boss," he said as soon as Duane reined up. "Old fancy pants has been like to blow his cork for two days watching for you. The whole camp's wondering what he's to hot about. That is all but a half dozen of his personal gunslingers that he's been talking to private-like."

"It's the kind of ranny he is," Duane said. "Always jealous of the other fellow."

"You can't blame him," Bart said, looking over at Juana. "Anyway, Boss, it looks like trouble. What I want you to know is, if it comes to a showdown I'm with you. We won't be alone either by the looks of things. His high-and-mighty lordship ain't too popular with the boys. Him an his bodyguards an' special grub an' whiskey an' all. Even that fancy half-Mex of la Jim Dancer come to me quiet-like the other day. Tell you to watch the wind close, he says."

"Thanks, Bart," Duane said with real sincerity. "Believe me, I appreciate the way you feel and you won't suffer for it. Not while Buck Duane can still pull trigger, you won't, and that'll be for years to come. I don't think there'll be any blowoff today. Keep your eyes and ears open and pass the word along I'll stand by any man who stands by me. Let the boys know, too, that we can bring the Indians in on our side. That should make them think."

"I get you," Bart said. "You can count on me."

"Fine. Get me a tally, if you can, of the men who ride with us."

The Old Man and several of his bodyguard of gunmen had started to walk out from the camp towards the little group of riders. Buck Duane and Juana spurred their horses and the girl waved a greeting. The rustlers stopped and waited for them.

A short way from the group, Buck dismounted and tossed his reins to Poco. If there was to be a showdown he wanted solid ground under his feet and both hands free. A couple of the herders saw what was up and started to ride over. This was the outlaw's chance to gun down Duane and seize the girl for a hostage, if he was desperate enough to try it.

Juana must have had the same idea. She sprang down from the palomino and ran out between the two groups calling out, "Hold on. Let's talk this over."

The big rattler came up out of the grass ahead of her, its wicked triangular head waving to and from on a thick neck and the rattles whirring menace. She tried to stop, but it was too late. The hideous mouth opened to show wicked fangs as the big snake struck.

Duane's hand blurred into motion so swift that no eye could follow. The Colt .45 seemed to leap into his hand of its own violiton and the hammer fell even as the muzzle swung level. With the crash of the shot the headless body of the snake fell back to lash convulsively at the girl's very feet.

She turned white and would have fallen except for Duane's strong arm about her waist.

The oncoming riders, the gunmen, and the people around Duane all stared with unbelieving eyes.

"My God," said one of the gunslingers. "It ain't true. It can't be true even if I saw it. No man living can out-draw a striking snake. It just can't be."

"He did it," the Jackrabbit Kid yelled to the riders and the world in general. 'He let the snake strike and drew and killed it before the fangs hit! No gun ever equalled that before."

Buck Duane put his gun back in the holster. It wouldn't be needed now, and everyone there knew it. The men behind Dawson were tough professional killers, but no one of them would face that fabulous draw.

"We'll go in and talk," Dawson said. "It's time this herd moved out of here."

All round the rim of the valley little knots of Comanche riders had come out of the woods. Watching the camp, they'd seen that shot. When Buck Duane stepped forward they raised their rifles and lances in salute and wild whoops sounded in applause.

XI

In four more days the riders drove their stolen stock down the last foothills of the Chisos range and out onto the comparatively open plains. It was here they saw the last of the Comanches who had watched their flanks every step of the way. Half-naked, painted and whooping young braves brought their ponies into camp at a dead run to collect the beeves, horses, guns and boxes of ammunition and supplies promised them for a safe passage.

They departed presently, yelling their contempt of the white men who paid rather than fought them.

With them went Juana and Poco.

She had protested bitterly to Duane. "I can't leave you alone, and I won't. That wicked old man is full of hatred for you. He won't rest till he kills you. I know it, and I could not bear that."

Duane had laughed and tried to seem perfectly unconcerned. "The rattler robbed him of his chance to kill me," he said. "There's not a gunman on his payroll that would face me in a fight after that. Besides half the men—maybe more—would take my part in a fight anyhow."

"Then why stay with that stupid drive, Buck? Come back to the valley with me, dear. Let's live and love and learn to know each other there. There is safety and peace for a time. If we want to leave later on, there is money enough to go anywhere in the world that we please. There. A woman can't speak plainer than that."

She kissed him passionately, and he returned her kiss.

"I can't," he said flatly. "God knows I want to, Juana. I must finish this drive, and you know why. I made that promise to captain MacNelly before I ever knew that you were alive, let alone that we loved each other."

"You can trust me, Buck."

"I know—and this time you must trust me. Go back to the valley and wait for me. When what I have to do is finished, I will come and tell you about it. I promise you that."

She could not shake him and she was too proud to plead, so she rode out of camp with the Comanches. Just before she left, she had a talk with Dawson and he made her promise to wait word from him and guide future herds through as in the past. Neither of them believed what they said, but this was a matter of form. As long as they had the talk there was no open break, and they were free to deal with the future as might seem best to each of them.

For Duane's part, he felt that his job was almost done. He was sincere when he told Juana he didn't think the Chief would dare make an open attempt to have him killed. The odds were too evenly balanced if fighting broke out in the band. Besides, no matter who won such a fight, it would ruin the Old Man's whole carefully worked out setup.

It was more likely Dawson would wait to see if his suspicions were correct. If he could not get through the Chisos route another time, then he might hire men to seek out and kill Duane.

Duane planned to finish the drive. Once he knew who the buyers were, he'd head back for the valley. Juana said the Indians would let him through. Then they'd go back to Texas together and he could give Captain MacNelly all the facts he needed to keep Dawson or any other rustler from using that route again. The mountain Indians needn't be bothered as long as they refrained from raiding down into Texas or otherwise provoking official reprisals.

His plan was to leave the drive as soon as he had definite proof of the identity of the buyers and the market where they in turn took the herds.

He hadn't long to wait. Dawson put the herds into a sheltered valley close to where Juana had left them and sent off one of his bodyguards on a fast horse to go ahead. All the other men were told to stay in camp. Men were coming to take over the herd, and they'd be paid off at that time.

Buck Duane knew that they were somewhere south of a line from the tiny settlement of Marathon to Fort Davis. A short drive would put the stolen animals on well-traveled trails going west or north. A hard turn to the south would put them over the Rio Grande into Texas. From the direction in which the rider had gone, he figured the new buyers would come from Fort Davis. Meanwhile there was nothing to do but wait.

He kept the Jackrabbit Kid close to him at all times on the pretext that "I need somebody I can trust to watch my back, Kid. A man hasn't eyes in the back of his skull."

Mostly he wanted to be sure Dawson didn't grab the Kid and try to make him tell what had happened in the mountains. The Kid would be loyal, and get himself tortured as a result. Duane was worried anyway. Now the Kid followed him out of a boy's hero worship. What would his reaction be when he found out Duane was a Texas Ranger? That's when the youngster would really be put to the test. A boy is as unpredictable as wind—Duan knew it and it worried him.

About noon of the third day in camp Dawson's bodyguard brought the buyers in. There were two of them, hard-bitten characters in long black frock-coats and Stetson hats. Each man also had a bodyguard sporting two guns and carrying Winchester rifles across their saddles. The men led a pack horse which quite evidently carried the coin and banknotes to pay off for the herds. They rode straight for Dawson's tent.

The Old Man's crew gathered around the tent in a big circle as close as they dared come. They knew the payoff was imminent and the money drew them like a magnet.

Jim Dancer came out and talked to them. The buyer's drovers would be along later in the day to relieve them. Any who wanted could sign on with the new leaders for the rest of the drive, as they were short of hands. The buyers were called Miller and Dongan.

They were taking the herd all the way to California, dropping off small bunches as they could be sold along the way at Army posts and towns and to ranchers needing stock. A couple of days' drive would get them out of Texas to safety.

The rest would go north with the Old Man to intersect the Goodnight-Loving trail. They'd be paid off in Colorado.

Duane knew what that meant. Dawson was afraid to pay off his men till he got them out of Texas. They'd head straight for the saloons and fancy houses and some might talk.

The men didn't like the idea of a delayed payoff. There was a howl of protest. "We want our money. We earned it and we want it now. Give us our money."

Dancer tried to argue with the men, but they wouldn't

listen to him. Guns were waved in the air. Finally Dancer went back into the tent for a conference.

Dawson's personal following of gunmen drew into a circle around the tent. There were eight of them besides the two guards who had come with Dongan and Miller. Outside their ring almost forty men yelled for their money. Only a few of them were real gunslingers, but all were armed and looking for trouble.

Loud voices came from the tent. Apparently the buyers were telling Dawson to pay off and stop the uproard. They'd come to buy cattle, not to fight for their lives.

Dawson came out by himself.

"All right," he yelled. "Let's talk it over before somebody gets hurt. Back off a ways and my boys will too. Then send in a man to talk for you. We'll work it out."

The men backed off about fifty yards. The gunmen, except for Dawson's bodyguards and the two strange bodyguards went the same distance in the other direction. They stood facing each other and trying to decide what to do next.

"Send Buck Duane in," one of the men suggested. "He can talk for us—him and that snake-killing gun!"

The last thing Duane wanted was to become totally involved at this point. He had what he'd come for and wanted to get clear with the information. But the men demanded it and there was nothing he could do. The Kid insisted on going with him.

"Remember your back, Buck," he said.

As Duane walked forward he saw that the men waiting for him had split into two groups. On his left, and a little in advance of the others stood the Old Man and one of his body servants. The black had a shotgun tucked loosely under his arm. The Chief showed no guns, but Duane figured him for at least a couple of hidden derringers, probably one in a forearm clip under his shirt.

About thirty feet to the right and a little behind these two Dongan and Miller and their two hired guns stood in a loose grouping. They were actually out of the conference and only there as observers.

Duane walked easily, letting his hands swing at the end of his arms, but never letting them get far from his gun butts. Walking into such a setup was always a little like smoking over an open keg of gunpowder. He didn't really expect trouble, but long years on the outlaw trail had taught the Ranger that the price of life was all too often eternal vigilance.

As he came forward he heard one of the buyers' gunslingers say to his boss, "Mr. Miller, I've seen that man some place before."

Every nerve in Duane's body tightened to the killing pitch. The icy knot that came before crucial and sudden action was in his stomach. Adrenalin poured into the blood.

"You might have, Tom," Miller was saying. "They say he's fast. He's the one they said shot the snake, I think."

Duane's hands poised almost on the butts of his two guns. He sensed what was coming next. Because of that, he'd have the edge he needed. The trouble was there were two groups. He couldn't watch and fire at both at once. No man living could.

The man Tom watched him intently. "I know I've seen him," he said. "I've seen him kill a man." Suddenly he started. "My God, Boss, that's the Ranger killed Tulsa Harrow. I saw him."

For a second everybody froze. Then the Old Man yelled, "Ranger! Kill him, boys! Cut him down!"

Duane made his life-and-death decision in a split second. The Old Man and his personal bodyguards weren't professional guns. The two men with the buyers were. He'd have to take them first, trust that the buyers were slow and try to get Dawson and the shotgunner next. It was an impossible gamble, but not to try was certain death.

He walked on in and the guns bloomed flowers of flame in his hands. The man Tom was fast but he never reached his gun. Duane's first shot cut him down.

His sidekick was a shade slower to react, and that meant he never had a chance. The second and third slugs from

Duane's right-hand gun sounded almost as one report. The slugs punched out his right lung and heart.

The two buyers were businessmen, not killers. They bought their corpses instead of making them. They started to put their hands in the air.

Duane saw movement flicker out of the corner of his eye where one of Dawson's bodyguards brought the shotgun around. He tried desperately to turn head and arm for a left-hand shot. The buckshot would cut him in two at that range. Every muscle pulled with tigerish strength to pull him round even as he knew the best he could do was a dead heat.

Behind him a .45 thundered once and again. The big bodyguard came straight erect with the impact of the first slug. The second slammed him over on his back. Both barrels of the slug gun fired uselessly into the sky.

Dawson was trying for his derringer, but it was snagged on his linen cuff. When he saw Buck Duane's guns come round to him, he opened his hands and squealed for help like a goat caught under a fence. Then he put his hands up as the buyers already had.

Both the Chief's gunmen and the rustlers behind Duane had been too far away to hear the accusing cry of "Ranger!" All they knew was that killing had started. The two groups milled and yelled.

Buck Duane turned to his three prisoners. "If one of you opens his mouth, he's dead," he said. "Watch them, Kid."

Then he turned to wave to both gunmen and rustlers. He raised his voice to a shout they could hear. "It's all over, boys. The money's in the tent there. Go get it."

Both groups understood the logic of that. They ran for the tent. Under the rush it went down. Men trapped inside fought blindly to reach the money bags, while those outside tried to get the canvas off. Hostility between the groups were forgotten. Even the herders in the valley came galloping up, leaving the stolen stock to mill aimlessly about.

Duane and the Kid herded their disarmed prisoners over to the remuda where saddled horses were picketed. Bullet came to Duane's whistle. The others took what horses they could.

"Ride for the hills," Buck Duane ordered. "We're taking you back the way you came."

They hadn't far to go. At the very crest of the valley they were met by a wave of whooping Comanche braves whom Juana had been holding to watch the camp—"In case any harm came to Buck."

Juana joined them with a picked guard of Indians. The rest took the unguarded cattle and horses out of the valley with a single screeching rush while the rustlers were still fighting each other for the cash in the tent.

"We'll take these fellows back to face Texas law," Buck Duane told Juana. "Captain MacNelly will arrange that this is the last of the 'invisible' drives. Nobody will repeat what the Chief started ever."

"What about me?" the Jackrabbit Kid said. "I killed a man."

"I think you wiped the score clean this time," Duane said. "Captain MacNelly will think the same. He's that kind of man, and the Rangers have friends in this end of Texas. We'll get you a verdict of self-defense, and you can ride like a man again."

The Kid grinned from ear to ear. "I'll go for that," he said. Then his face changed. "Why didn't you tell me before you could do that?"

"I wanted to see if you were a man," Duane said. "A man makes his own decisions for himself. Just like you did when you saved a Ranger's life."

He rode ahead with Juana, Bullet matching the palomino stride for stride in a magnificent and joyous burst of speed.

THE OTHER SIDE OF THE CANYON

ROMER ZANE GREY

THE OTHER SIDE OF THE CANYON marks the return to print of one of Zane Grey's strongest characters, Laramie Nelson, first introduced in Grey's novel RAIDERS OF SPANISH PEAKS. Laramie was a seasoned Indian fighter, an incomparable tracker, and one of the deadliest gunhands the West had ever known.

In these stories, Romer Zane Grey, son of the master storyteller, continues Laramie's adventures as he takes on a gang of train robbers, a gold thief, and a sharpshooting woman wanted for murder!

WESTERN
0-8439
2041-6
$2.75

GUN TROUBLE IN TONTO BASIN

ROMER ZANE GREY

Gun Trouble In Tonto Basin signals the reappearance of Arizona Ames, the title character of one of Zane Grey's most memorable novels. Young Rich Ames came to lead the life of a range drifter after he participated in a gunfight that left two men dead. Ames' skill earned him a reputation as one of the fastest guns in the West.

In these splendid stories, Arizona Ames comes home to find his range and his family haunted by the shadow of a terror they dare not name!

WESTERN
0-8439-2098-X
$2.75